COS 21

USA TODAY b
London, Englan at v
sons—which give ra
insight into the ma
film journalist. She
getting swept up in a v
excitement, funny and r men, sexy and
tortured men and glamorous locations where laundry
doesn't exist. Once she turns off her computer she
often does chores—usually involving laundry!

When **Kali Anthony** read her first romance novel at
fourteen she realised two truths: that there can never
be too many happy endings, and that one day she
would write them herself. After marrying her own
tall, dark and handsome hero, in a perfect friends-to-
lovers romance, Kali took the plunge and penned her
first story. Writing's been a love affair ever since. If
she isn't battling her cat for access to the keyboard,
you can find Kali playing dress-up in vintage
clothes, gardening, or bushwalking with her husband
and three children in the rainforests of South-East
Queensland.

A FORBIDDEN NIGHT WITH THE HOUSEKEEPER

HEIDI RICE

REVELATIONS OF HIS RUNAWAY BRIDE

KALI ANTHONY

MILLS & BOON

First Published in Great Britain 2020
by Mills & Boon, an imprint of HarperCollins*Publishers*
1 London Bridge Street, London, SE1 9GF

A Forbidden Night with the Housekeeper © 2020 Heidi Rice

Revelations of His Runaway Bride © 2020 Kali Anthony

ISBN: 978-0-263-27824-8

MIX
Paper from
responsible sources
FSC® C007454

This book is produced from independently certified FSC™ paper
to ensure responsible forest management.
For more information visit www.harpercollins.co.uk/green.

Printed and bound in Spain
by CPI, Barcelona

A FORBIDDEN NIGHT WITH THE HOUSEKEEPER

HEIDI RICE

To the squad—Daisy, Susan, Fiona and Iona—
my writing support posse.
And my wonderful sister-in-law Isabel
for her help translating Maxim's French!

CHAPTER ONE

CARA EVANS STOOD at the graveside, listening to the priest drone on in French, and stared at the miles of vines owned by the neighbouring Durand Corporation covering the adjacent hillside like a patchwork.

She didn't understand all the words in the eulogy; her French wasn't fluent. But still she felt sad, and stunned, at the loss of her employer, Pierre de la Mare, the owner of the small vineyard on which they stood.

Not just her employer, her husband, she corrected herself.

Although it felt ridiculous to call Pierre that. He had been old enough to be her grandfather, she'd only been married to him for three days...and now she was his widow.

'Marry me, Cara. Take pity on an old man who does not wish to die alone.'

She could feel the eyes of the tiny group of Pierre's friends and associates who had arrived for the burial staring at her as she watched the sun dip towards the crest of the hill.

And could hear what they were thinking.

Gold-digger. Opportunist. Whore.

But she refused to feel guilty about accepting Pierre's proposal. Pierre had told her the vineyard would have to be sold. All she stood to gain from their brief marriage was a small legacy from his will to cover the wages he had been unable to pay her for months.

Towards the end she'd been more like a carer than a housekeeper. She'd bathed Pierre, fed him, helped him dress, wheeled him into the fields he loved each morning so he could watch the vines ripen and had endless conversations each evening about everything from Simone Signoret—his favourite French movie star—to the latest news of Maxim Durand, the billionaire vintner who owned all the land surrounding Pierre's much smaller vineyard. And who Pierre said had been trying to put him out of business for years.

She had never just been Pierre's employee. She'd been his companion and eventually his friend. Theirs had never been a sexual relationship, although she'd be damned if she'd humiliate Pierre by letting anyone know that. They'd struck a deal: if she married him he would be able to pay her the wages he owed her after his death, and she needed that money to help her settle somewhere new.

The pang of loss and anxiety tightened around her chest. She would miss Pierre but, more than that, she would miss La Maison de la Lune because the house had become her home.

She'd been living at the ramshackle old farmhouse for eleven months, scrubbing the stone floors until they gleamed, dusting the worn furniture, learning how to work the temperamental washing machine, planting a vegetable patch to save money on their food bill.

She'd never stayed anywhere this long, never felt so settled and secure, and it hurt more than it ever had before to know she would be forced to move on soon.

She sighed. She ought to be used to it by now. So why did it feel harder this time? Was it just because she was getting older? She'd turned twenty-one two weeks ago.

One thing was for sure, La Maison de la Lune held a special place in heart.

She squinted into the setting sun as a large black SUV appeared on the far ridge. A cloud of dust rose in its wake as it bounced over the rutted track towards the family cemetery on the edge of the de la Mare property.

Probably another of Pierre's casual acquaintances come to judge her.

But then she noted the Durand logo on the side of the Jeep as the vehicle stopped and a man got out.

He was tall and muscular, wearing worn jeans, battered work boots and a grubby white T-shirt, his jaw covered in stubble.

She recognised him instantly, even though she'd never met him and never seen him in such casual attire—only in tuxedos and designer suits in snapped shots online and in tabloid magazines.

Maxim Durand, Pierre's billionaire neighbour. And France's most eligible playboy, according to *Paris Match*. Who else could look that ruthless and commanding—and annoyingly handsome—while dressed like a labourer? And who else would be arrogant enough to attend a funeral straight from the fields?

Anxiety skittered up her spine. What was Pierre's business rival doing coming to his funeral? There had been no love lost between the two men, or certainly not by Pierre. Her employer had talked about Durand often, with utter contempt and surprising venom. She had loved Pierre— he was charming and paternalistic towards her—but his hatred of Durand had shown a side of her employer she had never quite understood. Pierre had been fixated on the other man. Every time they had a problem at the vineyard—a small fire, a spring flood, one of the field hands leaving—Pierre had blamed Durand, as if the other man was personally responsible for everything that had gone wrong over the years. Cara had tried not to encourage it. She'd thought Pierre was paranoid—yes, the Durand Corporation had bought up all the land surrounding the de la Mare estate, but Durand had never attempted to buy out Pierre—but now she wondered. Was it possible Pierre had been right? Had Durand simply been waiting for Pierre to die before making his move?

Durand slammed the door of the Jeep and marched across the dry earth to the graveside, his movements supremely confident. He certainly didn't look as if he were in mourning. A strange liquid pull worked its way through her system.

A blush burned her neck as Durand dipped his head and she could feel his gaze, behind dark aviator sunglasses, assessing her in the retro fifties black dress she'd found at the market the previous day. The dress had been too tight, but with its wide skirt, fitted bodice and hourglass shape it had looked elegant. She never wore dresses, feeling more comfortable in what Pierre had laughingly called her 'work uniform' of shorts and T-shirts. But she'd wanted to look elegant today, for Pierre. And the dress had suited the occasion. Or so she'd thought until this moment. Durand's perusal scorched her skin, insulting her and exciting her at one and the same time—and making her feel more exposed than elegant.

But he didn't speak to her, his gaze leaving her burning face as he approached the graveside and said something to Marcel Caron, Pierre's lawyer.

The priest finally stopped talking and handed her a trowel. She bent to scoop up a shovel of earth, far too aware now of her breasts straining against the tight bodice.

She sprinkled the chalky red earth on Pierre's coffin.

'Give Simone a kiss from me, Pierre,' she whispered in

English. Handing the trowel back to the priest, she said a silent goodbye to her friend.

Swallowing to hold back the emotion closing her throat, she turned from the graveside and walked past the graves of the de la Mare ancestors, heading down the hillside to La Maison de la Lune.

She'd decided not to arrange any kind of wake. Pierre had told her he didn't want any fuss.

Pierre's lawyer, Marcel, was due to come to the farm-house after the service to give her a cheque for the money Pierre had promised her from his pension when they'd wed. She already had one of de la Mare's best wines open and breathing—the way Pierre had taught her to do—on the kitchen counter ready for Marcel's arrival.

She heard some hissed whispers in French as she headed past the other mourners, but no one approached her.

She needed to pack her rucksack and start thinking about where she was going to go next. She doubted there would be much time once the estate had been settled. And if Durand bought it he would want her off the land quickly. She wanted to be ready to go before she was pushed. And Durand's presence here today—in his work clothes—suggested he wasn't going to stand on ceremony.

Should she go to Paris? To London? To Madrid maybe? She'd never been to Spain before.

But as she tried to muster some enthusiasm for her new adventure all she felt was weary. And sad. And heartsick.

Sod it. She wasn't going to pack tonight.

Tonight she wanted to remember her friend—a sad smile curved her lips—her husband. So once Marcel left she would sit out on the terrace, sip Pierre's beautiful wine and enjoy the twilight magic of the vines she had come to love. The vines that had become a rare oasis of calm and security and safety amid the chaos of her nomadic life.

She could feel the laser-like intensity of Durand's gaze behind his sunglasses as she made her way past him to the path out of the graveyard. A disturbing prickle of need ran riot over her skin and the hot, heavy weight settled low in her belly.

She struggled to rationalise the strange, unfamiliar sensations.

Durand was rich and forceful, a notorious womaniser, and exuded an animal magnetism it would be hard for any woman to ignore. And she had so little experience with men. As a foster child, she had learned to hide her light under a very big bushel. It was always better not to be noticed, then you might get to stay a bit longer. And as a teenager she'd been a tomboy, determined not to conform to the stereotype of an unwanted girl looking for love in all the wrong places. She was still a virgin, for goodness' sake. Thanks to her rootless existence since leaving foster care she'd never settled down anywhere long enough to build a meaningful relationship with a guy. Well, apart from Pierre! But Pierre—despite their last-minute marriage—had been forty years older than her and frail, not a forceful, magnetic man in his physical prime.

Given her history, it was no surprise she found Durand's attention a bit…disconcerting.

But the good news was she didn't know him and she never had to meet him—so this weird heady feeling would pass. Eventually.

Before too much longer Durand was probably going to own the two-hundred-year-old de la Mare vines that produced the best vintage in the region and the beautiful old stone farmhouse that had become the first real home she had ever known.

But tonight the vines and La Maison de la Lune were

hers. And she did not need to get Durand's permission—
or anyone else's permission—to enjoy them.

'How long before the estate goes on the market?' Maxim
Durand asked Pierre de la Mare's lawyer in French as he
watched the girl—de la Mare's housekeeper, or nursemaid,
or whatever the hell she was—walk past him without making eye contact.

Her curves moved sinuously in the vintage dress, the
black silk shimmering gold in the sunset, the reddening
dusk turning her mass of blonde hair, pinned in a haphazard chignon, to a rich gold. His pulse beat a lusty tattoo in
his crotch. Infuriatingly.

Someone had said the old man had got himself a new
housekeeper a while ago. He'd expected her to be young
and pretty, but not young enough to be de la Mare's grand-
daughter. How old was she? Early twenties at the most.
Which would make her up to a decade younger than his
own thirty-one years. And as much as forty years younger
than de la Mare.

Did the old bastard have no shame whatsoever?

Despite her apparent youth, though, he would guess the
girl had supplied more than just pastoral care for the old
roué. De la Mare would have charmed her into his bed the
way he'd charmed so many other women. She looked like
just his type too. Hot and available.

But still the pulse of desire and a grudging respect,
rather than the distaste he wanted to feel, persisted as she
strode into the shadow of the trees with her head held high.

What was it about the woman that had captivated him as
soon as he had arrived? Perhaps it was the flush that hit her
cheeks as he checked out her impressive breasts—provoca-
tively displayed for every man here to enjoy in the revealing dress—or the flicker of surprise in her cornflower blue

eyes as they met his. Or maybe it was just that he hadn't slept with a woman in close to three months and he was fatigued after getting up before dawn this morning to assess the new yield. But whatever the reason, he didn't like it.

Now de la Mare was finally dead, Maxim intended to claim what was rightfully his—not get distracted by the old man's leftovers.

'Your haste is quite unseemly, Monsieur Durand,' the lawyer murmured. 'Monsieur de la Mare only died a few days ago.'

'This is business, not personal,' he lied easily. 'I wish to be informed as soon as the estate is on the market.'

He'd waited long enough to get hold of the de la Mare Estate. He'd refused to deal with the old bastard, but had ensured that no one else would offer for the land while the man was alive. Now de la Mare was dead, the vineyard was his for the taking.

'It is not as simple as that; we must meet tonight at La Maison de la Lune,' Marcel Caron said, 'for the reading of the will. Actually, it is good you are here. It will save me sending for you, as Monsieur de la Mare requested you attend.'

'What?' Maxim's attention switched to the lawyer—the girl had already disappeared anyway—as he struggled to hide his shock. He ruthlessly quashed the foolish kernel of hope. He knew there would be nothing for him in the man's will.

'Monsieur de la Mare requested you attend two days before he died when he made his will.'

'Why did he even make a will?' Maxim said, his voice hoarse with anger. 'He had nothing but debts to pass on and no heirs to pass it to as I understand it.'

Or none he was prepared to claim.

Bitterness rose in his throat like bile.

He swallowed it down as he had so many times before. Ever since he was a small boy and his mother had tied him to his bed to stop him from running through the woods to La Maison de la Lune in a desperate bid to see the man who did not want to see him.

'You have not heard?' The lawyer looked sheepish.

'Heard what? I only returned from my business in Italy yesterday and I've been in the fields all day,' Maxim demanded as the sick dread—which had been a large part of his childhood—churned in his gut.

'Mademoiselle Evans, La Maison's housekeeper, and Monsieur de la Mare were married three days ago, and she is now his widow.'

Bitterness knifed through his gut as his mother's face seared his memory—fragile and drawn and exhausted—the way he remembered her, the last time he'd seen her, on the morning he'd left Burgundy as an outraged and humiliated fifteen-year-old.

'*Merde*,' he murmured as his anger became icily cold.

The little English whore hadn't just been screwing de la Mare, she'd managed to seduce the old bastard into doing something no other woman ever had—putting his wedding ring on her finger.

CHAPTER TWO

'MADAME DE LA MARE, thank you for receiving us at this difficult time.'

Us?

Cara nodded as Pierre's debonair lawyer Marcel stood in the farmhouse's doorway an hour after the funeral. 'It's good to see you, Marcel. Is…is someone else coming?' she asked. Marcel's English was usually flawless. But then the SUV she'd seen at the cemetery drove into the farmyard. And Maxim Durand stepped out of the car.

He'd changed out of the grubby T-shirt and jeans he'd worn at the graveside into a pair of designer trousers and a white linen shirt rolled up at the sleeves. His dark hair was damp and slicked back from his face as if he'd recently showered and his jaw clean-shaven. But he still looked untamed and intimidating as he strode across the yard.

He'd also lost the sunglasses, the piercing gaze even more devastating than it had been at the cemetery when it raked over her figure. Thankfully, she'd changed out of the too-revealing dress, but she wished she had dressed in something more formal than the pair of shorts and the thin cotton camisole and shirt she was wearing. Marcel had visited the house often, especially in the last few weeks, to see Pierre and she'd stopped standing on ceremony with him months ago. But Durand wasn't a friend or even an acquaintance.

'*Bon soir*, Madame de la Mare. Marcel asked me to attend at your husband's request,' Durand said with a perfunctory nod of greeting. His perfect yet heavily accented English though, like his gaze, was ripe with thinly veiled contempt.

Cara ruthlessly quashed the shiver of distress, and the heady ripple of sensation which hadn't died as she had hoped.

She hadn't realised quite how large he was at the cemetery, his shoulders wide enough to block out the glow of twilight as he stood in the doorway. The top of her head barely reached his collarbone.

Why had Pierre requested his presence? This made no sense. The will was just a formality, a chance for Pierre to pay her the wages he owed her, wasn't it?

Had Durand already bought the estate? Was that possible? Would she have to leave tonight? Or first thing in the morning? She'd thought she would have more time, a few days at least.

And why couldn't she control the liquid pull tugging at the deepest reaches of her body? This was worse than seeing him from several yards away at the graveyard. Up close and personal, Maxim Durand was a force of nature, who seemed to have a control of her senses she could neither rationalise or deny.

She didn't want to invite him into her home. Her sanctuary.

But as Marcel and Durand stood on the doorstep she knew she didn't have a choice. The realisation made her feel like she had so many times as a child, being told she was going to be uprooted again and moved to a new family.

Powerless.

'I... I see,' she said, although she really didn't see. 'Please come in,' she murmured, but her arm shook as she held the door open.

Durand's shoes echoed on the farmhouse's stone flooring as he walked past her, the scent of expensive sandalwood soap tinged with the distinctive salty scent of the man filling her senses.

She shifted away from him, feeling like Red Riding Hood being stalked by the wolf.

Without waiting for another invitation or any directions, Durand strode down the corridor towards the visitors' salon at the back of the house where she had laid out a light meal for her and Marcel.

The shiver of distress, and unexplained heat, was joined by a spike of anger.

Durand didn't own her home yet.

Given his height, he had to duck his head to get under the door lintel before entering the large airy room now suffused with the golden glow of full dusk. That he did it instinctively and seemed to know exactly where she would have laid out the wine and food she had prepared only rattled Cara more.

How did Durand know the house so well? Had he been here before? Pierre had certainly never mentioned that he had met his nemesis in all the conversations they'd had about his business rival.

Pierre had been obsessed with the man, but she'd always assumed that was simply because the Durand Corporation had been encroaching on the shrinking de la Mare estate for so long.

But now she wondered. Was Pierre's dislike of this man, his enmity towards him, more personal? It was just one more reason to be wary.

Durand stood in the large room, somehow managing

to make it look small, with his back to the butcher's block table where she had arranged an array of cheeses, a fresh baguette and a platter of fruit. He stared out at the de la Mare vineyard, his legs wide and his arms crossed, making the seams of his shirt stretch over his shoulder blades. The rolled-up sleeves revealed the bulge of deeply tanned biceps. The sun had set half an hour ago, but there was enough light to see the gnarled roots of the ancient vines that were the de la Mare legacy.

Durand's stance looked nonchalant, dominant, as if he were already surveying his own property, but tension vibrated through him too, almost as if he were a tiger waiting to pounce.

She covered an instinctive shudder by hastily lifting the carafe of wine she'd left breathing on the sideboard.

'Pierre asked that I serve the Montramere Premier Cru tonight,' she said, taking an additional glass from the sideboard.

But as she began to pour the wine Durand's gruff voice intervened, the husky purr stroking her skin despite the brittle tone.

'Don't bother pouring me a glass. I prefer not to mix business with pleasure.'

If she'd been in any doubt the enmity between Pierre and Durand wasn't personal, she wasn't in doubt any more.

'Very well, Monsieur Durand,' she managed, pouring a glass for herself and Marcel. She lifted the wine to her lips, attempting to appear calm and unruffled by Durand's surly presence. 'To Pierre,' she added. 'And the de la Mare vines.'

Durand's features remained schooled into a blank expression. But she noticed a muscle jump in his jaw when he dipped his head in acknowledgement then murmured, *'Aux vignes, mais pas à l'homme.'*

Perhaps he thought she didn't understand him, but she got the gist of what he had said.

To the vines, but not the man.

'To Pierre,' the lawyer said, raising his glass without acknowledging Durand's inflammatory comment. Either Marcel was trying to defuse the tension or he was deaf.

After sipping the excellent vintage, the lawyer sighed with appreciation. '*Magnifique.*' He indicated the chairs at the table. 'Let us sit,' he said before taking a seat, 'and enjoy the refreshments Madame de la Mare has provided while I outline the terms of Monsieur de la Mare's will.'

'I don't wish to sit,' Durand announced, 'or eat. I wish to get this over with.'

The lawyer nodded and opened his briefcase, drawing out a laptop.

Cara sat opposite Marcel, determined to ignore Durand.

Clearly she wasn't to be afforded any respect as Pierre's widow. Or even as the host for this evening's meeting. But she could agree on one thing with Durand.

She wanted this over with now too, as quickly as possible, so she could get this man and his disturbing effect on her out of her home. She had never felt this unsettled, this disorientated and yet oddly exhilarated in the presence of any man. And she didn't like it. Why couldn't she control her elemental response to Durand, especially given his apparent contempt for her?

Marcel took several painfully long minutes tapping on the keyboard of his laptop and retrieving documents from his briefcase while Durand continued to stand on the opposite side of the room, his presence like a shadow—crowding out all her memories of Pierre.

Cara downed a huge gulp of the fragrant Pinot Noir as she waited, not caring that she wasn't fully appreciating the delicious notes of clove and smoke and white pepper in the exceptional vintage. Right now, all she wanted to do was forget about Durand and the strange sensations he aroused. And find out if Pierre had left her enough to stay solvent over the next month while looking for a new job.

'To avoid too much legal language I shall summarise the main portion of the will,' Marcel said, passing a copy of the document across the table to her and another towards Durand, who didn't approach but left it on the table.

'Monsieur de la Mare has left the property known as La Maison de la Lune and the surrounding vineyards of the de la Mare estate to his widow. Unfortunately, as the estate has considerable debts he understood she would have to sell part or all of the property. He was happy for her to do so, but has added a clause: Madame de la Mare must not sell any part of the estate to Maxim Durand, the Durand Corporation, any of its subsidiaries or any shell companies in which Maxim Durand or the Durand Corporation has an interest or she will forfeit this inheritance.'

'*C'est pas vrai!*' Durand shouted, startling Cara, who was still struggling to get to grips with the news.

The bubble of hope expanding in her chest at the prospect of owning La Maison burst at his furious reaction.

Why had Pierre done this? As much as she loved the vineyard, if Pierre had wanted the de la Mare legacy to continue the only answer was to sell the vines to Durand. For all his sharp business practices, the man was known as an excellent vintner. And no other reputable vintner would buy the land if it meant defying Durand.

A stream of French swear words followed as Durand stalked across the room. The leash on Durand's temper was off now, if it had ever been on.

'This is nonsense,' he said, switching to English for her benefit. 'He cannot prevent me from buying the vines; I have waited long enough for them. And anyway, who the hell is she?' He glared at Cara. 'She knows nothing of vini-culture.'

Cara flinched—something about Durand's fury and the anger in his eyes felt so personal.

This wasn't about the vines. How could it be? Just as she had suspected at the graveyard, when Durand had appeared so unexpectedly. And when he'd turned up this evening at Pierre's request. There was something between Durand and Pierre. Something that went way beyond the business of winemaking.

Oh, Pierre, is this why you insisted on marriage? Not to help me, but to defy Durand?

Her stomach turned over. Had Pierre used her? Surely he must have known his bequest would put her in the fir-ing line of Durand's wrath.

'I don't… I don't understand,' she said, feeling betrayed. Pierre knew enough about her childhood and adolescence to know how much she hated conflict. 'Why would Pierre do this?'

'I cannot tell you, Madame de la Mare,' Marcel mur-mured, eyeing Durand with caution. 'I advised against this course, but Pierre was insistent. He did not explain to me his motives but I believe it was important to him you be allowed to remain at La Maison de la Lune. And that you take ownership of the vines.'

'She can't have the vines,' Durand announced, the curs-ing having stopped to be replaced by steely anger. 'The vines are mine; they belong to me, not to some English *salope* who has been here only a few months.'

Cara shot out of her chair at the derisive comment. She clenched her fists, determined to face him down, not car-ing that he was bigger and angrier and a lot more intimidat-ing than she was. Just because he was rich and powerful, and owned every acre of land surrounding the de la Mare estate for as far as the eye could see, didn't mean he could insult her.

'The vines are not yours, Mr Durand,' she said with as much dignity as she could muster while her hands were shaking and her whole body was far too aware of his nearness. His strength. 'And apparently they never will be,' she said, ruthlessly quashing the ripple of guilt. And confusion.

She didn't deserve this legacy.

She had been friends with Pierre, but she had only known him for a year; she wasn't his family and they hadn't been husband and wife. Not in any real sense of the word. She could see with complete clarity now, Pierre *had* used her as a pawn in his fight with Durand. How could he have had her best interests at heart if he had always intended to set her up against a man with Durand's power and influence? By leaving her the vines and stopping her from selling to Durand he was setting her up to fail, setting up the vineyard to fail. However sick he had been, he had never been stupid.

Had Pierre hated Durand more than he had loved the vines? Perhaps.

One thing was certain, though—he had hated Durand more than he had cared for her. And that hurt, more than she wanted to admit.

'What do you know about the de la Mare vines?' Durand asked, his handsome face ripe with contempt. 'About how to nurture and care for them? Or how to get the best out of them?' His gaze raked over her figure, the heat in his eyes so contemptuous it burned. 'You know nothing,' he replied, answering his own question. 'And yet you think you can take what is mine because you opened your legs for that bastard, *comme une pute*?'

Like a whore.

'Monsieur Durand! There is no call for such language,' the lawyer said.

But Cara couldn't hear Marcel, all she could hear was the blood pounding in her ears. She didn't care what Durand thought of her, what anyone thought of her, so why did his disgust cut through her composure to the wounded girl who had been called names so many times before? And why was his forceful fury only making the sensations racing over her skin more volatile, more electric, more uncontrollable?

'I'm not a whore, I'm his wife,' she said, her voice breaking on the words. 'You certainly have no more right to the vines than I do.'

'You think not?' Durand stepped closer, close enough for her to feel the heat of his anger pumping off him, and see the tension in his jaw, the brittle fury in the vivid brown of his eyes. But there was something else in the dark depths that was even more disturbing. Something hot and vibrant that she could feel deep in her abdomen.

'I have *every* right to these vines. I nurtured them and fed them, protected them from frost and fire and blight, picking off the insects until my fingers bled,' he said, the forceful words as compelling as the passion sparking between them. A passion she did not want to acknowledge but couldn't deny. 'I worked these fields for hours, when I wasn't even old enough to see over the top of the vines,' he murmured. 'And I promised myself then, some day they would be mine.'

Durand's origins were sketchy. She'd heard the stories whispered about him in the media, that his mother had come from a poor family and no one knew who his father was. That he had started out very young working in the fields, had little formal schooling and had worked his way up from nothing, eventually earning enough to buy his first stake, then expanded and grown his business. But no one had ever suspected he came from Burgundy, and certainly not from around here, or someone surely would have mentioned it before now.

'Are you saying you worked for Pierre and he didn't pay you?' Cara asked, her voice shaking. Was he lying to her? She could imagine he would be ruthless enough to do just that, but something about the tone of his voice, as if he were admitting something he was ashamed of, suggested the opposite. 'I don't… I don't believe you.'

It couldn't be true.

Pierre had been a complex man, perhaps more complex than she had realised, but he wasn't a monster. Was he?

'*Oui*, he paid me,' Durand snarled. 'The money he insisted I owed him for being born. And I did the work willingly until I realised that all he had ever wanted from me was free labour. That he never had any intention of acknow—' He stopped short and something slashed across his features, something more than fury. Something that looked suspiciously like betrayal and hurt, as well as anger.

Cara recognised that emotion because she had endured the same feelings of confusion and inadequacy as a child, on the day her father had left her at the children's centre in Westminster and told her he couldn't look after her any more.

It was the last time she had ever seen him.

As she absorbed the echo of that shattering emotion now, tightening her ribs and making her heart thunder, she thought of the confusing statement he'd made—why would Pierre believe Durand owed him money for being born…?

Then she noticed the golden halo around the dark brown of Durand's irises for the first time.

'You were his son,' she murmured, the truth suddenly so obvious she didn't know why she hadn't figured it out as soon as Durand had stepped inside her home.

Or rather *his* home.

Had he lived and worked here as a child? And never been acknowledged by Pierre?

The wave of compassion towards this hard, indomitable man was so fierce it nearly knocked her off her feet. Because suddenly she understood exactly why the vines meant so much to him. Why he wanted them so badly. And why he hated Pierre—or wanted to hate Pierre—as much as she had once wanted to hate her own father. For abandoning her.

But as the wave of compassion flowed through her, the wave of desire surged too, that shocking feeling of connection breaking down the barriers she'd been trying and failing to construct ever since his gaze had raked over her at the graveside.

CHAPTER THREE

WHAT THE HELL did she just say?

'*Qu'est-ce qu'elle a dit, là?*'

Maxim was so shocked at the woman's whispered statement his English deserted him—and momentarily so did his fury at his father's vindictive attempt to deny him even from beyond the grave. He had said too much, far too much, but even so she couldn't possibly have figured out the truth so easily when no one else had ever suspected his link to Pierre de la Mare.

'You were...' She stumbled over the words but her blue eyes were so filled with sympathy he stiffened. 'You *are* Pierre's son. Your eyes, the shading...they're just like his.'

It wasn't a question this time, any more than it had been the first time she'd said it.

'What stupidity is this?' he said, instinctively denying it.

But his voice sounded rough with shock as the humiliation that had consumed him as a boy—when he'd discovered what a fool he'd been to believe even for a second that a man of Pierre de la Mare's breeding and wealth would ever have claimed a bastard like him—threatened to engulf him again.

He didn't want her pity. And he had no intention of claiming the legacy; all he wanted was the vines. Vines he'd sweated and laboured over for years, believing his father loved him, or at least respected him, when all he'd ever been to Pierre de la Mare was a mistake.

'Even if you are mine, as your mother claims, do you really think I'd want a whore's brat to carry the de la Mare name? However good he is with the vines.'

The words his father had spoken to him the day he'd turned fifteen rang in his head. That was the day he'd finally got up the courage to tell Pierre de la Mare he knew they were father and son. The day he'd told his father how proud he was to carry on that legacy. The day his father had laughed in his face and told him he had no right to any legacy because Maxim would never be more than a field hand, a labourer, a bastard.

Pierre de la Mare had *never* been his father, whatever his mother said. It had taken him years to figure out the blood tie between them meant nothing to his father and it never had.

How the hell his father's ten-second wife had figured out their connection, though, was beyond him.

He forced himself to breathe, to calm down as everything inside him rebelled against the pity in her eyes and the volatile mix of emotions it caused to roil in his gut—shame, humiliation, anger.

'I can see him in you,' she said, searching his face. 'Pierre spoke of you all the time; you were like an obsession of his. I thought it was because you'd been so successful in this business so young. But I can see now it was always more personal than that.'

Maxim's stomach tightened into a knot of fury at the softly spoken words.

'In his own way, although he feared you, I think he was proud of you too,' she added.

The comment knifed into his gut. Was she serious? Was this some kind of sick joke? Did she think he gave a damn about what de la Mare thought of him or his business? He'd stopped seeking his father's approval sixteen years ago. He'd run away from the vineyard that night and left Burgundy the next day to make his own way in the world, after years living on the outskirts of his father's land, effectively begging for scraps by doing everything de la Mare asked of him in the hope he would one day acknowledge their connection.

No one here had recognised him when he'd returned. No one except de la Mare—which was precisely why he had enjoyed remaining aloof and at the same time stymied all the old man's attempts to save the vineyard from its debts. He hadn't had to get his hands dirty because the old fool had run the place into the ground on his own. And when de la Mare had come to him, begging for help and investment, thinking that Maxim still wanted his acknowledgement, Maxim had taken great pleasure in laughing in his father's face.

He had promised Pierre de la Mare at that meeting that once the old bastard was dead he would buy the vines and stamp the Durand name, his mother's name, his low-class gutter name on them—and the de la Mare legacy that his father had been so proud of, and so determined to deny him once, would be gone for ever.

The old bastard had married this woman in a last-ditch attempt to trick Maxim out of the legacy that was rightfully his. And for that alone he should despise her…

Although…

Devoid of make-up, the girl's face—fresh sun-burnished skin, high cheekbones, wide too-blue eyes and a mouth ripe for kissing—was all the more compelling. And her body, even disguised in the shorts and work shirt, looked ripe for a great deal more. No wonder his body had responded to her. She was a beautiful woman. The fact that she was his father's widow did not detract from her physical allure.

He huffed out a harsh laugh, determined to break the spell she had weaved over him so effortlessly. 'Do you actually think I care what that bastard thought of me?'

She blinked, obviously taken aback by the savage tone.

He realised too late he had made a tacit admission that the girl was right about his biological connection with de la Mare when the lawyer—whom he'd forgotten was in the room with them—murmured, 'Is this true, Monsieur Durand? Pierre de la Mare was your biological father?'

He glanced at the lawyer, who looked shocked to the core.

He could continue to deny it. He had no desire to have it become common knowledge. But, feeling the girl's eyes on him, he realised he didn't want to lie. Lying made the truth more powerful. Made it seem as if he cared about the connection when he considered it nothing more than an unfortunate accident of birth.

'My mother was one of de la Mare's mistresses,' he said, careful to keep any inflection out of his voice. 'Elise Durand Pascale. We lived here—' he glanced around the room '—until he got bored with her.' He shrugged. 'Then he allowed us to live in a small shack on the edges of the estate. But as soon as I was old enough, de la Mare insisted I work for him to pay for that privilege as my mother was too weak to work full-time.' The bile rose in his throat, but he swallowed it down, the details of that devil's bargain, a bargain he had only become aware of when he'd confronted de la Mare years later as a fifteen-year-old, still sickened him. What a fool he'd been to believe his father had wanted to train him in the art of winemaking so he could eventually take over the business, when all the old bastard had really wanted was a free field hand. 'But I have no desire to claim a connection I take no pride in,' he continued. 'If you don't keep the information private you'll be facing a lawsuit.' He turned back to de la Mare's widow, although calling her anyone's widow seemed absurd. Her young heart-shaped face was surprisingly guileless for a woman who had slept with an old man to get a hand on his property. Somehow he couldn't quite get himself to think of her as a *putain* any more, though, when the disturbing mix of pity and under-standing in her expression looked genuine.

'And that includes you, Madame de la Mare,' he said, just in case she was in any doubt.

Instead of looking surprised, she simply nodded. 'Of course,' she said. 'Your connection to Pierre is private, I understand that.'

He doubted she did understand. Perhaps she thought she had a better chance of keeping the land if no one knew of his relationship to de la Mare. If so, she was mistaken. He didn't need to be de la Mare's son to take the land... And complete his revenge on the man who had sired him. And then discarded him.

'If you wish to dispute the will based on this information you would have to submit to a DNA test,' the lawyer said, obviously fearful for his job. He had to know Maxim had an impressive legal team and enough money at his disposal to keep the guy's practice tied up in litigation for years over the legality of this last-minute bequest.

'I have *every* intention of disputing this will,' he clari-fied. 'But I certainly don't need to prove I am de la Mare's flesh and blood to do it. All I have to do is prove the man wasn't of sound mind when he made it.' He let his gaze rake over the woman in front of him, lingering on the rise and fall of her breasts under the worn cotton camisole she wore beneath her shirt.

The visible outline of her nipples had the now familiar

heat settling low in his belly. He knew he should ignore it—
he didn't want de la Mare's leftovers—but then her breath
caught and the heat intensified, despite his best efforts.

So she could feel it too? This pull between them that had
disturbed him so much at the graveside.

'I doubt it will be hard to persuade a judge that de la
Mare was enthralled by the charms of his new wife when
he made this will,' he said, the husky tone hard to disguise.
'And the ludicrous stipulations contained within it.'

In truth, he doubted the girl had had anything to do
with the will—de la Mare had probably planned this final
slight ever since their meeting two years ago, and she had
simply been a willing participant. But that didn't make his
instinctive attraction, and his apparent inability to control
it, any less baffling. Or annoying.

The girl's flush rose up her neck and her breathing became shallower. Her nipples were so prominent now, he felt
sure they must be painful. The heat throbbed and swelled
in his groin as he imagined easing down the soft cotton
to relieve her pain with his lips. He inhaled, capturing the
scent of wild flowers and the vague musk of her arousal.

Damn, but she was exquisite. Beautiful, fiercely desirable and apparently unable to disguise her sexual needs.
The veneer of innocence—however fake—was also captivating.

While it pained him to realise it, he couldn't fault the
old bastard for his taste.

'Monsieur Durand, I assure you the will is watertight.
Monsieur de la Mare was entirely cognisant when he made
it,' the lawyer said. 'And Madame de la Mare had no knowledge of the contents of it before today, as per my client's
wishes.'

'We will see,' he replied, never taking his eyes off the
girl. For that was what she looked like to him. Exactly how

old was she? He'd wondered earlier, but he was wondering even more now. She had to be more than a teenager, but in the casual clothes, and out of the revealing dress, she didn't look like much more. And his father had been in his sixties.

For a moment he considered that age difference. Her gaze darted from Marcel and back to him, her nervousness only increasing his desire.

Exactly how desperate must she have been to consider spreading her legs for an old man? And how could he hold that against her, when he had done things he wasn't proud of himself as a boy, simply to survive.

He glimpsed the table, where an array of fresh local cheese and fruit and bread had been artfully arranged. And the thick fog of desire finally cleared enough for him to start thinking... If not clearly, then at least coherently.

The solution to this problem was simple. Why hadn't he thought of it sooner? Surely if she had married an old man for his property, she could be bought. All he had to do was make her an offer she could not refuse—controlling this inexplicable surge of desire would also be a good start.

'I will stay to eat after all—and try out the wine—so we can discuss the situation further,' he said.

'I am afraid I must leave,' the lawyer said. 'My wife will have dinner waiting for me.'

The girl's brows lifted, and wariness flashed across her features. She didn't like the suggestion that she be left alone with him.

Good, he had the upper hand at last. And that was all that mattered in a negotiation of this sort. He needed to be ruthless now—and stop obsessing about her rigid nipples.

Walking to the sideboard, Maxim poured himself a glass of de la Mare's wine to keep his hands busy. And concentrate his thoughts on what he wanted to achieve—namely getting his hands on de la Mare's ancient vines, not his nubile young widow.

He watched an array of emotions cross the girl's face. Concern, panic, maybe even fear.

But was she scared of him, he wondered, or the hunger her rigid nipples and shallow breaths had acknowledged, even if she could not?

Satisfaction surged at the evidence that she was finding it even harder than him to control her responses. Whether she was scared of him or the provocative passion that had blindsided them both, he could make her fear work in his favour. If he kept his head.

Before she could formulate a polite way to kick him out of the house he added, 'This may be my last chance to eat a meal in the house where I was born.'

He couldn't care less about having a final meal in La Maison. He barely remembered living here; all he could remember was the early mornings spent racing across the fields from the shack where he and his mother had ended up, and working with his father's field hands in the pre-dawn mist, or after school long into the night and watching and waiting for his father to arrive, and hopefully notice him and how hard he worked. And the day he had come to claim that connection, full of pride and longing, and had been left standing at the back door to meet his father—because he was considered too low-class to enter the house.

His deliberately wistful comment had the desired effect, though, when the sympathy and misplaced sentiment for his plight he had noticed earlier crossed the girl's face again, and she nodded. 'I understand, Monsieur Durand.'

The lawyer packed up his laptop and his papers, then snapped his briefcase shut. 'If you have any questions, Madame de la Mare…' He inclined his head towards Maxim. 'Or Monsieur Durand. Feel free to contact me at my office.' He laid down a business card for each of them. 'But I do hope we can be civil about this.' He gave a hearty if strained laugh. 'I think a quiet meal together to discuss amicably how to proceed makes perfect sense. While de la Mare did not want the vines sold to the Durand Corporation, I see no reason why Madame de la Mare should not lease them to you, Maxim, if you wish to carry on producing the Montremare Premier Cru in your father's honour.'

Maxim nearly choked on the salty cube of Brie de Meaux he had popped into his mouth. He swallowed his outrage with a sip of his father's famous wine. 'That is an interesting possibility,' he managed, thinking Caron was an imbecile.

He had no desire to do anything in honour of that bastard. And he didn't want to lease the vines, he wanted to own them. Because only then could he obliterate the last of de la Mare's legacy. And complete his revenge on the man who had rejected him all those years ago.

But he had no intention of revealing that to either the girl or her lawyer. He had exposed himself enough already. He wasn't usually a man given to emotion. In fact, he was famous for his cold, clinical business practices. But right now he wasn't feeling cold or clinical. He was feeling hot and on edge. Somehow he needed to find a way to use that to his advantage in his negotiations with the girl.

As the lawyer left, Maxim watched his father's widow make a point of sitting in the chair on the opposite side of the table. She picked at the grapes.

She was nervous, as well as turned on. Good—at least he wasn't the only one unsettled by this inconvenient attraction.

'How old were you?' she asked. 'When Pierre expected you to come work for him to pay for the use of the shack you lived in?'

'Ten. Eleven. I don't recall exactly.' He shrugged, but the movement was stiff. He could see that damn sympathy clouding her eyes again and it was the last thing he wanted. 'It wasn't a hardship,' he murmured. 'I enjoyed the work. And I came to love the vines.'

She took the hint, her flush igniting again. 'I'm sorry, it must be hard for you that he made that bequest.'

'Not at all, I expected no less from him, Madame…' He paused. He disliked calling her by that old bastard's name. 'What is your *prénom*?'

'My first name?' she said, and he realised he had lapsed into French again. Why did he find it so hard to concentrate around her?

'*Oui*, your Christian name.'

'It's Cara. Cara Evans… Or, rather, Cara de la Mare, I guess.' She didn't sound sure.

'Cara Evans is a better name,' he said, oddly pleased by her hesitation.

Bright flags of colour hit her cheeks and the heat in his groin surged—which only confused him more.

'As you were only married to the old bastard for a few days I think you do not need to take his name,' he added.

'Please don't call him that,' she said. 'I'm sorry he wasn't a good father to you. But Pierre was my friend.'

My friend. What a coy way to describe the man she had a long-term affair with.

'You do not understand,' he said, annoyed by the warmth in her voice.

Why couldn't she get it through her head that he had no need of her compassion? Whatever his father had or hadn't done to him a lifetime ago had no bearing on who he was now.

'I did not need for him to be a good father to me, or any kind of father,' he said, determined to spell it out to her.

He tore off a chunk of the fresh baguette and spread it with Brie, then bit into the snack and let the creamy, salty taste melt on his tongue—determined to look nonchalant if it killed him. He had never spoken to anyone of that time in his life when he had tried so desperately to win Pierre de la Mare's admiration and affection, not even to his mother.

In some ways he was still ashamed of that boy—how weak and foolish he had been to need validation from a man who felt nothing for him. But Cara Evans needed to know that desperate child was long gone.

'I survived very well on my own,' he continued. 'In fact my father's decision to deny our connection, to reject me as a boy because I was a bastard and my mother was from a poor family, made me a much stronger man, prepared to fight for everything that is mine—and I will never allow anyone to have what is rightfully mine ever again,' he finished.

Her eyes widened but, instead of the fear he had hoped to instil with the veiled threat, her gaze filled with that infuriating compassion—even rawer and more intense now than it had been moments before.

'Pierre rejected you as a child because you were illegitimate?' she said, clearly having completely missed the point of the disclosure. 'How dreadful. I'm… I'm so sorry.'

She reached across the table in an instinctive gesture of comfort—and sympathy. The touch of her fingertips was like a naked flame, searing his skin and his pride and making the fire in his loins ignite.

He flipped his hand over and clasped her wrist, preventing her from drawing those incendiary fingertips away again, when she realised her mistake.

'Do not feel sorry for that boy,' he said, wanting to revel in the shock and wariness in her expression, but still disturbed himself by the fire that continued to spark and spit as her pulse went wild under his thumb. 'He is long gone.'

Damn it, he was a billionaire, as far removed from that impoverished, rejected child as it was possible to get. He was rich beyond his wildest dreams now and wielded all the power that boy had been denied, and he was soon to be the master of *all* he surveyed… Including de la Mare's ancient vines.

She tugged her hand free and he let her go, infuriated by the blood still pounding in his groin.

He could have any woman he wanted. Why the hell should he want this woman—a woman who had once warmed his father's bed—so much?

But, even as he asked the question, his gaze landed on her mouth. Her small white teeth dug into her bottom lip and his breathing accelerated at the thought of biting that lush lip too and then soothing the soreness with his tongue, before plunging his fingers into the silky soft hair piled on her head and…

Arrête.

He drew a deep breath into his lungs to halt the erotic visions bombarding him, and fuelling the need to transform the wary heat in her eyes into a raging fire, only to have his whole body intoxicated by the scent of her arousal.

'It would be a grave mistake to pity the man he has become, Cara,' he said, but even he wasn't sure what he was talking about any more.

CHAPTER FOUR

CARA.

The way Maxim Durand caressed her name sounded so intimate, his husky French accent roughening the R in the middle. The intensity in his eyes, though, was as terrifying as it was exciting.

Cara rubbed her wrist where the light touch of his fingers had burned the skin, desperately trying to escape the explosive sensations which had taken her body captive.

He made a point of lifting the bread and cheese back to his lips, taking a bite and swallowing, then licking his fingers. But she could see the hunger in his eyes because it compelled her too.

She dragged her gaze away from his sensual lips and stared down at the grape in her hand. 'I don't pity you,' she said.

She doubted anyone had ever pitied him, despite the horrors he had let slip about his childhood. He didn't strike her as a man who would ever inspire anyone's pity; he was far too forceful, far too commanding, far too controlled.

Except…

He hadn't been able to disguise his response to her any more than she had been able to disguise her response to him. Why did that seem so significant? Why was the thought making her feel so giddy, so light-headed?

She forced the grape she'd been fidgeting with past her dry lips, made herself swallow it, to buy herself time to think—something that was next to impossible with his dark gaze fixed on her.

Maxim Durand was Pierre's illegitimate son. And he'd once worked in the fields here. No wonder he wanted the vines. And Pierre had rejected him in the cruellest way possible when he was still a boy. And for the cruellest of reasons, because he was poor and illegitimate.

The fruity sweetness of the grape burst on her tongue.

As charming as Pierre had been to her, and however much she had come to care for him, she knew he could be ruthless when it came to his business. And after what he had done in his will it was hard to ignore the fact that his suggestion of marriage—and the legacy he had left her— had been a means of hurting his son, again, rather than of helping her.

Perhaps she should give Durand the vines? After everything he'd suffered, did she really have a right to keep them from him?

'How much?'

She jerked her head up and found herself trapped in Durand's intense golden-brown gaze again. 'Excuse me?'

'How much do you want to disappear? I am a rich man and I can be generous. You're clearly a woman who appreciates the value of money and I respect that…' His gaze dropped to her breasts, and lingered, before rising back to her face. The contempt in his gaze was so clear—and so brutal—it shocked her.

Her back straightened, even as her nipples squeezed into tight points of need.

'I don't want your money,' she said as she wrapped her shirt around herself, attempting to hide her physical response to him.

'Really?' His sensual lips lifted into a cynical smile and she felt like Little Red again, being baited by the wolf. 'Even if I offered you half a million euros to disappear, which is considerably more than the property is worth?'

'Yes,' she said, releasing the breath held hostage in her lungs.

She didn't want his money. Only moments ago she had been considering giving him the vines. But she wanted to be able to stay at La Maison de la Lune.

She didn't want to have to disappear. Again.

How many times had she been forced to do that in the past? Because of the whims of others. Whatever his motives, Pierre had given her the house she had come to love. And she had earned this chance. 'I want to stay living here, as Pierre planned. But I'd be more than happy to lease the vines to you, as Marcel suggested.'

His smile flatlined. 'I don't wish to lease them; I wish to own them. And you can't remain here, as I intend to demolish this place.'

'But… What? Why?' She jumped from her seat, distressed not just by the suggestion but the chilling conviction in his tone. 'Why would you do that?'

He stood too, the cynicism replaced by a thunderous frown. 'I do not have to explain my reasons to you.'

She crossed her arms over her chest to try to stop the trembling in her limbs—and to disguise the ache in her treacherous nipples. 'Well, you can't demolish La Maison de la Lune because it belongs to me.'

'And once I have challenged the will, it will belong to me.'

He was actually serious. She stared, trying to gauge why he would do such a thing. Pierre had treated him appallingly, she understood that. But he'd said himself he wasn't that rejected boy any more. And what was the point of obliterating the legacy of a dead man?

'But you can't,' she pleaded again. 'La Maison is beautiful…' She let her gaze roam over the old furniture, the worn armchairs and sturdy table, the beautiful vista beyond—not just of the old vineyard, but the ancient forest that rimmed the property, the small stream that bisected the land, gilded now by the full moon. 'It deserves to be here for generations to come.'

'No, it doesn't. The only thing that matters are the vines.'

He walked around the table, bearing down on her, making her more aware of his strength, his size. But, instead of feeling intimidated, she felt energised, exhilarated, mesmerised by the fierce passion in his eyes.

Was it for the grapes? It had to be, but why then did his passion feel as if it were infecting her body, rushing like wildfire over her skin, making the hot sweet spot between her thighs burn?

'If you knew anything about viniculture, Cara, you would understand,' he said, saying her name again like a caress, the harsh cynical anger morphing into something rough and raw with a devastating promise. 'The soil here is unique, rich in complex minerals that give a specific flavour to the grapes.'

The thickness in his throat seemed to echo in the deepest reaches of her body. She didn't know what was happening to her. But for the first time ever she felt truly seen.

He cupped her face, the rough calluses on his palm making her shudder as his thumb brushed across her lips. She should step back, away from that incendiary passion, but she felt trapped, owned and so desperately needy, the pulse between her thighs spreading out to ignite her entire body.

'Once I own the vines,' he murmured, 'I can propagate

them and replant on the land, creating a new vintage, even better than the Montremere.'

She was breathing heavily, they both were. She licked her dry lips and the passion in his eyes exploded, darkening the pupils to black. She felt the answering explosion in her sex.

But, instead of drawing her closer, his hand began to slip from her cheek.

The need seemed to spring from nowhere, more than passion, more than desire. Something deep and elemental, that probably went all the way back to that rejected girl.

And in that split second all she could see was the boy he had been too. The child who had been rejected and betrayed and exploited. She covered his hand with hers, the way she had attempted to do before at the table, to comfort him.

But this time comfort wasn't the only thing she felt. She didn't want to lose his touch.

Lifting on tiptoe, she placed her lips on his, needing to strengthen that connection, wanting to feed the hunger so she could obliterate his pain. And her own.

She heard him groan, but then his hands were gripping her cheeks, pulling her against him and his mouth was on hers.

Wild, hungry, demanding.

Her mouth opened on a gasp and he captured the sob as he angled her head, giving him better access. Her own hands dropped from his face and she found herself clinging to him, her fingers fisting in his linen shirt. She shuddered, too aware of the overwhelming heat of his body, the press of his chest against her swollen breasts, her thrusting nipples becoming more engorged as she rubbed against the muscular strength like a cat desperate to be stroked.

His tongue branded the secret recesses of her mouth. She tried to respond in tentative darts and licks. She had no idea what she was doing, all she knew was she needed more of his taste, his passion, his heat. His fingers threaded into her hair, releasing the pins she'd used to keep the wild mass aloft. She could hear them scattering on the stone flooring, hear the pounding rush of the blood pumping around her over-sensitised body and plunging into her sex.

At last he yanked his mouth free. His dark eyes stared down at her, his expression stunned. But not as stunned as she felt.

He swore softly, the searing gaze rising up to her hair then concentrating on her mouth. 'I want you,' he said. 'Even though I should not. It is madness.'

The raw honesty in the confession spoke to something deep inside her.

'I know...' she said, because she understood exactly how mad it was.

They were in Pierre's house. A house Durand wanted to destroy, a house she had come to love, on the day of Pierre's funeral and she was Pierre's widow. She shouldn't want him and he shouldn't want her. But all she could really feel was the need pounding in her blood, fuelled by the heady feeling of connection—their shared pain a living, breathing thing.

And all she could see was the possessive desire in his eyes.

No man had ever looked at her with that furious hunger, that passionate intensity. And, before she could stop herself, she said the words that had been echoing in her head ever since she first saw him climb out of his Jeep that afternoon.

'I want you too.'

He frowned, and tensed, his body poised, shocked but undecided, and for one agonising moment she thought he was going to refuse her.

But then the confusion cleared, almost as quickly as it had come, and he scooped her into his arms.

'*Bien*,' he murmured.

She grasped his neck, struggling to catch her breath as he strode out of the room and down the hallway. He took the stairs two at a time to the first landing.

'Show me to a room you did not share with de la Mare,' he demanded, his voice gruff and broaching no argument.

The answer was simple. She pointed to her own bedroom at the end of the landing—the one she'd lived in ever since becoming Pierre's housekeeper.

He kicked open the door and flicked on the light with his elbow, then let her down beside the narrow double bed.

She stood trembling, her body like a leaf being buffeted by the winds of her own desire. She'd never felt this way before, excited, exhilarated, out of control.

He cupped her cheek, pressed a kiss to her lips, his large hand slipping down to cradle her neck and drag her against him. His lips devoured her cheek, her chin, the rioting pulse in her collarbone, sending the unbearable need darting into her sex, her breasts, and everywhere his mouth conquered.

He wrapped an arm around her limp body, tugging her against the hard line of his, and the thick evidence of his arousal pressed into her quivering belly through their clothes.

His hands were frantic but gentle as he tugged off her shirt, skimmed his fingers under the cotton camisole. Her bra released with a sharp snap and he drew away to watch her reaction as his thumbs found her aching nipples beneath the soft cotton. The tight peaks swelled and hardened as he played with them—circling and plucking and making them ache even more.

'I need to see you,' he groaned.

She nodded, not sure if he was asking a question or making a demand. But, before she had a chance to second-guess herself, he had stripped off her bra and camisole. And she stood naked from the waist up.

'*Trop belle*,' he murmured, the reverent growl making her feel truly beautiful for the first time in her life.

He cupped the underside of one breast in his callused palm and then bowed his dark head to capture the ripe, throbbing peak in his lips.

She sunk her fingers into his hair, the sensations so exquisite as he suckled her that a raw moan broke from her lips.

He teased and tortured her, circling the areola with his tongue, nipping at the swollen peak then drawing it deep into his mouth, the hot suction driving her wild. Her moans became sobs, her fingers fisting in the silky locks of his hair to draw him closer, demanding he give her more. The fire sparked and sizzled in her sex, threatening to consume her.

'Please… I need…' What did she need? She didn't even know.

'Tell me what is good for you,' he rasped in her ear, hugging her trembling body close, notching the ridge of his erection against the melting spot between her thighs.

The heat swelled and strengthened, but not enough… she needed to feel him, his strength, his hardness, filling the empty spaces inside her.

'I need you naked too,' she managed, shocking herself with the explicit request.

He chuckled, the sound harsh. '*Mais oui*, Cara.'

Placing a last kiss on the crest of her breast, he drew away to strip off his shirt.

His chest was as broad and strong and magnificent as the rest of him. She devoured the sight of him, so bold and unashamed in the yellow glow from the ancient light fixture.

The defined muscles of his pecs and the brown discs of

his nipples were scattered with hair that arrowed down in a thin line bisecting the ridges of his abdominal muscles. She folded her arms over her breasts, trying to hold onto her sanity as he unbuttoned his trousers. Her heart slammed into her throat and pounded harder in her sex as he kicked them off and then lowered the stretchy black boxer shorts.

The massive erection sprang free from the nest of hair at his groin.

She'd never seen a naked man in his physical prime before, and certainly not one who was fully aroused.

She swallowed heavily, unable to take her eyes off the hard shaft, which thrust up towards his belly button, so long and thick.

How on earth was that supposed to fit inside her? But, even as the panic rippled through her, her sex moistened and softened, the muscles tensing and releasing in anticipation.

She didn't know if she could take something so huge, but she wanted to try.

'Cara?' he murmured as he nudged her chin up, forcing her gaze to meet his. '*Ça va?*' he asked, the flash of concern crossing his face making her heart thud against her ribs.

She nodded. 'Can I...? Can I touch it?'

Creases appeared in the tanned skin at the corners of his eyes, the dark depths sparkling with amusement as his lips quirked in a curious half smile. 'Of course—you do not need to ask permission.'

She nodded again, cursing her inexperience. She didn't want him to know he was her first. Didn't want him to suspect what a big deal this was to her. Because it was not a big deal to him.

Reaching out, she touched his erection. Her fingertip glided along the rigid length, exploring the velvet softness of his skin, the hardness beneath.

The erection jumped against her palm, thrilling her. He let out a rough groan as her thumb glided across the broad tip, gathering the bead of moisture that seeped from the slit.

He grasped her wrist. '*Arrête*, Cara. You are killing me,' he said as he lifted her fingers to his mouth and kissed them. The sight was so erotic her breath seized in her lungs. How could she be this turned on and not dissolve into a puddle?

Releasing her hand, he dipped his head. 'Take off your shorts, *ma petite*,' he said, the gruff endearment caressing her senses. 'I cannot wait much longer to be inside you.'

She fumbled, her fingers trembling, and couldn't seem to get the buttons free.

Brushing her hands away, he knelt in front of her and released the fastenings to draw the rough denim down her legs. She stepped out of her shorts, placing her hand on his shoulder to keep her balance, so shaky now she knew she needed to get to the bed before she collapsed.

But, before she had a chance to move, he stood and lifted her easily into his arms. She knew she wasn't particularly light but she felt fragile and even precious as he placed her gently on the bed.

He loomed over her, his broad shoulders cutting out the light, his lips finding hers again, the kisses more demanding now, more insistent. The atmosphere changed. Not tender and seeking, but urgent and relentless.

He cupped her sex, his fingers exploring the slick swollen folds. She bucked against his touch, the pleasure becoming raw and jagged as two blunt fingers pressed inside her. The tight needy flesh stretched, making the throbbing ache pound so hard in her veins she thought she might pass out.

And then his thumb found the very centre of her struggle, gliding over the hot, wet nub, circling and flicking until she was riding his hand, holding onto his shoulders for purchase.

'Yes…yes!' she sobbed, unable to control the pleasure battering her body.

'Come for me, Cara,' he commanded and her body obeyed, the coil at her centre tightening to pain and then releasing in a shattered gush of sensation.

She opened her eyes to find him watching her. She was dazed, disorientated, the waves still ebbing through her as the pleasure rippled throughout her body, startling in its intensity.

She'd pleasured herself before, but it had never felt this good, this right, this devastating.

He looked dazed too, but then the shadows cleared to be replaced with a fierce, desperate need. He grasped her hips, angling her pelvis as the large head of his penis probed, demanding entry.

'Open for me,' he said. And again she obeyed instinctively, hooking her legs around his waist, opening herself fully for the onslaught, so desperate now to feel the thick length inside her she was ready to beg.

He surged deep in one hard thrust.

The pleasure turned instantly to rending pain, the heavy weight tearing her fragile tissue.

She stiffened, biting into her lip, her nails scoring his back to contain the shocked cry which would give her away.

But she knew it was already too late when he stilled. His face was rigid with shock, his gaze sharp with accusation as it locked on hers.

'Es-tu vierge?' he said, his English deserting him.

Are you a virgin?

She turned away from his probing gaze, wanting to lie but unable to get the words out with his erection still lodged so deep inside her she felt conquered, owned.

He grasped her chin and forced her gaze back to his. 'Tell me, how is this possible?'

Maxim couldn't focus, he could hardly talk, her body clasped so tight around him it was like a vice. A hot, sweet, unbearably pleasurable vice, about to tip him over the edge. He wanted to move, to dig deeper, to find the place that would make her moan and beg again. But he resisted the urge to thrust into the tight, wet warmth. And forced his mind to engage.

The guilty shadow in her eyes told a shocking story.

Her innocence, her inexperience, that strange feeling of something not being right that had assailed him as soon as he had brought her upstairs. The blush suffusing her ripe body, the shocked gasp as his lips closed over her nipple and suckled, the jolt of adrenaline as her fingers fumbled with her shorts. He'd assumed it was all an act, a beguiling, artless act that had captivated him even though he knew it couldn't be real. And now to find it was all true?

He shuddered, still lodged inside her.

She didn't speak, didn't answer his accusation, her eyes glassy with shock, but there was only one explanation. The marriage had been a sham. A trick in more ways than one.

He should withdraw. But he could still feel the pulse of her pleasure, the tight clasp of her body milking him, and the relentless need hammered at the base of his spine.

'Am I hurting you?' he asked, unable to withdraw, not caring any more about her reasons, her complicity in his father's scheme.

She shook her head. 'It's… You're so big, but it doesn't hurt so much now.' She stumbled over the words. And he found himself cradling her cheek, feeling the heat of her humiliation.

Maybe that was faked too, but he didn't think so, as he

drew his thumb across the full lips, felt her body relax a little.

'I need to move,' he said, deciding all that mattered now was feeding this hunger. The questions could wait because he couldn't focus on anything but the spasming grip of her muscles threatening to drive him insane if he didn't rock his hips.

She nodded. But a tear leaked from the corner of her eye. He brushed it away with his thumb.

'Why are you crying?'

'I… I've never felt this way before,' she said, the honesty in her pure blue eyes pushing at his chest. Surely this couldn't be faked, this intensity, this desperation, this emotional upheaval. Did she feel it too? And what the hell did it mean?

But even as the panic ricocheted against his ribs, he dismissed it.

This wasn't an emotional connection, this was just sex. And an insane chemistry that had exploded between them from the first moment he'd laid eyes on her.

He eased out of her then pressed back in, slowly, carefully, feeling her tight flesh soften to receive him more easily this time. She moaned, her fingers clinging to his shoulders, as if he were the only stable thing in the middle of the storm consuming them. As he withdrew and pressed into her again, her back arched, bringing her sex up to meet his invasion, welcoming it, revelling in his possession.

He began to rock his hips, in, out…slowly at first, establishing a rhythm that would satisfy them both. But as her moans became pants, her pants became sobs, the frenzy overtook him—and one shocking realisation charged through his brain.

He was the first man to touch her, to taste her, to feast

on her fragrant flesh, to hear her sob in his ear as she surrendered to him.

The surge of possessiveness, the need to claim her overwhelmed him as his smooth moves became clumsy, faster and more frantic, the thrusts deeper and more demanding. His fingers dug into her hips as he clung onto his own climax, needing her to shatter first.

Her body bowed back and she cried out, the spasms of her orgasm gripping him as she flew over that final peak.

He let go at last, to tumble over that high ledge behind her, the climax shattering him, as his mind blanked and his body became boneless. And one word reverberated in his head.

Mine.

CHAPTER FIVE

As THE BLISSFUL wave of afterglow cleared, Cara lay staring at the crack in the ceiling moulding, the crack she'd mapped each night before she fell asleep, for the last eleven months. But tonight everything was different.

The musky scent of sex and sweat surrounded her. The heavy weight of Maxim Durand's body pressed hers into the old mattress as the thick length of him pulsed inside her tender sex.

She dragged in a shattered breath and sunk her teeth into her bottom lip to control the stinging tears that threatened to spill over the lids.

But there was no controlling the emotion sitting on her chest like a stone and threatening to crush her ribs.

What had she done? And why?

How could she have slept with her husband's biggest rival on the day of his funeral? The man who was threatening to destroy La Maison de la Lune?

She shifted under Durand's weight, gently shoving his shoulder blade, which was digging into her collarbone. She needed to get away from him. He was still firm, still *huge,* inside her—and all she wanted to do right now was curl up into a tight ball and die.

He groaned and shifted and she gasped, unable to disguise the tenderness in her sex as he eased out of her, ashamed of the renewed prickle of yearning.

'*Pardon*,' he murmured as he rolled off her.

She edged across the bed, every part of her aching now, but most of all her heart.

What Pierre had done to Maxim all those years ago was wrong, terribly wrong. But surely what she had just done was even worse.

As she tried to leave the bed Maxim Durand's hand shot out and grasped hold of her upper arm.

'Where are you going?'

'I need… I need to wash,' she said, heat climbing into her cheeks as she became all too aware of the sticky residue of their lovemaking between her thighs.

He hadn't used a condom. And she hadn't asked him to.

She dismissed the new ripple of panic. She couldn't think about any consequences now. She'd deal with those later. First, she had to get away from that assessing, intense gaze. And regroup, rethink, re-evaluate her position—her thoughts were so tangled now she could hardly breathe, let alone think.

Could she still stay here? Did she deserve to live in Pierre's home after sleeping with his enemy? But how could she not when she was the only thing standing between La Maison de la Lune and destruction?

She tugged her arm but Maxim held on, his thumb stroking the inside of her elbow and making the prickle of renewed desire distress her even more.

'Please, I need to…' she began.

'Let me help you clean up.' He sat up, swung his long legs to the floor and stood in one smooth move, still keeping a firm grip on her arm.

While she was frantic and awash with guilt, he seemed

composed and unperturbed by what had just happened. Her panic increased.

'What?' she asked, the blush burning her cheeks as she tried to avoid looking at his nakedness and deny the melting sensation in her chest—and her sex—at the abrupt but painfully intimate offer to help her wash herself.

How could her body still want him when everything they'd just done was wrong? On so many levels. She'd never really considered her virginity of particular importance. But if that were the case, why had she held onto it for so long? And how had this man been able to destroy all her fears about intimacy so easily—and so quickly?

He tugged her off the bed until she was standing in front of him, then cradled her cheek in his palm. 'Did I hurt you, Cara?'

She shook her head, but the gruff question had the tears she couldn't shed burning the back of her throat. She swallowed hard.

Don't cry, don't you dare cry. It doesn't mean anything. It happened and now it's over and it was a massive mistake.

Her chest felt as if it were imploding.

Not a mistake, an aberration. Brought about by stress, and chemistry. And incredible stupidity.

He doesn't care about you. All he cares about are the vines. And his feud with Pierre. And you don't care about him. Not really. You don't even know him. Your loyalty is to La Maison now. It has to be.

Just because he was Pierre's son. And Pierre had neglected him. He was powerful and successful now. And he'd slept with hundreds of women.

Just because he was your first, it doesn't make this special. First is just a number.

He planned to destroy La Maison, and she couldn't let

that happen. That made them enemies, no matter what had just happened in her bed.

'Really, I need to…' She couldn't seem to find the words, so ashamed now she could hardly talk. She should ask him to leave, but she was so shaky, so confused, she couldn't seem to say anything.

'Breathe, Cara,' he said, taking control, just as he had before.

He threaded his fingers through hers and led her into the bedroom's small and spartan en suite bathroom. Snagging the robe she kept hooked on the door, he handed it to her. She shrugged it on, pathetically grateful for the layer of protection. And even more grateful when he lifted a towel from the pile she kept by the sink and hooked it around his waist.

He slapped down the toilet seat. 'Sit.'

She perched on the seat, trying to focus, trying to find her equilibrium again. But all she seemed capable of doing was gazing at him, mesmerised by his assured, efficient movements.

If he'd made La Maison's reception room look small he made her bathroom look minuscule. Finding soap and a flannel, he ran water into the sink until it was warm, then soaked and lathered the washcloth.

He squatted in front of her and drew apart the robe to expose her tightly closed legs. His gaze met hers as he placed a warm hand on her knee.

'Open for me, Cara,' he murmured, the husky words reminding her of a similar demand earlier, which she had obeyed without question.

'I can… I can do it,' she said, stuttering, her blush radioactive as she reached for the flannel.

'I would like to,' he said. 'I want to be sure I did not hurt you.'

It wasn't a demand, she could have refused him, but the

yearning in her chest had her dropping her hand. And allowing him to ease her knees apart.

He washed her gently, carefully, wiping away the evidence of her innocence and their lovemaking with a tender efficiency that stole her breath and had the hollow yearning sinking deep into her abdomen. Her thighs trembled, the renewed pulse of desire impossible to disguise. He touched his thumb to the reddened skin on her hip where he had gripped her in the heat of passion.

'I have bruised you, *ma petite*,' he murmured, sounding genuinely contrite.

'It's okay,' she said. 'It doesn't hurt.'

To her surprise, despite her denial, he leant forward and placed a kiss on the spot. 'You must accept my apologies,' he murmured, his eyes shadowed.

She nodded.

Dumping the flannel in the sink, he pressed her knees back together and smoothed the robe over her nakedness before meeting her eyes. The rueful smile which twisted his lips made her heart beat in an erratic tattoo.

'As much as I would enjoy taking you back to bed, I do not wish to hurt you again.'

'You didn't hurt...'

He touched his finger to her lips, halting her denial. 'Don't lie, Cara, there are enough lies between us already.'

She stared at her hands clasped in her lap, and nodded. 'I know.'

What was wrong with her? One act of tenderness and she was ready to throw herself at him again, even though she knew it was wrong. Exactly how desperate for affection was she?

Tucking a knuckle under her chin, he raised her gaze back to his. 'Now you must tell me why you were untouched.'

'I…' She let out a tense breath. 'Pierre and I didn't have that kind of marriage,' she managed.

He straightened from his crouched position and let out a harsh laugh, the look in his golden eyes not so much suspicious as unconvinced.

'There is only one kind of marriage, Cara. One where a husband takes his wife to his bed.' His gaze roamed over her. 'If you were mine I would not let you out of my bed for a week after we were wed.'

The blush burned her neck and spread across her collarbone, the hunger in his words so compelling it made the hot spot between her thighs throb.

She scrubbed her hand over her cheeks, hoping to calm the colour as she looked away. The sight of his naked chest and the red score marks on his shoulder—which she must have made with her nails—was not helping with her breathing difficulties.

'Pierre was an old man,' she said. 'He wasn't capable of…' Her throat seized. 'Even if I had been willing,' she continued. 'We were just friends. He wanted to marry me so he could give me some security when he was gone, that was what he said.' She didn't tell Durand about the wages Pierre owed her because it would just make her feel more pathetic and expose her marriage to even more of this man's contempt. 'It was never a sexual relationship.'

Maxim stared at the riot of blonde curls, fighting against the desire still pulsing in his groin and the strange wave of elation.

Even if I had been willing.

So she hadn't ever contemplated sleeping with his father. That was good to know.

But then his disgust with the man returned.

He wished Pierre de la Mare wasn't dead, so he could murder the bastard himself.

De la Mare had used Cara Evans to get his revenge against him. But Maxim very much doubted his father's decision to marry this girl had just been about the vineyard, as she clearly believed. The bastard had always had an eye for women, claiming this young beautiful woman as his wife had probably given him some kind of sick ego boost—even if he had never been capable of consummating the relationship.

A sick ego boost that left Maxim with a problem.

He had always planned to raze La Maison to the ground as soon as he purchased the property. It was what he had told de la Mare he would do, all part of the promise he had made to the boy he'd been—an important part of his final revenge for the cruel slights that child had endured.

But how could he in all conscience kick this girl out of her home? Wouldn't that make him as much of a bastard as his father? Especially after he had just taken her innocence?

Not only that, but he hadn't used protection. Something he'd become brutally aware of as he'd cleaned her up.

He frowned. What the hell had possessed him? He hadn't even thought about it. He'd never been that impulsive or reckless before in his life, even as a teenager. Not only did he have no desire to become an accidental parent, but he knew precisely what it was like to be that accidental child. Unwanted, unloved, unimportant. Even now a child could be growing inside her because of his thoughtless behaviour.

The irony of the situation was so apparent it was almost funny. That he should impregnate his own father's widow with an unwanted child—and thereby repeat the old man's crimes.

Except he wasn't laughing. Nothing about this predicament was amusing.

'Are you using contraception, Cara?' he asked, surprised at his ambivalence when her head jerked up, and he deemed the answer from the abject misery on her face.

She shook her head.

'When did you last have a period?'

Embarrassment scorched her cheeks, which would almost have been charming if the possible consequences of their foolishness weren't so dire. 'A few days ago.'

He nodded. 'Then at least we are not in the middle of your cycle.'

There was still a chance their recklessness would have a far higher price than either of them was willing to pay, however. And there was only one solution that he could see which would ensure that didn't happen.

He would take Cara Evans as his mistress. That way, they could arrange for her to take the necessary precautions now to prevent an unwanted pregnancy and he could offer her a place to live while he demolished La Maison— at Château Durand.

Strangely, the thought of supporting Cara and inviting her to live in his home didn't make him as uncomfortable as he would have expected. He had never invited a woman before her to share any of his homes. And he'd never taken a mistress. Up until now, he had always kept his dating habits casual.

He had a business to run. He didn't have time for romance. And he saw no benefit in long-term commitments of any kind. But Cara, for a number of reasons, was different.

Not only did he need to ensure there was no pregnancy, and find her an alternative home, to finally break the last of her ties to his father—but she was the first virgin he had ever slept with, and they shared an insane chemistry which he could see no good reason not to indulge, once all the other issues between them had been resolved. It made

sense therefore to have her live at Château Durand and—
once this insane chemistry had run its course—he would
give her the pay-off he had already offered her.

She had been reluctant to take his money earlier, because
she wanted to stay at La Maison, but surely she could see
her marriage to his father would never hold up in a court
of law now he knew what a sham it had been?

'If there's a…' She sighed. 'If there's a consequence, I
can take care of it,' she said, her voice unsteady.

She didn't look him in the eye, and he found his usual
cynicism returning. However innocent she might appear,
he was not about to trust any woman to 'take care' of the
consequences, as she had so coyly put it.

He was a wealthy man and, although she had been un-
aware of his father's true motives for suggesting marriage,
the fact remained she had already married one man she
didn't love. What if she were setting her sights on trapping
him into marriage too?

Weirdly, the prospect didn't appal him quite as much as
it should. But he suspected his magnanimity would disappear once the afterglow still washing through his system
had subsided.

'If there are consequences, it is as much my responsibility as yours,' he said, broaching no argument. 'I think
the best solution is for you to live at Château Durand. I can
arrange for a doctor to attend you as soon as possible to
ensure no pregnancy occurs.'

Her head rose, her blue eyes so luminous anticipation
surged in his chest.

The truth was, she would make him an excellent mistress. Not only was she exquisite, and surprisingly forth-
right, but he couldn't remember ever wanting a woman this
much. Just thinking of all the things he could teach her, all

the pleasure they could share while he did, was making the blood pound straight back into his groin.

But then she said the most ridiculous thing.

'You're offering me a job? As a housekeeper?' she said, sounding wary but hopeful. 'That's… That's amazing and it could solve our problems,' she continued, her voice eager with hope now as he struggled to get his head around her misconception. What had he said to give her the impression he was planning to employ her? 'I'd be happy to give up my right to the de la Mare estate, if you'd just reconsider your plans to demolish La Maison? I know you need the land, but there must be a way to save…'

'I am not offering you a job, and my plans for La Maison will not change.' He interrupted the frantic flow of excited words, allowing his impatience to show. 'I have no need of a housekeeper,' he added, gentling his voice as he watched the hope in her eyes die—and suddenly felt as if he had kicked a kitten. 'And you do not need a job as you will have a generous allowance.'

'But… But what exactly would you be paying me for if I'm not working for you?' she asked, sounding confused.

He frowned. This was ridiculous, she could not be this naïve? Surely.

'Cara,' he said with a sigh, dialling down his impatience—her cluelessness was quite captivating in its own way. And another thing that made her unique. 'I would not be paying you for anything, I would simply be supporting you while you are my mistress.'

CHAPTER SIX

'Your...*mistress?*' The word came out on a horrified gasp as Cara struggled to contain her shock, not just at Maxim Durand's bold offer but the pragmatic way in which he delivered it. As if it were perfectly rational to offer to pay a—how had he put it?—'generous allowance' to a woman he was sleeping with.

Perhaps it *was* perfectly rational in the world in which Maxim Durand lived.

What did she know of that world? A world of lavish parties and show-stopping events, of elegant balls and expensive soirées, held on enormous super yachts on the Côte d'Azur or grand hotels on London's Strand or picture-perfect white-sand beaches in the Bahamas. All she'd ever done was read about Maxim Durand's extravagant world in magazines. Perhaps the women he dated—the glamorous supermodels and actresses, the sophisticated hostesses and smart, stunning career women she'd seen on his arm at those events in those same magazines—*didn't* think there was anything amiss with expecting Durand to foot the bill. And maybe there wasn't, *for them.* Because they had money and status and agency too. They would never be dependent on his largesse because they belonged in his rarefied world and knew how it worked. And if they'd ever been powerless, they certainly weren't powerless any more.

But for someone like her, who had fought for every scrap of dignity and respect, and against people's low opinions for most of her life, how could she not be compromised by such an arrangement? Not just compromised but owned. Because without a job, with no way of paying her own way, she would be not just completely dependent on him but little more than his property.

'Yes,' he replied, his puzzled frown only making her feel more compromised, more undermined. '*Ma maîtresse*... Is mistress not the correct word for this in English?' he added.

'I... Yes, but I can't... I don't want to be your mistress,' she said, feeling desperately exposed, and even more ashamed than she had when she'd been lying naked under him, with the orgasms he'd given her still echoing in her sex.

'Why not?' He seemed genuinely confused.

Couldn't he see how belittling, even insulting such a suggestion was? Especially given the names he had called her earlier.

Downstairs, he had accused her of being a whore and a slut. She'd dismissed those insults, once she'd figured out his connection to Pierre and why he was so determined to own the de la Mare vines. Those cruel words had been said in the heat of the moment, while he was processing the reality that his father had rejected him again, even from beyond the grave. And if there was anything Cara understood it was how that kind of rejection made you feel—insignificant, angry, vulnerable, hurt—because she'd felt every one of those emotions herself as a child, when she'd waited for her father to visit her, or to at least call, until she'd finally figured out what his silence meant... That the promises he'd made to her on the steps of the Westminster children's centre had all been convenient lies to get her to go with 'the nice lady' without a fuss.

But the names Maxim had called her haunted her now. Was that what he really thought of her?

'We have a rare chemistry, Cara. We would be foolish not to enjoy it while it lasts.'

Taking her hand, he tugged her off the toilet seat. Wrapping his arm around her waist, he pressed his lips to her neck. She shuddered with a need she couldn't disguise, but found the strength this time to place her hands on his bare chest and push him back.

'Maxim, please don't,' she said.

He let her go but then he smiled, the twist of his lips as cynical as it was amused. 'Why not? When I can smell how much you still want me?'

She tightened the belt on her robe, aware of her nakedness beneath it, and his nakedness beneath the towel—and the ease with which he could turn her own body against her.

But she didn't just feel hurt and insulted now, and compromised, she felt foolish. He was laughing at her naïveté. She got that. She *had* been naïve—to fall into bed with him without a thought to the consequences, and to give him her virginity without realising how much power that would give him. She had also been foolishly optimistic a moment ago, probably because she had been scared and desperate after what she'd done. Foolish to think the solution to a situation which had been decades in the making could ever be solved by him offering her a job.

'I think you should leave,' she managed, straightening her spine and welcoming the spike of anger because it helped steady her nerves.

His smile died. 'What foolishness is this, Cara?'

It hurt to hear him say her name with such gruff intimacy, the desire still thick in his voice. Because a part of her wanted to sink into that intimacy, to take anything he wanted to offer her. But she knew from grim experience there was always a catch to taking that easy road. And if this evening had taught her one thing it was that instant gratification was not the answer.

He lifted his palm to her cheek but she jerked her head out of his reach. 'Please, Maxim,' she said. 'I need to think.'

'What is there to think about?' he said. 'You are mine now, you need medical attention and a new home. This is the best solution.'

A spark of anger burned under her breastbone.

'The best solution for you, you mean.' The flush rose into her cheeks but she'd be damned if she'd be embarrassed about it. She wasn't the only one who had given in to their desires. 'I don't want to be your…your kept woman.'

'What is this ridiculous term?' he said. 'Kept woman? What does that even mean?'

'It means you'd own me.'

'I would support you—not own you,' he said through gritted teeth, clearly holding onto his temper with an effort. 'You would live at Château Durand, but you would be free to leave whenever you wished.'

'But *this* is my home, Maxim, and I don't want to leave it,' she said, trying to make him understand. If he couldn't see that him supporting her was the same as him owning her, maybe he would understand this. 'And I don't want to let you destroy it, just because you can. I realise your situation with Pierre was complicated, but he left La Maison to me. You can have the vines, there must be a way to get past Pierre's will there. But I owe it to him not to let you destroy his home.'

She'd said the wrong thing, she knew it as soon as she mentioned Pierre's name. Maxim's expression became stormy, but what disturbed her more was the steely determination in his eyes.

'You owe that bastard nothing. He used you to get to me, if you cannot see this you are even more naïve than the evidence suggests. And I will not change my mind about La Maison. I told him I would destroy this place as soon as he was cold in his grave and I will.'

'You...you told him?' Shock came first. '*When* did you tell him?' she asked, her voice thick with horror as a sickening understanding of what was really going on here took root. Maxim's determination to destroy La Maison had nothing to do with his business and everything to do with his need for revenge against a dead man.

'Years ago,' he said dismissively.

'How many years ago?' she asked, the horrifying truth becoming a knot of anguish in her stomach. Had Maxim seduced her deliberately? Had the heat that had flared between them even been real? Or had sleeping with her, in Pierre's house, only hours after his funeral been just another way for Maxim to get revenge against the man who had rejected and exploited him? Had she been used, not just by Pierre but also by his son? 'Was it ten years ago? Five? Two?'

'Why does this matter?' he snapped, the cold steel in his voice a far cry from the furious heat in his eyes. 'You gave your virginity to me. Any loyalty you had to him means nothing now.'

'This isn't about my loyalty to Pierre,' she said, feeling broken inside. Why had she trusted him? A man she barely knew. A man who didn't care about her, had never even pretended to care about her. She'd believed they had some connection, through shared pain, but had that just been a convenient excuse to feed the hunger, and take what her body desired without having to pay the price of her foolishness? 'It's about your need for revenge,' she finished.

'This whole conversation is madness,' he said. 'Pierre is dead. You need a new place to live because La Maison will soon be gone—which means you must grow up and stop talking nonsense.'

Before she could even process the possessive, dictatorial response, he stalked out of the bathroom and flung off the towel.

He dressed as she stood shaking in the doorway.

Leaving his shirt unbuttoned, he returned to her and captured her cheek in his hand. He pressed a kiss to her lips, delved deep with his tongue and her traitorous mouth opened instinctively, her treacherous body melting against his, even as her palms flattened against his abdominal muscles, trying to find the strength to resist him.

When he finally released her from the erotic spell they were both panting, her rigid nipples poking against the silk of her robe, begging for his attention.

'Your body knows you belong to me, even if you do not.' He rubbed his thumb across one nipple, making the brutal sensations dart down to her core. 'When you are ready to face reality I will be waiting,' he added softly, belying the anger she could feel reverberating through his body.

She stood transfixed as she listened to his footsteps disappear down the hallway.

The front door slammed below and she crossed to the window, her limbs still shaky, to see him climb into his SUV. He didn't look up, the headlights illuminating the ancient vines as he backed the car out of the yard in a squeal of rubber.

His clipped parting words echoed in her head as the roar of the SUV's engine disappeared into the night.

Your body knows you belong to me.

Not a threat but a promise. And one she couldn't deny.

She had thrown herself into the wolf's den but, unlike Little Red, she wasn't sure she was smart enough or strong enough to get out again before Maxim Durand devoured her.

CHAPTER SEVEN

Madame de la Mare, there has been a significant development in the settling of your husband's estate. May I come to La Maison this morning to discuss the situation?

CARA WOKE TO find the message from Marcel on her phone. She typed out a reply, telling him she would be ready to see him in half an hour, shocked to realise it was past ten o'clock in the morning.

She dragged her aching body out of bed. She'd had a fitful night's sleep, every one of her dreams—so hot and febrile—haunted by her overwhelming encounter with Maxim Durand.

Opening the shutters of the bedroom she'd moved into after Maxim had stormed out, she allowed her tired eyes to adjust to the morning sunlight and then breathed in a fortifying lungful of the September air. It didn't help.

She squeezed her thighs together to ease the pulse of tenderness.

After a long hot shower, in a vain attempt to clear her groggy thoughts and understand the shameful echo of desire that still lingered, she dressed in her usual outfit of shorts and a T-shirt. Returning to her own bedroom, she stripped the sheets from the bed, careful to avoid looking at the spots of blood left by the innocence she'd lost—not lost, thrown away. She carried the sheets downstairs to the laundry room and stuffed them into the ancient washer.

She turned it on and listened to the old motor whirr into action.

If only she could wash away her stupidity—and the memories of her forbidden night with Maxim—as easily.

Was it her imagination or could she still smell Maxim's scent—sandalwood and salt—lingering on her freshly washed skin?

She needed coffee, and lots of it, before she faced Pierre's lawyer. The last thing she wanted was for Marcel to figure out what she'd done last night.

She was still struggling to pull herself together, sipping her second cup of coffee, when she heard Marcel's car in the driveway. He'd arrived five minutes early.

A thread of unease worked its way into her stomach as she considered his text again. She'd assumed this was some kind of formality. But why was he eager to see her so early?

The argument with Maxim tormented her as she walked down the hallway to answer Marcel's knock.

Had Maxim taken legal action to dispute Pierre's will already? She supposed she should have anticipated this, but after last night… She'd had some vague hope he would wait, to find a compromise with her.

While the thought of seeing him again wasn't doing anything to alleviate the knots in her belly, it felt better than the wave of foreboding that hit her as she opened the door and saw Marcel's expression.

This was no formality.

'Madame de la Mare, there is a problem with the will,' he said. 'This morning Maxim Durand's legal team have made some outrageous claims which we must dispute immediately. May I come in?'

'Yes, yes, of course.' She held the door open. But her

mind couldn't seem to engage with what this all meant as she followed Marcel into the kitchen. It was almost like being in a bad dream as she poured the lawyer a cup of coffee and he set his briefcase down on the kitchen table.

'What claims?' she murmured, but the horrifying reality of what Maxim might have done was already making her stomach hurt.

'Durand has sworn an affidavit that you and he had sexual relations last night and in the process he discovered you were a virgin.' Colour stained the usually staid lawyer's cheeks, the outrage in his voice making the knots in Cara's belly tighten, her mind struggling to comprehend what Marcel was saying.

Maxim had told his legal team she was a virgin, but why would he do that?

She didn't have to wait long to get the answer as Marcel continued in a furious rush.

'Durand's team are looking to have the marriage annulled on the grounds it was never consummated. Of course, this is not a precedent in French law, the marriage does not have to be consummated for it to be legal, but as he is trying to assert that you were *never* in an intimate relationship with your husband, even before your marriage, this might have some weight with the court. But what is more outrageous, his legal team have released a press statement detailing Durand's claims against you, no doubt to force your hand and get us to withdraw to avoid further scandal. It is only a matter of time before the press turn up here. Maxim Durand is a…' The usually congenial Marcel bit off the swear word she suspected was about to come out of his mouth. 'Our path is clear, we must counter the man's lies immediately with a written affidavit from you disputing these claims which we will also release to the press, showing the whole region what… How do you say it in English? What *trash* he really is.'

Marcel finished with a flourish, his hazelnut-brown eyes full of fighting spirit.

Cara's knees gave way and the coffee cup dropped to the floor, but the crash of breaking porcelain was muffled by the deafening punches of her heartbeat.

The harsh reality of what Maxim had done began to seep into her bones like a virus, both debilitating and unbearably painful. This was all her own fault, for thinking she could take on a wolf, and survive.

She hadn't just been foolish and naïve, she'd been a fantasist. She'd realised last night how much Maxim hated his father, but she hadn't believed he would be this cruel, this callous. That he would be prepared to destroy her reputation as well as her home, simply to exact his revenge.

She sniffed as the tears she'd refused to shed last night slipped over her lids.

'*Madame*, do not despair,' Marcel said, sitting next to her and resting a paternal hand over hers on the table. 'We will dispute his claims. In truth, he may have given us a tactical advantage; telling such lies means we can make a counterclaim for defamation.'

'But we can't,' she murmured, scrubbing the pointless tears off her cheeks and forcing herself to meet the lawyer's trusting gaze. 'Because everything he said is true.'

'Maxim, is that your communications guy?' Victor Dupont, Maxim's estate manager, said in French, clearly amused. 'What is he doing here, where the real work takes place?'

Maxim glanced up from tying off the twine on the new vines he and Victor had been inspecting all day—well used to Victor's scathing opinion of the marketing end of wine-making.

He squinted into the sun, wiping the sweat off his forehead. 'I think so,' he murmured. Victor was right to be amused, Rick Carson looked incongruous in his designer suit, picking his way through the rows of vines.

Spending the day out in the fields had seemed like a good way to sweat away his concerns over the Cara Evans situation—and the lingering desire that would not die—not to mention his discomfort at the move he'd been forced to make this morning.

He'd rung his legal team early, after spending the night figuring out a solution to Cara's stubborn refusal to even consider his offer.

The affidavit he'd signed about their night together had made him uncomfortable; it was ruthless, but he'd done ruthless things before to get what he wanted, and she had left him with no choice. He needed to break her misguided loyalty to de la Mare. And because of the problem of a possible pregnancy, he did not have time to do this gently. He wanted her safely installed at Château Durand and the purchase of de la Mare's estate set in motion before he left France next week for his vineyards in California. By the time he returned, she would be over her stubbornness and ready to see the benefits of becoming his mistress.

The truth was he had lost his temper last night when she had mentioned his father. Blindsided by a surge of possessiveness... And, yes, dammit, jealousy. Which didn't make a lot of sense. But then very little about his reactions to Cara made sense.

After spending a sleepless night thinking about the way she had come apart in his arms, he had come to several important conclusions, however. He had no need to be jealous of his father. Not only was the man dead, but Cara had never given herself to him, only to Maxim. Perhaps he had also been too hasty insisting that La Maison be demolished.

He had made that threat to de la Mare because he had been furious when the man had dared to ask him for his help, attempting to play on Maxim's sentiment for a place he had never been allowed to even step inside. But his goal when returning to Burgundy had always been to create his own legacy and make wines that were better than de la Mare's had ever been. Owning the vines he had sweated over as a child was enough. If Cara was willing to come and live at Château Durand, perhaps he could be magnanimous about the house?

By the time Carson reached him and Victor, he was sweating profusely. 'Maxim, why don't you ever answer your cell phone?' he said in his broad Californian accent.

Maxim shrugged. 'I don't have it with me,' he replied. He'd left his phone in the car. The whole purpose had been to get back to basics today. And get away from the endless thoughts of Cara.

'What is the problem?' he asked, because there was obviously a problem or Carson wouldn't have risked ruining his two-thousand-dollar shoes.

'We need you back at headquarters. The internet has blown up. We've got local news reporters doorstepping the office and the story's threatening to spread to the nationals.'

'What story?' Maxim snapped, annoyed now as well as confused. He did not appreciate getting dressed down by a subordinate.

'The one your legal team broke at nine thirty this morning…' Carson paused to take a breath. 'The one in which you question the validity of Pierre de la Mare's recent marriage, thanks to your seduction of Madame de la Mare last night.'

'*C'est quoi ça?*' Maxim's shout rang across the fields, the trickle of irritation turning into a flood of volcanic rage. 'I never sanctioned such a thing.'

Someone at Brocard et Fils, his solicitors, had released the details of the affidavit he'd signed this morning to the press? The lava rose up his chest like a fire-breathing dragon, threatening to blow his head off. He threw the last of the twine to Victor, who caught it one-handed. 'Finish this, Victor. I must go.'

The estate manager nodded.

Maxim stalked across the fields towards his vehicle, his fury building with every step.

'But if you didn't sanction it, who did?' Carson asked, running to keep up with his long strides.

'I don't know but I will find out,' he snarled through gritted teeth.

Reaching the SUV, he jumped into the driver's side, the fury firing through his veins at the imbecile who had done this—but right behind it was the dread making his stomach heave towards his throat.

Cara.

As uncomfortable as he had been taking the nuclear option to make her see the reality of her position, and his, he had never intended to publicly humiliate her. And having the details of their first night together—details he had given in confidence to his attorney—become the subject of a media storm would do exactly that.

He had seen the shame in her eyes last night as she sat in the bathroom. Shame which made no sense. She had been innocent. In fact, the chemistry between them had been so strong, neither one of them would have been able to deny it for long. What had happened was inevitable. And it had been good, for both of them. Very good, despite her inexperience. So good he hadn't been able to stop thinking of having her in his bed again.

His fingers flexed on the steering wheel.

Was that the real reason he had taken action this morning to force her hand? Not because he wanted to ensure no pregnancy occurred from their night together, but because he wanted her?

He shook off the thought as he hunted for the car keys in the glovebox.

No, that was madness. However much he might want her, it was only sexual desire. And sexual desire always died.

But as he jammed his keys into the SUV's transmission, the memory of Cara's wary expression the night before clouded his vision. He could picture her now, her hands clasped in her lap while he washed her as gently as he could, and examined the red skin where he had bruised her during their furious coupling. And for the first time in a long time his stomach dropped, and his heart rammed his throat.

He recognised the feeling as the same one that had pursued him for years after he'd left Burgundy. Guilt.

He turned on the ignition, swung his head round to start backing down the track, and hit the gas.

Carson jumped back as the dirt sprayed his suit and the SUV lurched into reverse.

Maxim swung the vehicle round and sped down the track, heading for the back road that led through his property towards de la Mare's estate.

Towards La Maison de la Lune.

And mentally prepared himself to do something he hadn't done since the morning he had told his mother he was leaving Burgundy…

Apologise to a woman.

He arrived at La Maison ten minutes later, to find a local news crew outside that looked to be in the process of packing up their equipment.

As soon as he stepped out of the car, the reporter rushed towards him with a microphone in her fist, the cameraman not far behind. She shoved the microphone in his face, firing a string of questions at him about his scandalous 'tryst' with Madame de la Mare.

'*Sans commentaires*,' he snapped, brushing them aside before pounding on the door of the farmhouse. 'Cara, open the door. I need to speak to you.'

After five agonising minutes the door opened, and Marcel Caron glared at him.

'You? What are you doing here? Haven't you caused enough...'

'*Tais-toi!*' He cut the lawyer's diatribe off, then barged past him to slam the door shut. 'I have no wish to give those parasites more to talk about,' he continued in English, just in case the bastards could record them through the door.

'I find your sudden discretion hard to believe,' the lawyer sneered back, keeping the conversation in English. 'Given the damage you have already...'

'Where's Cara?' he demanded as he stalked past the lawyer. He didn't have time for the guy's micro-aggressions.

He reached the reception room and was immediately struck by the sense of emptiness which lingered over the room that hadn't been there the night before. Where was the warmth, the touches of personality and hospitality he had noticed yesterday when he had walked in here? The spray of wild flowers in a glass jar on the mantel? The scent of rosemary and lavender? The erotic aroma of Cara herself which had invaded his senses and driven him wild?

'Cara?' he shouted again, the hollow ache tangling with the heavy weight of foreboding which sat in his stomach. 'Stop hiding, we need to talk.'

'She is gone,' the lawyer interrupted softly, the bitter accusation in his voice replaced with weariness. 'She left this morning before the media hounds arrived, thank God.'

Maxim swung round. 'Where did she go?'

'I do not know,' the man said, then lifted a sheaf of official-looking papers from the briefcase he had open on the table. 'But she left you these.'

Maxim frowned down at the papers and shoved his hands into his pockets. He didn't want to take them, whatever they were.

Cara had left? Without contacting him? Without giving him a chance to explain?

'Take them,' Marcel said, the edge of accusation returning. 'It's what you wanted.'

The harsh stab of regret dug into Maxim's stomach. Whatever those papers contained, this was not the outcome he had planned.

What if he could never hold her again? Hear her sighs? Her sobs? Feel her body close around his?

What surprised him, though, was the realisation that it wasn't just the chance to have her back in his bed that he regretted the most.

What if he never saw her face again? So open, so trusting, the flags of colour on her cheeks when she was aroused? What if he never heard her voice again either? Crisp and smoky, arousing him and antagonising him at one and the same time…

Caron dumped the papers onto the table. The thud yanked Maxim out of the unfamiliar reverie. The lawyer let out a hefty sigh. 'She has relinquished any claim on the de la Mare estate and this property. I will file the papers with the court tomorrow morning and the estate will be put up for auction to pay the debts very soon.' The lawyer's gaze met his, the accusation back full force. 'I realise you are a ruthless man, but I never realised you were this ruthless.'

He could refute the man's claims. He hadn't intended for the affidavit to become public, certainly hadn't planned for it to be leaked to the press. And he hadn't seduced Cara with any ulterior motive. But he didn't really care what Marcel Caron thought of him. The threat of public or private censure had never stopped him from doing what he had to do to grow his business, and destroy his rivals, before now.

Which only made the numbness spreading through his body all the more confusing, and unexplainable. How was it that he found he did care what Cara thought of him?

'Here—' the lawyer lifted a sealed envelope with his name written on it in neat black lettering '—she left you this too.'

He snatched the envelope from the man's hand and ripped it open.

Maxim,
I realise what happened last night was simply a
means to an end for you—and it was naïve of me to
think it was anything else.
I hope you can be at peace with your father now.
Goodbye,
Cara Evans

He let the paper drop, then thrust his fingers through his hair. His guts churned as the numbness was replaced with anger. Not just with himself, but with Cara.

Did she think he'd planned this? That he'd seduced her to get hold of the estate? That he would stoop so low as to use his body to further his business ambitions? Did she think what had happened between them hadn't been as spontaneous for him as it had been for her?

She'd run without listening to his side, without giving him a chance to explain, but, worse than that, she had folded her hand because of what? A few press enquiries?

Yes, his legal team had made a catastrophic error, and

heads would soon be rolling because of it, but why hadn't she stayed to fight this thing? Why had she given up so easily?

And that nonsense at the end of the letter about his father. He didn't give a damn about that old bastard. He'd moved on from that rejection a long time ago. Why hadn't she believed him?

'You need to tell me where she's gone,' he demanded, focusing his rising fury on the only person there. He needed to find her, to get her back. To get rid of this growing emptiness inside.

'I told you, I have no idea,' Marcel said.

Although Maxim suspected the other man wouldn't have told him where she'd gone even if he knew, he also suspected he wasn't lying.

'I'm not even sure she knew,' Caron added wearily. 'It took all of my powers of persuasion to get her to take a few hundred euros so she could buy a train ticket and survive until she finds a new job.'

'She has no money?' Maxim asked, his fury building. 'How can she have no money? Was she not working for de la Mare? Surely she must have saved something?' From what he could see of La Maison, for all the homely charms she had added to the place, she and de la Mare had been living very frugally.

'Pierre hadn't paid her for months,' Marcel announced, and Maxim's temper shot into the stratosphere. 'That's how he persuaded her to marry him,' Marcel added. 'Apparently he told her he would be able to leave her the money he owed her in his will from his pension, if she were his widow. If I had known this before now I would have told her: there was no pension.'

'That bastard.' Maxim stalked back towards the farmhouse entrance. The surge of guilt wasn't helping to contain his rising fury at Cara's foolish actions.

His father had always been a bastard. So it was no surprise the conniving cheapskate had found a way to cheat his housekeeper out of her wages before he died. And trick her into marriage in a pathetic last-ditch attempt to stop Maxim owning the de la Mare legacy.

But if Cara was destitute, why hadn't she accepted Maxim's offer? And why had she capitulated so easily over the will? Surely this was madness.

He understood pride, but you couldn't eat pride, and it didn't put a roof over your head. Was the thought of becoming his mistress really so repugnant that she would rather starve?

He shoved past the waiting reporters, ignoring the lights flashing in his face and the probing questions being shouted at him. Not to mention the hit to his ego at Cara's foolish decision to run, rather than accept his help.

He tugged his cell phone out of his pocket and started dialling. Once he'd climbed into the SUV, he stuck the phone on hands-free and began issuing orders while he reversed out of the yard.

He needed Cara Evans found.

The guilt stabbed into his gut as he drove off the de la Mare property. But more than that was the crippling feeling of loss—that he did not fully understand—and the terrifying sense of *déjà vu*.

His mother's voice echoed in his head... A voice which had haunted his dreams for so many years after her death, a voice he hadn't heard for years.

'Maxim, ne t'en vas pas. Je ne peux pas vivre sans toi.'
Maxim, do not leave. I cannot live without you.

As he accelerated along the country road, he allowed

his fury to overwhelm the memories. He would bring Cara back. And make her see reason.

He took the turning to the local train station.

She only had a few hours' start on him—she wouldn't be that hard to find. Especially not with the resources he had at his disposal.

This wasn't over. It couldn't be. He wouldn't let it be. Not like this.

CHAPTER EIGHT

Five months later

'YOU SHOULD SEE the crowd out there tonight. I swear I've spotted more movie stars already than are at my local multiplex.'

'That's cool.' Cara sent a wan smile to her new friend Dora, whose excitement at their latest waitressing gig would have been infectious if only she weren't so exhausted. She eased the zip up on the short black skirt she wore for her waitressing work but left the button at the top undone. But as she donned her white shirt, she encountered another problem. She hunched her shoulders, attempting to hide the way the shirt's buttons threatened to pop out of their holes over her ever-increasing bust.

How much longer was she going to be able to hide her condition? And what would she do when that day came? This job was the only thing keeping her afloat. But working any and every shift she could get was starting to take its toll.

She slammed the locker door and slipped on the four-inch heels the luxury hotel on London's Embankment insisted on, then stretched her back to alleviate the ache which had set in a week ago.

She pressed her palm to the curve of her stomach, and

the trickle of panic receded. The wave of love she already felt for the child swept through her and a tired smile edged her lips. This baby was hers, and only hers, something she could love and cherish the way she never had been.

'How far along are you, honey?' Dora murmured.

Cara's head swung round, to find Dora's gaze on her, full of concern and curiosity.

She dropped her hand from her stomach, the panic returning to tighten around her throat. 'I... How did you know?' she managed. Dora was her friend, surely she wouldn't tell their line manager.

'Because you've got that dreamy look on your face I had with my two,' Dora said easily. 'And that bump...' she glanced pointedly at Cara's tummy '...is becoming harder and harder to miss.'

'Is it really that obvious?' Cara whispered, the exhaustion threatening to envelop her. 'I can't... I can't afford to lose any shifts.'

'Isn't there anyone who can help you out, luv?'

Cara shook her head, grateful Dora hadn't asked the obvious question—where is the father?

'I'll pick up all your drinks then. And you can take my canapés, okay, they're lighter.'

'Thank you.' Cara blinked, feeling stupidly emotional at the other woman's kindness.

'You never know, you might find a sugar daddy tonight.' Dora grinned as they made their way up the back stairs of the Regency hotel towards the huge ballroom where the Valentine's Day event they had been hired to work on was taking place. 'There's certainly enough mega-rich men at this thing.'

'I wish,' Cara said, forcing a smile to her lips at the renewed blip of panic, knowing there was one rich man she really did not want to see.

She entered the kitchen from the staff entrance. Surely even she couldn't be that unlucky. And anyway, serving staff like her were all but invisible at these events.

After the kitchen staff loaded up her first tray, she walked into the ballroom.

Chandeliers sparkled, hanging from the room's vaulted ceiling. Towering sprays of roses and lilies were arranged in crystal vases and added a heady aroma to the cloying scent of expensive colognes and fragrances. Conversation hummed over the delicate strains of classical music. Shelves full of leather-bound books lined the walls, a nod to the cavernous room's former life as a historic library. Mullioned windows looked out over the Embankment, framing the spotlit majesty of Big Ben and the purple glow of the Millennium Wheel on the opposite bank. The room was packed with people—men in dinner suits and tuxedos and women in elaborate designer gowns of every conceivable hue, their precious jewels glittering in the low lighting.

Cara's heart fluttered as she absorbed the splendour of the scene and she edged into the crowd to serve the delicate lamb skewers with a tamarind dipping sauce.

She pasted a bright smile on her face. Every one of these people belonged to a world in which Cara would never belong. This was Maxim's world, she thought. Rich, beautiful, arrogant and entitled.

She shifted the weight to her other arm, mindful of the baby bump she had hidden beneath the tray. And willed away the ache in her chest that thoughts of Maxim and their one night together always caused.

She had struggled with the question of whether or not to tell Maxim about the pregnancy when the doctor had confirmed it. She'd tortured herself with all the obvious questions, racked by a guilt she still hadn't quite been able to shake.

Didn't every man deserve to know he was going to be a father?

And didn't every child deserve to know its dad?

Despite his actions later, Maxim had been tender towards her that night, after he'd discovered her virginity. And she knew he could feel deeply from the way he'd reacted to Pierre's will.

But then she thought of her own father, and how easily he had discarded her. And the cruel way Maxim had discarded her too. She knew she'd made the right choice.

These weren't normal circumstances. And Maxim wasn't any normal man. Not only was he rich and powerful, and overwhelming, he had proven how ruthless he could be. He'd also made it very clear he had no desire to become a father.

She kept her head down as she weaved through the opulent crowd, grateful for the cloak of invisibility she wore as one of the waitstaff, and forced her mind back to the job at hand—keeping her elbow braced and her arm steady so she didn't end up spraying tamarind dipping sauce over anyone's designer ballgown before her shift was over…

In six never-ending hours' time.

'Maxim, darling, what are you doing out here? The party's inside!'

Maxim turned from the view of the Thames to find his so-called date, Kristin Delinski, strutting towards him as if she were still on the catwalk, carrying two champagne flutes. Her legs had to be freezing in that short leather skirt, he thought dispassionately, as he took a deep breath of the chilly night air. Air he'd needed as soon as they'd walked into this mayhem twenty minutes ago. Not for the first time, he wondered what had possessed him to attend tonight's event and invite her along. When had he ever celebrated Valentine's Day?

His gaze flickered over his date's expertly made-up face as she handed him one of the glasses. He'd probably had some vague notion of taking her to bed, but the minute she'd climbed into his car he'd known that wasn't going to happen. The sexual spark which had once been there for her, and all the other women he'd dated casually over the years, was gone—blown away by the tornado that had hit his sex life five months ago and still wasn't finished wreaking havoc on his libido.

When was he going to be able to stop obsessing about that one night? A night that had meant nothing.

Cara Evans had vanished. He'd searched for her for months, but every avenue he—and the different investigators he'd hired—had tried had hit a dead end. The woman was a ghost, without a family, any known acquaintances and, most infuriating of all, not even a social media footprint.

'It's Valentine's Night and you never know...' Kristin paused to flutter her heavily painted eyelashes. 'You might get extremely lucky if you make more of an effort.'

'Duly noted,' Maxim murmured as he sipped the champagne—and assessed the vintage. Not as good as Durand's best champagne, but not bad.

The problem was he didn't want to make the effort, because he had no desire whatsoever to get lucky with Kristin, despite her mile-long legs and that provocative self-confidence, which had once made her such an appealing distraction whenever he was in London on a business trip. He could barely even remember those encounters now, because his memory was still full of another woman's sighs, and sobs. Luminous bright blue eyes filled with shame and confusion, soft dewy skin that smelled of wild flowers and arousal, ripe nipples begging for his…

Merde! Stop thinking about her—she's gone; she didn't want you…

Kristin ran a fingernail across his jaw, interrupting his frustrating thoughts. 'Really, Max,' she said, using the nickname he hated as she pouted. 'Are you even listening to me?'

Non.

Just as he opened his mouth to tell her the truth, something caught his eye at the far end of the balcony.

A serving girl in the standard waitressing outfit of white shirt and short black skirt had walked out of the ballroom to offer a tray of canapés to the only other couple on the terrace. Her lush figure was barely contained by the fitted uniform. Desire sizzled along his nerve-endings, the heady fizz of recognition a great deal more intoxicating than the vintage champagne. He grasped Kristin's wrist to pull her hand away from his face so he could get a better look at the waitress.

Was it her? Could it possibly be her? Or was his mind playing tricks on him again?

He'd conjured up this image a dozen times before in the last five months. Fleeting glimpses of Cara's hair, her figure, that heart-shaped face—on the streets of Paris and Rome and even Johannesburg—had stirred his senses, only to destroy him seconds later when he looked closer and realised the woman wasn't her.

But as he studied the apparition this time, instead of dissolving into reality, the yearning became stronger.

The waitress's blonde hair was piled in a haphazard chignon, glowing gold in the flicker of lamplight on the balcony. His fingers tensed on Kristin's wrist as he recalled the silky feel of Cara's hair as the pins scattered across the floor of La Maison and the locks tumbled into his hands.

'Max, what is it?' Kristin's tone was annoyed, but he could barely hear her above the thundering of his own heartbeat. 'Why are you staring at the waitress like that? Do you know her?'

'*Oui*,' he murmured, but he wasn't talking to his date any more as he watched the girl turn and head towards them with her tray.

'*Lève la tête*,' he whispered, willing her to lift her head so he could get a better look at her face. But he already knew, from the sensations charging through his body, making his sex harden and his breathing accelerate. He'd found her. At last.

Just as she had done all those months ago, she obeyed his command instinctively and their gazes locked. She stopped dead. Stunned surprise crossed her face first, followed by panic and guilt, but then her gaze flicked to Kristin and what he saw in her face—could it be envy, hurt, regret?—had adrenaline firing through his system like a drug.

And he had the answer he had been looking for, for five months, without even realising it. She still wanted him too.

The tray clattered to the floor, making everyone but him—and her—jump as the food splattered across the stones. She stood transfixed, her body trembling as if she were in a trance from which she couldn't escape.

Reaching into his pocket, he pulled out his wallet and shoved some notes into Kristin's hand. 'Find your own way home,' he murmured, tucking his wallet back into his jacket pocket, his movements deliberately slow and cautious, his gaze fixed on his runaway lover.

'Well, really, Max, I…'

He tuned out Kristin's indignant response as he walked past her, towards Cara, his gaze devouring every inch of her.

Something about her was different. Her figure? Why did it seem fuller, even more lush than he remembered it? She edged back a step and the lamplight hit her face.

Concern lanced through him.

Where had those dark circles come from, under her eyes? Why did she seem so fragile despite her curves?

The wave of possessiveness and protectiveness, which he'd convinced himself didn't exist, surged up his chest.

'Cara,' he said, her name rough on his tongue as he lifted his hand to beckon her towards him, scared to make any sudden movement in case she vanished and he discovered he had been dreaming all along.

Like a young deer scenting the hunter, she snapped out of her trance and spun round.

He cursed as she shot back into the ballroom.

'Cara, *reviens ici!*' he yelled, demanding she come back, but she'd already disappeared into the throng of guests.

He shoved his way through the crowd after her, not caring about the drinks he spilled, the stern looks and shouted admonishments he received from the people he pushed out of the way. He craned his neck to look over the heads of the other guests. Relief rushed through him as he spotted her golden hair disappearing through a door at the end of the great hall, marked Staff Only.

The crowd parted as he barged past, the relief and adrenaline—and the sharp swell of desire—joined by a rising tide of fury.

This was no dream, it was real. *She* was real.

She'd run from him once. No way was he going to let her run again.

Cara kicked off her shoes as soon as she got through the staff door and picked them up, to race past the wait stations where the other servers were having their trays filled, her exhaustion forgotten in a rush of pure unadulterated panic.

Maxim! Maxim was here and he'd found her.

'Cara, is everything okay?' She shook her head at Dora's shocked question as she rushed past her friend towards the stairwell to the locker room.

Maxim, who had been with another woman.

Kristin Delinski, a world-renowned supermodel who Cara had recognised instantly from the magazines she'd once loved to read. But had avoided in the last five months.

She swiped away the tear that slipped down her cheek as she made it to the stairs.

Good God, why are you crying? Of course he's with another woman. He's probably had tons of other women since that night, all of them more beautiful and accomplished than you.

Her line manager, Martha Simpson, was coming up the stairs from the staff locker room as she headed down. 'Cara, where are you going? There's two more hours left on your shift!'

'I'm sorry, I've got to go,' she said, then rushed past, not waiting for the woman's answer. She wouldn't be able to come back, not now he knew where she worked.

She made it to the locker room.

He wasn't following her. Why would he? But, even so, urgency made her hands clumsy as she grabbed her bag, shoved the heels inside, slipped on her flats and untied the apron. She was reaching for her coat when she heard footsteps enter the room, and a deep voice had her fingers jerking on the coat.

'Cara...why did you run?'

Hearing the roughened R, the husky intimacy of her name said in his gruff French accent—a sound which had woken her from dreams so many nights since she'd left

France—had so many conflicting emotions hurtling into her chest. She turned to face him without thinking, the urge to see him again riding roughshod over all her instincts of self-preservation.

She realised her mistake as his gaze tracked down to her stomach, and the baby bump, which was no longer hidden by the apron.

His eyes met hers, the golden-brown rich with passion and fury and yet dark with accusation, and something she didn't understand—because it looked strangely like hurt.

'The child, is it mine?'

She wanted to say no, to protect herself and her baby from that caustic cynical gaze, and the character of the man she knew lay behind it. Powerful, arrogant, demanding, ruthless. More committed to his revenge against a dead man than he would ever be to someone like her. But something about the flash of pain which had been there and then gone in a heartbeat had the lie catching in her throat.

She turned back to the locker, releasing the coat, and pressed her forehead against the cool metal. The weariness that had haunted her for weeks returned to sap the last of the energy from her limbs, but this time it was accompanied by the bone-sapping guilt she had wrestled with for months. She thought she'd conquered it, thought she'd come to terms with her choice not to contact Maxim. But if she had, why could the truth still punish her?

She placed a hand over her stomach and silently apologised to her child before saying the only words that would come out of her mouth.

'Yes. Yes, it is.'

CHAPTER NINE

MAXIM WAS IN SHOCK. Or at least he thought he was. Because it was hard to tell, so many emotions were bombarding him at once he could hardly control them, let alone differentiate or identify them.

Cara was carrying his child.

The only emotion he knew he didn't feel was regret—that he had found her. For a man who had never intended to become a father this didn't make a lot of sense, but there was no denying the surge of protectiveness that had blindsided him when he'd first identified Cara on the balcony.

'Why did you not contact me?' he demanded, allowing his anger to show—to cover the hurt he didn't want to acknowledge.

She raised her head, the tiredness in her eyes and those dark shadows under them that had disturbed him so much making his fingers clench into fists.

He swallowed hard, forcing himself to resist the urge to pick her up and cradle her against his chest. She looked as if she were about to collapse. How long had she been working like this, late into the night, constantly on her feet?

'Because I didn't want you to know,' she said.

The pain caused by the softly spoken words arrowed into his gut, making him stiffen.

He stepped forward and grasped her arm. 'You carry

my child and you had no intention of telling me? *Ever?*' he said, not quite able to keep the whisper of shocked betrayal out of his voice. Things had ended badly between them, and part of that had been his fault, but he did not deserve this.

She tugged her arm free. 'This is *my* child, Maxim. I chose to have it. You don't have to be a part of this.'

'Are you mad?' His gaze roamed down to her stomach, where the baby grew. 'This is my flesh and blood. Do you really think I would choose to abandon it?'

She looked down, breaking eye contact, but he could hear the distress in her voice when she murmured, 'Men do it all the time.'

He cursed under his breath. 'Not this man,' he said, more frustrated than he had ever been in his life. 'I am not my father, if that is what you believe.' Would he never be free of that bastard's crimes? To be judged now by the sins of his father would almost be laughable if it weren't so unjust.

She glanced up, the guilt in her eyes tempered by the shadow of doubt, and regret. And, although she remained silent, he could hear again what she had said that night.

'This isn't about my loyalty to Pierre... It's about your need for revenge.'

And the question that had tormented him a thousand times since in his nightmares.

If you are really better than him, why did you insist on your revenge, insist on destroying La Maison, when letting her keep the house might have persuaded her to stay?

'I don't want to argue with you,' she said, clasping her arms around her waist in a defensive gesture that had the guilty recriminations receding.

What the hell was she protecting herself against? Him?

Whatever his crimes against her that night, whatever he had done, or failed to do, she had taken the decision not to tell him about his child.

'I deserve a better answer than that,' he said. 'You had no right not to inform me I was going to become a father.'

She lifted her chin, the spark of defiance in her eyes somehow better than the exhaustion, or the guilt, or the regret. 'I didn't think you'd want to know,' she said.

'When did I give you that impression?' he demanded, the fury and frustration threatening to strangle him. 'I asked you to come to Château Durand that night, I offered you my support.'

'While making it very clear you thought a pregnancy would be an inconvenience,' she fired back. 'A problem to be solved…' Her blue eyes darkened with sadness. 'To be taken care of.'

'Because at the time it was,' he barked out, no longer able to contain his anger. She flinched and he forced himself to lower his voice again, to remain calm. Shouting at her was not the answer. 'But the choice would always have been yours.' He ground out the words, annoyed that he had to spell it out. Did she think he was some kind of monster? The kind of man who would have insisted she have an abortion? 'But whatever I said then hardly applies now. The child is now a fact.'

She nodded, the flicker of guilt in her eyes some compensation. 'Okay,' she said.

A part of him was still furious with her, still angry, and still upset that she had run without giving him a chance to explain. A chance to change his mind about the damn house. But the protective side that had surged to life on the balcony… Hell, all those months ago, when he had tended her in the bathroom in La Maison de la Lune, went some way to calming his fury now. He had searched for a glimpse of her for months in every crowd and been unable to forget her, no matter how hard he tried. However shocking the news of her pregnancy was, and however hurtful her decision not to tell him about it, his first priority now had to be to take care of her, and ensure she didn't run from him again.

So he went with instinct and cupped her cheek.

Her head jerked up, but she didn't draw away from his touch as he ran his thumb over her bottom lip.

The surge of desire and the urge to feast on that mouth again was so fierce he had to force himself not to act on it. Giving in to this hunger now was not an option, but he took some consolation from the dazed arousal in her eyes.

'You look exhausted,' he murmured. 'Are you well?'

'I'm just tired. It's been a long night,' she said, the weary resignation in her tone crucifying him. He made no effort to control the shaft of tenderness, of possession that knifed through him this time.

They had a lot of talking to do. And probably arguing too. And he had no clue whatsoever how to handle the news that he was going to become a father, the fact of the child an abstract concept that he would have to deal with another time.

But right now she looked barely strong enough to stand.

Nudging her aside, he took her coat from the locker and wrapped it around her shoulders then lifted her bag out of her hand. 'Come, we will go back to my hotel.'

'It's okay. I live in East London. I can get the Tube home,' she said, reaching for her bag. He whisked it out of her grasp and she frowned. 'If you tell me where you're staying, Maxim, I'll come over tomorrow and we can talk then about the baby.'

He let out a harsh laugh at her earnest expression. 'Do you truly believe I would be so stupid as to let you out of my sight again?'

She didn't say anything, clearly stunned by his question.

He couldn't imagine why she would be so surprised. Why would he trust her, after what she had done?

He cupped her elbow and guided her out of the locker room and through the back entrance of the hotel into the street. Her body was limp, her demeanour passive. The fight had drained out of her. He would have been more pleased if his concern for her well-being wasn't starting to gag him. Was it normal for pregnant women to be so fragile?

Yes, it was.

Fear knifed through his gut at the thought of his mother.

He whistled for a passing cab, which skidded to a stop at the kerb. He helped her in then climbed in behind her, giving the name of his hotel to the driver. It was only a few streets away, but he wasn't taking any chances.

She scooted to the other side of the bench seat, to stare out of the window into the night. He saw her brush a lone tear from her cheek, her face illuminated by the passing cars and the neon signs of the Strand as the cab arrived at their destination, the landmark six-star art deco hotel where he kept a suite whenever he was in town.

He stepped out of the cab and paid the driver, then took her elbow again when she climbed out. He signalled a bell-boy.

The teenager shot over. 'Yes, Mr Durand, how can I help you?'

'I need *un obstétricien* to come to my suite immediately. Ask the concierge to contact the hotel doctor to find the best available at this hour. Money is no object,' he said, giving the boy a twenty-pound tip before the kid shot off towards the concierge's desk.

Cara's arm tensed in his as he led her through the lobby to the lifts, but she didn't resist him.

'I already have a doctor, Maxim,' she said, the exhaustion in her voice so apparent now he decided not to resist his instincts any longer. He scooped her into his arms and carried her into the lift, ignoring her efforts to protest.

'*Bien*,' he said, stabbing the button to the penthouse. 'Now you will have two doctors.'

'Your girlfriend is healthy but undernourished, Mr Durand, and exhausted. I've given her a supply of vitamins, but what she needs most right now is rest. And someone to make sure she eats three square meals a day. No more working on her feet for hours would also be a good idea,' the doctor said, giving Maxim a judgemental look.

He ignored it. He didn't care what the obstetrician thought of him, as long as she could reassure him that Cara was well.

The doctor packed the last of her instruments into her bag. 'Your child is certainly much livelier than its mother at the moment. It has a firm, steady heartbeat and quite an impressive kick.'

'It kicks?' he asked, the words catching in his throat as his heart somersaulted in his chest. He'd been trying not to think too much about the baby.

The doctor smiled. 'Your child is very active and big for dates, from what I can tell by touch. Cara says she missed her last prenatal appointment.' The doctor sighed as she snapped the bag closed. 'Apparently she overslept.' The woman shot him the same judgemental look, probably wondering why a man as rich as he was had allowed the mother of his child to work long into the night for the minimum wage.

Maxim tried not to care what the doctor thought of him. Cara would no longer be risking her health working dead-end jobs. She might not have wanted him to support her, but everything had changed. He had a responsibility to her now that he had no intention of shirking, so he was going to give her no choice in the matter.

She was coming to live in Burgundy with him, as soon as he could make arrangements for them to be married. He'd considered the pros and cons of the arrangement while the doctor examined Cara and he could see no other solution that would satisfy him. He couldn't trust her not to risk her health and well-being. And—while he doubted he would ever be capable of having a relationship with this child—he refused to allow it to be born without his name.

The doctor passed him her card. 'If you want to bring her to the clinic tomorrow we can do a proper blood workup and an ultrasound scan to give the baby a thorough check. But, for the moment, I'd suggest leaving her alone to get a good night's sleep.'

The implication was clear in the doctor's stern expression—no sex tonight. Perhaps she had heard of his 'insatiable appetites' from the tabloid press. While he had earned that reputation in the past, the doctor's stern look was ironic now, given that he hadn't had the inclination to touch any other woman since he had left Cara's bed five months ago.

'Do not worry, I have no intention of demanding any sexual favours from Cara tonight,' he said.

Or ever, he thought as he stuffed the doctor's card into his back pocket, the sting of guilt unmistakable.

Having Cara in his arms earlier, as he'd carried her into the suite, had caused a string of conflicting, confusing and contradictory emotions but even he could not deny the relentless surge of desire.

How could he have become aroused so easily? When she had been so fragile. Exhausted by a pregnancy which he had failed to prevent. Perhaps he wasn't that unlike his father after all. The thought sickened him, bringing back memories of his mother, and giving him an even more compelling reason to insist on marriage. He would not abandon the mother of his child while her health was at risk, the way his father had abandoned his mother.

'Mr Durand, please don't misconstrue what I said.' To his surprise, the doctor paused at the door, her face a picture of empathy. And understanding. 'I didn't intend to imply sexual intercourse between you is dangerous. It's not. As long as you're both willing, many couples continue sexual relations well into the third trimester. And, as I said, Ms Evans is healthy. She just needs a good rest. I think it would be wise, though, for you to bring her into the Harley Street clinic tomorrow so we can do an ultrasound.'

'You feel this is necessary?' Maxim asked, unable to hide his anxiety.

'Not necessary, but desirable,' the doctor said, touching his arm. 'To put both your minds at rest. It's not unusual for men to experience a loss of libido when their partner becomes pregnant. But I can assure you the changes to Cara's body are all perfectly natural.'

'Okay,' he said, feeling like a fraud. The doctor had mis-understood. A loss of libido was not the problem. 'I will bring Cara to the clinic tomorrow,' he added reluctantly.

He didn't want to think too much about the child just yet. Only Cara. But ensuring all was completely safe with the pregnancy made sense. Especially given the answering desire he'd seen in her eyes today.

She would be living in his home, with his ring on her finger, for four long months until the child was born if he got his way, which he would. The chances of them both being able to keep their hands off each other for that length of time were minimal, at best.

He could not let Cara out of his sight again, until he had her promise that she would let him do what was best for her. And that meant getting her to agree to marry him.

CHAPTER TEN

CARA'S EYELIDS FLUTTERED open and she found herself in an enormous room. The gold drapes of the four-poster bed in which she'd slept were illuminated by a strip of sunlight shining through the gap in the curtains drawn across a large picture window opposite the bed.

Was she dreaming? she wondered as her eyes adjusted to the half-light.

This was not the cramped, chilly room in the house she shared in Leyton, where the traffic noise from outside rattled the windows and woke her up at dawn each morning. Her limbs felt light, her mind refreshed, despite the familiar ache in her toes from the high heels she wore for work. When was the last time she'd woken up feeling this well rested?

She sat up and the sheet dropped into her lap, making her aware she was wearing nothing but her bra and panties. Where were her fluffy PJs?

The ripple of sensation became a flood as the sleep cleared from her brain, and the events of the previous evening rushed in to fill the gap.

Maxim. Maxim had found her last night and brought her here.

The memories assailed her. His dark eyes—shocked, aroused, accusing. His voice—rough with tightly leashed outrage, then deep with reproach. The scent of him—sandalwood soap and man—invading her senses as she sat in the cab on the ride to his hotel, struggling to stay awake and focused. The strength of his arms—powerful, unyielding, supportive—as he scooped her up when her knees turned to water in the lift. His hands—gentle yet brusque in the shadows of the ornate room as he undressed her and tucked the quilt around her after the doctor's visit, and she lost her battle with exhaustion.

She shivered, even though the room was the perfect ambient temperature, and the familiar heat at the memory of his touch glowed in her belly.

This is my flesh and blood. Do you really believe I would choose to abandon it?

What had she done? She had assumed he would be furious if he ever found out about the child, and her decision to have it, but all she could remember from his expression was the flash of hurt.

I am not my father.

The heat in her stomach became sharp and jagged.

She'd judged him and condemned him. And while her decision to run away had been sound, he was right: everything had changed once she had discovered her pregnancy. She placed her palm on the firm bulge of her stomach, felt the flutter of movement which had scared her a week ago but now reassured her.

'Good morning, pipsqueak,' she murmured, as she did every morning. She let a tear trail down her cheek—because there was no one to see it. 'I'm so sorry,' she whispered, swiping the tear away with the back of her hand.

Running had become a default after she'd left care, because it had always been easier to start afresh than to face her fears. She should have realised as soon as the doctor had told her she was expecting Maxim Durand's child that now was the time to stop running, but it was pointless beating herself up about that panicked decision now.

He'd found her, and last night, despite his shock, he had seemed much more furious about the fact she hadn't told him about the baby...*his* baby...than he was about the pregnancy itself.

The choice would always have been yours.

She'd made a mistake not contacting Maxim. Maybe she'd made it for the right reasons. He was still rich and ruthless and as overwhelming as he'd always been. But recognising her mistake now was the only way to move forward.

She slipped out of the bed. Her bare feet sunk into the thick luxurious carpet as she padded over to an armchair upholstered in embroidered silk, where someone had draped a thick bathrobe.

She shrugged it on, and then opened the curtains on the room's huge picture window to find a balcony overlooking a striking view of the River Thames.

She shoved her hands into the pockets of the robe, then glanced back at the bed. The pillow next to hers lay untouched. He hadn't joined her during the night.

She recalled his touch the evening before. Not urgent and intense, but gentle and impersonal. The weight in her stomach twisted and plunged.

For goodness' sake, Cara, what did you expect? Of course he isn't interested in you any more. And why would you want him to be? You're a pregnant woman, and it was your inability to resist him that got you into this fix in the first place.

She pressed her fists towards her belly, sending a silent apology to the life growing inside her.

You're not a problem, pipsqueak. Or a fix. And you never will be, okay?

Although pretty much everything else in her life was, she thought ruefully.

She'd lost her job last night. Martha would never rehire her after she'd run out on her shift like a madwoman. And somehow or other she was going to have to set aside her guilt at not contacting Maxim a lot sooner and find a solution which would suit them both—without letting him steamroller her.

She drew in a breath, overwhelmed at the thought of navigating that conversation.

Maxim, being Maxim, had been forceful and demanding last night, riding roughshod over her protests and basically taking matters into his own hands—or, rather, arms. She'd been way too exhausted to object. But this morning she was going to need to start standing up for herself.

She brushed her hair back from her face. It was still early, she realised, analysing the angle of the sun over the Thames. The first order of business was to have a shower and find her clothes, then she'd be ready to face him. And ready to face the mistake she'd made not contacting him.

But she wasn't the only one to blame for what had happened, she told herself staunchly.

She wasn't the one who had chosen to use their night together in a cynical bid to acquire a property—the one who had been so hell-bent on revenge he had decided to throw her to the media wolves.

Maxim was not blameless in this calamity. Once she was washed and dressed, she'd be ready to point that out to him—a bit more forcefully than she had last night.

Twenty minutes later, Cara was clean and dry, her damp hair brushed. Unfortunately, she still only had the bathrobe and yesterday's underwear to wear because she'd been unable to find her clothes. Or her shoes. Even her coat had disappeared.

Had Maxim stolen them? Or hidden them? To keep her docile and trapped in this room?

Bolstering her newfound courage, she tightened the tie on the robe and eased open the bedroom door.

Expecting him to be waiting for her in the sitting room, she let go of the breath she'd been holding as she scanned the suite's large, luxuriously decorated lounge area and couldn't see him anywhere.

But then a gruff sound had her gaze zeroing in on the back of the three-seater sofa facing another large picture window, which was the feature aspect of the lavish room. A pair of bare feet, long and tanned, hung over the cream silk arm of the sofa.

Maxim?

Her throat tightened as she walked round the sofa to find his tall frame stretched out on the cushions, taking up all the available space. A thin blanket covered the lower half of his body, the waistband of his boxer shorts peeking out. Her heartbeat throbbed in her throat and the weight in her stomach plunged as her greedy gaze studied him unobserved. His bare chest looked as magnificent as she remembered it, while his flat stomach rose and fell in a steady rhythm which echoed in her abdomen. There was a tuft of dark hair under one arm where he'd lifted it over his head, probably in a vain attempt to get comfortable. His usually swept-back wavy hair was ruffled, and mushed on one side, while the shadow of beard scruff covered his jaw.

She assumed most men looked less intimidating while they were asleep.

Not Maxim.

If anything, the sight of him, his body relaxed and yet

no less powerful, his nakedness making him all the more
compelling, was having the opposite effect.

Her breath shuddered out.

The quiet huff had his eyes snapping open. Instantly
alert, his golden gaze narrowed. And she found herself
taking a step back.

'*Bonjour*, Cara,' he said, clearly having no problem remembering exactly what had happened the previous evening.

He yawned and stretched then sat up, his movements
indolent and yet focused.

Why did she suddenly feel as if she'd ventured into the
wolf's den? Again.

Every one of her pulse points throbbed, the edgy tension in her body intensifying as he threw off the blanket
to reveal hard thighs and long legs, furred with hair. She
could also see the prominent length pressing against the
front of his boxers.

The weight in her stomach became hot and achy, beating a chaotic pulse in her sex.

He thrust his fingers through his hair, sweeping the silky
waves back, scrubbed his hands down his face—then sent
her a humourless smile.

'Ignore it. I get one every morning. Especially if I have
been dreaming of you.'

The blush climbed into her cheeks, making her feel painfully gauche. And stupidly light-headed.

What on earth was that about? She didn't want him to
dream about her… Did she?

'Where are my clothes, Maxim?' she blurted out, unsettled, not just by the intimacy of the moment but also her
ludicrous reaction to it.

She needed to leave. They could talk about everything
later, when she'd regained her equilibrium. When she

wasn't standing in his hotel suite too aware of her naked-ness under the robe... And his prominent morning erection.

Instead of replying, though, he stood and arched his back, then tilted his head to one side then the other. She heard the joints popping in his neck, making the tightness in her throat increase—at the thought that he had slept all night on the couch in his own luxury suite so she could get her first good night's sleep in weeks.

'I had them destroyed,' he said, the husky tone completely unapologetic.

The statement had all her warm feelings evaporating.

'You...*what*?' She wanted to be outraged at his arrogance, but all she felt was more exposed. And wary. 'Why?'

'To prevent you from running away while I was asleep,' he said without even a hint of remorse.

'But... You... That's... You had no right,' she sputtered, finally managing to grab hold of some outrage. She'd had to pay for that uniform out of her own money.

'I had every right,' he said as his gaze strayed down to her midriff. 'I don't intend to let you vanish again until we have a few things settled.'

'But I wasn't going to vanish,' she said, stunned by the inflexible tone. And the arrogance behind it. And wondering what things he intended to settle. 'I told you last night I'd come back here to talk to you today.'

He didn't even give her the benefit of an answer this time, simply lifted one sceptical brow, his expression saying in all but words: *Do I look like an idiot?*

She wanted to shout and rail against his lack of trust. But she was forced to concede he had a point, given her previous disappearing act. 'Those clothes were my property. I paid for them and I need them because I'm going to have to find another job today. So thanks a bunch for that,' she said, trying to hide her distress behind a wall of sarcasm.

Showing weakness to Maxim Durand was not a good idea. She'd shown him weakness last night in her exhaustion and he'd steamrollered over all her protests, not to mention destroying her property.

The cynical expression disappeared but, just when she thought she'd finally scored a point, he said in a voice so calm and forceful and pragmatic it took a moment for her to register the outrageousness of what he had said, 'You do not need those clothes, as I will buy you better ones. And you don't need a job, because we are to be married in France as soon as it is possible, in ten days' time.'

'Are you…? Are you crazy?'

Maxim watched the light flush on Cara's cheeks deepen to magenta—and the wary concern in her bright blue gaze turn to panic.

Okay, perhaps that had not been the best way to propose. She'd retreated another step, as if trying to edge away from a dangerous animal which was about to pounce.

She was right to be cautious. His emotions had never been this volatile before, this uncontrolled. As soon as he'd opened his eyes, and seen her standing by his makeshift bed, her hair damp and her curves swamped in the fluffy bathrobe, he'd had to quell the primal urge to leap forward and claim her, scared she would disappear again, as she had so many times before in his dreams, and nightmares.

In fact, for one split second he'd thought she might be an apparition, caused by the loss of blood from his head fuelling the painful erection which had woken him every morning for five long months.

'Let me explain, Cara,' he said, taking a step forward. 'Marriage is the obvious solution.'

She scuttled back another step. 'Don't… Don't touch me, Maxim. I mean it.' She held her hands up in the universal sign of surrender, her gaze darting across the suite to the door. 'I have to leave. I can't…'

She made a dash round the sofa. Without thinking, he leapt over the obstacle and captured her wrist, drawing her to a halt.

She struggled, trying to tug her hand free. 'Let me go, Maxim… I want to leave.'

'Stop, Cara. You will hurt yourself,' he said, drawing her against his body, quelling her struggles in his embrace as he pressed her gently against the wall, caging her in.

He inhaled her scent, wild flowers and woman, the scent that had driven him mad last night as he undressed her—and forced himself not to touch her more than was absolutely necessary.

At last she stilled and he heard the stifled sob as her forehead pressed against his sternum.

He felt like a brute, a beast. The jagged sound of her breathing—the painful attempt to hold onto her tears, and the hopelessness that he suspected lay behind it—cut into his composure, his equilibrium. His heart expanded in his chest and his throat closed. But he couldn't let her go, not like this. Not now he had found her. If he let her run, he might never find her again, and he wouldn't be able to live with himself—knowing she was out there somewhere, surviving on nothing, endangering herself, when he had the means to protect her. He had failed his mother once. He would not fail her.

'Shh, Cara,' he murmured against her hair.

She shuddered, the sounds of her breathing cutting off as she tried to hold onto her emotions.

'I would never hurt you,' he said, as softly as he could. 'You have my word. But I cannot let you leave until you have agreed to marry me.'

She sniffed, the sound enough to unlock the strangling feeling in his throat.

How had they come to this? And how could they repair the damage between them? He had planted a child inside her. A child which had sapped all of her strength. Given her virgin state five months ago, he had to take full responsibility for that.

He brushed the damp hair back from her cheek, then cradled her face to lift her gaze to his. Her cheeks were dry but he could see the moisture in the deep pools of shattered blue.

Heat surged in his groin. He steeled himself against it. Now was the time to soothe rather than demand—not a skill he was particularly adept at. He must not ignite the passion between them, even if he could smell the musky scent of her arousal. And see the stunned desire in her eyes.

She did not understand the depth and power of their physical connection because she had so little experience. But he did.

He placed a light kiss on her forehead, felt her shudder of response and then forced himself to drop his arms and release her from the protective cage.

She stood watching him. Unsure, shaky, but he took it as a major concession that, rather than try to run, she simply wrapped her arms around her waist, as if attempting to hold onto the emotions cascading through her body.

Emotions he recognised because they were cascading through his body too. Emotions she probably didn't understand any more than he did.

'The marriage would be time-limited,' he said, his voice rough as he struggled to get his mind to engage with the plans he'd made last night. Detailed, pragmatic, sensible plans before he'd managed to shoot them to hell with his knee-jerk demands.

Her eyes widened and her expression was still stunned, still confused, still a little panicked. But she didn't speak and she didn't move, so he forced himself to continue in a voice he hoped was more persuasive than demanding. Another new experience for him.

'I want the child to be born with my name—and to always have my protection.'

And I want you to have my name and my protection too.

He swallowed, forcing himself not to add the qualifier, the truth of which surged through him as she stood before him, virtually naked, and utterly defenceless.

'I want you to live in Burgundy at my *château*, to have the best possible *prénatal* care. No more working, no more hunger, no more exhaustion. I will…' He paused, forced himself to counter the desire to demand. 'I *wish* to provide for you everything you need while you bear this child. This is very important to me.'

She watched him but, instead of refusing his help out of hand as he half expected her to do—for she was nothing if not contrary, and fiercely independent—she simply said softly, 'Why?'

'Why do I wish this?' he asked, confused. *Was this not obvious?* 'Because I do not wish for you to put your life at risk…' He breathed, paused, before blurting out too much. 'Simply to survive, when I have the money you need.'

'My life's not at risk, Maxim.' Her gaze softened, drawing him in, while only frustrating him more. 'Why would you think that?'

His brow knotted. Was this a trick question? But she didn't look conniving, she looked guileless and unsure, so he was forced to answer the question. To spell out the obvious.

'Pregnancy and childbirth *is* dangerous, Cara. Women can be…' He breathed, the memories burning like acid on his tongue. 'Women can be weakened by childbirth, especially without the appropriate care. We shouldn't have had sex without a condom.' He allowed his gaze to stray to the pronounced bulge of her belly, the guilt he had tried to qualify and mitigate during the night starting to overwhelm him. 'It is through my carelessness that you are now facing this danger. So it is my duty to ensure you are well cared for until the child is born.'

He lifted his gaze to hers, ready to demand, beg, cajole, even blackmail her if necessary into agreeing to the marriage. But he stopped, shocked by the sheen of tears in Cara's eyes. 'What is wrong?'

The stab of guilt lanced into his belly. He hadn't meant to distress her more. Had only wanted to give her the explanation she sought—so she would see why marriage was the only answer.

'Maxim, I'm really not in any danger,' Cara said. 'And, even if I were, you're not responsible.'

'Of course I am,' he said, his voice prickly with impatience. But for once she welcomed the caustic reaction because it revealed so much.

Going with instinct, she pressed a hand to the rough stubble on his jaw.

A muscle in his cheek tensed before he drew back, his expression confused and wary, but also more vulnerable than she had ever seen him. Or ever suspected he could be.

'How can you pretend this is not my fault?' he said.

'Because I made a conscious choice to have this child,' she said, trying to pick her way through the minefield he had exposed. She had underestimated him in so many ways, she realised. That he should feel such responsibility for her health and well-being was ridiculous, but she had helped exacerbate it because of her own stubborn pride, her refusal to bend.

She should have contacted him as soon as she'd found out about her condition. If she had asked for his support she would not have had to work herself into exhaustion. And scared him to this degree.

'I could have ended this pregnancy but I didn't want to,' she said. 'You're not responsible for the choice I made to have this child.'

She'd been a coward, scared he would object to her keeping the baby. And, because of her fear, she hadn't given him a choice.

'This is a pointless argument, Cara.' His gaze slipped to her stomach again, and she could see the anxiety about her condition flicker across his face before his gaze met hers.

What was it about the pregnancy that disturbed him so much?

'The fact is you are pregnant, you are having this child.' She saw his Adam's apple bob as he swallowed and realised how hard it was for him to say the next word. '*My* child. I do not want you to be harmed.'

Her heart swelled painfully in her chest. 'I won't be harmed, Maxim,' she said, struggling not to make too much of his determination to care for her, when no other man ever had. 'I'm pregnant, not sick.'

'Pregnancy is dangerous. My own mother…'

He stopped, his eyes becoming shuttered, the naked emotions she'd seen flash across his face ruthlessly controlled. But it was already too late. She'd seen the agony when he'd mentioned his mother.

'What happened to your mother, Maxim?'

He shifted back, withdrawing even further. 'It is of no importance,' he said.

But she could see it was of considerable importance. Was

this why he was so determined to marry her, to provide for her? Was his mother the reason why he was so concerned about the pregnancy?

'Did she… Did she have a difficult pregnancy?' she asked softly. 'Is that why mine scares you?' she probed gently, covering her bump with her hand.

He thrust his fingers through his hair. But she'd seen the shocking answer to her question, the shudder of remembered trauma in his eyes before he could mask it. 'I was a big baby,' he said. 'She was a small woman. And he refused to pay for the care she needed.' He looked away, his voice brittle with anguish. 'And I was not the only child he failed to prevent. She had two miscarriages before he finally discarded her.'

'Maxim, I'm so sorry,' Cara whispered, touching his arm, feeling the muscles tense. Had he witnessed these miscarriages? He must have, the shadow of trauma in his eyes was unmistakable. 'I wish I'd known him for what he really was,' she said forcefully, realising how foolish she had been to ever stand up for her old employer. 'I never would have agreed to marry him.' How could she have been so blind to Pierre de la Mare's faults?

'You are not to blame,' he said, and she could see he didn't blame her. 'My father spent a lifetime manipulating women. He was very good at it.' He blinked, the flush of colour on his cheeks making her realise how hard it was for him to talk about his parents' relationship. 'My mother never stopped loving him, despite the way he treated her.' He huffed out an unsteady breath, the confusion in his eyes so poignant she felt her heart butt her tonsils. 'But none of that is important now. What *is* important is that you do not suffer, the way she did. I cannot let that happen, or I will be no better than him.'

She nodded, tears welling in her eyes—he'd said yesterday that he wasn't his father; she hadn't realised how much he'd meant by that. 'I… I understand.'

'I would not have chosen to become a father, Cara,' he said, gruff pain in his voice, devoid of accusation but so full of regret it made her heart hurt. 'But I did not take the precautions I could have to ensure this did not happen, and now you must face the consequences of my actions.' He made the baby sound like a terrible burden. And obviously to him it was, she thought miserably. 'I also know what it is not to have a father's protection, a father's name and wealth. So I cannot allow my own child to grow up without these things.'

Cara nodded again.

But a good father could provide so much more than that. When her own mother had died, she'd looked to her father to provide not just financial but also emotional security. And he'd failed. He'd discarded her and rejected her—because she was too much trouble and he had never really loved her. The same way Pierre de la Mare had discarded and rejected Maxim.

'Would you…? Would you be able to offer this baby more than that, Maxim?' she asked, scared to hope, but more scared not to ask.

'What do you mean?' he said, looking genuinely perplexed by the question, and her heart stumbled in her chest.

'Do you think you could offer the child more than just your name and your protection?'

He frowned, as if he hadn't expected the question. 'I doubt that is a possibility. As I said, I never planned to become a father, Cara, precisely because I do not think I would be good at it.'

The words were said gently, firmly, but even so the spurt of hope refused to die. He hadn't categorically ruled the possibility out.

Both their fathers had been incapable of love. But she refused to believe it had to be like that. She already loved their child so much. And while the kind of marriage Maxim was talking about—a time-limited marriage, simply for the purposes of protecting her and giving his child his name—wasn't enough, the fact that he was so desperate to offer her and their child security was a start.

Maxim had been rejected the same way she had. She knew exactly how much that hurt. How it could make you doubt yourself, make you lose confidence in your ability to love. She'd discovered in the last five months—from the first moment when the blue line had appeared on the test kit to that flutter of movement a week ago—a vast well of love she'd never realised she was capable of.

The baby wasn't real to Maxim, the way it was to her.

But from their interaction that first night, when he had tended her and the next morning, when he had tried to persuade her to become his mistress, she knew he wasn't an insensitive man. Even blinded by his need for revenge against Pierre, he'd tried to do the right thing by her.

She also knew that he'd witnessed enough of his parents' relationship to be deeply cynical about love. But surely that didn't mean he couldn't one day be a good father.

'Is that why you were so determined to destroy La Maison?' she asked, as what he had said about his mother and the trauma of the miscarriages he must have witnessed shed new light on his actions that night, and the morning after. 'Is that why you exposed me to the press? Because of what happened to your mother—and you—in that house?' she finished softly. The memory of how he had betrayed her still hurt, but maybe that betrayal had never been about her, maybe it had always been about his past—a way to avenge his mother as well as himself, against the man who had used his mother so callously, and then discarded them both.

'What? No.' He swore softly, looking shocked. 'It was just an error. Some intern at the *advocat*'s office forgot to delete the attached affidavit before sending out a press statement that I was challenging the will. Believe me when I say I would never have revealed details of our sex life to the press deliberately. And I am not so insane as to blame my mother's suffering on a house.'

She smiled at his indignation, as the tightness in her chest, which had been there ever since that morning, dissolved. 'That's good to know.'

His gaze intensified, searing her skin all over again.

'Surely you can see we must be wed now, Cara?'

The roughened 'R' as he said her name seemed to stroke across her swollen clitoris, making her powerless to deny the yearning this time. The silence in the room seemed to vibrate around them both, making her more aware of the liquid pull which had been there ever since she had first set eyes on him.

'*Épouse-moi, Cara*,' he murmured in guttural French. *Marry me, Cara.*

He closed the gap between them and kissed her neck, sensing her weakness and exploiting it.

She arched against him as a sob of desire burst out of her mouth.

Need arrowed down, making her tender breasts ache and swell, and the sweet spot between her thighs engorge in a rush as he suckled the pulse point under her earlobe.

His breathing became as ragged as hers but, before she could surrender to the sensations surging through her body and give him the answer he wanted, she felt the familiar flutter of movement in her womb.

Maxim jerked back, his brows launching up his forehead.

'*C'est le bébé*?' he asked.

She nodded, unable to contain her grin—or the choking sensation in her throat—at his horrified expression. 'Yes, it likes to kick.'

Going with instinct, she untied her bathrobe, took his limp hand, placed it on her naked belly, then pressed down. The baby responded instantly, not that impressed with having its living space impeded.

His dark gaze was stunned and wary when it met hers. '*Il est très fort, ce bébé,*' he murmured. 'It does not hurt you?'

'No,' she said, unable to resist a sad smile at his question, knowing it came from a place of fear. 'The obstetrician last night said it's just extremely active… Most women don't feel the baby's kick until twenty-five weeks in a first pregnancy. But it's perfectly natural and just a sign of how healthy the baby is.'

She knew she was babbling but he didn't seem to notice as he stared at her stomach as if he were trying to see right through the skin to his child beneath.

His hand slipped away from her stomach, before he nodded. 'Dr Karim suggested we go to her clinic this morning for an ultrasound,' he said. He glanced at his watch. 'The concierge can bring some new clothes to the suite this morning to replace the ones that were destroyed. Once you are dressed, we can leave for Harley Street.'

It wasn't a question, it was a demand, his gaze fixed on her face with its usual intensity, daring her to refuse him.

She sighed. Even though Dr Karim had been wonderful last night, she didn't need an expensive Harley Street doctor when she already had a great obstetrics team at her local NHS hospital. But now she knew why it was so important to him to give her the best medical care money could buy, she didn't have the heart to refuse him.

'All right, Maxim. If you insist,' she said.

'I do,' he said, as she knew he would.

'I guess I should be grateful you're going to supply me with clothes first,' she managed, trying to lighten the mood before the emotion in her throat strangled her. Perhaps she was being naïve and too hopeful. But it felt like a positive step to have him care about the baby's welfare, even if it did come from an irrational fear.

'I am being very magnanimous,' he murmured as he braced his hands above her head, caging her in again. 'As I much prefer you naked.'

She laughed, but the sound came out husky and strained, the heat in her core flaring again. Surely his willingness to flirt with her again was also a good sign, she thought a little desperately.

Pressing his forehead to hers, Maxim murmured, 'Cara, you must marry me. Please say yes.'

Unlike before, the proposal wasn't a demand. Instead, he sounded tense, wary, concerned. Her stomach dropped, the faint flutters of the baby's kicks almost as if their child was giving its assent.

He lifted his head, his expression strained but conciliatory. 'I want you to be safe. Can you not see it is madness for you to work when there is no need? I have money. Let me spend it on you both, at least until the child is born.'

The emotion that had been so carefully contained welled up her chest. She dropped her gaze. 'I don't... I don't feel comfortable having you support me,' she managed round the huge boulder that was starting to choke her.

She understood why he needed to do this. He wasn't trying to take her independence away from her. She understood that now too. This was about protecting her, the way his mother had not been protected by his father.

But it was still hard for her to contemplate putting her life into his hands, however temporarily—it had been so long since she'd been able to trust anyone with her well-being. She'd always relied on herself. And, okay, maybe she had taken some foolish risks, working long hours for minimal pay. But she wasn't fragile.

He tucked a knuckle under her chin and lifted her gaze. 'There is no shame in needing support,' he said.

Her lips quirked. Did he realise how ironic that sounded coming from him, a man she suspected had made a point of never needing anyone's support?

'What is funny about this?' He frowned, the prickly frustration back. But this time she could see his temper was simply a mask for his deeper feelings—feelings that compelled him to do whatever it took to be a better man than his father.

She shook her head. 'Nothing, really,' she said, her thoughts sobering. 'Why couldn't I just come to live in Burgundy until the baby is born? We really don't need to be married.'

'Yes, we do,' he said in that dictatorial tone she had come to recognise. But somehow, this time, she could hear the emotion behind the command. 'I do not want my child born without a father,' he added. 'If you will agree to marry me, we can work out an arrangement that will satisfy us both. I would need you to sign a prenuptial agreement, so that we can dissolve the marriage as soon as the baby is born with the minimum of fuss.'

She tried not to let the thought sadden her that this marriage—if she agreed to it—would already have a sell-by date. Surely that would be in her best interests, as well as his? Ultimately the marriage wasn't important in itself, what mattered was that while she was living in his home, and preparing to bear his child, he would have the chance to come to terms with the reality of his role in its life. And perhaps overcome his objections to being its father in more than just name only.

'What about… What about custody?' she asked.

'A child must stay with its mother,' he said without hesitation, which had the bubble of desperate hope twisting in her chest. Did he have any intention of seeing the child after its birth?

Don't despair, Cara, he's only known about his child for one day—you've known about it for months.

'But I would ask that you allow me to support the child once the marriage is over,' he added.

Emotion welled in her throat, at the simple and unequivocal statement.

'Of course,' she said, determined to give him the time he needed. The truth was she wanted so much more from him for this child than just financial security. She wanted him to forge an emotional connection to it.

At the moment, that was not what he was offering. But surely that could change, if she could break down some of the barriers he had put around his heart? And overcome his fear of fatherhood, which was the hideous legacy of his own childhood. This marriage would give her four precious months to do that…

'So will you marry me, and come to Burgundy until the child is born?' The curt demand had a sobering effect.

Was she seriously considering saying yes?

This was a business arrangement for Maxim in many ways. A way for him to discharge his responsibilities to his child, make amends for the wrongs done to his mother and ensure that he was better than his father. And she was fairly certain her reasons for wanting to spend more time with Maxim weren't nearly as pragmatic.

But surely the chance of giving her child something she had never had—a father, in every sense of the word—was worth the risk?

'Okay, Maxim,' she murmured, determined to focus on the hope and not the fear.

She didn't want to be a coward any more. She'd taken so many crucial decisions away from Maxim with her silence, decisions she couldn't and wouldn't change, but this was a decision they could make together. And maybe, just maybe, it could lead to more.

'I'll marry you,' she said.

CHAPTER ELEVEN

'DO YOU WANT to know the sex of the child?'

Maxim blinked, barely able to register Dr Karim's question, still stunned by the image on the screen, and the loud, rapid tick coming from the ultrasound equipment, which the obstetrician had informed them was the heartbeat.

It had a head, a face, tiny fingers and toes already forming, its long legs folded up and practically touching its nose. No wonder it kicked so much, it looked cramped in there.

His child. His baby. Not abstract now, but tangible, and real… And so terrifying he was struggling to breathe.

'Can you tell?' Cara asked the doctor, breathless and excited. 'At my last scan they didn't know.'

'We just got a very good shot of the genitals,' the doctor said. 'So I can say with some degree of certainty. But it's really up to you if you want to know, or would rather wait.'

'Maxim? What do you think?' Cara asked him, her face flushed with pleasure.

He didn't have an answer for her. He didn't know if he could stand to have this moment be any more real than it already was. He was starting to sweat, the blue walls of the luxury suite closing in around him and the memories of that day so long ago playing through his head on a loop.

'Ne me quitte pas, Maxim. J'ai besoin de toi.'

Don't leave me, Maxim. I need you.

How could he possibly protect this tiny vulnerable creature from harm? When he had failed to protect his own mother?

'I don't…' He coughed to ease the tightness in his throat, and banish the vicious memories. 'I don't have a preference. You can decide,' he managed. Did it really matter what sex this child was, when he could never be a part of its life?

The sparkle of excitement in Cara's eyes dimmed. He steeled himself against the vicious stab of guilt. He had already told her what he could offer, and what he could not. The child would have his name, his wealth and his protection, always, and that would have to be enough. He had nothing more to offer.

'I'd like to know then,' Cara murmured, turning back to the doctor.

Dr Karim smiled and pointed out something on the monitor with a wand. 'Obviously, I can't be one hundred per cent certain, but I'm fairly sure what we have here is a penis,' she said with a chuckle.

'A boy?' Cara said, her tone thick with a hushed reverence that only made the hollow weight in Maxim's stomach plunge. She turned and gripped his fingers. 'Did you hear that, Maxim—we're having a son.'

He nodded, then lifted her fingers to his lips, barely able to speak round the shame threatening to choke him. 'I should go,' he said. 'To make the rest of the arrangements.'

'Arrangements?' she said, looking confused.

'I must return to France today. I have arranged for you to remain at the hotel in London until the marriage can be performed at the *mairie* in Auxerre in ten days' time.'

Why had he agreed to come to this appointment? It had been a foolish impulse that he now regretted. He'd never expected the child to be recognisable this early in its gestation. 'I will see you at the airport in Burgundy. Remember to rest.'

'I won't see you for ten days?' she asked.

He steeled himself against the tightness in his chest caused by the stunned dismay in her eyes. 'Yes, I am afraid it takes ten days to do the documentation before we can be married.'

Something he was pathetically grateful for.

He had planned to suggest they marry in London, but he was far too aware, even now, of Cara's lush figure beneath the clinic's starched robe. He still wanted her too much, even knowing that a life grew inside her. He needed this ten-day separation to ensure he got his hunger for her under some semblance of control.

'You must rest,' he said to Cara. 'Doctor, thank you,' he murmured, turning to the obstetrician.

Saying his goodbyes, he placed a kiss on Cara's forehead, then made his escape from the airless room. Leaving the fear, and the memories and the insistent hunger behind him. For the time being at least. The weight in his stomach expanded.

He had ten days to pull himself together and seal off the raw, aching hole that had opened up in the pit of his stomach on seeing the image of his child.

His son.

And ten days to figure out how he was going to survive four endless months of marriage without jumping his son's mother every single chance he got.

CHAPTER TWELVE

THE CAVALCADE OF black SUVs crested the hill. Cara's breath caught as Maxim's home appeared in the distance. Château Durand's centuries-old stone architecture dominated the surrounding fields, making a defiant statement about the power and wealth of the man she had just married in a short civil ceremony at Auxerre town hall.

She'd never ventured onto Durand Corporation land during her months in Burgundy as the de la Mare housekeeper, but she'd heard all the local whispers about the derelict *château* Maxim Durand had bought and then spent a fortune renovating in the last few years.

Nothing could have prepared her, though, for the magnificence of the property as they drove towards it from the heliport at the winery complex where they'd touched down twenty minutes ago.

They drove through the gates in the high stone wall, making their way past a series of brick outbuildings before travelling along the driveway that led through lavish, perfectly manicured gardens designed in a geometric pattern Capability Brown would have been proud of. The house itself—not a house, a mansion—loomed large at the end of the drive, three storeys of elegant arched windows with pale green shutters. Wisteria and ivy clung to the stonework to add a fanciful charm, while the intricate wrought iron balconies on the upper levels and the red tiled roof blended perfectly with the turrets on each end of the imposing building, giving it the appearance of a castle fit for a king.

Cara risked a glance at her husband, who was busy speaking to someone in rapid French on his mobile phone. Maxim might not have been born a king, but he suited the role perfectly.

Had it really been ten days ago that she had agreed to marry him? The last week and a half had gone by in a blur. The days had merged into one, each one dominated by some new task: the meetings with Maxim's legal team to outline the prenup he was offering her, which seemed scrupulously fair; the appointments with a barrage of stylists; the fittings with the couturier who had designed and made a whole new wardrobe for her in record time, not to mention the chauffeur-driven trip to say goodbye to Dora, who had been starry-eyed at the mention of who Cara was marrying.

But during the nights Cara had missed Maxim, feeling alone and confused in the hotel's luxury suite.

Her fevered mind had had far too much time, going over every moment of their relationship so far, and especially the last time she'd seen him, in Dr Karim's surgery in Harley Street—and the stricken look on his face when their baby… she breathed…their *son* had appeared on the monitor.

There had been no sign of that haunted look this morning when he'd met her at the airport. Perhaps she had imagined it?

There had certainly been no time to question him before they'd been whisked to the *mairie* to say their vows, before heading to a heliport for the breathtaking ride to the Durand estate.

She pulled the brand-new smartphone she'd been given by one of Maxim's army of assistants out of the pocket of the new linen trousers she wore—part of the beautiful new trousseau that had arrived yesterday. Maxim had arranged to have her belongings brought from her room in Leyton, but her battered rucksack now sat in the back of this pristine SUV, among a pile of matching hand-tooled luggage with her initials stamped on them.

Her *new* initials. CED. Cara Evans Durand.

She checked the time, trying to ground herself, and get rid of the tightness that had gripped her chest ever since she'd stepped out of his private jet, to see him waiting for her on the tarmac.

Two o'clock in the afternoon. She huffed out an unsteady breath and stared through the car's window as the line of vehicles entered a leafy courtyard at the side of Maxim's palace. She could see a large pool shaded by trees, covered now for the winter months, at the far end of a manicured lawn which led down from the *château*'s back terrace.

Of course he had a pool! She'd never even visited somewhere this lavish, let alone lived in such a place.

She'd known Maxim was wealthy. But she'd had no idea of the extent of his wealth, and power, and how he wielded that power so effortlessly, until the last ten days. His home was simply the crowning glory.

The car stopped and Maxim ended his latest call. After stepping out of the car, he skirted the bonnet, spoke to one of his assistants then arrived to grasp the door handle before she could open the door for herself.

'Welcome to Château Durand, Cara,' he said, sending her a distracted smile. He clicked his fingers and two footmen rushed out of the long line of uniformed staff waiting at the *château*'s door to greet them.

'Your new French obstetrician and her team are waiting to check you over,' Maxim said as the footmen began collecting her luggage from the boot. His large hand settled on the small of her back, to direct her up the marble stairs to the *château*'s entrance. Shivers rippled up her spine where his fingers touched.

'But I had another check-up with Dr Karim yesterday,' she said.

'It is only a formality,' he murmured, rubbing her back as he guided her, making the shivers increase. 'Once the doctor is happy,' he said, 'it is probably best if you take a rest in your rooms before tonight.'

Her *rooms*? Why did she need more than one? And what was happening tonight? Was he talking about consummating their marriage?

He glanced at his watch. 'Does six o'clock suit you?'

'You're scheduling sex?' Her shocked question burst out before she could think better or it. After all, she'd had far too much time to think about this aspect of their relationship in the last ten days, while lying alone in her hotel bed.

His lips quirked in a wry smile, but his intense gaze had a blush firing into her cheeks.

'I was talking of the wedding, Cara,' he said, the arousal in his eyes unmistakable at the mention of sex.

'Oh, I… I see.' She'd never felt more gauche or stupid—or needy—in her life. 'But aren't we already married?' she murmured.

She'd assumed the quick ceremony at the town hall in Auxerre was all they needed to do. Had actually been grateful for the secular, perfunctory nature of the proceedings. It was going to be hard enough to keep the reality of their marriage clear in her mind while living in Maxim's lavish home for the next few months.

'Yes, but we need a wedding ceremony, so that I can introduce you as my wife,' he said. 'There is a chapel in the grounds which has been prepared for the event, and my kitchen staff have arranged a wedding banquet in the *château*'s great hall.'

A *banquet*?

'But, I… *Really*?'

How had he arranged all this in little more than a week? And why?

She'd assumed there would be no ceremony. The less this felt like a real marriage the better. But Maxim seemed to have other ideas.

'Do not concern yourself,' he said. 'The stylist assured me she has provided a suitable dress in your trousseau.'

She had? Was it one of the numerous outfits she'd tried on? Why had no one told her it was a wedding dress?

He proceeded to introduce her to a few of his senior staff. Cara dutifully shook hands and spoke to them in her faltering French. The whole episode started to feel surreal as Maxim directed her into the house.

The *château* was as lavish inside as it was outside. Her breathing became ragged as Maxim led her past the downstairs salons and parlours and she glimpsed the bespoke antique furniture and a selection of stark modern pieces which looked equally expensive and intimidating. They walked up the wide sweeping staircase at the end of the entrance hall to the first floor, his hand on her back the only thing that was anchoring her now.

He left her at the door to a series of bright, airy, lavishly furnished rooms—*her rooms*, apparently—and introduced her to the obstetrician and two nurses he'd flown in from Paris.

'Wait, Maxim.' She stepped onto the landing to grasp the sleeve of his suit jacket. 'Will there be a lot of people at the wedding banquet?'

'Just some local dignitaries and my friends and colleagues,' he said. 'No more than a hundred in total.'

A hundred people? She actually felt sick.

He laughed, an indulgent sound that didn't do much for her panic attack, then cradled her cheek with his palm. 'Do not worry. It will be over sooner than you think.'

At which point…what? Were they going to consummate this relationship? Not that she'd been obsessing over that question… Much.

Stop worrying about sex… attending a wedding banquet with a hundred people is quite intimidating enough.

'But I… I'm not… I have no experience of these sorts of social events,' she said as the fierce need continued to throb in her sex.

He placed his hand on her neck, stroked the rioting pulse point with his thumb and placed a kiss on her forehead. 'Do not panic, Cara, it will be okay. My assistant, Jean-Claude, has invited Marcel Caron to attend on your behalf, so there will be a familiar face. Marcel has offered to give you away, if you are happy with that arrangement?'

'I… I guess,' she said, surprised he had gone to the trouble of inviting Pierre's lawyer. 'But I really don't…'

'Shh…' He silenced her with another kiss. 'As my wife, you must get used to attending such events.'

She must? She'd had no idea he was going to expect her to behave like a real wife. She'd thought she was just supposed to be living here until the baby was born.

'But… I…?' She tried again to voice her fears, but he covered her mouth with his, silencing her again. The gentle kiss quickly became firm, seeking, persuasive, taking on a life of its own.

She answered his passion instinctively, desire rising to suffuse her whole body in undulating, unstoppable waves. She was panting, trembling with need, when he finally tore his mouth away.

'Do not fear, Cara. I will not leave your side once the

ceremony starts,' he said, his gaze shuttered, and so intense it burned.

She stood shaking on the threshold of her rooms, watching him jog back down the stairs as the passion he had ignited so effortlessly continued to flow through her body.

One thing was certain: having Maxim by her side throughout the ceremony was not going to calm her nerves one bit.

'*Ta femme est très belle, Maxim.*'

At his estate manager and best man Victor's whispered compliment, Maxim shifted round from his position at the front of the church to glance over his shoulder.

The soaring strings of Pachelbel's *Canon in D*, which had been picked by the wedding organiser he had hired at great expense a week ago, filled the small chapel as Cara made her way down the aisle on Marcel Caron's arm to the hushed reverence of the crowd.

He stood, transfixed. His bride had her head bent, watching her steps in the golden slippers, the simple but supremely elegant silk dress she wore shifting colour from gold to rose in the flickering glow of a thousand candles. Her blonde hair had been arranged in a pile of unruly curls threaded through with blue flowers to match her eyes. She wore no veil.

The air gathered in his lungs, threatening to strangle him as heat rose through his body like wildfire—the surge of pride and possessiveness like a tidal wave.

Mine.

The word echoed in his head again, unbidden, as it had on their first night together.

He tried to qualify and control it—the way he'd been trying to do for a week. Ever since he'd left her in London.

The wedding had been a necessary charade, for his business, the press and his personal standing in the community.

But as his eyes devoured the stunning woman walking towards him, it was hard to stick to the script he had written so carefully for himself when making the arrangements.

He noticed her knuckles whitening where she gripped the elaborate bouquet in her fist and realised that while Victor was correct—his wife was indeed exquisitely beautiful—she was also extremely nervous.

He tried to calm his breathing, finally forced to admit that his insistence on this ceremony was not quite as pragmatic as he had wanted to believe.

He'd had no hand in choosing the dress, but as Cara approached him he realised he was glad the couturier had made no attempt to disguise her pregnancy. The child was a fact. A fact neither one of them could ignore. So why deny the strange surge of pride and possessiveness at the evidence that she was his?

While he had not wanted the affidavit he had signed to become public all those months ago, he couldn't deny he was pleased that everyone would know she had been untouched by his father. That while the old bastard had married her first, he had never known the pleasures of her beautiful body.

Perhaps the crowd would think her pregnancy was the only reason *he* had married her, and until this moment he had been determined to convince himself of the same. But as Cara's head finally lifted and her shy gaze met his, he was forced to acknowledge the basic biological urge to claim her he had never been able to contain.

Mine.

Marcel presented Cara's trembling hand to him as they drew level. Maxim captured her fingers in a firm grip and lifted them to his lips. He buzzed a kiss across her knuckles and whispered above the fading music, 'Do not fear, Cara. This will soon be over and then we can schedule the sex.'

It was supposed to be a joke, a poor attempt to ease the tension, but when the familiar blush ignited her cheeks—and the heat surged in his groin—the joke was on him.

He folded her arm under his and tucked her against his side to face the priest.

The cleric began to say the blessing—there would be no vows as those had already been made at the *mairie* in Auxerre. But Maxim barely heard the man's words, far too aware of Cara's body, ripe with his child, standing stiffly beside him as the cleric blessed their union before God, the local community and Maxim's employees and friends.

This marriage would be over once the child was born. He could never give her more. His panicked reaction to seeing his son ten days ago was all the proof he needed of that. But as they stood together in the candlelight, the eyes of everyone who mattered in his life upon them, the pressure in his chest refused to go away.

As the blessing finished and the priest gave him permission to kiss his bride, the primitive urge charged through his bloodstream like a living, breathing thing.

As he gathered Cara's lush body into his arms and conquered her lips in a searing, incendiary kiss, their audience and the reasons for the ceremony faded from his consciousness. All he could smell was her light flowery scent and the musk of her arousal, all he could comprehend was the feel of her soft, pliant, responsive body surrendering to his.

And all he wanted to do was brand her as his in the most basic way imaginable, as soon as was humanly possible.

CHAPTER THIRTEEN

'You made a very beautiful bride, *madame*.'

'Thank you, Antoinette,' Cara murmured as she watched her new maid pluck the pins out that were holding her elaborate hairdo aloft.

She was tired, and grateful the festivities—or at least the festivities she was expected to participate in—were over. She sighed as the heavy locks of hair tumbled down.

'Would *madame* like me to run a bath?' Antoinette asked in her perfect English.

'That would be wonderful,' Cara replied, still unused to having anyone wait on her.

The battalion of stylists and beauty therapists who had arrived in her suite to prepare her for the wedding had done a spectacular job. At least she had looked the part of Maxim's sophisticated society bride. But the truth was she had been terrified as she'd walked down the aisle on Marcel Caron's arm, the hauntingly beautiful classical music, played expertly by a string and woodwind orchestra in the corner of the chapel, only making her feel like more of a fraud.

The dress had been so close-fitting no one could have missed her baby bump and, while she could never be ashamed of her pregnancy, she had felt as if she'd had a sign round her neck saying 'shotgun wedding'.

But when Maxim had gripped her hand and brought it to his lips, the fear of exposure had been replaced by a more visceral fear. In that second, as his gaze roamed over her, rich with appreciation, she had felt beautiful, and truly seen, for the first time in her life… And it had terrified her. Because it could not possibly be true.

But what terrified her more was how much she had wanted to look beautiful, for him.

She stared at herself in the mirror.

She couldn't go there, she mustn't. Because she knew what would happen if she allowed herself to think that if she changed who she was it would make a man like Maxim truly care for her. It wouldn't.

She'd tried to change before, with the foster families she'd stayed with. Even tried to change for her own father as a young child, after her mother's death, when she'd sensed he was going to leave her too… It didn't work, it never had.

She let out a guttering breath and heard Antoinette's carefree humming while she prepared the bath in the adjoining room.

For goodness' sake, lighten up, Cara.

Tonight was an elaborate show. Maxim had said so himself. She mustn't take it so seriously.

The heady scent of lavender and rose drifted into her bedroom from the bathroom, and she recognised the tune Antoinette was humming—the sensual melody from their first waltz.

More unhelpful memories flooded back, of the rest of the evening, the romance of the *château*'s Great Hall, illuminated by thousands of candles and sprays of hothouse flowers. And that waltz with Maxim, as he had banded his strong arms around her, gathered her close and led her effortlessly through the steps of the dance so she didn't stumble or fall.

The twist of panic in her belly tightened. How could he have managed to make her feel so cherished, so adored, when none of it was real?

Everything he had done had been for the benefit of their audience, so why hadn't it felt that way? Was she really so desperate for affection she could be fooled by romance and spectacle—and the glow of desire in his rich brown eyes?

She pushed the memories into the furthest reaches of her brain. She had to remain a realist, or she would be destroyed at the end of all this. The way she had been destroyed as a child.

She went to pick up the heavy silver brush on the dressing table and clashed fingers with Antoinette, who had returned from the bathroom.

The maid laughed. 'I can brush *madame*'s hair, if you would like?'

Cara smiled at the young woman in the mirror, who was so much more sophisticated than she was. 'Would it be okay if I did it myself?'

'Of course.' Antoinette smiled. 'Would you like me to leave you to bathe?'

Cara nodded, desperate to be alone as her gaze strayed to the large four-poster bed which dominated the bedroom. She needed to get her thoughts in order before… Well, before Maxim arrived tonight, assuming he was coming. The comment he had made when she'd reached him at the altar had sounded like a joke. So why couldn't she stop fixating on it…and wanting desperately for it to be real?

'Should I return to help you dress for your wedding night?' the maid asked boldly.

'I think I can handle that,' Cara murmured, almost choking on her embarrassment. 'But thank you so much for your help this evening, Antoinette.'

The maid grinned, making her look very young. 'You

are welcome, *madame*. I think Monsieur Durand chose very well for his wife.'

Before leaving, Antoinette laid out a gossamer-thin piece of lace on the bed then added with a sparkle of humour, 'The *couturière* left this for you to wear tonight. But as Monsieur Durand did not take his eyes from you all evening, I do not think you will need it for very long.'

'Right…thanks, Antoinette.' Cara's blush incinerated her cheeks as the maid left. And the pulse of need between her thighs—which was always there—pounded even harder.

Brushing the last of the wild flowers out of her hair, she laid the brush on the dressing table with trembling fingers and headed towards the bathroom. A claw-foot tub stood in the centre of the lavish room, facing tall French windows which looked out over the dark fields of vines beyond the estate's gardens. Slipping off the robe, she climbed into the steamy, fragrant bathwater, but as she soaked tired muscles, trying to loosen the kinks caused by this overwhelming day, and the last overwhelming week and a half, the throbbing ache between her thighs strengthened and the panic intensified.

She had already lost too much of herself during tonight's events. If only she had more experience. Should she risk sleeping with Maxim? Was she even capable of denying herself that pleasure? And if he did come to her tonight, how did she remember that this marriage was one of convenience, not love?

Maxim tapped gently on the door to Cara's suite of rooms. No reply. Was she already asleep?

But as he contemplated returning to his own rooms across the hallway, the sensual tension that had been tormenting him throughout the day—ever since she'd stepped off his private jet that morning—clawed at his gut again.

He didn't feel rational, or focused. He felt desperate—driven by a craving stronger than he had ever known.

Every time he had got a lungful of her scent today, each time he'd seen the heat warm her cheeks when she'd glanced his way, the hunger for her had increased. Their first dance had been torture, as her body softened in his arms and she'd allowed him to lead her in the steps—while all the time he had been thinking of another dance he wished to lead her in.

Every single thing about his wife turned him on. But was that really so surprising?

He had searched for five long months to find her and then forced himself to leave her for ten days while preparations for their marriage were made. And during all that time he had dreamed about her continuously—sweaty erotic dreams which had turned his hunger into something more than it was ever meant to be.

He wasn't a man used to having to deny his natural urges, and every one of them had been focused on Cara for months. And now she was his wife, was it any wonder he wanted to consummate their marriage? Surely they both deserved something more from this union than simply security for the child? Madame Moreau, the Parisian obstetrician he had hired, had confirmed what Dr Karim had said in London. Cara and the child were healthy; there was nothing to fear from sexual intercourse.

Damn it, stop second-guessing yourself. You can hardly satisfy this hunger from the hallway.

He knocked again, then tentatively opened the door, wondering if she was asleep. As he entered the room, the light coming from the bathroom illuminated the empty bed, and a scrap of something lacy and insubstantial laid upon it.

Just the sight of the negligee and the thought of Cara's

full curves barely concealed by it had the heat surging into his groin.

He could hear splashing in the adjoining bathroom and smell the heady fragrance of flowers.

He cursed softly to himself then walked across the room, unable to resist the pull of a desire so strong it had been driving him crazy for hours, days, weeks…hell, even months.

He stood in the bathroom doorway to absorb the sight of his bride in the free-standing tub unobserved. Her heavy breasts were misted with moisture, while damp tendrils of hair clung to her high cheekbones.

He groaned.

Her head shot round, and what he saw in her eyes—stunned desire, naked need—echoed in his gut and turned the erection to throbbing iron. The emotion that gripped his chest felt like more than desire, more than passion, more than the basic urge to mate—he struggled to beat it back, to control it.

This was just hunger, nothing more, nothing less; it only felt like more because he desired her so much—and the fact of her pregnancy had resurrected emotions, vulnerabilities, that were best left buried.

'Maxim?' she said, folding her arms over her beautiful breasts to cover her nakedness. 'You're… You're here.'

He could hear the wariness in her voice, see the shyness in her flushed face. Damn, why did her innocence make her even more exquisite? It made no sense. He had always preferred the women he slept with to be bold and assertive, ready to tell him what they enjoyed, but, with Cara, her pleasure was like a rare gift waiting to be unwrapped. And, weirdly, her innocence made him feel untouched too, discovering the limits of his own pleasure for the first time.

The thought was so damn intoxicating he had to swallow another groan.

'Do you wish me to leave?' he asked, even though it was the hardest question he had ever asked. If she said yes, he would have to go, even though the thought of stepping away from the feast before his eyes might well tip him over the edge into insanity.

He saw her slender throat tighten as she swallowed, but then she shook her head.

He sent up a silent prayer of thanks to whoever might be watching over him in that moment. And sent up a silent vow too, that he would do his very best to treat her with the respect her inexperience—and her condition—deserved, even if the hunger clawing at his gut was already more than he could bear.

An idea sprung into his mind, erotic but also playful, and his erection stiffened even more.

'Would you like me to wash your back?' he asked, trying to keep his voice light, the opposite of what he felt.

'Um…' She chewed her lip, considering, and every one of his pulse points throbbed in agony, waiting for her decision. 'That would be nice, if you're sure you want to.'

He masked the inevitable groan with a husky half laugh. She was going to kill him before the night was out. *'J'en suis certain*, Cara.'

He sat down on the gilded chair in the corner of the room to unlace his shoes and had managed to strip off his shirt and tuxedo trousers before her shocked voice asked, 'Maxim, what are you doing?'

'Joining you in the bath,' he said as he lowered his boxer shorts and watched her gaze drop to the painful erection. Stunned need—and panic—flared in the blue depths and he laughed again, the sound considerably more tortured this time. 'It's the only way to do a thorough job.'

She didn't take her eyes off the mammoth erection as he crossed the room. He climbed in behind her, the water rising to lap over the lip of the tub as he sunk down, his erection now snug against her bottom. She trembled, and moved, instinctively rubbing against the stiff length.

Oui, she was definitely going to kill him, but at least he would die in a state of bliss.

He reached past her to pluck the soap from the side of the tub. He lathered his hands, then placed them on her shoulders. Beginning at her nape, he worked down her spine as far as he could reach, kneading the tight muscles, glad when the sinews began to loosen under his thumbs. She still had her arms clasped across her chest, but he could feel the tension gradually releasing. At last her arms softened enough for him to draw them down.

He covered her breasts with his hands, and leant over her shoulder to watch the nipples—rosy from the water—elongate under his focused caresses.

'Maxim, I… That's not my back…' Her voice broke on the husky comment, the raw need in her tone a potent aphrodisiac.

'Yes, but I feel they need my attention,' he teased, desperately trying to keep the mood playful. 'It's my job as your husband to make sure you are properly washed.'

'It… It is?' she said, her body relaxing enough to lean into him.

Unable to bear the tension any longer, he leaned over her shoulder and, holding the heavy weight of her breasts in his palms, whispered in her ear, 'Turn your head for me, *ma femme*.'

She did as he asked, and he claimed her lips. The angle was too awkward to go deep, but even so her tongue tangled with his, meeting his shallow thrusts. He lifted his head first, her soft sigh of disappointment like a siren call to his senses. Standing, he lifted her from the water and stepped out of the tub with her in his arms.

'Maxim, be careful, you might slip,' she said, gripping his shoulders.

He placed a kiss on her nose, pink and delicious, and laughed at her practicality.

Dieu, could she be any more exquisite?

He brushed his feet on the damp bath mat and strode into the adjoining bedroom with her held high in his arms. 'Take a towel,' he said as they walked past the pile on the bathroom dresser.

Placing her on her feet beside the four-poster bed, he took the fluffy bath sheet from her and proceeded to dry her wild tumble of curls, then her body, taking the opportunity to run the soft towelling over her flushed fragrant flesh, marvelling at the changes—surprised by how much they aroused him.

He would not have believed he could want her more than he had that first night. But he did. Her breasts were fuller and firmer, her curves more lush where her body had ripened in pregnancy.

Was she more sensitive? he wondered.

Sinking to his knees, he discarded the towel and gripped her hips, suddenly desperate to taste her.

'Maxim!' She grasped his shoulders, her whole body trembling as if she were in a high wind. He knew how she felt, every inch of his skin was alive and raring to devour her, the erection so hard it hurt.

'What are you doing?' she said.

He looked up and smiled at the stunned desire in her face. He ran his fingers over the seam of her sex—and decided to taste her another time. If he feasted on her tonight he might not be able to hold onto the frenzy building in his blood.

'Making sure you are ready for me,' he said, exploring the swollen folds.

She jolted and moaned as his thumb stroked across the slick nub of her clitoris. 'I'm… I'm very ready,' she said.

'*Bien*.' He stood and licked his fingertips then watched her pupils expand. He'd done his best to take this slowly, to woo her, but he couldn't hold back much longer. Despite the need rioting through his system, though, he took in the firm mound of her belly—aware of the life that grew inside her.

'Climb onto the bed, Cara, on all fours,' he managed, his voice raw, as violent need sparked along his nerve-endings.

She seemed confused, so he took her elbow and guided her onto the bed, then rolled her over gently and lifted her hips. The lips of her sex quivered, swollen and shiny with her juices. He placed himself at her entrance, the sight of the thick erection entering her so erotic he felt dazed.

He slid deep in one slow, careful thrust, filling her to the hilt. Her muscles clenched around him, tighter than a fist, her shocked sob making his erection grow to impossible proportions.

He began to move, rocking his hips, out and back, to claim every centimetre of her sex. This part of her, at least, still belonged to him.

But as he plunged deep, took more, branded her as his… the words of the ceremony in the *mairie* that afternoon—words which shouldn't have meant anything—poured through his mind all over again, this time binding, and true. Too true.

Her sex clenched around him in orgasm, massaging his length and triggering his own titanic climax. A shout was wrenched from his throat as his seed emptied inside her.

But as they shuddered through the devastating orgasm together, a disturbing thought occurred to him. She was his, but only until the child was born, so why did this need feel too huge to ever be sated?

CHAPTER FOURTEEN

CARA AWOKE THE next morning to find the light shining through open shutters… And the bed beside her empty.

She'd tried to convince herself last night, as the after-glow had suffused her senses and Maxim had held her while she fell asleep, that all her fanciful feelings about him, about her marriage, were just endorphins. An industrial-strength hormonal rush which had only become more potent because of her pregnancy. Her feelings for Maxim, for this marriage, were nothing to be terrified of, because they were just a chemical reaction she couldn't control.

But as she stretched in the bed alone, the luxury linen sheets like sandpaper on her over-sensitive skin, she couldn't help fixating on the empty space beside her, and struggled to explain away the tenderness beating under her ribs. And the wave of disappointment… And longing.

Or the questions that bombarded her.

Where had he gone? Had he returned to his own rooms? Why hadn't he stayed?

She pushed the questions back, tried to stop the tender spot in her chest becoming the hollow ache of inadequacy that had defined her childhood as she slipped out of bed and walked into the bathroom on unsteady legs.

The damp bath mat had been hooked over the heated towel rail and the bath had been emptied. Even so, the erotic memories from yesterday evening, his tender ministrations as he'd joined her in the bath and the powerful, passionate sex that had followed assailed her senses again. But as she searched the room for Maxim's clothes, or any sign that he had ever been there, her confidence faded.

After taking a quick shower, she managed to find a pair of designer jeans and a pretty blue blouse in the wardrobe full of expensive new clothes in the suite's dressing room.

She could hear the bustle of activity downstairs as she stepped onto the landing. The clean-up operation was in full swing. After wandering downstairs unobserved, she headed past the Great Hall and saw a small army of staff, busy packing away the remnants of last night's wedding banquet.

The show was well and truly over.

She spotted Antoinette amid the mêlée.

'Antoinette, *bonjour*!' she called out, glad of the distraction. While she had no aptitude for social events, she knew a lot about housekeeping. And cleaning. Perhaps she could help? And it would take her mind off last night, and Maxim's absence from her bed this morning.

Antoinette rushed over, looking concerned. '*Madame*, I am so sorry. Monsieur Durand gave us instructions not to wake you.'

'It's okay. I'm an early riser.'

'We did not expect you to be up so early. I am so sorry I didn't attend you immediately.'

'That's quite all right, Antoinette, really,' Cara said, feeling a blush work up her neck on cue. Did everyone know what they'd been doing last night? 'Do you know where Monsieur Durand is?' she asked, feeling a little foolish.

Antoinette nodded enthusiastically. 'Monsieur Durand is in the breakfast room.'

The maid led her through the house, leaving her at the

entrance to a huge glass conservatory. The lush planting inside the room contrasted with the bare wintery gardens shrouded in an early morning mist outside. She walked through the foliage, and spied Maxim seated at an ornate iron table in a picturesque alcove, sipping coffee and reading something on his phone.

Her husband. Her lover.

The emotions she'd worked so hard to control during the night rushed towards her again like a tidal wave, threatening to knock her off her feet.

How could they be even stronger now and more volatile? And what was she supposed to do to make them stop?

Dressed in a crisp white shirt, his jaw clean-shaven and his hair recently brushed, his gaze was locked on the screen. With the flaky remnants of his breakfast on the plate in front of him, Maxim looked focused, alert, confident and every inch the captain of industry.

She cleared her throat and his gaze rose from his phone. Passion flared in his eyes but, before she could respond to it, he frowned.

'Cara, why are you awake so early?' he said, not sounding pleased to see her. 'After last night, you need your sleep.'

All her questions about what time he'd left her and where he planned to sleep in the future died on her tongue. It wasn't exactly a reprimand, but it was close enough. Heat flushed through her at the mention of 'last night' but she forced herself to walk towards him.

'It's not *that* early,' she said in her defence.

He stood and pulled out a chair. 'Sit,' he said, placing a perfunctory kiss on her cheek as he tucked the chair in. He seemed distracted but the buzz of his lips still set off a shiver of reaction. She tried not to dwell on it. Her response to him was physical not emotional. Why couldn't she remember that?

'What would you like to eat? I will have the chef prepare it for you,' he said, sitting down.

'I'm… I'm not that hungry,' she said.

'Cara—' his brows furrowed '—you must eat.'

She nodded, remembering his obsession with her health and where it came from. 'A croissant then, I guess.'

'That is not enough,' he said, then lifted the phone and barked an order for an array of breakfast dishes.

'I'm not sure I can eat all that,' she said when he ended the call to the kitchen.

He didn't seem too pleased with that response, but simply nodded. 'There is an app on the phone Jean-Claude supplied you with. It has a direct link to the staff. If there is anything you require, just let them know. I have hired a nutritionist to suggest meals suitable for pregnant women, you can consult with her, also through the app.'

'Okay.' She wanted to be pleased with his thoughtfulness, but instead she felt overwhelmed again. And a little frustrated. Where was the man who had made such passionate and provocative love to her last night? And where was the woman who had made that commanding, confident man moan?

She didn't feel powerful any more, she felt inadequate and out of place—the way she had so many times before when she'd arrived at a new foster home, desperate to fit in, to find a place for herself. Only to discover there wasn't one.

'It is good you are here,' he said, surprising her, but, just as her heart lifted at the encouraging statement, he added, 'I am about to head to the winery for the day.'

'But it's Sunday!' she heard herself say. *And it's our honeymoon*, she almost added, but managed to stop herself—after all, this wasn't a real marriage.

But, even so, his imminent departure made her feel strangely bereft. She'd hoped to have a chance to talk to him this morning, to get to know him better and maybe discuss her role at the *château*. Was there anything he needed her to do as his wife? She wanted to be useful.

He smiled indulgently. 'Yes, but unfortunately the vines do not respect weekends.'

'When will you be back?'

'This evening. Do not wait up for me, I may be late.'

'Okay,' Cara replied, trying hard not to feel abandoned. Why was she being so ridiculous? This marriage wasn't real, however real it had seemed last night.

'By the way,' Maxim continued, wiping his mouth with his napkin, 'I will be travelling to Tuscany for a week in March. I will need you to join me at the end of the trip to attend a ball being held in honour of the man who, I hope, will be selling his vineyards to me.'

A spike of anxiety at the thought that he was going to leave her for a whole week sent her thoughts into a tailspin. 'A ball?'

'Yes. Jean-Claude will make all the arrangements and the *couturière* has been asked to supply suitable clothing,' he murmured.

His hand covered hers on the table. The warmth of his rough palm sent the familiar desire sprinting up her arm to tighten her nipples. 'Do not panic, Cara, you have a few weeks to prepare.' He squeezed her fingers and lifted them to his mouth. The press of his lips and his teasing smile had her heart doing a jitterbug in her chest.

'I enjoyed last night immensely,' he said, the rough intimacy in his voice stroking her senses. 'Would you like me to come to your rooms tonight, if it is not too late when I return from the winery?'

'I… Yes, that would be…' She swallowed. What? Fun?

Wonderful? Exciting? All of those things and more? 'I would like that very much,' she managed, disturbed not just by her instant, instinctive response to him—and her complete inability to say no—but also by how much she was already looking forward to his visit.

When he released her hand, she clasped her fingers in her lap.

How did he do that? How did he disturb her and excite her at one and the same time? Was this need inside her normal? She'd tried to persuade herself it was last night, but if her response to him was just about endorphins, why did she feel so empty inside at the thought of not seeing him all day?

'Is there anything you'd like me to do today?' she asked.

His frown reappeared. '*Do?*' he asked, clearly confused.

'I mean, as your wife?' she said. If she kept busy, surely it would help to alleviate the hollow feeling of inadequacy. 'I'd love to be useful.'

She certainly didn't want to sit around all day doing nothing, or she was likely to spend too much time dwelling on this marriage that wasn't a real marriage, and how much she was going to miss her husband who wasn't a real husband.

Maxim huffed out an incredulous laugh. 'There is nothing for you to do, Cara. You are my wife. The staff are here to wait on you. Not the other way around.'

As if on cue, a parade of footmen arrived to deliver the breakfast Maxim had ordered for her. An array of food, enough to feed several people, was laid out on the breakfast table. Plates filled with buttery pastries, fresh fruit, a selection of bread and cheese and even a fluffy omelette were revealed with a flourish before the staff bowed and left. Fragrant scents filled the room and made her stomach growl.

'*Bon appétit*.' Maxim smiled then stood as he glanced at his watch. 'I must go. Hopefully I will see you tonight,' he said, leaning down to give her a kiss on the cheek. 'Eat,' he said. 'You need food.' Her heart squeezed and her stomach knotted at the casual reference to her welfare. Was he thinking of the child too, as well as her? 'And do not concern yourself with unnecessary chores.' His lips skimmed down to her earlobe. The nip of his teeth had a shuddering sigh issuing from her lips. He laughed, the husky sound reverberating in her sex. 'You will need your rest—I intend to keep you very busy when I return.'

Before she had a chance to gather her thoughts again, he was gone.

She forced herself to tuck into the delicious omelette, knowing he was right about her nutrition, and tried to control a pang of melancholy. But as she devoured the delicious food, much hungrier than she'd realised, a plan formed.

Maxim hadn't said she *couldn't* find a role for herself here. He'd simply said she didn't need to.

Keeping busy, having a role, had been her way to cope with the constant feelings of isolation she'd experienced as a child.

After finishing the omelette and most of the fresh fruit, she headed off to find Antoinette.

She hated confrontations, but she didn't need to get Maxim's permission to figure out her role here for the next few months. Ultimately, it was up to her to decide what being Maxim Durand's wife meant, because she was the new *temporary* mistress of Château Durand, not him.

CHAPTER FIFTEEN

'Your wife is exquisite, Durand.'

'Hmm…' Maxim barely registered his business rival Giovanni Romano's observation, thanks to the blood pumping through his body at breakneck speed ever since Cara had arrived at the Donati Ball half an hour ago.

He'd made a point of not leaving Donati's palazzo to collect her from their nearby hotel when he had been informed she had arrived in Italy, knowing if he saw her before the event, in a bedroom, after seven days—and nights—of separation, they would probably end up missing the ball altogether.

She looked stunning in a shimmering blue satin gown, her figure even more lush and gorgeous than when he had left Burgundy a week ago for this business trip; her blonde curls were artfully arranged with diamond pins which sparkled in the overhead light of the chandelier. He had not been able to take his gaze off her since he'd greeted her.

They had been married now for nearly a month. She had settled into life at the *château* with surprising ease. While he had not been pleased with her decision to befriend his staff, and take on the domestic duties of the mistress of the *château*, he had been forced to accept she needed something to keep her busy or she would be bored. His wife, he had discovered, had a prodigious work ethic and was incapable of being idle.

So he had indulged her, on the understanding that she would not take on any tasks that required physical labour. He had also had Jean-Claude send a confidential email to the *château*'s staff without Cara's knowledge, telling them they would be fired if they allowed her to do anything more strenuous than lift a teapot.

Over the weeks he had begun to notice her presence in ways he had not expected—little touches, small changes that made the house more charming, more welcoming, more liveable—the bunches of fresh flowers that had begun to appear as spring bloomed over the estate, the smiles of the staff, who all seemed to adore her, and the smooth running of the household which allowed him to concentrate on his business instead of having to waste time making domestic decisions that didn't interest him.

And the sex each night, when he returned from work, continued to be addictive.

In fact, he had become so eager to see her each night, and so reluctant to leave every morning, it had begun to make him feel extremely uneasy. He'd promised himself after their wedding night that he would not spend the whole night with her, but each time he went to her bed he found it harder and harder to leave.

He'd planned this trip precisely so he could break the habit of keeping her in his arms until daybreak—and begin to re-establish the distance between them that a month of marriage had eroded.

He stared at Cara, standing a few feet away at the elaborate buffet, talking to Donati's elegantly dressed seventy-five-year-old wife, and was forced to admit that his plan had failed miserably. She looked so luminous to him, she was practically glowing.

Anticipation thrummed through his system like an electrical charge. Tonight was important to his business. Tomorrow he was supposed to be sealing the deal with Eduardo Donati and beating out Romano to the best vineyards in Tuscany—and completing Durand's expansion into the Italian market—but he couldn't concentrate on anything, because all he could think about was taking his wife into his arms and making her sigh and moan and beg.

She was like a drug he was finding it increasingly hard to live without. He'd torn himself away from her for seven days to control his obsession with her and it had done exactly the opposite. All he'd been able to think about in the past week was her.

All he'd dreamt about was her. And not just sexual dreams, but more disturbing ones—dominated by the vision of her eyes filled with compassion the day they'd first met, the feel of her exhausted in his arms when he had carried her away from the Valentine's Ball in London, the joy on her face when they had sat together in the Harley Street clinic and seen their son for the first time, the open smile that spread across her features each night when he arrived in her bedroom.

How had he become so attuned to even the most subtle of her reactions? He always tried to be considerate with the women he dated, but with Cara it was more than that. Every one of his senses was more focused, more alert, more desperate if he was near her, and now, he'd discovered, also when he was not.

No woman had ever distracted him from his business before now. But it was taking every ounce of his control not to stalk towards her, scoop her up and march out of this godforsaken event so he could take her somewhere private and relieve the insistent craving to have her again.

Apparently seven days of denial—during which he'd

forced himself not to contact her—had only increased his addiction.

'Pregnancy suits her—when is the child due?'

Maxim turned at Romano's wry observation, his temper spiking at the man's mocking smile. He'd had to force himself to leave Cara's side five minutes ago—to calm his racing heartbeat—and had been waylaid on the way back from the restroom by Romano. The last damn person he wanted to speak to.

'In the summer,' he said. The twist of anxiety that thoughts of the child usually brought with it sharpened.

He had married Cara to keep her safe, and give his son a name, but every time he thought about the baby now, the guilty weight in his stomach seemed to become heavier. The fierce protective instinct he could not contain had begun to torture him every time he thought of the child growing inside her, and then his mother's face—the last time he had seen it—would swim into his mind's eye.

'Ne me quitte pas, Maxim.'

He cut off the debilitating memory. Again.

The same memory that had first assailed him in the ultrasound suite, and then returned when he had left Cara's bed on their wedding night—sated, exhausted and yet still aroused.

He had understood, as he'd cleared away the evidence of their night together in the bathroom, desperate to return to her bed and hold her throughout the night, that he couldn't allow such a foolish indulgence. So why hadn't he been able to stick to his promise?

The novelty value of sex with Cara, sex with his wife, had made their physical relationship more intense than any he had ever experienced. But he must not let that blind him to the limitations of this marriage, for Cara's sake as well as his own.

He could not let her become dependent on him. The way his mother had been. Or he would fail her too.

'You don't sound too pleased about the prospect of fatherhood,' Romano said, still with that wry mocking grin on his face. 'Although I take it the pregnancy was planned?'

'And this would be your business, how exactly?' Maxim planted his fists firmly in his pockets, resisting the urge to knock the smug smile off Romano's face.

Flattening the bastard at Donati's eightieth birthday ball would defeat the purpose of the whole trip—namely to earn the old vintner's trust so he would sell him the legendary Donati vines.

'So you don't deny it?' Romano laughed, the sound rough with contempt. 'I have to admire your dedication to the vines, Durand.'

'What are you talking about?' Maxim snapped, the control he had always been so proud of fraying dangerously at the edges. He wasn't a thug, a gangster, an ill-bred upstart, as so many people had claimed when he had first had the audacity to enter the wine trade—he had ignored all those insults, determined not to live up to people's low expectations, or his own father's scorn, but Romano's attitude was starting to irritate him. Big time.

'Oh, I think you know,' Romano said, the smug twist of his lips enough to send Maxim's temper into a tailspin.

'Really?' Maxim's hands shot out to grab the lapels of Romano's dinner jacket and haul him forward until they were nose to nose. 'I think you should spell it out.'

He ground the words out, not caring about the gasps of the nearby guests, who had shuffled back to give them room for their altercation.

'All I'm saying is impregnating old man de la Mare's hot little widow before the guy was even cold in his grave was a smart, and I'm sure very enjoyable, way to get his land.'

Romano's accusation sliced through the last frayed threads of Maxim's control like a rusty blade. His fist shot out and connected with Romano's jaw, the shudder of pain in his knuckles worth it as the man flew backwards and landed on his backside with a thud.

'Don't ever talk about my wife again,' Maxim growled as he flexed his fingers, ignoring the shocked gasps of their audience and the sight of one woman fainting into the arms of her partner.

The red mist of rage refused to clear as he watched Romano jiggle his jaw. 'Good right hook, Durand,' the man said as he laughed.

'Durand? What is going on?' Donati's horrified shout did nothing to calm Maxim's raging heartbeat or the fury pounding through his veins at Romano's insult. The man had insinuated that Maxim was a whore but, worse than that, he had implied that Cara was a whore too. A woman who had been innocent until he had touched her.

'Maxim, is everything okay?' Cara's concerned voice seemed to tether him to reality as she gripped the sleeve of his jacket.

He turned to see her face, sweet, worried, compassionate. The red mist cleared, to be replaced by something even more disturbing. Grasping her cheeks, he kissed her, the meeting of their lips making her soften instinctively. The heady rush of blood to his groin drowned out the indignant whispers of the crowd, and Donati's threats to cancel the sale.

Lifting his head, he grasped her hand. They needed to get out of here so he could feed the hunger that would not stop.

He turned to Donati. 'We're leaving. If you want to sell to Romano instead, that is your decision, Eduardo. But no one insults my wife.'

He marched out of the ballroom towards his waiting car, with Cara's hand gripped in his. She stumbled and he stopped, to scoop her into his arms. The crowd parted before him like the Red Sea before Moses, the whispers of outrage only feeding the adrenaline rush.

Damn them.

He didn't care. He couldn't wait, couldn't stop—he needed her. The desperation intensified as her body softened against his and her scent filled his senses. The way he had dreamed of for seven long nights and every day he had spent away from her.

'Maxim, what did Mr Romano say?' Cara asked as she clung to her husband's neck and tried to ignore the people gaping at them as Maxim carried her out of the ballroom and down the wide sweeping staircase to the palazzo's entrance.

The truth was she'd known something was wrong as soon as she'd arrived at the ball. Maxim had been on edge, curt and annoyed, the intensity in him even more pronounced than usual.

She'd tried to swallow her unease. She'd been disappointed that he hadn't been waiting for her when she'd arrived at the lavish hilltop hotel in Tuscany three hours ago. Instead there had been the familiar battalion of beauty therapists and a stylist waiting to dress her for the ball, and a lonely drive in a limousine—while she chewed on her newly manicured nails—before Maxim had greeted her at the palazzo's entrance then whisked her inside to introduce her as his wife.

While the usual rush of endorphins had assailed her as soon as his hand had settled on the small of her back, and his fierce gaze had darkened as it roamed over her, she'd felt like a decoration, an accessory, as he'd introduced her to an array of people she didn't know.

If only he'd contacted her during the last seven days, told her something about the event, she might have been able to get involved in the conversation, and control her nerves.

It had been a struggle not to feel inadequate, or invisible. Or confused again about her place in his life. She'd worked so hard in the last three weeks to be useful at the *château*— and she'd managed it, despite Maxim's initial objections.

She'd come to love her 'work' as the mistress of Château Durand. Here, at last, was something she could do to help Maxim. Something she was good at.

Maybe Maxim had never said that he appreciated her input. Perhaps he didn't even notice the changes she'd made—he spent very little time at the *château* after all. But she noticed, and it made her happy—which was why tonight had felt like a step back.

And now he'd hit a man.

'That bastard insulted you.' Maxim bit the words out as he marched out of the palazzo's main entrance and demanded his car be brought round by the wide-eyed doorman. The limousine whisked to a stop in front of them moments later.

'What did he say?' she said, confused, not just by the searing comment itself but by the inappropriate flutter of something in her chest at the thought that Maxim had punched a man to defend her honour. 'He doesn't even know me.'

Maxim let her down but, before she had a chance to climb into the car and escape the stares of the staff still watching from the *palazzo*'s entrance, Maxim grasped her hips and pulled her into his embrace.

'It doesn't matter, he won't be repeating it,' he said, before covering her mouth with his.

The kiss was firm and hungry, devouring her gasp of surprise. His hands roamed over the bare skin of her back and sent her senses reeling. As always, she reacted instinctively, the flutter turning into a vibrant hum as she kissed him back like a starving woman.

This, at least, was something she understood, something she knew how to do.

He groaned, and ripped his mouth away. 'Get in the car. I can't wait much longer to have you.'

The urgency in his voice, and the desire flaring in his eyes, sent her senses into overdrive. She scrambled in.

'Take us to the Castillo. And don't disturb us,' he said to the driver, before pressing the button to raise the privacy screen, plunging them into shadows.

The car drove off into the night.

She could hear her own breathing, and his, before he reached for her and dragged her across his lap. She straddled him, her hands gripping his strong shoulders, trying to find purchase as the giddy rush of emotion—that he needed her so much—threatened to overwhelm her.

Her thighs quivered as his strong hands skimmed up her bare legs, lifting the gown to the waist.

'Release me, Cara,' he demanded as his fingers found the lace gusset of her panties and sunk beneath to torture the molten spot with his thumb.

She bucked against the delicious torment, fumbling with his fly in the darkness, her hands clumsy with need. Her body was already on the edge of the familiar precipice. At last she found the tab and eased it down, then captured his solid length in her hand.

He moaned, the guttural sound like a benediction. The desire to take him into her mouth—the way she knew he loved—was overwhelming but, as she edged back to give herself room, his hands clamped on her hips, preventing her.

'No, Cara, not like that, not tonight. Tonight I need to be inside you.'

She nodded, unable to speak, desperate now too.

The shocking sound of ripping lace barely registered as he tore away the last impediment to their joining, then lifted her hips to lower her onto the rampant erection.

His size and girth stretched her as he impaled her, making her shudder. She clung to him, her nails digging into the fabric of his tuxedo jacket as she tried to control the waves already threatening to annihilate her.

It was too much and yet not enough.

Holding her hips, he began to move her on the huge erection, guiding her to ride him in a slow, sensuous, all-consuming rhythm.

Their pants misted the car's windows, the hum of the engine vibrating through her as the waves of release crashed over her and then receded to build again…

She couldn't take any more, her body battered and bowed, another orgasm hurtling towards her. Freeing her breast from the satin, his mouth found her engorged nipple and suckled hard.

The strong drawing sensation sent her crashing over again. She collapsed on top of him, a sweaty heap as his roar of completion echoed in her ear.

She came down slowly, spent and exhausted and raw, as she struggled to contain the familiar rush of emotion.

But, just as she attempted to lift herself free, she felt the little dig inside her body of their baby, making its presence felt. She clasped her belly, and his whole body tensed.

'You are okay?' he murmured in the darkness, sounding stricken.

'Yes, it's… The baby moved, that's all.'

He lifted her gently off him, carefully pulled up the bodice of her gown to cover her exposed breast. It was only then that she realised the car had stopped moving.

She adjusted her gown, painfully aware of her husband's sudden withdrawal as the lights of the Castillo Hotel flickered through the misted windows.

He tapped on the partition. 'We are ready to disembark.'

The driver opened her door seconds later and helped her out, keeping his eyes downcast. Had he guessed what they had been doing? He must have done.

But somehow she didn't care. Why should they be ashamed of their need?

Maxim got out of his side of the car, then strode round to capture her hand. He led her into the hotel. They travelled in silence in the lift. What had happened? Why did she feel bereft, unable to bridge the gap between them? How could the sex be so intense and yet change nothing?

As they approached the door to the suite, he dropped her hand. 'I will see you at the estate in a few days' time.'

She clasped her arms over her bosom, her nipple still raw, the hum of sensation from their frantic lovemaking still *there* in her sex. 'You're not… You're not coming in?' she asked.

'I have my own suite,' he said.

The news was like a blow. She had assumed, had hoped, that tonight they would be sharing a bedroom… And that Maxim would wake up with her in the morning.

Maxim always left her rooms after their lovemaking, but she knew it had become more and more of a struggle for him. Each night he had held her longer and waited longer to leave. And she had rejoiced at this sign of progress. But why had she deluded herself that tonight would be the first night they would spend the whole night together when he hadn't even bothered to call in the last seven days?

'Maxim, wait,' she said, gripping his arm. 'Did I... Did I do something wrong tonight?'

He pressed a finger to her lips, his expression no longer blank but filled with regret. 'Shh, Cara, you were exquisite. You are the perfect wife.'

If that were so, why did she feel like even less of a wife than she had a week ago? She gulped down the fear expanding in her throat. And forced herself to ask the question that was torturing her. 'Then why don't you want to stay in my bed for a whole night?'

'I cannot stay.' He cupped her cheek, stroked his thumb across the sensitive flesh, tender from the rub of his stubble. 'If I did, I would exhaust you and the baby.'

It was an excuse he had used before, to leave her bed at dawn, and she'd never challenged it because she knew where his fears about her safety came from. But this time the truth spilled out of her mouth, regardless.

'You wouldn't exhaust us.' She gathered every last ounce of her courage. 'I'm fit and healthy and so is our baby.'

His gaze dipped to her stomach, prominently displayed in the close-fitting gown. Had the baby's movement spooked him? But he didn't look spooked, just distant. And suddenly so aloof.

'You need your rest,' he continued before she had a chance to gather her wits and question him more. 'You must travel back to Château Durand alone tomorrow.'

'You're not returning home with me?' she blurted out, the panic twisting into something more painful.

His eyebrow quirked at the mention of the word *home* and she realised Maxim still didn't see the *château* as a home, even though she had tried so hard to make it one.

'I need to repair the deal with Donati, if I can. If not, I have other business in the Loire before I return. But I should see you in a few days.'

He lifted her numb fingers and buzzed a kiss across the knuckles. The stupidly gallant gesture made her want to cry.

He'd made no promises, and she had no doubt at all that he wouldn't contact her before he returned. But somehow it wasn't enough any more.

'*Au revoir*, Cara,' he murmured, before leaving her standing in the doorway to her suite.

She watched him go, his broad shoulders stretching the seams of his suit jacket. A jacket she had gripped for dear life only minutes ago, while he took her apart with his lovemaking.

But it wasn't lovemaking, she thought as she stepped into the suite and closed the door. Not for him.

How many times had she been rejected in her life? So why should this rejection hurt so much more?

She leant against the door, blinking back the stinging sensation in her eyes and swallowed around the tightness in her throat as she finally acknowledged the truth she had been denying for weeks—every time Maxim took her with such passion, every time he stayed a little bit longer in her bed, every time he smiled at her, his eyes dark with approval, every time he frowned, concerned for her well-being or that of the baby...

She had fallen hopelessly in love with her temporary husband.

She pushed away from the door, kicked off her shoes, walked into the lavish bedroom and gazed at the four-poster bed where she would sleep alone tonight, while her husband slept alone down the hallway.

She was scared, terrified really, of her feelings for him. But as she lay down on the empty bed, inhaled the smell of him still clinging to her skin, she wondered...

What if Maxim were running scared too, of his feelings for her?

She rolled onto her side and curled up into a tight ball to cradle the precious bump of her pregnancy.

When Maxim returned to the *château* she had to find a way to confront him, to show him how she felt. And somehow, eventually, she had to find the courage to demand from Maxim something she had believed she could never have, never deserve, ever since her father's desertion all those years ago. His love.

It was a risk, a huge risk. If she failed, she would feel like that abandoned child again, alone and unlovable. But if she succeeded? Her heart lifted into her throat. *If* she succeeded, perhaps she could finally let go of that girl for ever and have Maxim's heart, as well as his body.

CHAPTER SIXTEEN

'WHERE SHALL WE put this bunch?' Antoinette asked, her eyes bright with excitement.

Cara grinned back, feeling like a naughty schoolgirl with a secret. Not that she'd ever been naughty as a school-girl, she'd always been too scared that if she caused any trouble her latest foster family would chuck her back into the system.

But she wasn't that insecure child any more, she thought staunchly as she grasped the ribbon on the bunch of gold-and-silver balloons Antoinette and two of the estate's foot-men had been helping her blow up to decorate the dining room.

Maybe part of that child still lived inside her, she would have done something like this a lot sooner if she didn't. But it was way past time she put that child aside.

'Move the ladder and I'll put them up there,' she said, pointing at the cornice above the table she and Antoinette had laid out that morning.

Maxim was due back in less than an hour. He'd stayed away for a whole week in the end, supposedly to repair the deal with Donati. But in a way she was glad, because now she was sure she had been right to think he was run-ning scared too. And right to know she couldn't let him do that any more.

Cara swallowed around the ball of anticipation—and fear—lodged in her throat. His absence had given her a chance to muster her courage but, more than that, it had also, completely by chance, gifted her with the perfect way to show him how much she felt for him.

'Is everything okay, *madame*?' Antoinette asked.

'Yes.' Cara smiled at the maid, determined to believe it as she tied off the ribbon on the balloons and climbed the ladder.

Maxim was a workaholic, who had an almost preternatural ability to focus on the now. She also knew, from what she knew of his past, that the reason he worked so hard was to overcome the deprivations of his childhood. She also suspected he was nervous about becoming a father. She understood that, because she was nervous about becoming a mother too. But shouldn't that give them an even better reason to forge a bond that went beyond sex?

'Be careful, *madame*,' Antoinette said as she steadied the ladder.

'I will be,' Cara said as she stretched to pin the balloons to the cornicing, her baby bump pressing against the metal.

She wanted this small celebration to be ready for Maxim's arrival. She knew he was unlikely to want a big fuss—he hadn't even mentioned to her that today was his birthday. But, as someone who had rarely had the chance to celebrate her own birthday, she suspected he had also missed out during his childhood. She knew his mother and he had been left living in abject poverty after Pierre had thrown them out when he was young. And she also knew he had left Burgundy at only fifteen to make his way in the wine trade. While her childhood had been blighted by the care system, she suspected Maxim's had been non-existent— ever since he was a young child and he had witnessed the way his mother had been neglected by his father. What better way to show him she loved him—without scaring him off—than to mark this special occasion? To show him he mattered to her.

Of course it had taken every ounce of her newfound confidence as the mistress of Château Durand to suggest it to Antoinette and the other staff but they had happily agreed to the idea.

This marriage didn't have to be an end, it could be a beginning. They still had two and a half months before the baby was due and she already felt as if she belonged here.

'What do you think?' Cara asked, admiring her handiwork.

Antoinette leaned to one side to look and loosened her grip on the ladder. The slight wobble had Cara's body shifting.

'*Cara, descends tout de suite!*' The shout in French from behind her, demanding she get down immediately, startled Cara so much she swung round too fast.

The ladder tilted sharply to one side. Antoinette gasped.

Cara felt herself falling in slow motion, as she watched Maxim run towards her, his face a mask of panic. And pain.

Strong arms banded around her, breaking the fall. She inhaled a shuddering breath of pure relief. And caught the joyous scent of sandalwood soap and salty sweat.

Maxim. Maxim had saved her.

Her husband swore as she grasped his neck and clung on, pressing her face into the warmth of his pectoral muscles, feeling them tense and quiver under her nose.

Love rushed towards her, the threat forgotten.

'Cara, what were you doing? Are you mad?' He was shouting, his voice trembling.

But as she looked into his face, saw the dark eyes wild with concern, love flowed through her on a wave of hope.

Why had she waited so long to show him how she felt about him?

'I'm sorry, Maxim. I was…' The surprise was ruined, but she let it go. 'It's your birthday, and we wanted to surprise you.'

'You… What?' He glanced around the room, taking in the bunches of balloons pinned to the cornicing, the banner she and Antoinette had made yesterday afternoon, the delicious *croquembouche* the chef had prepared on her instructions and the present she'd knitted herself over the last week, wrapped in paper and ribbon and arranged on a small side table with a bunch of early summer blooms she'd picked from the estate gardens that morning.

He placed her on her feet and stood back, his eyes widening as he studied the celebration she'd worked so hard on in complete silence. The muscle in his jaw tensed. He looked stunned, she realised.

And not happy.

She struggled to ignore the tightness in her chest at his reaction. He'd had a shock. They both had.

'Are you okay, *madame*?' Antoinette asked, still holding the ladder. 'I am so sorry I lost my grip.'

'Don't worry, Antoinette, it's—' Cara began, but Maxim interrupted.

'*Sortez*,' he said, the barked command for Antoinette to leave making both Cara and the maid jump. 'You are fired. I never want to see you on these premises again.'

The maid nodded and rushed out of the room in tears.

'Maxim, stop…' Cara touched his forearm. 'You can't fire Antoin—'

He swung round to grip her upper arms.

'Why? Why did you do this?' His voice broke on the words. This wasn't unhappiness, she realised, he looked undone, broken.

'Maxim, what's wrong?' she asked, the tightness like a vice now around her ribs.

Had she made a terrible mistake, confused her feelings with his? Projected emotions onto him that weren't there—had never been there?

He brushed a frustrated hand through his hair. 'You had no right.'

'I just wanted to do something for you, after all you've done for me,' she said, her voice shaking now at the sight of his distress.

'Any man would do it, to protect their child,' he said, the words clipped.

But when his eyes locked on hers, his gaze tortured, wild with pain, she knew she had to come clean about her real reasons for organising the celebration.

'No, they wouldn't, Maxim,' she answered, trying to remain calm, trying to quell the riot of emotions pressing against her ribs, thundering in her heart.

Fear, panic, but most of all love.

'But you're right. That's not the real reason I did this,' she said, the truth pushing against her larynx and making her throat close. The moment had arrived when she couldn't hide behind that frightened, lonely child any longer.

'Then why?' he demanded.

'I wanted to celebrate your birthday, because I've fallen in love with you,' she said. 'And I want this to be a real marriage, for this house to be our home.'

He remained rigid, his eyes blank and unresponsive, so she found herself babbling the things he had never asked her about herself. And her past.

'I spent the whole of my childhood in a succession of foster homes,' she managed. 'Some were good, some were okay, some weren't. But I was never able to stay in any of them for very long. And when I came of age I spent years travelling around Europe, looking for something I finally found at La Maison de la Lune. I thought at first it was my friendship with Pierre, but it was much simpler than that—it was the home I made there. I discovered that I didn't need anyone else to make a place for me. I could make it for myself. But with you…' She swallowed down the lump of raw, unadulterated emotion. 'With you, I've discovered I want so much more than just a place to call my own. I want a real home. And I know, even though you've never said it, it's important to you too, or you wouldn't have reacted so strongly to becoming a father. Been so determined to care for me.' She could hear the painful hope in her voice, despite the rigid expression on his face. 'We could make this place into a home, Maxim. Make our marriage into a real marriage. For the baby, and for ourselves. All we have to do is admit that's what we need.'

She had hoped against hope to make a life for them both, but the last embers of that hope flickered and guttered out as she watched his blank expression harden.

'This marriage can never be real.'

'Why not?' she asked, desperation setting in.

'Because I will never love you back.'

'You don't have to love me, Maxim. Not yet,' she said, still trying to rescue a dream she knew had already died. 'All you have to do is open yourself to love.'

'I can't,' he said.

She nodded slowly, carefully, scared she was about to shatter into a million pieces at the finality in his statement. Not shatter, crumble into dust, feeling so insignificant, inconvenient, the way she'd been her whole life.

She hadn't asked him to love her, all she had asked for was the hope that one day he might. But he didn't even want to try. Anything she had to offer him would never be enough.

The little girl inside her who had watched her father walk away without a backward glance was screaming in pain. But the woman she had become simply nodded. 'Okay.'

She needed to leave before he saw her crumble, before he saw how much his rejection hurt. Or she would be nothing again.

It had taken her a lifetime to become somebody. And she couldn't let any man take that away from her. Not even him.

'You must not be upset,' he said stiffly. 'This is for the best.'

No, it's not.

'I need to be alone for a while,' she murmured.

He caught her wrist as she tried to leave. 'Cara, I'm sorry,' he said. 'But I thought you understood I can't offer you that.'

A spark of anger fired in her chest, and she clung to it. Anything to disguise the pain. 'You said to me once, Maxim, that you didn't need my pity,' she managed. 'I don't need yours either.'

She'd exposed herself to these feelings by accepting so little from him. And if this pain could teach her one thing, it was never to accept so little again.

'Where are you going?' he said from behind her as she walked away from him.

'To my rooms. I'd appreciate it if you didn't disturb me tonight,' she said, her voice coming from far away, as it occurred to her for the first time ever that she was glad they had separate bedrooms.

She couldn't make him love her. And she didn't want to. He'd seduced her with sex, but she had let him, revelling in the physical and wanting it to mean more when it never had. At least to him. All she could do now was repair her broken, foolishly misguided heart.

'Don't do anything foolish, Cara,' he said. 'We can talk more about this in the morning.'

She pressed her hand to her stomach, imagining the life inside her. And acknowledged how pathetically eager she would have been to take him up on the offer to talk about their relationship only minutes before. Why had she been prepared to accept whatever scraps of affection he was prepared to offer her?

She didn't feel tired as she headed up the stairs to her rooms, she felt exhausted, her feet like lumps of lead as she trudged up each step.

But one thing she did know: there was nothing left to talk about.

CHAPTER SEVENTEEN

'MONSIEUR DURAND, *MADAME* asked me to give you this.'

Maxim glanced up from his breakfast—the breakfast he hadn't been able to eat—to find the young maid he had fired the day before, and then reinstated because none of this was her fault, holding an envelope in her hand.

It was ten o'clock and he'd barely slept last night. He'd wanted to go to Cara's rooms a dozen times during the night, to soothe her and beg her to forgive him for his harsh words. To hold her in his arms and take the shattered pain in her eyes away the only way he knew how, by bringing her to the peak of ecstasy and watching her revel in her own pleasure. A pleasure only he could give her.

But he knew he couldn't, because that would only give her more false hope.

When she had told him last night of her childhood, the home she had been denied, all he'd been able to think about was her as a little girl, shunted from family to family without anywhere to belong. He'd wanted to hurt every single person who had rejected that little girl, had made her believe she wasn't enough.

But how could he punish them when he'd hurt her more? And made her believe she was the one who wasn't enough when it had always, always been him.

'*Merci*, Antoinette,' he said, remembering the girl's

name and taking the envelope. 'Is my wife awake then?' he asked as he sliced open the envelope with his knife.

'The mistress woke hours ago, sir,' she said. 'She left at about nine o'clock.'

'She…left?' His fingers paused on the letter. 'Where did she go?' The hollow weight in his stomach turned into a sharp slice of panic.

'I do not know,' Antoinette said. 'She told me not to give you this letter, though, until ten o'clock. I think she took a car; she said she was going for a drive.'

No. No. No. No.

He flicked open the letter the girl had handed to him and read the words written in black ink.

Maxim,
I'm sorry I can't be the wife you need. I think it is best in the circumstances if we divorce now.
I cannot bear to live with you and know you feel nothing for me, when I feel so much for you.
I hope you understand.
Cara x

His fingers shook, making the paper tremble.

She had run. He leapt out of his chair, the fear turning to terror—and the unbearable pain of longing. He forced his mind to engage. If she'd taken one of the estate's cars it would have a GPS tracker. He stormed out of the *château* towards the garage, praying each step of the way that she had not managed to get to the station already.

He couldn't lose her. Not again. Not like this. What had he done?

Cara took the turning into the short lane through the woods that led to La Maison de la Lune. She'd been driving aimlessly for over an hour, trying to get her thoughts in order before she went home. Not home, she thought miserably.

Back to Château Durand to talk to Maxim about the divorce.

He would have received her letter by now. She'd left her phone at home precisely so he couldn't contact her. But she would have to go back soon. She didn't want him to worry unnecessarily.

She wasn't even sure how she had ended up here. She knew Maxim would have knocked down La Maison last September when she'd run away from him, but even so she hoped that just being in this place, where everything had begun, might help her get some perspective on her pain—and her grief—at the end of their marriage.

Despite everything, she was still struggling to accept that everything she'd believed about her and Maxim's relationship—the intimacy she had believed had been growing between them—had been wrong.

The car took the short bend in the road through the woods but, as she steeled herself for the empty plot that awaited her, she spotted a shape through the trees that had her heart—her bruised and battered heart—bouncing into her throat.

The house—the house she had once loved so dearly—still stood. The shutters were closed, the door boarded up, the flowers she'd planted in the boxes on the windowsills wilted. But the structure itself—the stone walls, the wooden gables, the red slates of the roof—were all still there, just as she'd left them that morning, when she'd run away from Maxim—and, she now realised, feelings that even then had terrified her.

She drove into the yard in the SUV she'd borrowed and braked, then rubbed her tired eyes. Was she dreaming, imagining this?

Why would Maxim not have destroyed the house? He'd been so determined to do it all those months ago—she now knew because of the cruel way his father had treated him and his mother—and, after discovering the full extent of Pierre's cruelty, she didn't blame him.

So why was it still here, whole and solid and, from the way the yard had been brushed free of autumn leaves, also cared for in the months since her departure?

She got out of the car, walked to the door and laid her cheek against the worn wood. After all the months she'd lived here with Pierre, all she could remember about her life inside these walls was that one forbidden night with Maxim. The hunger, the panic, the joy and then the pain. But most of all the tenderness that she'd failed to acknowledge then, but couldn't help but acknowledge now.

The tears that she'd shed during the night returned. God, it hurt to know that even though he'd rejected her, she loved him still. And she knew she always would—that was why she'd asked him for a divorce. She couldn't go on living with him, sleeping with him, knowing that he would never be able to love her back.

She heard the purr of an engine, getting louder, cutting through the chirping cheerfulness of a goldfinch's song. As she turned Maxim's car drove into the yard. The squeal of brakes was followed by the slam of the car door as he jumped out.

'Cara…you're here…you didn't run?' he said. His eyes were wild, as wild as they had been yesterday in the moments before he had told her he didn't love her, when he'd saved her from falling.

She wiped the tears off her cheeks. 'Of course not,' she said, shocked when he ran across the yard towards her. 'I just needed some space.'

Suddenly she was in his arms and he was hugging her

so tightly her heart was hammering against her ribs like a jackhammer.

'*Ne me quitte pas, ne me quitte jamais,*' he murmured against her hair, his tone urgent, desperate.

Don't leave me, don't ever leave me.

'Maxim?' She pulled back, her heart swelling in her chest and clattering against her ribs. 'I wouldn't have run away. Not again. Not now.'

He sunk to his knees, clasped her thighs, pressing his head into the mound of her belly. 'I thought… I thought you had left me.'

She sunk her fingers into his hair, drew his face up, and saw something in his eyes that had her swollen heart bursting in her chest. She glanced back at the house—the first home she had known. But that home had meant nothing until she had welcomed him into it.

'Maxim, why didn't you destroy La Maison?'

'Because I couldn't,' he said, his expression stark, naked with the longing he had never allowed her to see, until this moment. 'After you left it was the only thing I had that reminded me of you.' He swore softly and dropped his head. 'My revenge against him seemed unimportant once I had lost you,' he said. 'I don't want to lose you again. I can't.'

Her heart did a giddy leap, despite the hopelessness in his voice.

Had she been wrong to give up so easily, to believe what he'd told her instead of following her own instincts, her own emotions?

Gripping his cheeks, she forced his gaze back to hers. 'Maxim, you don't have to lose me. I love you,' she said again, but she refused to bask in the fierce emotion in his eyes. She couldn't settle for less, the way she had settled so often before. 'But you made it very clear yesterday you can never love me back. Is that really the truth?'

He shook his head, but his expression became bleak. 'I lied,' he said, his voice full of emotion as he covered her hands with his and stood up. 'Because I'm a coward,' he said, dragging her hands from his cheeks. 'Because I'm afraid of what I feel for you.' He placed their joined hands over her belly. 'And for our child. Because I am scared I can never be enough. And that I will fail you, the way I failed my mother.'

Cara looked stunned, Maxim realised, but so beautiful his heart broke just looking at her. She still loved him, but how could he take comfort from that until she knew the truth—until she knew what he'd done all those years ago? How could he ever hope to deserve her love if he did not tell her what he had done to his own mother?

'How did you fail your mother, Maxim?' she said, the sweet compassion in her eyes wrenching the truth he had never wanted to reveal out of his mouth.

'She was frail, fragile, as I told you, ever since I was a young boy. My birth and the miscarriages she had suffered had hurt her, both physically and mentally. She had dark moods, days when she could barely function, and when that happened she needed me to cook for her, to talk to her, to get her out of bed. The day I came here…' he looked at the house he had always hated, until he had found his salvation inside it '…to tell my father I knew I was his son. I was so excited. It was my birthday. I was fifteen and I believed myself a man. I thought he would want me. But he didn't. And I was so devastated, so hurt and angry, I took it out on her. I left Burgundy, even though she begged me not to. Even though I knew she would struggle on her own. She needed me and I left anyway. Five months later, she was dead.'

Once the words were out, he waited to see the love in

Cara's eyes curdle and die, to turn into the disgust with himself he had felt for so many years. But the warmth in his wife's deep blue eyes didn't falter or fade, it didn't even flicker, she simply absorbed his confession and then wrapped her arms around his waist, pulling him away from the darkness—and back into the light.

'Maxim, that's madness. You weren't responsible for her death. You were her son, not her parent. Whatever you did or didn't do for her, you weren't responsible for her pain or her fragility, or her depression.' She glanced over her shoulder at the house he'd saved because he couldn't bear to lose the one thing he had that would remind him of their one night together. 'If anyone was responsible,' she added as she turned back to him, 'it was your father. He didn't deserve a son like you.'

Her faith in him seemed to seep into his bones as they stood in the sunlight together. He held her too tightly. But he knew he wouldn't be able to loosen his grip. Not for a while.

'Can you give me another chance?' he asked. 'To make this marriage a real marriage. To become a real father to our son. To figure out how to love you.'

It was the hardest but also the easiest question he'd ever asked of anyone.

The bright smile she sent him reached into his soul and lightened his heart, until it bobbed into his throat.

'Yes,' she said. 'But first I want something from you.'

'Whatever it is, it is yours,' he said, knowing he would be willing to give her anything she desired. If she wanted a palace—if she wanted two—he would buy it for her. She was worth every penny he had, every second of his time it took to earn those pennies. Whatever he had to do to be worthy of her love, he would do it.

'I want you to promise that you will stay in my bed until morning,' she said.

'That is all?' He blinked, baffled not just by the simplicity of her request but by the strength of the wonder that barrelled through him at the thought of waking up with her soft body in his arms and never having to let go of her again. Ever.

She nodded.

He threw back his head and laughed, the joy—that he had found her and would never ever have to lose her—almost too much to bear.

'Do I have your promise?' she asked, her voice stern but her eyes sparkling with the same joy exploding in his chest.

'My beautiful wife,' he murmured as he lowered his head to hers, ready to kiss them both into oblivion then kick in the door of the old farmhouse and carry her upstairs to the bedroom they had shared all those months ago, 'I promise I will hold you until morning, every day for the rest of our lives.'

EPILOGUE

'LET ME TAKE *le bébé*. You must sleep.'

'Go for it, Papa.' Cara smiled as her husband leant across the wide double bed they had shared all night, every night, for the first time three months ago—the day their marriage had become a real marriage—and scooped their week-old son into his arms.

Tucking the tiny body against his naked chest, he placed a firm hand against the baby's back and crooned in a deep, gentle voice, 'Shh, *mon petit garçon*, it is time to sleep. Your mother has fed you enough for one night.'

The baby stopped fidgeting on hearing his father's voice, and gave a loud burp.

Cara chuckled wearily.

'Our son is very greedy,' Maxim murmured, but she could hear the fierce pride in his voice. 'Hopefully, he will give us both some rest now.'

'Fingers crossed,' Cara said around a huge yawn. Tucking her now empty breast back into her maternity bra, she snuggled back under the bed's summer quilt, contentment rolling through on a wave of fatigue as Maxim whispered instructions to his son and the baby's eyes drifted shut. At last.

The fatigue was joined by a wave of love—for both the

guys in her life—which crested as her heart beat a strong, steady tattoo against her ribs.

Seriously, was there anything more wonderful than watching this man become the father he was always meant to be? How could Maxim ever have believed he wasn't capable of loving her, or their child?

Her husband climbed out of the bed and carried their baby in strong arms to the bassinet, then laid him down gently on his back. She forced herself to stay awake so she could watch the familiar ritual.

She couldn't help noticing the muscles in his backside flexing beneath the pyjama bottoms he had started wearing a few weeks ago—when she'd been so huge that sex had become impossible. She felt the familiar flutter of appreciation. It would be quite a while yet before she'd want to act on it—hello, ten hours of labour!—but she could still enjoy the show as Maxim concentrated on stroking his son's cheek to lull him into a deeper sleep.

She gave another jaw-breaking yawn and noticed the glow of the summer dawn through the large bedroom's shutters. She should probably go to sleep too. In two hours, three at the most, their insatiable son would want another feed.

Instead she blinked furiously to keep her tired eyes open, as she waited for Maxim to return to the bed. She had something important she wanted to ask him.

At last, satisfied that their son had finally fallen into a deep enough sleep, Maxim padded back to the bed. Climbing in beside her, he dropped a quick kiss onto her nose. 'Go to sleep, Madame Durand.'

'I will…but, Maxim, I've got another name for you first.'

They'd spoken—or rather argued—about what to call their son on and off for over three months now. Which had basically consisted of her coming up with names and

Maxim vetoing them all. She loved that he was so determined to get it right, but seriously, their son would be in university before they came up with one they could agree on if they didn't get a move on.

'And this cannot wait until morning?' he sighed, yawning himself, and then wrapped his arm around her shoulders to pull her against his side.

'No.' She snuggled into his embrace, the scent of sandalwood soap and baby's milk that clung to his skin making the flutter of appreciation become a definite hum—and the warmth in her heart spread.

'Okay,' he sighed. 'What is your latest terrible suggestion?' he said.

'Stop it.' She gave him a playful slap. 'My suggestions are not terrible.'

'Hugo? Eugene? *Mortimer*?' he teased.

'Mortimer was a joke.'

'And the other two?' he said, pressing his lips into her hair in one of the many absent gestures of affection he always showed her, that she had come to adore. 'For them there is no excuse.'

'How about Pascal?' she blurted out.

He stilled, the easy smile dropping from his lips in the half-light. She could hear his heart thumping against her ear. And feel hers beating in time.

He frowned down at her. 'What made you think of this name?' he said, his tone gruff. But she could tell, from the emotion in his voice, which he never hid from her any more, that he had already guessed the connection.

'You said once that your mother's surname was Pascale.'

He stared at her and her heart thundered.

'You remembered this?' he asked, his voice raw with surprise but also rough with love.

She nodded, peering up at him. 'Do you like it?'

He brushed a hand over her hair, then leant down to cover her lips with his, the intensity of the kiss all the answer she needed.

When he drew back his face was a picture of raw emotion. 'Pascal Evans Durand,' he murmured softly, his voice rich with love as he tried out the name. '*J'adore*,' he said. 'But not as much as I adore him… And you, Cara.'

* * * * *

REVELATIONS
OF HIS
RUNAWAY BRIDE

KALI ANTHONY

To my mother, Dot.
Wish you were here to enjoy the journey with me.
You'd have loved the ride.
Always in my heart.

CHAPTER ONE

THEA STRUGGLED IN the near darkness to tear free of the wedding dress she'd been forced to wear. The cursed laces of its bodice trussed her as tight as a chicken ready for roasting. She fumbled with the tangled bow at the small of her back, then stopped to steady her trembling fingers. Her breaths blew sharp and fast, and the cloying scent of citrus blossom from her bridal bouquet threatened to overwhelm her. No time for clumsiness. Tonight was about speed and execution. Because this plan—her only plan—allowed no room for failure.

'It's never going to work.'

Thea faced the quavering voice. Sheathed in soft cream silk, her best friend huddled in a shadowy corner. The brim of an oversized hat swooped across her face.

'We've been over this, Elena. It will.'

It has to.

There were no second chances. Outside, the hungry crowd and her husband waited. The man now entitled to all of her. Thea shuddered. He wouldn't get her mind, her body or her soul. This was her moment to escape. Tonight she'd break free and show them all.

'How do I look?'

Elena moved into what dim light shone through a lavishly curtained window from the dreary alleyway beyond. She smoothed her hands over the front of the dress, which swirled barely above her knees. Demure. Perfect. The dress Thea should be changing into now.

'Like more of a bride than I feel. Nobody will realise.'

Till it was too late. Till she was gone.

Everyone said she and Elena could pass as sisters, or as

each other. And they regularly did—with laughable ease. Allowing Thea a shred of freedom otherwise denied her.

Now all the years of planning her escape were over.

She walked to her friend and held her in a tight hug. Elena's body quaked in the embrace.

'Thank you. For this. For everything,' Thea said.

Elena returned the hug, then pushed away, wiping at her eyes. 'Let's get you out of that wedding dress and away from here.'

Thea turned and flinched as Elena's frantic hands fought the laces which bound her.

'Can we put on some lights?' Elena whispered. 'I can't see to do this quickly.'

'What if someone walks in? Like this, it's hard to tell who's who. Now, remember what I said?'

Elena laughed. There was nothing cheerful about the sound. 'Skirt the edges of the room. Keep the hat brim down. If anyone tries to talk to me pretend to cry and hide my face in a handkerchief like I'm overwrought by the sheer joy of this blessed marriage. Easy.'

One final pull and the bodice fell free. But Thea wasn't quite free yet. Her friend started on the laces of the corset.

'No time!' She wriggled away to search for the rest of her clothes. 'And it *will* work. We've told everyone about the hat and dress I'm wearing to leave here. People will be looking out for that, not for me.'

No one saw *her*. Sure, they saw her clothes, her jewels. Evidence of her father's money when he decided to show her off like some prize pony. That's why she and Elena were interchangeable. People were told about a sensational dress and hat and that was all they'd see—not the person wearing it.

Because to her father's friends she was nobody. A shadow who could slip away. And when somebody finally did notice, it would be too late.

'But Christo...'

Thea's heart dropped a beat at the sound of his name. She licked the perspiration beading on her top lip.

Christo Callas.

My husband.

No need for pretence now. Yet she'd slipped in those last moments. When Christo had lifted her veil. She'd looked into his unfathomable olive-tinged eyes and hadn't been able to quell the serpent inside. The knowledge that she'd been forced into this marriage to save her half-brother Alexis. Potent emotion had coiled and then reared, begging her to strike out at the man who'd effectively bought her. And in that moment he'd hesitated. As if he *knew*.

So she'd painted a sweet, soft smile on her face. Waited for the kiss which would transform her from Thea Lambros to Thea Callas. And, for all the horror of it, Christo's lips had been warm and soft with something that had felt like understanding…

No! She scrubbed at her mouth, smearing the shell-pink lipstick. Wiping away the strange tingling the memory had wrought.

'Thea?'

'Christo won't notice either.'

He didn't understand her—hadn't even tried.

Thea thrust Elena the bridal bouquet which had lain wilting on a side table.

'He's not interested in me—only in what this marriage can do for him. One woman's the same as another to men like that.'

To Christo she was simply a commodity. Like she was to her father, who'd made it clear she must agree to the marriage as part of a business deal. If she didn't, Alexis would go to jail.

But now, with Alexis's freedom bought, she could run. Extract herself from whatever questionable scheme her father had concocted. Her plan all along.

'I hope you're right,' Elena said.

There was no time for doubts now. Thea stepped out of her dress and flung it into a dark corner, where it flopped like a discarded marshmallow. The suffocating corset could wait till she was safely hidden. She'd cut the damn thing off if she had to.

'I fit the job description,' she said, pulling on a practical black knit top. 'A compliant bed-warmer.'

Her blood ran hot with a furious roar. She knew her own worth—and it was *not* playing that role. Not for any man.

Thea shrugged into a heavy leather jacket, then zipped and buckled the front. Earlier she'd hidden her jeans and boots under the ridiculous confection of a dress now deflating in the corner.

It was almost time to go.

Thea walked to Elena and took her hands. The chill of them shivered through her. 'Are you sure you'll be okay?' She squeezed Elena's fingers in reassurance. 'I'm not asking too much?'

Elena squeezed back. 'You're like my sister. What wouldn't I do for you? And I can look after myself. Time to live your life. You've been caged long enough.'

In the Lambros family cage.

For most of her twenty-three years she'd only known one sibling. Demetri. A cruel thug disguised in civilised clothes. He'd always been her father's enforcer, and Thea his first victim. Her father hadn't cared. Not about the little girl who looked too much like her mother. The wife who'd had the temerity to leave him.

No. Thea never wished to set eyes on Demetri or her father again. But Alexis…

She pulled her phone from the pocket of her jeans. From the moment he'd inveigled himself into their home as her bodyguard two years earlier things had become almost bearable. His presence had kept her going. But since this morning he hadn't responded to her texts.

Elena frowned as Thea checked her phone. 'Still no word?'

'Nothing… But it'll be okay.'

Thea chewed her bottom lip till she tasted the tang of blood. Surely he'd left Athens? She rubbed at the ache in her chest. The pain of having to leave him so soon ran soul-deep. Only the knowledge that her marriage had freed him kept her going.

She took a shuddering breath. 'And when you're discovered?'

Because Elena would be—it was only a matter of time. But everyone had to believe what they were told so they'd search in the wrong place.

'Where have I gone?'

'You've taken a hire car.' Elena's bottom lip quivered. Her eyes brimmed with the glitter of tears as she played her role with breathless innocence and trembling perfection. 'You're driving towards Karpathos. To visit your mother's grave.'

Thea had wanted to go before the wedding. Her father had refused to allow it. Try as he might, he'd never excised her mother's memory from her life, so her visiting there would make sense to him. It was a subtle mix of truth and fiction blended into a believable enough concoction.

Still. It didn't feel right.

'I hate using Mama's memory this way.'

Elena shook her head. 'Maria would have approved. Anything to get you away from men like those. But forget that. Was I good enough?'

'You should become an actress,' Thea said. 'After that flawless performance Christo's minions will definitely head south looking for me.'

'And you'll be starting your new life.' Elena smiled—her first display of happiness on this bleak day. 'Can't you tell me where you're going?'

'No. It's safer this way.' It would protect Elena as much as herself in the little time they had.

Thea grabbed her motorcycle helmet from the chair behind her, hesitating.

'How in Hades am I going to get this over my stupid hair?'

All that teasing and plaiting… The style had taken aeons to create, with the hairdresser cooing over what would be a wasted effort.

Elena pulled at a few of the sculpted curls. 'It'll take an hour to get rid of these pins!'

'No time for that. I'll squash the helmet over the top somehow. How much time have we spent already?'

Elena checked her watch. 'We haven't been long. Anyhow, they're too busy drinking your father's ouzo to care. Everyone's going to think you're spending ages to look beautiful for Christo. And once you leave they'll have to go—which none of them want.'

It was the sad truth. Thea had no idea who most of the people at the wedding were. Business associates, she suspected. More deals and alliances being sealed over the carcass of her blighted union. Vultures, the lot of them. They were interested in the food, the alcohol, *the spectacle*.

'I'll never forget what you did for me. When it's safe, I'll try to let you know where…'

Thea swallowed the lump tightening her throat. There were few people she loved. Elena. Alexis. The thought of leaving them crushed her.

Elena waved her away. 'I'm holding you to that. One day when we're both grandmothers we'll drink coffee together and laugh about today,' she said, searching through a bag, then thrusting Thea an envelope. 'Don't forget this. Passport. Money. Bank details. It's all there. Now, go! Be happy.'

Thea hesitated. She slipped her hand into her jacket pocket and rubbed the worn St Christopher medal on its fine chain, safely nestled there. Then she grabbed her padded gloves and secreted rucksack, moving to slip out of the door at the back of the room, which led to the alley where her motorcycle was hidden.

The door was usually kept locked, but she'd been able to charm the manager of the venue into leaving it unsecured for a fictional delivery. *A surprise for the groom.*

'Wait!' Elena squeaked.

Thea whipped around, her heart pounding with the electric spike of adrenalin. They'd been discovered?

All she saw was her friend, a slender shape framed by the light from the doorway behind.

'What?'

'Rings!'

How could she have forgotten her engagement ring? The dead weight of the baguette diamond. Huge. Impossible to miss. And her wedding ring wasn't far behind, with its twinkling encrustation of pure white gemstones. Her husband's mark. His claim.

Thea prised the pair of them from her finger and handed them to her friend. *Now* she was free.

Time to go.

'And that is where this absurd charade ends.'

The deep, growling voice rumbled like thunder as a shadow loomed from a darkened alcove.

Christo.

Christo strolled over to a petite side table and turned on a lamp. The room shone with a soft glow. Such a pretty space, with delicate gilt furniture and swathes of brocade fabric draping the walls. Perfect for wedding preparations. Not so perfect for the curious machinations of the two wide-eyed females now frozen before him.

He'd been prepared to allow their odd scene to take its course. There was no chance of his sparkling new bride running away. One of his men stood waiting outside the door. She would have walked into a wall of immovable security.

He gritted his teeth. Breathed through the heat blistering his veins. *The rings.*

Holding out his hand, he nodded to the Drakos girl. She placed Thea's bouquet on one of the fine chairs and dropped the glittering tokens into his palm. He curled them into his fist and they burned in his hand. Hundreds of thousands of euros in jewellery sat there, abandoned without care.

Christo slid them into the pocket of his trousers and addressed Thea's bridesmaid. 'Leave us.' He kept his voice level and calm. His bride and his future were secure for now. Any further emotion was misdirected.

'You can't make me. I'm staying here.'

Such a brave statement. Christo smiled. He'd been told he looked wolf-like when he did, so he tried for a less predatory edge. Elena shuddered, and wilted a fraction. Ah, so he'd failed. Again.

He sighed, reaching into his pocket for his phone. Pressed speed dial. 'Raul,' he said evenly, 'I need you. Miss Drakos would like to dance.'

He'd attend to Thea soon enough. From the corner of his eye he glimpsed her, standing straight. Stiff. Glancing at the door. Would she run or hold her ground? He suspected the former and hoped for the latter. Why? It was hard to say. He was used to women running when life didn't meet their expectations. His mother had been the finest advocate of *that* coping strategy.

Raul, his appointed head of security and best man, arrived at the door. Elena was the maid of honour. She was required to dance with Raul at some point. Now was an opportune time as any.

'Elena stays.'

The lady speaks. Although it was more like a hiss. Quiet. Serpentine. Curling a chill tight on his spine.

He ignored it. 'Elena, you'll dance with Raul *now*.'

Christo had little doubt she'd leave. His commands were invariably followed. Raul held out his hand. His prospective dance partner took it, removed her ridiculous hat, placed it on a chair and left the room with a tearful *'Sorry...'* to Christo's bride. Such a touching moment.

He turned his attention to Thea.

She didn't wilt. She stood rigid. Head held high. So fierce and proud. Dressed in jeans and leather with exquisitely coiffed and braided hair. All contradiction—such a heady mix.

A tantalising buzz thrummed through him.

'How long were you hiding there?' she asked.

Christo would allow her some questions. He had a lifetime to get answers of his own.

'Long enough.'

'And you watched us dress?'

He shrugged. 'There was nothing to see.'

She'd been half dressed already. Yet even in the darkened room Thea had blinded him. Her gentle curves. The slender waist. That crushing corset. An interesting foil for jeans and heavy boots... Everything about her had proved interesting tonight.

'I didn't realise my husband *lurked.* I would never have married you if I'd known. Lurkers can't be trusted.'

He laughed. Such an unfamiliar thing it sounded more like a bark. Thea didn't flinch. Most people would have.

'That's something I've never been accused of. I'll add it to the list of my many documented achievements.'

His laughter seemed to increase her courage. She took a step forward. Still clutching her gloves, helmet and a white envelope. He wanted that envelope.

Instead of taking it, as he would in due course, Christo allowed her another question. He knew it was coming. Her brows creased in a slight frown and her mouth was opening and closing a fraction, as if silently practising the words.

'How did you find out?'

Her voice stroked soft as a feather over his skin. The perfect balance of seduction and wheedling. Lashes downcast. Deferential. If she'd been close enough no doubt she'd have placed a fine-boned hand on his. Gazed into his eyes. Perhaps granted him a few false tears. Such a subtle act, and all too familiar.

He despised it.

'Take care, Thea. I don't endure theatrics.'

She tossed her head and the artfully placed curls of her hair flicked and bounced. 'I'm no performing seal.'

'Then what's today been about, if not a performance?'

He'd known she had spark. That much had been evident in the interminable parades he suspected her father had imposed upon her each time Christo had visited their ostentatious home. Thea's beauty shone fierce and bright, and such beauty came from intelligence. Yet she'd attempted to hide it from him until today.

When he'd lifted her veil there it had been, boiling through her icy veneer. Those eyes…tight and burning with hatred. He'd almost recoiled, witnessing the wild creature beneath. And then her face had smoothed, as if a wave had washed away writing on sand, and it had gone.

But he'd watched her at the reception. She and her friend wandering to and from this room. The furtive whispers between them. After one trip Thea's skirt had hung more loosely. After another the hem had dragged on the floor. So he'd schooled Raul, had the door to the alley placed under guard and silently thwarted her plans.

Creeping into this room to wait in the darkness was beneath him, perhaps. Still, he'd needed to witness the deception personally. It would serve as a reminder of why he couldn't trust.

Thea hadn't taken long to reveal herself.

'Today? It was about escaping *you*.'

The words might sting, but he was used to his parents' rejection so what did one more matter? He'd been the child they'd weaponised to hurt each other, not loved for being their son. That was what the people closest to you were capable of.

He'd inured himself against the pain of those boyhood lessons years ago. Never again would he beg for meagre crumbs of affection from another's table. All he dealt in now were cold truths and hard cash. And Atlas Shipping, the company his grandfather had founded, was his ultimate and only reward for being born into the misery of his family.

Christo walked towards Thea, towering above her. At six foot four, he towered above most people. It was an edge which many might exploit, but he refused to be known as a bully.

He rolled his tight shoulders. Swallowed down the anger roiling in his gut. Tried again for a smile which was conciliatory. Who knew whether it had worked? As she looked up at him Thea's face was as blank as a fresh sheet of paper.

'You want an escape, and yet I still have you.'

Christo plucked the envelope from her hand and slid it into the inner pocket of his tuxedo. Thea wasn't expecting it. She broke a little. A slump of her shoulders. A tremble in her bottom lip. Her freedom had been stolen, as his had been.

Would she understand? He almost felt sorry for her in that moment, but finer feelings had no place here. Later he might make time to regret what he had to do. Not tonight.

'Wait. I can't… I won't…'

Emotion ran high in her voice as it quavered and cracked. Nothing moved him. He had no choice. She'd realise soon enough and then a deal could be struck—although only on his terms, because her compliance was essential.

'Did you really think your childish plan would work?' He schooled his voice, low and sharp as a blade. He'd witnessed grown men crumble at this tone. 'That I wouldn't notice the switch immediately with only that monstrosity of a headpiece as a disguise?' He nodded to the discarded hat.

She dropped her helmet and gloves onto a chair. Brushed

a fine strand of hair behind her ear. 'It was all about mis-direction.'

'So now you're playing conjuror's tricks?'

'I was supposed to be a happy, blushing bride—not a prisoner planning an escape. People saw what they wanted to.'

Well, her confidence was misplaced. Time to show her.

He cupped her chin in his right hand, felt Thea's perfect skin, silky and warm under his fingers. Her lips thinned, but she didn't move.

'I see your cognac eyes. Your skin like mountain honey. And your hair rich as dark chocolate,' he said, his voice pitched soft as a caress. 'I see your haughty grace as you walk. The ferocity in your gaze. I see who you try to hide. I see *you*, Thea.'

A new look flickered across her face. *That* look he understood. Those incendiary eyes were all flash and fire. He wanted to set her alight and watch her burn. But he wouldn't. He wasn't weak, like his father. Falling for lies about love. Letting a woman trap him into marriage. Love was for vulnerable fools. Not him. Having once been a weapon, he'd learned how to defend himself. And love was the deadliest weapon of them all.

Yet as he looked down at her, Thea's glorious lips parted. Her pupils went dark and wide. So he dropped his head and brushed his lips across hers as a test. For effect. She gasped when he pulled away.

'Elena is a pretty dark-haired, brown-eyed girl,' he said, his lips burning where they'd touched hers. 'But she could *never* pass as you. You're a fool to imagine it.'

He released this new Thea. This aware Thea.

She raised shaking fingers to her lips. He took her free hand, dropped the rings back into it. She snatched her hand away and looked down at them, eyes still wide. Not so good at hiding now. Her mouth fell open, her skin paling to ivory.

He knew that look too. Horror.

His stomach clenched. He'd felt much the same when he'd realised he required a bride. A cruel trick of his father's. Christo had sworn off marriage until Hector's actions made it necessary. His father had procured secret loans from Thea's. Failed to pay the crippling interest. Become indebted to a man who had demanded Christo's marriage to his daughter to stop the impending foreclosure.

Christo didn't want this debacle any more than Thea did. Still, no matter how distasteful the task, he'd do whatever was required to save Atlas Shipping. To secure his birthright, his inheritance and the company his father had nearly destroyed.

'It would have worked,' Thea whispered. 'It *would* have.'

'Perhaps if you'd married anyone else. Unfortunately, you married me.'

Thea's hand clenched into a fist, tight around the rings. 'And what's so special about you?'

'I understand people.' He'd learned as a child. So he knew when to hide from his hostile mother. To avoid his mercurial father. For Christo, people were transparent as glass. 'It's why I'm unparalleled in business.'

'I'd say you have an unparalleled ego.'

He stalked past Thea and opened the rear door of the room. The gritty smell of real life wafted in from the alley behind. He spoke to the man outside and ordered him in.

'An ego's only worth something if it's backed by ability. Which I have. You see, Thea, your plan *wouldn't* have worked.' He stood back and let her take in the hulking security guard he'd posted outside. 'There was no chance you'd escape. Every exit was being watched. Your transportation is now safely in my garage. You'd failed even before you'd begun. Accept it.'

He nodded to his man, who left the room. Thea watched him go, realisation spreading across her face.

'I'm not a slave to be traded. I won't stay with you. This marriage is a sham.'

In some ways, he agreed with her. Yet here he stood, with a gold wedding band prickling on his finger. Thea still held her rings. He needed her to put them on. If she did, he'd won—for tonight.

'You're asking me to return you to the tender care of your father?' A man Christo suspected didn't have a sentimental, loving bone in his body.

Thea grabbed the back of a spindly chair, clutching it till her fingers blanched. 'I'm asking you to let me go.'

'No.'

Christo had heard whispers about Tito Lambros. He was reported to be cruel and vindictive. The bitter burn of loathing coursed like poison through his veins. That his father's negligence had allowed such a man to hold Christo's future in his hands...

There was a great deal he needed to learn about Thea's family—some of which he might be able to use. But that could wait. Now it was time to give her something to cling to. *Hope.*

'You'll come with me as my wife and we'll discuss the situation in which we find ourselves. That's my promise. But we're leaving now.'

She looked down at her clothes and back at him. Her liquid amber eyes glowed in the soft lights. 'I can't go dressed like this!'

No more delays. She glanced at the door again. He didn't want a scene. Her tantrums could occur at his home, where any witnesses would be paid to hold their silence.

'You look perfect,' he said, waving his hand in her direction. 'It shows a flair for the dramatic—which you've proved to have in abundance tonight. Our exit will be unforgettable.'

She seemed to compose herself. Thrust her chin high, all glorious defiance. 'But my hat... I told everyone about it. I can't disappoint them.'

'Life's full of disappointments. Tell them it wouldn't fit over your magnificent hair.'

Thea's lips twitched in a barely suppressed sneer, her eyes narrow and glacial. The look she threw him would have slayed a mere mortal. Luckily for the most part he felt barely human.

'Rings,' he said.

She jammed them carelessly on her finger. *Victory.* He held out the crook of his arm and she hesitated before slipping hers through it. All stiff and severe. But her body still fitted into his in a way which enticed him. Caused his heart to thrum, his blood to roar. Strange. Intoxicating. All Thea.

'Now, smile,' he said.

She plastered on a mocking grimace.

He leaned down and whispered in her ear. 'Like you mean it, *koukla mou.*'

'I'll smile when you say *that* like you mean it, Christo.'

And he laughed.

This second laugh was more practised. More familiar—like an old memory. But the warmth growing in his chest was real. Beyond all expectations, he was enjoying her. For his sanity, perhaps a little too much…

CHAPTER TWO

THEA TUCKED INTO a corner of the limousine, far away from her newly minted husband. No one had noticed her biker chic clothes as they'd left the reception venue. They hadn't paid much attention to her at all. Everyone had been congratulating Christo. Shaking his hand. Wishing him happiness. The only tears for her had been shed by Elena.

Thea didn't have time for tears. She had to pull herself together. Devise another plan. Her focus needed to be on the future—which now sat in a white envelope in the pocket of Christo's jacket.

But how to get it?

She looked over at him. His long, lean legs stretched out, relaxed. His face illuminated by the cool glow of his phone. Some might call him handsome. Incredibly so, with his regal nose, strong jaw and high-cut cheekbones, all cast in a way to make a sculptor swoon. She, on the other hand, loathed the sight of his testosterone-fuelled perfection.

Though seduction might work… It was their wedding night, after all. She could try. Croon something…she wasn't sure what…slip a hand beneath his jacket, kiss him…

Christo's mouth formed a disapproving line as he tapped at his phone. She'd already had a taste of that mouth. The soft, chaste kiss at the altar. That shocking moment when he'd brushed his lips against hers at the reception venue and they'd sparked as if touched by a live wire.

She lifted her hand to her mouth, which still tingled.

Even if she could grab the envelope at the perfect moment, what then? She shook her head. A few grains of rice clattered from her hair onto the leather seats. The element of surprise was gone, so she couldn't try that approach. There must be something else.

Christo turned to peer at her. One eye was shadowed in darkness. The blue light from his phone turning the other inhumanly green. The effect made him look something like a pirate.

There was no way she was going to let him plunder *her* treasures. Her fresh plans started now.

'Where are we going?'

'Home.'

'No honeymoon? Christo Callas—ever the romantic,' she said, placing a hand to her heart. 'I'm *so* lucky.'

'You want romance?' He raised an eyebrow. 'You're the one who pronounced our marriage a sham. Had you not, we'd have been on our way to a week of wedded bliss on my island.'

An island? Typical. Though, come to think of it, not even her father had one of those. 'You had to cancel? How inconvenient.'

'For my staff, perhaps. Though I admit standing down the jet *was* an irritation.'

Something about being the cause of one of his irritations irked her. 'So…what? If I'd been a good girl, in exchange for my freedom I'd have been rewarded with a joy-ride and some time at the beach? Lucky me. Would you have supplied chocolate mints on my pillow too?'

He wasn't looking at her now. Instead he studied the dull glow of the city, which washed his imposing form with gold light. The breath caught in her throat. For a moment she forgot who he was, transfixed by the beauty of the picture.

'An island in the Echinades, a home in the mountains, a yacht berthed in…' he opened the calendar on his phone and checked something '… Monaco and an apartment in New York—any of which you could have flown to in my jet. And that's amongst other things. The rewards are many and varied for a *good* girl, as you put it.'

Thea had come from wealth—though nothing like this. She and Elena had discussed it when her father had made terrifyingly clear she had to marry to prevent Alexis rotting in a jail cell. They'd talked about Thea enjoying the considerable fruits of Christo's fortune.

Could she do it now? Christo would spend his days in the city, working. She could go anywhere. New York? That was where her mother had promised to take her all those years ago. Before she'd died, when life had held some hope. She'd like New York, she supposed.

And then came the reality of the price she'd have to pay. Because there was always a price. Her body was the currency of this union.

Never.

'I'm not prostituting myself for a chance to dip my toes in the Aegean or for a ride on your boat!'

'Yacht. Crewed by forty. And that's what marriage is about. Fair exchange for services rendered.'

Yes, marriage was a cruel snare. She'd seen it imprison her mother, and other women too. The wives of her father's friends. Locked in gilded cages where they fawned and simpered for attention from callous men. She'd planned never to be fooled by that trap, no matter how cunningly laid. The lure of money or circumstance…or love would never bind her to another…

'So cynical,' said Christo. 'On your wedding day too. You could have refused the offer at any time until we were pronounced man and wife. Yet here we are.'

'*Offer?* You never *asked* me to marry. I was an afterthought. You and my father negotiated the terms of my servitude. One day I woke up engaged and was thrown a ring in a box. Stop trying to turn this into some grand sacrifice on your part.'

'Don't presume to know *anything* about my sacrifices!'

Christo's words snapped like a whip-crack. Thea couldn't see his face, shrouded in darkness as they were. But the cut of his voice carved right to her soul.

'I was informed that you were satisfied with the arrangement. So you wanted a man on bended knee, professing love and adoration? If I'd done that what would your answer have been?'

Thea dropped her head, toying with the wedding and engagement rings which itched and burned her finger. She'd refused her father's demands to marry at first, and so he'd cut off any meagre freedoms she'd still had.

Demetri's methods of persuasion had been more brutal. The twin threats of social seclusion and physical force usually ensured her compliance, but she'd become braver since Alexis had entered her home. That day he'd stepped in to protect her had changed everything.

Her father then realised his importance to Thea. Not only as her bodyguard, but her half-brother. He knew she'd do anything to save him—the love child her mother had been forced to give up before entering a loveless marriage.

She wrapped her arms round her waist. Closed her eyes.

'As I thought,' Christo said. 'You're having a tantrum because I didn't play Prince Charming.'

'You can think what you like.'

'I invariably do.'

She turned to look out at a world which had always passed her by. 'I don't care. Your good opinion of me doesn't matter.'

Self-recrimination ran riot through her head. She should have run earlier. But when Alexis had confessed who he was, everything had changed. He'd told her of the promises he'd made to protect Thea if their mother couldn't and each day had become a little more tolerable. So she'd stayed. Worked to ensure her future so she would be able to do more than eke out an impoverished existence like her mother had.

Yet when it had almost been time to leave, fate intervened. With Alexis paying the price for her cowardice.

She slumped in the seat.

'Perhaps you should learn to cultivate a friendly benefactor,' Christo said. 'It could make your life easier.'

She adjusted one of the loathsome hairpins, now pricking into her scalp. 'There's no vacancy for the role of friendly benefactor in my life.'

'Shame. If there was, I'd be available to fill it.'

Something had shifted his tone. Now there was a lightness. Was he entertained by this?

She looked over at him, and even in the dim light of the cabin she glimpsed the hint of a smirk. She wouldn't be baited.

'Since you're more *unsociable detractor*, fortunately you don't meet the job description.'

'I'm known to be extremely affable in the right circumstances.'

The car's interior closed in on her. She needed to get out of here.

Breathe. She must stay calm.

But how? In this claustrophobic space? Drowning in the scent of Christo?

It was something more than expensive cologne. A dark, intoxicating essence whispering of wild places. Of powerful, untamed male.

Thea shivered. Clenched her fists till the nails bit into her palms. She could *do* this. Christo had promised they'd talk. She'd hold him to it.

The car drove up to a wrought-iron gateway which slid open before it. As the vehicle slowed to a halt outside the front entrance of Christo's mansion Thea moved to open the door. Escape the confines of this space threatening to crush her.

'Stop,' Christo said.

She did—without thinking. His voice, quiet as a whisper on the breeze, had carried such force she knew he wasn't someone she could trifle with. She must make no mistake. Whatever liberties she took, it would only be those that he allowed her to take.

'You will play your part as a happy new bride. Even if…'

His eyes traced a path from her head to her toes and back again. Everywhere his gaze touched ignited in a flare of heat.

'Even if you don't look like one. Freedom is bought. You start paying now.'

Christo didn't wait for the driver. He exited the limo, bending down to hold out his hand for hers.

She looked at it for a heartbeat. Long, elegant fingers. Square, perfect nails. The shiny wedding ring that caught the light and glinted. She placed her hand in his. Warm, strong. Curling possessively around hers.

A strange feeling wove through their connected fingers. A sinuous tempting thing that whispered to her, heated her cheeks, made her pulse thready and panicked. There was power in his touch. And the sense of possession was overwhelming as he squeezed gently.

Snakes of fear uncurled in her belly. Slithering. Contorting. Knotting into one another. She couldn't take her eyes from the place where he held her tight. Held her prisoner. Would he ever let her go?

'Now look at me.'

She couldn't resist. His voice was like the sprinkle of rain on a summer's day, the breath of a warm breeze. Then there was his stillness. It terrified her more than any lashes of emotion.

'*Not* like that.' He frowned.

'Like what?'

'Like I'm a Cyclops,' he said. 'I want you to look at me in a way that tells everyone what you crave is a locked door, a big bed and me inside you for hours.'

His words cut off her breath as surely as if he'd grabbed her by the throat. She tore her hand free of his, almost crawling back into the car as she did so.

'I can play my part, but I'll never look at you like that.'

He raised one mocking eyebrow. 'Afraid you might like it?'

'Enough!'

She was no coward. Thea slid out of the limo. Stood. Waited for a moment to suck at the air before Christo placed a heated palm on the small of her back. And then she allowed herself to be escorted through the monolithic front doors to where a line-up of staff waited.

'Let's get this over with,' she said.

His home was a vast display of modern, elegant lines in whites, golds and blues. Though she didn't have much time to survey the place as Christo swept through it like a tidal surge.

He introduced her to each staff member by name. All of them were eager to meet the new Mrs Callas, but they slid by in a blur as he led her up a winding staircase, past artwork bursting from white walls.

Yet she couldn't take her mind from Christo's hand at the base of her spine. Strong. Possessive. She supposed it was meant to appear affectionate, but the staff had long ceased watching and had melted away as if they were ghosts. There was no need for it now.

'Where's my bag? My phone?' Thea asked, trying to take her mind off the burn of his palm.

She'd hardly brought anything with her—only enough to maintain the ruse.

'I have your phone. Your bag's being unpacked together with all your other possessions, which the removal company delivered this morning.'

Yet again she hadn't been consulted. Choking bile rose in her throat. There was nothing at her father's she wanted. Her life was meant to be starting elsewhere. Fresh, clean. Something she could create for herself, not borrow from others.

'How efficient. And unnecessary. I won't be here long.'

'You'll be here as long as I need you.'

His voice was all quiet intent. They were deep in the house now. Away from everyone—especially prying eyes.

'That's something we need to discuss,' she said.

He looked down upon her. Cold. Unreachable. Her heart slammed into her ribs.

'And we will.'

'Where?' she asked as they stopped before a set of double doors.

Christo turned the handles and thrust them open. 'In the bedroom, *koukla mou.*'

'I'm not sleeping with you!'

Her words were a breathy gasp as she stopped, rocking back on her feet.

Christo ignored her and strode inside, a hot burst of irritation running through him. What was she thinking? He'd never force himself on her.

Her presumption that he would made him reckless.

'Really, Thea? It *is* our wedding night. That's what newly married couples do.'

He turned. Thea was frozen like a statue on the threshold of his room. Eyes wide. Surveying him up and down.

'This isn't a real marriage. It was arranged.'

'Marriages are "arranged" for people like us all the time. This could be a real marriage.' Or as real as possible for someone in their position.

He'd anticipated a relationship with no passion. A performance of duty for them both. But a lack of passion was not something he could imagine now. This new Thea intrigued him. His heart throbbed with a curious rhythm, as if charged with a fresh energy.

What he'd been promised by Tito Lambros, when Christo had realised the position his father had forced him into, was a sweet, obedient, chaste girl. He didn't hold much value in chastity. Better a woman who knew what she was doing, in his opinion. So he'd steeled himself for a wedding night of tutelage. The sweet and obedient type didn't thrill him either, but she would make a trouble-free sort of wife.

The woman in front of him was another creature altogether. One he didn't recognise from the quiet investigations he'd asked Raul to conduct, to ensure there was at least a modicum of truth behind her father's words.

He needed to check the work Raul had been asked to do.

'This can't be a real marriage. It'll never be consummated.'

Christo reached for a phone in the corner of the room and called the kitchens. 'Cognac. Two glasses, please.'

He shrugged off his jacket, cast it onto the chair next to him and tugged at his bow tie, letting it hang loose.

Thea hadn't moved, still standing in the doorway.

He undid the shirt button at his throat. Her gaze lowered, watching the flick of his fingers.

He undid the next. And the next. Then he stopped.

Her eyes hesitated at the open shirt showing part of his chest. As they burned on him with that strange heat, a crackling tension tightened in his gut.

'Come in. Close the door. Sit.'

A small flush whispered across Thea's cheeks and was gone. She looked away.

His stomach clenched at the loss of her eyes on his body. It was too much like disappointment. He ignored the sensation, removing his phone from his trouser pocket and tossing it on a table before sprawling on a plump couch.

His bedroom was more of a suite—the size of a small apartment and the one place in his home where he was rarely disturbed. They were safe here, for whatever histrionics were about to come.

He motioned to an armchair on the opposite side of an occasional table.

'I'm not your lap dog.'

'No, a lap dog would be less trouble. And it would at least jump all over me and be happy when I came home.'

She perched on the edge of the chair and glared at him as if she had murder on her mind.

A quiet knock at the door disturbed the uneasy silence.

A young woman in a crisp black uniform entered, carrying a silver tray.

'Thank you, Anna,' Christo said. 'Please leave the bottle.'

He suspected at least one of them might need fortifying for the negotiations to come.

The young woman placed the drinks on the table between them. 'Congratulations again, Mr and Mrs Callas. It's a happy day for you both.'

He tried to appear as pleased as his staff were. 'You have no idea…'

'Will that be all?'

Christo nodded.

Anna smiled at Thea and left the room.

He picked up one of the brandy balloons and swirled the glass in the light. Amber liquid coated the glass in a slick film of gold.

'A toast,' he said.

'What is it?'

Thea took a glass and sniffed it, wrinkling her nose. There was an unexpected cuteness about her when she did so. He smiled.

'Cognac.' Christo took a sip. Enjoyed the burn. The same type of burn as Thea's gaze upon him now. 'The colour of your eyes.'

She stopped and cocked her head. There was something so cool and unreachable about her. Yet her ferocity shone through. Those eyes of hers, spitting golden fire. The need to witness more of it, to experience her and the wildness she hid, grabbed him in a breath-stealing grip.

He hadn't expected to feel this way. The natural desire from contemplating a night with a beautiful woman, yes. Not this consuming sensation which thrummed through his every nerve, making him heavy and tight with lust for a woman he couldn't touch.

Thea placed the glass on the table without tasting it and slid it towards him. 'I've nothing to toast.'

'Shame… It's twenty-five years old. Obviously more mature than you.'

'I'm not the one being childish. I'm not the one playing games.'

She still refused to accept her part in the position where they now found themselves. 'Yes, Thea. You are. You've been playing games with me since the beginning and now I want answers.'

She leaned back into the armchair, feigning disinterest. But he could see by the tense set of her shoulders and the way her bottom lip puckered as she chewed at the inside that she was deeply concerned about what was happening here.

He reached over to his jacket, slung on the chair, and pulled out the white envelope. It might well have been a glass of water for someone parched in the desert the way Thea watched it, with a desperate craving stare.

Christo slid his thumbnail to unseal it. Made a show of inspecting the contents. Two thousand US dollars. Not so much. Certainly not enough for an escape. A passport. Nothing unusual there.

He unfolded a white piece of paper with account numbers written on it.

'Who taught you to ride a motorcycle?' he asked.

Her eyes widened a fraction. She hadn't been expecting that question, he was sure of it. Which had been his intention all along.

Thea licked her lips. They shone moist and pink. 'M-my brother… Demetri.'

Her brother was a dissolute, soft, rich boy, who only knew how to drive so he could show off his newest supercar. The thought that he could ride a motorcycle was absurd.

He let her lie sit unanswered, for now, and returned his attention to the paper in his hands.

'What bank is this?'

Thea crossed her arms.

'How much money is in the account?'

The silence stretched till it was thin and fragile. He waited.

When the thread was so thin Christo thought it would snap, Thea spoke. A low hiss, but he heard it nonetheless.

'That's none of your business.'

'You're my wife. Everything about you is my business. We can treat this…' he waved the paper about '…as your dowry.'

'No!'

He didn't need her money. The gift her father had granted him, halting the foreclosure, was greater than any paltry amount she no doubt held. But this was a battle he'd win. Her antics wouldn't put Atlas Shipping at risk. Not in the company's seventy-fifth year. It was a year for celebration, not failure. He'd never allow it. *Never.*

'One call to my personal banker and I'll have not only the name of your bank, but the balance of your account transferred into mine and secure.'

Thea twisted her small, delicate hands in her lap. 'You can't…'

'He was at the wedding,' Christo said, picking up his phone. 'All I need to say is that you've forgotten the details and want me to take care of it. Would you like me to get him now? No matter the time, he'll take my call.'

She looked at him. Eyes narrow, lips thin. Hatred evident. Once, long ago, he might have cared. Tonight, he didn't.

'Four million.'

He put down the sheet of paper. Leaned forward. He couldn't have heard properly.

'How much?'

'Four million US dollars or thereabouts.'

She lounged back in the chair looking like the fox who'd stolen a prized chicken. How had she accumulated that kind of money? Tito Lambros was known for being stingy. A banker who made money through frugality and question-able practices.

'Your father gave it to you?'

She snorted, before catching herself. There was his answer. Tito Lambros would never have given his daughter those sorts of funds. She must have stolen it, somehow.

'I'm thrifty.'

'Or a criminal. Should I ask your father to check his accounts? Perform an audit to look for a missing four million "or thereabouts"?'

When she spoke it was with pure derision. 'I'm no thief.'

'So what *is* my beautiful new wife? Not thrifty... Your clothes and shoes are exclusive designer.' He should know—he'd spent enough on former lovers to understand that much. 'Unless you've acquired a goose capable of laying golden eggs or the touch of Midas?'

The twitch of a smile played at the corner of her mouth. She was dying to tell him how she'd done it, so he let the statement linger. He needed to know how she'd acquired her money. It would inform what he did next, because he was beginning to watch Thea *very* closely.

Thea crossed her legs, wrapped her hands around her knee and studied him. He could see the thoughts behind her golden, intelligent eyes. She was calculating. Weighing up her options.

'My clothes and shoes were all given to me by Elena when she'd finished with them.'

'Then where—'

'In exchange for letting you know, I want something in return. To discuss our short and unfriendly future together.'

Negotiation was something he understood all too well. His parents had never offered him anything out of affection, but out of anticipation that they'd receive something in return. *Him*—a convenient tool in their hostilities. His inevitable conclusion? They didn't love him. They used him.

He'd become an expert on navigating that kind of emotional quicksand. And, with Thea, he'd get his own way. Still, he was prepared to allow her to think she might win.

'We'll discuss our options after you answer my question.'

She raised her eyebrows. 'That's meant to be my incentive? You'll have to give me something more than a promise.'

Thea sat straight-backed in the chair, seemingly impenetrable in leather and denim. She wanted more?

His imagination meandered down paths she surely wouldn't have intended. Visions of cracking through that tough veneer with his questing lips on her body. Peeling away those layers till he had her in her corset and boots. Laying her out on the bed. Fingers stroking her honeyed skin. Burying themselves in her hair...

No.

He wasn't like his father, succumbing to a beautiful face and living with the consequences.

Christo swallowed. Shut down his errant thoughts.

He'd give her something, since before the night was over she'd need to trust him—if only a little. Christo reached for his jacket again, put his hand into a front pocket and retrieved her phone. He slid it across the table towards her.

Thea picked it up, checked the screen and frowned. Her eyes were tight with concern.

'Now, call for help and try to get someone to believe I'm holding you prisoner here on your wedding night...' He nodded to the mobile clasped in her hands. 'Or tell me how you got that money.'

She hesitated a short while, then her expression changed as if she'd dismissed whatever had been troubling her. A soft, knowing smile played on her lips. She was making him wait.

It had the desired effect. Christo savoured the warm lick of anticipation curling on its seductive journey through him. He might have smiled too, but he didn't want to show her he was enjoying this far more than he should.

'My father thought paid work beneath any daughter of his. But he always expected me to dress impeccably so people wouldn't talk,' she sneered. 'He paid me an occasional allowance, which Elena banked in that account. So I wouldn't be discovered, she gave me her clothes once she'd worn them a few times. Her father was a generous man, so he never noticed her constantly needing new things.'

A clever scheme—as far as it went. 'Well, it seems you're more frugal than I imagined. Lucky me. But that still doesn't explain how you accumulated so much.'

'I've been planning from the moment I turned eighteen and received my first *"pay"* for being a compliant daughter. Five years of saving. But that was never going to be enough. So I learned the stock market, investing… Turns out I was quite successful.'

Thea sat forward, talking with her eyes and body and hands. Bristling with an uncommon fire and passion. Dangerously sparking his. This woman—his wife… He now questioned whether he should have married her, or employed her.

'Do you have any investment tips for me?' Christo took another sip of his cognac.

Thea smirked. 'I hear Atlas Shipping's doing quite well. Perhaps even better now, with an advantageous marriage between its owner and the daughter of Greece's biggest banker.'

On paper, of course, she was correct. But his father's unfortunate dealings with hers had risked more than anyone knew.

'Since I own the company, investing there would be pointless. I want to diversify.'

Of course he didn't own the company quite yet. He shared it with his father. Which was what had necessitated this impossible situation.

She sighed. Rolled her eyes. 'There's a tech start-up in the States. The talk is that they've increased the capacity for solar cell efficiency to eighty percent. It'll make a small fortune.' She looked him up and down, as if inspecting something unpleasant. 'Not that you need it.'

'Name?'

'I'll let you know tomorrow,' she said. 'Once you've agreed to a divorce and given me the contents of that envelope.'

CHAPTER THREE

THEA SMILED. CHRISTO'S face wasn't so impassive now. His head was cocked to one side, pinning her with his hard green eyes. He slowly rolled the brandy balloon in his hands and took another sip.

Christo didn't want a clever wife; he wanted a compliant wife. She'd never be that, ceding her precious freedom to a husband. A quick divorce and he could find himself another woman. One who might even *like* to be with him, or to sleep in that bed which looked big enough to have a party on.

Heat flooded to her cheeks, slid through her blood. Not that she'd ever think about parties in his bed, or what sort of parties he might have there. No way.

'Unfortunately, I require a wife. Since I have you, I don't see any point looking for another.'

She clenched her hands, the edges of her mobile phone cutting into her palms. There had to be a way out of this. Alexis would know what to do if she asked, but her texts lay unanswered.

She took a few deep breaths, trying to calm the nerves roiling in her stomach. She'd come too far to fail. Time to start negotiations to release her from this disastrous union.

Although she doubted Christo had any, Thea appealed to his better judgement. 'I don't want to be your wife. And you don't want me. I *know*. Why settle for this? You could find someone else. Someone you love.'

He lounged back on the couch, impossibly masculine with his shirt part open, showing a dark sprinkling of hair on that strong chest. A shadow of growth now adorned his jaw. She'd never looked at a man before—not unfiltered like this—and he was mesmerising. He drained his drink. As he leaned forward to place his glass on the table he licked his full bottom lip. A seductive pulse sparked deep and low in her belly.

'I've no interest in love.' His lazy, heavy-lidded gaze fixed on her. Assessing. 'So, for now, I'm keeping you.'

The folded paper with her account numbers gleamed a taunting white in his hand. Christo turned it over in his fingers, flicking it backwards and forwards. But his eyes never left her.

She slumped in her chair. There was going to be no negotiation here. She was a prisoner. Just as with her father and Demetri. A pawn in some scheme between rich, powerful men.

She clenched her teeth. 'You're a monster.'

He shrugged and smiled. It should have been friendly enough, but the way he bared his perfect white teeth looked a little...carnivorous. Still, she wouldn't waver. She wasn't scared of him—not this man.

'Yes. Though on some days I'm only human,' he said. 'You'd do well to remember that.'

She glanced over at the enormous bed again. Did he mean she could buy her freedom another way? There was a *presence* about him. Muscular, powerful, superior. Maybe some women craved that in a man. Would relish running their fingers through his spiky dark hair. Live to drown in the depths of his hazel-green eyes.

She wasn't one of them.

Christo followed her gaze and looked back at her through steepled fingers.

'Tired, Thea? It has been a long day.' His perfectly etched lips tilted at the corners. 'So let's stop toying with each other. My father's will stipulates that to inherit Atlas Shipping I must have a wife. Since you've married me, I'm not letting you go till he's dead and buried.'

Threads of fear wrapped around Thea's throat, tightening till she gasped for breath. Her heart pummelled her ribs. How old was Christo's father? This could go on for years.

She couldn't.

She wouldn't…

Christo leaned forward. 'There's no point hiding the truth from you. Not now.'

How could he sit there so calmly, as if this sort of thing happened to him every day?

Her phone fell from her hand into her lap. She curled her freed fingers into her palm, concentrating on the bite of her nails on the soft flesh. Her breathing steadied.

'How's your father's health?'

Christo smiled. 'My father's ill. Terminally so. Although his condition has stabilised of late. But I appreciate your concern.'

Thea stilled. She knew too well the pain of losing a beloved parent before their time. The emptiness that followed. No matter what was happening here, she wouldn't dance around his father's waiting grave.

'That's why he wasn't at our wedding? I wondered…' she said, though it didn't explain why his mother hadn't been there either. 'I'm sorry.'

Christo waved the words away. 'Don't be. He has time.'

A chill spread through her. The man was like a glacier. Frozen, immovable. A shudder racked her body. If he didn't care about his dying father, he'd never care about what she wanted. She clenched her fists even tighter. The sharp slice of her fingernails branded her palms, yet the trembling in her limbs wouldn't stop.

'I'm not a cruel man. Although I had some fine teachers.'

His voice was gentle. Were those words supposed to be something like reassurance? Because she knew about cruelty too. Her father and Demetri were masters. She'd lived with it all her life and she saw its hallmarks in Christo. The arrogance, the superiority. The assurance that there was no other way but his.

'If you're not cruel, we can divorce.'

Her voice sounded distant, even to her own ears. The

room folded in, its walls seeming too close. Her vision faded around the edges as her pulse sped to an inhuman speed.

Not here, not now.

She breathed through the moment until everything came back into focus.

'My father hasn't long to live. Twelve months at most. So his doctors say.' He looked down at his hands, now clasped in front of him. 'I don't have time to divorce and remarry. When he dies, I'll grant what you want.'

'Why me?'

She wanted to know why she'd been chosen as a piece in this game. Her father hadn't told her, other than giving her a list of information he required about Atlas Shipping.

'You were available.'

'And you say you're not a cruel man? If that's all it needed, no doubt there were any number of women who would have thrown themselves at your feet if you'd asked.'

'I need *you*, Thea.'

His words were rich and silky and they wound around her like treacherous ribbons, tying her to the spot. She should get up…shout, rage. But she couldn't. Her skin prickled uncomfortably. She unzipped her jacket as perspiration slicked the back of her neck.

Christo went on. 'You're clearly a businesswoman, so I don't expect you to agree to this undertaking for free. Your funds will be increased and returned.'

Freedom. At a price.

She could leave now—assuming Christo let her, and that was in some doubt—but she had little doubt that if she walked out tonight, she'd go with nothing.

The curl of fear gripped her again. She'd witnessed her mother being turned against by family and friends because of her choice to escape Tito Lambros. The man she'd never loved. Even as a child Thea had recognised her mother's deprivations. Maria had always looked so thin and starved… of everything.

She'd never forgotten her mother's words of advice. *Don't do what I did. Ensure your future above all things.*

And if she left, where would she go? Elena's father and Thea's father were friends. She'd be returned to Christo and then...

No. There was only Alexis. Surely he'd done what he'd promised? Taken his money and left Greece?

The fear that he might not have began to throttle her. Dark visions chasing her and biting at her heels.

'You're thinking too hard, Thea.'

Christo's voice dripped calm patience. He was trying to seduce her into a deal with the devil. She was trapped. Exchanging one silk-lined prison for another.

'How can I trust you?' she asked.

He relaxed in the chair, a slight smile tilting his lips. He saw victory in his sights—she was sure of it. She wanted to keep him talking so she could think.

'All that I ask is we stay married until I inherit Atlas Shipping in full.' He stood and began unbuttoning the rest of his shirt. 'I'll have our negotiations committed to a formal document. A post-nuptial agreement, so to speak.'

He shrugged the crisp cotton from his shoulders, grabbed his suit jacket, her envelope and account numbers, and then turned.

'I'll give you a few moments to think about it.'

Thea froze. All she could do was watch as he strolled into a huge walk-in wardrobe. Transfixed by his broad, powerful shoulders. The way his back muscles flexed and moved with every step.

Somewhere in the depths of the room she heard the rush of a shower. Imagined hot water running over the ridges and hollows of Christo's tanned skin, taut over muscle...

Thea shook herself, lifting the spell. She needed to speak to Alexis.

Grabbing her phone, she texted.

Their code if she needed help. The one word he'd never ignore.

She waited for a response. Something. Anything.

No answer came.

She clenched her fists. Concentrated on the bite of her nails into her palms as she slowed her breathing.

'Have you decided?'

That deep velvet voice rolled over her, interrupting her dark thoughts. Christo wandered into the room wearing only long black silk pyjama pants, slung low around his narrow hips, where they seemed to have found an unsettling home. She couldn't tear her eyes from his elegantly muscled torso. A sprinkling of hair on his chest arrowed down his body in a line between the ridges of his abdomen, before disappearing underneath the waistband of his pyjamas.

'What are you doing?'

Her voice came out a little too high. She took in a breath. The intoxicating scent of warm soap and clean male skin teased her senses.

Christo raised his eyebrows. His hair clung damp to his head. A few drops of water still sparkled on his shoulders. 'It's been a long and exciting day. I'm preparing for bed.'

'Put on some clothes. This…' she flapped her hand about in his direction, averting her eyes '…it's impolite.'

'Since I usually sleep naked, I consider the way I'm dressed to be the height of good manners. What's your decision?'

Out on the streets with nothing, there would be little she could do to help her half-brother, if that's what he needed. Here, she had a chance. Some resources even without her money. She would put up with anything to ensure Alexis was safe. She owed him that much.

'I agree.'

She hated the smug curl of Christo's sensual mouth as she spoke.

'There are other conditions,' he said.

Thea narrowed her eyes. Of course there were. 'And they are?'

'This must, in *every* way, appear like a real marriage.'

'How does a "real marriage" appear?'

She had no idea. Her mother had left the brutality of the marital bed when Thea was young. She had no memories of anything other than the beautiful, broken woman Maria Lambros had become.

'We're happy newlyweds. Being faithful to each other is one condition. I'm sure you can use your imagination for the rest. You talked about marrying for love before.'

He walked to the huge bed, threw back the covers and lay down in masculine splendour, patting the space next to him.

'I said I wasn't sleeping with you!'

'I assumed you meant sex,' he said. Thea flushed bright and hot. The way that word slid syrupy from his tongue sounded dark, decadent and very, very dirty. 'Which has nothing to do with sleeping.'

'No. I meant I wasn't going to share your bed. Where am I going to sleep?'

'There's plenty of room here. You can trust me.'

She looked again at that enormous piece of furniture. With him all bronzed perfection like a god, at its centre. 'I'm not—'

'So you can't trust yourself?'

He smiled. And this smile wasn't predatory or wolf-like. His face lit up with warmth in his lips, dancing eyes. It made her all tight and shivery, as if she was about to burst from her skin.

'I need my own room.'

'If you move to your own room when we're newly married we'll be exposed.'

And then it dawned on her what she had really agreed to.

She'd not been concentrating as they'd talked, and Christo had outplayed her. Still, there was a possibility of rectifying the situation…

Thea waved at the sitting room area. 'A gentleman would take the couch.'

Christo sat up and skewered her with a fierce, hot glare. 'When I married you today I assumed it would be real enough. Arranged? Yes. Unwelcome? Absolutely. But real, nonetheless. That means sleeping in my bed, with my wife. None of this arrangement means I'll be relegated to the couch. If you want it, it's yours.'

He flopped back down onto the covers, with his arms behind his head.

Infuriating man.

Thea peeled away her leather jacket. Tore off her boots. She stormed into the still humid en suite bathroom, removed her top and battled with her corset, breathing a sigh as the laces were released. She cast it into a corner, slipped on her black top again and pulled the pins from her hair. They scattered on the benchtop as she raked her hands through it to untangle the braiding. She wiped off her make-up.

All right, she'd play his little game. For now. But what was she going to wear to sleep? The maids had packed her an exotic trousseau, with a variety of the skimpy nightwear her father's latest mistress deemed she required to entertain *'a man like Christo Callas'*.

The horror of that woman taking her 'under her wing', barely older than herself… Thea shuddered.

Tonight she'd sleep in her clothes, and work out the rest in the morning.

Thea marched back into the room and settled on the couch, making a show of fluffing the cushions. She needn't have. They were soft as down. In a final act of defiance, she bashed a decorative pillow into submission under her head.

Christo chuckled. 'Sleep well, Thea.'

The lights flicked off and the room was plunged into

darkness. As Thea lay there she heard Christo shift on the bed. She imagined the crisp drag of cool sheets over his semi-naked body.

'I will,' she said sweetly as the intoxicating vision rolled through her head.

She curled onto her side. And as she sank into the plump cushions the adrenalin leached away to be replaced by leaden exhaustion.

Before she fell asleep, she muttered, 'Once I overcome my dreams of smothering you in your bed…'

CHAPTER FOUR

CHRISTO ROSE AS dawn bled pale yellow through the window of his bedroom. Thea hadn't stirred. He walked past the infernal couch she'd made her bed for the past three nights. Three *long* nights. Her resolve was commendable, but his was rapidly shredding.

When he'd struck their agreement, he hadn't really considered the implications of having her so close. Every movement she made as she slept, each muffled sigh in the darkness, and he woke. He was at risk of getting no rest so long as she stayed in the room with him. And what she wore… Her nights were spent clothed in an alluring array of silk and lace which clung to her delectable body and set his on high alert.

This morning Thea lay in luxurious blue satin, split to her thigh. As she sprawled the gown parted, to reveal long, slender legs. He craved to stroke her golden skin, to wake her with gentle caresses. To hear her breathy murmurs of surprise as he coaxed her into consciousness. In his imaginings she welcomed him with a sultry smile and open arms…

He shook his head, took a slow breath. Clenched his fists, reining in the desire to touch. Madness lay at the end of these current thoughts. Their marriage was a business relationship. Nothing more. Anyhow, Thea didn't want him. She never would.

Christo threw himself under a cold shower to douse the fever of Thea raging through his blood. The needles of icy water shocked some sense into him. Once dressed, he made his way to the terrace overlooking a glittering lap pool. He ignored the breakfast of pastry, fruit and meats adorning the table. Of greater interest was the report Raul's security firm had prepared on Thea's movements in the months before their marriage.

He'd commissioned the work with only a fleeting pang of guilt. Tito Lambros couldn't be trusted, and Christo had wanted to know exactly who he was marrying before sliding a ring on Thea's finger. He'd glanced at the document before their official engagement. Uninteresting reports of her having coffee with her best friend, shopping, the occasional nightclub. Always overseen by bodyguards. Nothing to alert anyone to the suspicion that Thea was anything other than the dutiful, obedient, innocent daughter her father described.

Christo yawned. He sipped his bitter black coffee and turned to the photographs. Grainy, night-time pictures. He hadn't studied them before the wedding, preferring to rely on the certainty of printed words. Had he chanced a look he'd have noticed immediately. Thea and Elena swapped clothes. Hairstyles. In a darkened venue people wouldn't notice the difference.

Thea was right. She hid in plain sight.

The click of heels on the tiled terrace alerted him to her approach. He slid the report into his briefcase and threw back the dregs of his coffee. She sauntered to the table in low-slung jeans and a heavy studded belt. A sheer, jewel-coloured top flowed around her torso. She presented the same contradiction now as on their wedding night: a picture of toughness softened by feminine grace.

For a startling moment he craved to strip her down and discover where the toughness ended and the woman began.

'Good morning,' she said, and sat.

Reaching for a fig, she tore the ruby flesh in half. Her lips wrapped around the luscious fruit as she took a bite. Watching her sleep was an ordeal for even the most pious man, but witnessing her eat was a study in erotic torture. He adjusted himself in his seat. Thanked all things holy that he could remain at the table for as long as it took to wrestle the pounding hammer of need into submission.

As Thea consumed the mouthful of fig she rubbed her neck, oblivious to his crushing desire to kiss the juice of that fruit from her lips till she moaned his name. He cleared his throat. Quelled the fantasy. She'd probably bite him, not kiss back.

'Poor sleep?'

'I'm sore from the couch.'

'You should've asked me for proper pillows.'

'I want my own room. There's no privacy. No way to keep the mystery alive between us.'

Thea fluttered her long lashes. The glorious flirtation of her... Was this how his father had been trapped all those years ago? At least Raul's report gave no indication that Thea had a lover stashed in some safe corner, ready to resume their relationship at a moment's notice, like his mother had. Sad how he counted that as a blessing rather than an expectation.

Christo poured another thick, dark coffee and leaned back in his chair. 'We're newlyweds. Tangling the bed sheets with passion every night. We don't want there to be any mystery.'

The carnal visions rioting through his head made him wish his words were true, rather than a pretence.

Anna came to the table. She bustled about arranging food, collecting plates. Thea's lips tilted in a wicked smile as she stabbed a piece of meat with her fork. He had little doubt she wanted it to be his flesh under those sharp tines.

'But, Christo, *darling*. I look haggard. Of course I need my own room,' she said, with the perfect pitch of complaint. 'Anna, come here. You'll agree. Don't I look exhausted?'

Anna sidled over to them, panic written all over her face. What was Thea up to?

'See—I look too horrid for Anna even to answer.'

The girl tried to run off, but Thea clamped a hand on her arm, pinning her to the spot.

'No, stay. I'm not getting any sleep.'

Christo took another sip from his cup, schooling his face to one of polite interest. 'There are good reasons for that. Which no one needs to hear…'

He understood now. He'd been witness to all his mother's games over the years. This was no different.

'Anna does.' Thea looked at Anna, brows drawn, face serious. 'He snores. Terribly. All night.'

The coffee caught in his throat. He lurched forward. Coughed.

'I don't!'

Thea's wide-eyed innocence continued. 'He doesn't want to admit it… I'm sure he's quite embarrassed.'

Nowhere in their bargain was there any term allowing her to make a fool of him in front of his staff. His voice was a low growl of warning. *'Thea…'*

She ignored him, focusing on Anna, whose look of horror might have been comical in other circumstances. 'Now I'm getting dark rings under my eyes. Soon I'll stop looking beautiful and Christo won't want me anymore.'

'I'll buy you some earplugs.'

Thea lowered her voice to a conspiratorial whisper. 'That won't work. He's a beast, I tell you. Why, last night—'

His chair scraped in protest along the tiles as he stood. Jaw clenched tight. Breathing hard.

'Enough.' The lies and manipulation stopped now. 'Let Anna go before you horrify her any further.'

Thea released her grip and Anna ran back into the house. He sat. Took a drink of water. Attempted to cool the anger boiling his blood.

'What is it about the words "real marriage" that you don't understand?'

'The pronouncement that I had to share your room came after I'd agreed to this arrangement of ours.' She crossed her arms, eyes narrowing. 'That was underhanded. And as far as I'm concerned it doesn't form part of our original agreement.'

He threw up his hands. 'You're trying to win this argument on a *technicality*?'

'No. I'd prefer to talk about what the marriages I know of are actually like. My parents didn't share a room. What about yours?'

His parents weren't an example of marriage to which he aspired. Not that marriage was a state he'd ever thought he'd find himself in until that final argument with his father. But he didn't want to give her any more ammunition.

He stretched his neck from side to side. It gave an audible and satisfying crack.

'My parents weren't traditional in many things.'

Their relationship had been one of mutually assured destruction. His father had loved his mother. His mother had loved the Callas fortune. A pregnancy and Christo's birth had secured her future in a neat package.

'So why do we need to be?' Thea flicked her hair over her shoulders and pouted.

For all her theatrics, her lips were pink and dangerously kissable.

'If you loved me, you'd let me have my own room.'

He'd learned from childhood that love and marriage were lies. And a caring family the biggest lie of them all.

Christo dropped his voice to a whisper. 'Since I don't love you, what you say is meaningless.'

'That's the problem.'

Thea leaned forward, her hands splayed on the table. Christo's gaze dropped as the front of her sheer top fell open.

'If you were pretending to love me properly it's what you'd do.'

Was she guileless enough not to know that her position allowed him a perfect view of her magnificent cleavage?

All silky skin and powerful temptation? Probably not. He suspected Thea didn't do anything without good reason and a great deal of thought.

He stared for a moment longer than he ought, then pinched the bridge of his nose. 'You're a manipulator.'

'You're heartless.'

Thea flopped back into her seat, hands clenched tight on the damask tablecloth. Her colour faded till she was as pale as the white fabric under her hands. Something about it twisted tight in his gut.

Since when had he started developing a conscience? This was a business deal like any other. Though how he was going to survive another night, let alone another year with her in his room was anyone's guess.

Then, over Thea's shoulder, he spied movement. He reached out to take her clenched hand in his. Her eyes widened and she tried to tug away.

'We're being watched by my staff,' he said, and she stilled. He pasted what he hoped was a warm smile on his face. 'Whilst they're paid well to be discreet, I'd prefer to give them nothing to talk about.'

Christo rubbed his thumb over Thea's knuckles, trying to appear affectionate and attentive. Her eyes dropped to where he stroked gently back and forth, and the barest flush tinted her cheeks. Such a beautiful colour on her golden skin. A glow kindled deep inside him.

'All I was trying to say is that a man would do anything for the woman he truly loves.' Her voice was a whisper, gentle as the breeze through the olive tree above them.

'Where did you hear that?'

Thea's hand relaxed, smooth and warm in his. Her skin was a marvel of liquid silk under his fingers. So soft… How would the rest of her feel?

'Someone told me once,' she said, 'when counselling me to demand more from life.'

Those words pulled him back from his silent imaginings.

He'd never had to compromise for anyone. Although what Thea said had a ring of truth to it. They were supposed to be an adoring couple. Their love would have the power to make them do irrational things. Like lifting her hand to his lips. Anna was still watching, after all. Anyhow, it was only a light touch over her perfect skin. Yet he couldn't stop.

'Wh-what are you doing?'

He closed his eyes for a moment. Savoured her exotic scent of honey and spice. 'Pretending to love you properly,' he murmured.

What if they made the physical aspects of this marriage real, for as long as they had each other? It would be some sort of solution to what promised to become a long stretch of sleepless nights.

Thea's lips parted, all of her soft and languid. Her pupils were huge and dark. He could lean across the table and kiss her now. Start a seduction so complete the word *no* would leave her vocabulary for ever.

But his father's words echoed in his mind. *'I know you, son. Marry, and nature will take care of the rest.'*

A chill ran through him. He was not that man.

He released her. Pulled away. Suffered the cold loss of her hand in his.

'Ask me,' Christo said.

Hector didn't know him at all. He was stronger than his father and he'd prove it.

'For what?'

Her voice was low and husky, scraping across his skin as surely as her fingernails would. So affecting he could almost feel the erotic sting. He craved it. Ignored it.

'Your own room. No lies. No manipulation.'

She opened her mouth. Hesitated for a moment, as if asking for anything was foreign to her. 'Christo, I'd like my own room.'

'See? That wasn't difficult.'

'You haven't given me an answer yet.' A faint frown

marred her brow. 'What about this needing to appear like a real marriage?'

'That requirement hasn't changed.' He knew of one solution, but part of him wanted her to give something herself. Then he'd consider it a small victory. 'What can you offer me in return?'

Another flush of pink coloured her cheeks as Thea reached up to toy with the pendant hanging from a fine gold chain around her neck. 'If I have my own room, I could come to yours for a little while each night, so your people won't ask questions.'

And there it was. Not ideal, but he supposed compromise never was. At least he might get some unbroken sleep without Thea's glorious temptation sprawled out before him each night, burning his blood.

'You'll stay for a *long* while,' he said, sipping at his now cool coffee. 'I'm supposed to be making insatiable love to a beautiful woman. That's something I like to take my time with.'

She licked her lips. It hit him like a kick in the groin.

'What will we really be doing?' she asked.

He shrugged as Anna began another nervous approach to the table. 'For all I care you can do a crossword.'

When Anna reached them, she gave a discreet cough. 'Mr Callas, your mechanic's here.'

'Thank you. And, Anna? Mrs Callas and I have discussed her request. Please make up the spare room next to mine and move all her things in there. Today.'

He looked over at Thea, softened his gaze. Tried to muster an enamoured expression. He wasn't sure whether it worked, so his words would have to suffice. 'I'd do anything to ensure my bride's happiness here.'

Thea flashed a smile in response, relieved and yet dazzling. It curled into him, flickered into life a beguiling warmth in his chest. Odd how this new agreement between them felt so enjoyable...

He stood, before the sensation ran away with him completely.

'Tonight, *koukla mou*,' he said, kissing her on the cheek, relishing her soft exhalation as he did.

And as he walked away he found himself counting the moments till he saw her again.

CHAPTER FIVE

THEA SAT ON the edge of her new bed, in her new room, hands tightly clenched. Concentrating on the cut of her fingernails into her palms.

Pretending to love. Pretending.

Her whole life was a pretence. Faking her role as a dutiful daughter, a happy bride.

The pain of it knotted inside her, tighter and tighter. She breathed slowly through the gnawing in her stomach. And yet for a fleeting moment she'd snatched a glimpse of another life. The touch of a man. Her *husband*. The soft press of his lips on her hand. The burn it had left. How, for a breathtaking second, she'd craved something more and her heart had filled with silly, jagged if-onlys which had cut on every beat.

But this was more pretence. Marriage formed no part of her plans. Even in her short life she'd seen enough. Knew that husbands ruled, and heaven help any woman caught by circumstance or, even worse, love. She'd never succumb to it. It was a romantic trap set for the foolhardy. That was when the bars truly fell, clanging into place for ever.

She shivered, wrapping her arms round her waist. She had her plan. What she needed was to find Alexis. To ease the constant ache of fear in her chest. To prove her agreement with Christo was good for something.

Time for the next charade.

She stood, smoothing her palms over her clothes, relieved that at least she didn't have to deal with the teasing caress of silken lingerie sliding over her body. Or the hot gleam from Christo's eyes which had taunted her for the past three nights.

That man pretended too. His appearance of a tightly

reined-in gentleman was an act. She'd seen the way he'd looked at her as she'd lain on the couch in his room. As if she was a meal set out for his pleasure. All that dark hunger had tempted Thea to spread herself out and be devoured.

But it would never happen. He'd used her for his own ends and she'd take what she could from him, no questions.

Having her own room was a win, and in her life she'd had too few. It wasn't as big as Christo's, and was all soft neutrals—a blank, pale canvas like her life so far.

Thea dreaded leaving its silence and safety, but she padded down the hall with book and pencil in hand, her toes sinking into the velvety carpet. The doors to his suite were closed when she arrived. She raised her hand and knocked.

'Come.'

His deep, low voice slid over her like a rush of warm water. Thea hesitated, then took a steadying breath and entered the room.

Christo sat on the couch in jeans and a T-shirt, the clothes soft and well worn. His shirt looked bound to the sculpted muscles of his chest and biceps. The jeans outlined his powerful thighs. Her stomach flipped with a curious disappointment. But no, she definitely *didn't* miss the expanse of bronzed skin and naked torso he'd subjected her to as he'd slept on his huge bed.

Out of suit trousers and bespoke shirts he looked young. Thea supposed he was—though at thirty-one Christo was hardly Greece's youngest billionaire. And, unlike his usual stern poise during the day when his employees were present, tonight there was something almost approachable about him, with his hair raked through and messy, a few strands falling across his brow.

The observation tugged low and warm in her belly, pooling in a way that made her shift on the spot. But it was something on which she refused to dwell. Instead, she did a prancing little twirl.

'I wasn't sure how to dress.' She waved her hands between them as she looked down at her black leggings and oversized grey top. 'For this…assignation.'

His eyes met hers, then took a meandering journey over her silhouette. Even though her body was hidden under formless clothes it was as if he could see right through them.

'What you wear is immaterial, since the aim of newly-weds is to get out of their clothes as quickly as possible.'

All she envisaged was searching hands and naked limbs entwined. Breathless sighs and a deep, unrelenting ache.

She shut out the errant thoughts and flopped into the overstuffed armchair opposite. 'Charming.'

The corners of his mouth tilted in a lazy smile. 'If you pretended to be more of an adoring wife, I'd show you how charming I could be.'

She ignored the invitation. 'I'm here, aren't I?'

'You could try to look happy about it.'

She tossed her head, meaning to look resolute, but the move seemed somehow childish.

'Never.'

'Never is a long, cold time to be alone.' He ran his thumb over the full curve of his lower lip.

Such a decadent mouth for a man…

'I'm used to being alone,' she said.

Christo's eyes tightened for a heartbeat, almost in a wince, then it was gone.

'So am I.'

She dismissed him with a bored, practised glance and tucked her feet under her, opening the book Anna had purchased for her that afternoon. The request had earned her a bemused look, but she'd assured Anna that Christo loved doing puzzles in his spare time. When Anna had cackled out loud at this revelation, she knew she'd found a friend in the house.

Thea grinned.

One down. Six letters.

The tallest mountain in Europe.

She scribbled the answer.

'Crosswords?' Christo chuckled, deep and low.

The sound rolled over her, making her thighs clench.

She shrugged. 'Your suggestion.'

He tossed down the papers he'd been studying. 'I'm flattered you listened. So you're planning on becoming an obedient wife? Lucky me.'

'I wouldn't get my hopes up if I were you.'

'Ah, so my luck's running out already?' he said, sprawling on the couch.

Thea nibbled the end of her pencil and a dark and slumberous look swept over Christo's face. She ignored the awareness of it prickling at the base of her spine.

'Now hope is all I have left,' he added.

'Whilst you're hoping for something which won't happen, you can help. Two across. Eight letters. *"A large Patagonian rodent that lives in communal groups."*'

He stretched back, hands behind his head. His shirt shifted to expose a glorious slice of golden etched abdomen.

'Capybara.'

She pencilled in the word, which fitted. 'How do you know that?'

'I've tasted it.'

'What?' she squeaked. 'But a rodent's a rat.'

'More like a guinea pig. No tail.'

'Well, having no tail obviously makes *all* the difference.'

'Not my fondest culinary memory, but I was in South America on business and politeness dictated I sample it.'

Christo smiled. A wicked, glinting thing.

'I didn't realise I'd find crosswords so enjoyable. What's our next clue?'

He was teasing her. It lit up his face with a mischievous sort of amusement. She tried hard not to smile herself. She shouldn't be having fun. She shouldn't. Reality would intrude soon enough.

Thea shut the crossword book. 'I don't want to risk hearing about any more of your odd culinary extravaganzas.'

'Not my experience with sea cucumbers in China? Where's your sense of adventure?'

'I've never been encouraged to have one.'

'Shame… I'm travelling to New York in a few weeks. I thought you might join me.'

Her heart leapt. He was going to the city her mother had promised to take her.

An awful yearning replaced the sense of fun. It clutched at her, twisting hard. She toyed with the corner of the book in her lap, staring out past filmy curtains to the floodlit balcony. The illuminated olive trees waved silvery in the night breeze.

'I've never been out of Greece.'

Christo leaned forward, forearms on his thighs. His wedding ring glinted in the lights. 'What was your father thinking?'

That if he kept her in a cage she wouldn't fall, like her mother had before her marriage.

'He's protective. There was always a driver. Always a bodyguard. Something I rely on now.'

The lie caught in her throat. Her father had been her jailer. Demetri his enforcer.

'Come to New York with me and you'll have a driver. I'll also organise one of my security detail to attend you. If that's what you want.'

It was. Desperately. Because here was her way to locate Alexis. Christo had power and reach she didn't. If anyone could find him it was her husband.

'I'd like to bring my own bodyguard.'

'My men are all provided by Raul. Highly trained and supremely trustworthy.'

Could she tell him the truth about Alexis? That he was

the child her mother had been forced to relinquish? Her half-brother, who'd kept her going on her darkest days?

No lies. No manipulation.

No. She couldn't trust anyone who did business with her father—especially if that business involved her.

She licked her lips. 'I only trust Alexis Anastos—the man my father engaged.'

Christo lounged in his chair, but there was a tension about him which told her he was watchful.

'Where is he now?'

'I'm not sure. He was released prior to our marriage. Said he was going to take a long holiday. Something about working with me making him need one.' She laughed. It sounded hollow.

Christo's eyes narrowed. His body stilled with predator-like intent.

'How close were you to him?'

The question was measured, quiet. But the implication of the words burrowed under her skin. What did he think she was? A hot roil of anger seethed inside her. Newly married and already seeking out someone else? Anyhow, they had an agreement—one she loathed, but she'd stick by it nonetheless.

'He was like the brother I should have had!' she snapped.

Christo cocked his head. *Stupid.* Her emotion would give everything away.

Thea levelled him with a steady gaze. 'Besides, I'm not his type.'

That seemed to relax the crouching panther a little.

Christo settled back into the comfortable cushions of the couch. 'Let me know the security firm he works for and I'll look into it.'

She breathed out slowly. 'Thank you.'

'I said I'd do anything to make you happy here.'

That voice. Soft as the caress of silk sheets. But his eyes held the promise of a brewing storm. And she wasn't even sure he was trying. If he did, Thea knew the man would beat the devil in his ability to tempt.

'Are you really going to insist on doing this every evening?'

'I seem to recall you offered.'

'It was the lesser of two evils.'

'A similar position for both of us,' Christo said. 'We could try to get to know each other, since we might be together some time.'

Thea's stomach churned like a twisting pit of vipers. This could go on for years. Yet she couldn't pray for his father's death to free her any faster.

Her pulse leapt, threatening to rampage out of control. Her breathing became short and shallow. These episodes had increased in their relentless frequency since her engagement. An old, bitter enemy challenging her from the shadows. But she wouldn't let it consume her in front of Christo.

Thea flipped the pencil in her hand and pressed the sharp point into the pad of her thumb, concentrating on the pain. Her heartbeat slowed. The twist in her stomach eased. She relaxed the pencil's pressure and rubbed the spot with her index finger, soothing the sting.

'So, what? We play twenty questions?'

He smiled in that wolfish way of his and her toes curled into the plush carpet.

'Would you prefer truth or dare?' he asked.

'I'm a bit old for that sort of game.' She sniffed. In reality, she'd never played *any* sort. Though she'd always craved the freedom to make mistakes of her own.

'What would you like to play?' Christo asked, his tone all soft invitation.

Could he have been one of those mistakes, if she'd been allowed to make them? In other circumstances might she have fallen for the ruinous gleam in those gold-green eyes or the dark promise in his midnight voice?

No. He wasn't her mistake to make. Now or ever.

She sighed. Rolled her eyes for added effect. 'Ask your questions, Christo.'

Christo stood and walked to the bureau, where he poured himself a cognac. He sipped the drink as he regarded her over the rim of the glass. 'My mechanic was impressed with your bike. Where did you develop an interest in vintage British motorcycles?'

Her heart stopped for a beat. In truth, before becoming *her* interest it had been Alexis's passion. She had to step carefully. Christo didn't really want to get to know her. He was littering their conversation with landmines to trap her.

'And here I thought you were going to ask me my favourite colour. Which, for the record, is red.'

'Why does that not surprise me?' he said, smiling. 'Mine's green.'

'Opposites.'

'They can attract.'

'I'm thinking oil and water.'

'And I'm thinking you're avoiding my question.'

Clever man.

She tried for her most guileless look. 'I like the glossy black paint and glistening chrome.'

Which was what she saw the day Alexis had proudly delivered her gift—a classic of British motorcycling. Then he'd taught her to ride. Hours with the wind in her face, as if she was flying. And she'd finally understood the glory of the machine and the joy of freedom.

'You don't strike me as the sort of woman who'd make a decision because something looks shiny.'

The corners of Christo's appraising eyes crinkled in amusement, softening the inherent hardness of him.

'Sorry to disappoint.'

Christo raised his glass to her with a slow smile. She couldn't take her eyes from his perfect lips, the sensual way they curved. A slick of warmth bloomed deep inside her, aching to be satisfied in a way she'd never allow.

'I find you intriguing. Plenty of time for disappointment later.'

Her breathing hitched. He wasn't supposed to find anything about her interesting. 'Aren't I supposed to be asking some questions too?'

'I'm not finished with you yet.'

Christo strolled back to his seat and sprawled on the couch in apparent indolence. She knew better. He watched her like a predator stalking from the shadows.

'I don't think this is how the game is supposed to be played,' she said.

'My rules.'

'It's unfair. And I'd never marry a man who was.'

He placed his hand over his heart. 'You wound me. As your husband, I can't have you thinking that. Ask your question.'

'Why did your father force you to marry?'

There was that tightness round his eyes again. Christo tossed back his drink. She watched the fascinating bob of his Adam's apple as he swallowed.

'Because I intended to enjoy a bachelor's life for ever. No marriage. No children.'

Children?

Thea tried to relax, resting her hands carefully in her lap. If only she could stop them trembling.

'Is there something you haven't told me? Your father didn't demand a child in the terms of his will?'

A dark, brooding shadow passed across his face. He wasn't looking at her, concentrating instead on the shimmering tumbler in his hand. It was her first sense that he had secrets himself.

The silence stretched. And then, 'No. Hector's uncouth, but that would be vulgar even for him. And I would have told you about the requirement if he had. Though who knows what he'd demand if he suspected this marriage is a sham?'

'When are we going to meet your father, to prove it's everything he hoped for?'

His eyes snapped to hers. That focus was relentless. She didn't look away. She'd never been cowed by a man before, no matter how many times her father had tried. She wasn't starting tonight.

Christo leaned forward with cautious deliberation, placing his glass on the table in front of him. 'You'll meet him when you've learned to play the role of wife to my satisfaction.'

'I'm doing an excellent job as your wife.'

'This morning?' His eyes narrowed. 'That fiction about my snoring like a hibernating bear?'

'Don't be dramatic.'

'You called me a *beast*.' A tiny muscle at his temple gave a satisfying twitch. 'Then at dinner you told Anna I had an obsession with ear and nose hair growth.'

'I was trying to be friendly. Women always complain about their husbands.'

It was another thing she and Anna laughed about. It had been such a long time since she'd laughed about anything.

'Anyhow, I read somewhere it's something men think about. Often.'

'Perhaps you need a lesson in what men think about.'

The low growl of warning made her shiver in anticipation. She glanced at the huge bed. The soft pillows. Crisp white sheets.

Thea turned back to him. 'There's *nothing* I want to learn from you.'

'Are you sure?' he asked softly. 'If you change your mind, all you have to do is ask. Nicely.'

'Your vain hope's begun to delude you. My presence is obviously a bad influence.'

That tight band in her chest gripped her again. Pressing harder. She needed to get out of here. To breathe something more than the scent of him, which curled through her with every inhalation and lit fires inside.

'May I go now?'

He shrugged. 'If you want.'

She stood. He watched, as if he'd assessed her and found her wanting. Like her father. But she could do this. If he found Alexis, everything would be worth it. She grabbed her book and made for the door.

'*Thea.*'

The cold command in his voice stopped her.

'No woman I'm sleeping with leaves my room looking like you do.'

A superior smile played on his lips. She wanted to wipe it from his face.

'And how's that?'

'So completely untouched.'

Was this simply a terrible game to entertain a bored rich man? Her blood pumped hard and hot. She tossed her book and pen on a table. Tipped her head upside down and scratched her fingers through her hair till it was a tangled mess. Wiped her palm roughly across her lips so the gloss smeared.

'There. Better?' she sneered, hands on hips. 'Or should I tear my clothes as well?'

His lips narrowed a fraction in displeasure. Excellent. Some hint that she'd affected him.

Thea whipped round to leave. She didn't hear the silent footsteps marking his approach. Only sensed his heat as he moved close. She turned, her back against the cool wood of the door, tipping her head up to look at him. She was trapped by his devilish lips, the slash of high cheekbones. And his eyes… Sparkling and shimmering, like water in sunlight. Angry. Arresting.

She couldn't move. His perfect fingers teased along her jaw, slipping down her throat and behind her head. An exquisite burn was left by his touch. She knew he could snap her. Break her like a twig. But the languid softness in his eyes said nothing of anger or hurting.

Another hand settled on her waist. Hot. Possessive. The atmosphere took on a life of its own. Trembling with the spark between them. His thumb traced the line of her lower lip. A whisper of a caress. Setting her body alight. The world blurred and her lips parted as if there would never be enough air to breathe.

He drew her close and she pressed into him. Hands on his chest. Liquid heat between her thighs. She should push him away, but those muscles under her palms... Sculpted. Like stone. Every morsel of him was too male, too much.

His mouth dropped to hers and her mind blanked. She breathed the scent of him, cool and crisp like the mountains, full of wild thyme and rosemary and pine. His lips coaxed. Encouraged. Probed. Too gentle for this man. She fought not to succumb, but his hold on her and his wicked mouth dragged her under. She'd give everything for the feel of his tongue as it explored and danced with hers.

His hand was in her hair, the hardness contrasting with his gentle lips. And the seduction of it drizzled over her like honey. Drowning her in its sticky sweetness. The dark, luscious kiss deepened and took her into the abyss. Her control shredded, ripped away as her body thrummed with primal need.

She wrapped her arms around his neck. Pulled him down. If she was to drown, he'd drown right with her. And as she fell into the intoxicating rhythm of their breaths and lips and tongues he pulled back.

She gasped. Christo turned her, his arms banding her waist. Holding her upright because she'd fall if he didn't. His lips at her ear. And she looked in the mirror opposite, saw herself. A wanton creature she didn't recognise. With wild hair and passion-drugged eyes. Red moist lips and her chest heaving. Her nipples tight and proud against the soft knit fabric of her top.

'That—' he pointed to the mirror '—is what a woman who leaves my room looks like.'

He let her go and she stumbled. The heat of him, gone. Everything, cold. He looked at her with a face which told her nothing. No sign of the kiss that had almost destroyed her marred his perfect features.

'Now you're ready to see my father.'

CHAPTER SIX

THE OLD MAN was hunched in a wheelchair in the oppressive wood-panelled library, a blanket round his legs, living the wheezing, broken half-life left to him by his dying heart. Though none of that stopped his rheumy eyes scrutinising Thea with an intensity belying his age and ill health.

Christo leaned against a dark-stained bookcase. She was executing her role as new bride to perfection. Hector would never guess their arrangement, so superb was her performance.

She was pandering to his father. And every glorious, gracious smile was driving Christo to hell.

He'd sworn never to succumb to Hector's weakness for a beautiful woman, only to find himself trapped by a viper cleverly disguised. Yet here he was, teetering on the brink. And all because of a kiss which had been meant to challenge Thea's claim that there was nothing he could teach her.

Vanity—that was what it had been about. The moment their lips had touched, when she'd responded as if he was everything she'd always craved, reason had escaped him. And now he couldn't think of anything but the drugging wonder of her plush mouth. Of immersing himself in her body till he drowned. Never coming up for air.

Her throaty, musical laugh dragged him to other thoughts. To the memory of her curves in his arms. To the smell of sweet spice and a warmth that had curled inside and licked at the cold heart of him.

He'd left the flame kindling for a while. Soaked in that tempting heat before extinguishing it. There were things about Thea he mustn't forget. His investigations into her former bodyguard, Alexis, proved she was a woman held together by lies. Cleverly woven, but lies nonetheless.

He knew all about lies. About a war of attrition being fought through a child.

'If your mother comes for your birthday, I'll buy you a puppy.'

As if he'd ever had any control over what his mother did. But he'd asked, and begged. Like any little boy wanting something badly enough. Extracting promises that had always been broken. His mother had never come. He'd never owned a dog. He'd been raised on lies, like tainted sugar stirred into his milk.

Christo clenched his teeth against the burn of acid in his gut.

'We should leave, Hector. You seem tired.' He motioned to a nurse hovering nearby.

'When I'm dead I'll have all the rest I need.'

His father didn't look at him. Only at Thea, sitting opposite. Ignoring Christo like he always did.

What irritated him more than discovering Thea's untruths was her obvious belief that he wouldn't find out. Did she think him a fool?

She laughed at something Hector said and his father gazed back, mesmerised. Yes, she did. Thea believed she could con them all.

Soon enough he'd show her how easy she'd been to expose.

'You're kind to an old man,' Hector said, patting her hand, which sat on his knee. 'A rare and precious beauty.'

She shone like an angel, perfect in a cream sheath dress that skimmed her curves and highlighted her honeyed skin.

'Not too old to pretend to charm,' Christo muttered.

Hector peered up at him, dusky lips stretched in a thin, disapproving line. A look so familiar it was etched for ever in Christo's brain. *This* was the father he knew—the one who had constantly reminded him he was a mistake. A child that no one wanted. A child who should never have been born.

'I speak the truth. She is beautiful like Maria.'

Christo pushed away from the bookcase. This can of worms shouldn't be opened. Not here. Not now. He suppressed a snarl. He'd never let Thea know the extent of his indebtedness to her father, because that would give her a power over him he couldn't allow. He *wouldn't* lose Atlas to his father's foolishness.

His eyes narrowed in warning, but Hector focused his attention on Thea.

'You knew my mother?' she asked. She toyed with a thin chain clasped at her throat, the hunger for any morsel of information written in wide-eyed desperation on her face.

'We all knew each other back then.' His father smiled wistfully.

That could be the reason why Hector had sought loans from the Lambros bank, believing an old acquaintance wouldn't foreclose on him. More poor judgement that Christo could not forgive.

'She was a bird of paradise. Your father wanted to cage her. He never could. So she flew away.'

'You think I'm like her?'

'Yes. Does my son try to cage you?'

The old man was no fool. He must have some inkling as to why Christo had chosen Thea as his bride.

Christo's stomach clenched as Thea turned to look into the soul of him with mournful, over-bright eyes.

'Why would you say that about your own son?' she asked, sounding incredulous, though the slight tremor in her voice betrayed her. 'He's taking me to New York.'

'Such pretty lies. You're a clever girl. I knew you'd make him a good wife.'

Bile rose sour in Christo's throat. The gall of it. This from the man who'd invited an enemy to slip craven fingers into his birthright. Into the company he'd earned with his own blood. Through each abandonment by his mother. Every rejection by his father. The debts Hector had incurred would take a lifetime to undo—if that Gordian knot could even be unravelled.

Christo had done his duty. This farce had gone on long enough. He strolled towards Thea. Touched her gently on the shoulder and ignored her tremble under his hand.

'*Koukla mou.* Our flight's this evening. We should leave.'

'You must come again,' Hector said, to Thea alone. 'This old man doesn't have enough company.'

She squeezed the parchment-thin skin of his father's arm. Did she see through the cruel glint in Hector's eye? Perhaps. But her voice was all sparkle and flirtation.

'How can I resist? Your son's overworked. Whenever you feel lonely, please call. No doubt I'll be feeling lonely too.'

Her words tugged at parts of him long dead. Threatening to rouse them from the grave where they'd been safely buried. Lonely was being shunted off to other people to be cared for on school breaks. Lonely was having only servants to talk to for days. Lonely was recognising the one truth in your life. That your parents didn't want you.

His father beckoned for the nurse. As she came to take the old man away he looked at Christo, his eyes filled with a wicked fire. He waggled his finger and cackled as the nurse wheeled him down the hall.

'Don't leave this one alone for too long, son, or she might run away too.'

Christo settled into the comfort of his limousine, the blood freezing through his veins. His father always did that to him—left him colder than the Arctic.

He looked at Thea and the chill thawed with a sliding heat. Her gaze dropped to his lips and a flush of colour swept over her cheeks. The throb of hunger started low in his gut.

Against his better judgement she intoxicated him. One moment all flash and fire, the next moment beautiful blushes. He could lean across the seat, right here, in this warm car filled with her scent of honey and spice. Slide a hand behind her neck and kiss her till she melted with wanting him. Call her out as the liar he knew her to be.

Which was all the reminder he needed to pull back from these delusions.

'You played your part well. There's no need to subject yourself to my father again.'

She cocked her head. 'Why do you hate him?'

Christo undid the buttons on his shirt cuffs. Rolled the sleeves up. Thirty-one years of parental contempt layered tarry and thick. Nothing could wash *that* stain away. And then, when it had come time to take what was his—when what he'd been born to do had been so close he could have caressed it with the tips of his fingers—Hector had almost thrown it away. He didn't care about Christo at all.

'Fathers and their sons.' He shrugged. These were weaknesses he'd never disclose, because weaknesses could be exploited. 'That's the way it's been even before Zeus and Cronus.'

Thea stared out through the window, absentmindedly scratching at her knee. 'Not in my experience. My brother and father are close. Partners in every crime.'

He stiffened. How much did she know about her father's and brother's activities? He suspected she despised both men. In that way, their views on their fathers were strikingly similar. The rest he could only imagine. Tito and Demetri were too careful. Even Raul had come up with nothing.

What would Thea share if she was asked the right way?

He watched her white-tipped nails digging into the flesh above the hem of her dress. Pricks of red bloomed under her skin.

'Are you all right?'

He leaned over and placed his hand on hers. Thea's slender fingers were cool and tempting under his. He drifted his thumb over the back of her hand. She turned to him, eyelids heavy and slumberous, her raspberry lips parted as if it were hard to breathe.

He looked back to where he touched her. Glorying at her silky skin, paler than his. Light to his dark. So tempting to slide higher. To stroke his errant fingers along the flesh of her inner thigh and watch those golden eyes glaze with need. See if she'd gasp and yield, relax her legs and allow him to explore all her honeyed dark places till she sighed his name and clenched around his fingers as she came.

He could do that in the back of this quiet car, with no sound bar her shallow breaths and the low thrum of the engine. Trapped in this tiny world of their own.

Time slowed, the moment pregnant with anticipation as his pulse pounded with desire. Did she feel it too?

As he looked up at her Thea's eyes widened, her gaze flicked away and she jerked her hand from under his as if burned.

No, clearly not.

Christo sat back in his seat once more, ignoring the roar of blood coursing in his ears.

'Something bit me.' Thea smoothed the hem of her dress over the red mark on her thigh and clasped her hands in her lap, fingers twisting. 'Anna says when we get to New York we're staying in your apartment near Central Park. She seems excited.'

Christo accepted the brisk change of subject. It was safer this way, when all he craved was to touch. To push. His body didn't listen to sense when he was around her. It *wanted*— like a fractious child grasping for a jar of sweets placed out of reach. And Thea was the last woman he should desire. He'd discovered things about her. Secrets and lies.

The time would soon be arriving to show her he was no fool. He'd never be fooled again.

'I've a gift to keep you company whilst we're away,' he said.

Now to see how well she'd handle what he'd found out, and how fine an actress she was.

'Ooh, goody.' She rubbed her hands together with mock glee. 'What is it? A puppy?'

Christo stilled. Ignored the pang in his chest. No. Assuming his specifications had been met, his gift wasn't something she'd be able to tame and train.

'I'm not sure you're mature enough for that responsibility,' he said as the car slid through his home's open gates and pulled into the garage.

He led her to his study. A quiet, book-lined room where fortunes had been made and lost. Nothing had been lost since he'd acquired the house. Thea was to thank for that, but she'd never know it.

He sank into the chair behind his huge desk.

'I can hardly bear the thrill of it all,' she said.

Yet she hovered in the corner of the room. Tense, as if she was a woman who hated surprises.

There was a rap at the door.

'Come.'

In walked a hulk of a man. Christo recognised him. He was one of Raul's operatives, who'd been assigned for a month to go over the house's security before he and Thea married. He was perfect. Taciturn. Incorruptible. Raul had chosen well. Thea wouldn't wrap *this* man around her little finger, as she'd obviously done to so many others.

'Thea, meet Sergei Ivanov.'

A deep frown marred her forehead as she looked Sergei up and down. 'Who the hell is he?'

Christo leaned back in the leather of his chair and smiled. 'Your new bodyguard.'

She stiffened. 'I don't want him. I want Alexis.'

Now the game began.

Christo moved from behind his desk to lean against its front corner. He'd investigated her former bodyguard out of curiosity, though he'd never have employed a man who'd missed so much. It meant Alexis was either careless or complicit. From what he'd learned, complicit seemed more likely. Although there was more to it than that...

'Sergei comes highly credentialed, with impeccable qualifications for the role.'

Thea wouldn't look at him, her eyes darting instead to Sergei's massive form. 'Impeccable qualifications for a jailer. Were they your instructions?'

'You said you'd become reliant on a bodyguard.' Christo folded his arms. 'Sergei's brief is to keep you safe.'

'I won't feel safe with him.' Her hand reflexively slid the small coin-sized pendant backwards and forwards along the chain round her neck. 'I want—'

'Alexis. I know.'

She was a clever woman—she had to see he'd caught her out. But Thea stood there, tall and defiant. He'd give her a chance to redeem herself, to tell the truth once and for all.

'I'm wondering why you want him so badly. Is there anything I need to know?'

She licked her lips. 'If you want someone to protect you, you have to trust them.'

'Perhaps. Sadly, Alexis is unavailable.'

She seemed to relax a little. Her shoulders rose and fell with a long, deep breath. How would she take the rest of the news?

'He's on the run. Your father alleges that he stole fifty thousand euros.'

'No!'

The colour drained from Thea's face till she was as pale as moonlight. She slumped against the wall. Was she going to faint?

Christo jumped up from the desk at the same moment Sergei moved towards her. She held up her hand, halting them both. Sergei stood down but remained within arm's reach. Thea's trembling fingers moved to touch the pendant at her throat and she seemed to compose herself.

'Alexis is no thief.' Her voice scraped the words out.

A hot throb of anger burned in his chest. He looked at Sergei. 'Excuse us.'

The bodyguard nodded acknowledgement and left the room.

Christo glared at Thea. 'You said the same of yourself.'

Her denial was futile in the face of his evidence.

'I think your professed skill at accumulating money is a myth, and that you stole it like I originally suspected. With the help of a complicit bodyguard.'

'You can think what you want.'

She chewed at her lip, teeth biting so hard she might draw blood. Mercifully the colour had returned to her cheeks, though she still used the wall as support.

'All you give me is lies,' Christo growled. 'One truth. That's all I ask. Tell me one deep, abiding truth about yourself.'

Thea's plump bottom lip quivered, then firmed. The hand fiddling with her necklace fell to her side, clenching in a tight fist. She pushed away from the wall, bringing her luscious body closer to his.

Every part of him stood on high alert. He didn't care that Sergei waited outside the door. He didn't care that Thea was a liar. He craved to slide his arm round her slender waist, to push her back against the wall and take her so hard the only word from her lips would be his name, screamed loud.

'A truth, Christo?'

She tossed her head. The soft chocolate waves of her hair swirled round her shoulders. Her mouth curled into a bitter smile as she placed her hand on his chest where it seared like a brand.

'I'm not very partial to ouzo.'

Then she stalked from the room with an exaggerated sway of her hips, slamming the door behind her.

Thea jogged away from the building which housed Christo's apartment. She took a route to Central Park in a steady rhythm, with Sergei following a discreet distance behind. New York rushed in its gritty, inexorable way around her. Every part vibrant, hustling and alive.

She should have been enthralled by this place—the city that never slept. Yet after five days here all Thea wanted to do was sleep. There was no way to ease the pressure winding inside her, tighter and harder. It crept up on her as she dressed. Tried to throttle her as she fastened around her throat the fine necklace her mother had given her as a child.

Alexis was on the run, and she couldn't help from this beautiful, blazing city. This place her mother had always wanted her to see.

Thea had once had childish dreams of coming here with someone she loved. Those dreams had died the day her mother had. Now she wanted none of it. The risk of losing her heart, and with it her freedom, was too high a price to pay.

Anyhow, Christo despised her. After that exchange in his office, the interminable silence on his plane, she had been left only with businesslike interactions before each function. Information so she knew who was coming, what to say.

It was preferable, all this sullen formality. Except when they were on show as a couple. Then he epitomised the perfect husband. Pretending to be interested, pretending to care. All those affectionate meaningless touches and still her treacherous body sang to every single one.

Those thoughts chased her. So Thea ran. Ran till the air burned in her lungs and she couldn't suck another breath. Ran till her heart thrashed in her chest as if to escape. She stopped at a tree, one hand gripping the rough bark. Retching from the exertion. And still she hadn't run far enough. From the people. The crowds. From herself. The feelings.

She folded at the waist, gasping for air. Her free hand was on her thigh, fingernails cutting into the screaming muscle. The cruel bite of pain helped. She'd focus on that. Wait till her heart stopped slamming like a battering ram at her ribs.

Still the air wouldn't come quickly enough, her lungs heaving. The clutch of panic grabbed tighter. Her vision blurred at the edges. She'd faint. She'd die. Here, in front of everyone.

Heavy footsteps thudded behind her. An arm under hers gave support. An urgent voice pierced the fog.

'Mrs Callas!'

Sergei.

She found her breath. Steadied it.

In for four. Hold. Out for eight. Repeat.

She moved to a seat somehow. Sat with her elbows on her knees. Head buzzing.

There was a water bottle. The murmur of words. Strange. Distant.

'Are you all right…? Do you need a doctor…? I've called Mr Callas.'

She sat up with a sharp intake of breath, hands trembling as her upside-down world righted itself.

'No!'

Sergei stepped back. He'd hardly broken sweat, whereas her skin was slick with it, stinging her eyes. Thea wiped at the hair sticking to her face. When was the last time she'd had an attack this bad?

She stood, legs on fire and shaking like a newborn lamb. 'I don't need Mr Callas. I'm going back to the apartment.' She tried to sound strong, but her voice cracked.

Soft rain fell as she walked, sprinkling over her skin. At the doors of the building she was welcomed by the ever-friendly doorman. Dripped water all over the marble floor of the lift to the penthouse, where Christo's apartment took up the whole level.

Sergei hovered close. 'Are you sure you're well?'

Panic, her old enemy, always followed her. Taunting from the shadows. She wouldn't let it win.

'I pushed myself a little hard.'

An ambush like today was a concern, because it normally heralded more attacks. But she'd fight back. Regain control.

'It was more than that,' Sergei said as the lift stopped at the top floor and they exited. He punched the key code to enter the apartment.

'Worried I'll die on your watch?'

'You might feel like you're dying, but I won't let that happen,' he said as he held the door open for her. 'I'll carry paper bags for next time.'

Thea shot a look over her shoulder. 'That won't be necessary.'

He shrugged and exchanged a concerned look with Anna, who'd rushed towards them. Sergei must have texted her.

'I'm fine. Really,' Thea said, as Anna opened her mouth to speak. 'I just need a shower and coffee.'

'I'll bring breakfast. You haven't been eating enough,' Anna chided.

Thea smiled. It felt stiff, unfamiliar, but if she faked it for long enough her smile might become reality. One day.

'In my room. Thank you.'

She went into her en suite bathroom. Discarded her sodden clothes and stood under the steaming shower as water pounded her skin, washing away the dark hand of fear threatening to strangle her.

She had to get help to Alexis. How dared her father accuse him of stealing the money she'd negotiated as part of her agreement to marry Christo?

But her father had lied and now her marriage was pointless.

Christo might help.

She silenced the inner voice. That would require trust she didn't have for another man who was using her for his own ends.

Thea turned off the water. Dried her now wrinkled skin and wrapped a robe tight around her body.

The food Anna had left held as much temptation as cardboard. So she lay on her side in the huge bed. Stared out at the drizzly view of New York sprawling below her. The place her mother would never see.

And, as much as she'd tried to outrun the feelings, now she let them overwhelm her. For Alexis. For this marriage. For that awful afternoon when she'd waited in the kitchen, clutching only her favourite doll and wearing her St Christopher medal for a safe journey. Waited for her mother to come through the small wooden side door and steal her away. Waited as the day had darkened and daylight had faded.

But the person she'd loved most in the world had never come. And the waiting had ended when her father found her and delivered the words which had changed her life for ever. *'Your mother's dead...'*

Thea curled tighter into a ball on her side, arms wrapped round her waist.

A shadowed reflection loomed in the window ahead of her. The prickle of awareness skittering along her spine announced that there was only one person it could be.

'Sergei says you were ill on your run.'

The voice was tight with concern. But Christo didn't care. He only wanted to ensure he inherited from his father. She was just a casualty along the way.

'I overexerted myself.'

'Sergei doesn't believe that.'

'I don't care what anyone believes.'

The bed dipped as Christo sat on the edge of the mattress. She didn't look at him. Only at the rain that beaded and slid down the window ahead of her.

'So you've made clear before. Would you like me to call a doctor?'

Thea shook her head. 'It's nothing. You shouldn't have interrupted your day.'

'Sergei called. I came.'

A cool hand rested on her forehead. She closed her eyes.

'No temperature...'

So few people cared about her. She could count them on one hand: Alexis, Elena. Anna and Sergei, perhaps, but they were paid to care, after all. Same as the servants at her father's home, who'd looked after her when her mother had left. And still, like the little girl she'd once been, she craved the caring with a bone-numbing ache.

'We have the dinner party tonight.' Christo's voice was gentle and soothing. 'I'll cancel it.'

'No, I'll be there as promised.'

Her voice quavered and caught. She cleared her throat. Stupid. To fall for these tiny scraps of kindness, tossed to her by a man who cared as little for her as her father did. Still, a yearning twisted in her stomach.

'Are you sure?' he asked.

'Yes.'

She turned to him. Sat up. Pretending for a little while longer. They were so close on the bed. Her dishevelled in her robe. Him in his immaculately tailored dark trousers. The fine herringbone weave of his white shirt. Close enough for her to catch the scent of his aftershave and that whispered undertone she recognised instantly. Something dark and primal. All Christo.

Heat bloomed inside her, unravelling the tight twist of fear. Smoothing it out till the only ripple left was a low, sultry pulse she tried to ignore. But harder to ignore was his mouth…so close. The sensual curve of his lower lip… The slight shadow of stubble grazing his jaw…

His eyes fixed on hers. Hazel rimmed with slate, soft with concern. She shouldn't crave this, but for once she wanted to pretend that Christo cared too. The ache of it twisted hard, till her eyes burned with tears she refused to shed.

Still, it must have shown on her face. He cupped her cheek, his palm hot against her skin. 'What's wrong?'

Christo was trying to peer inside her, and she couldn't allow him to see too much.

Perhaps she'd tell him why she felt this way. It was a truth. A *real* truth, as Christo had demanded. But she was so full to the brim with truths they threatened to choke her. Her mother leaving. Finding Alexis. The years of deprivation. Fighting to retain a part of herself when darkness threatened to devour her. She'd pasted so many false layers over her true self—one breach of the barrier and it would all fall apart. She couldn't risk it. Not for this man.

She closed her eyes to shut him out as he threaded his hands into the tangle of her hair. The warmth of his breath was close, so close. She might not be able to tell him anything, but she could allow herself to let go. For a moment. She was entitled to that at least, wasn't she?

'Thea…'

Her name was a whisper as his lips brushed hers. She didn't care any more about pushing him away. For once, all she cared about was succumbing to sensation. Forgetting the world was hard and real and taking pleasure for herself and damn the consequences. Losing herself and ignoring the fear of gilded cages and the trap of marriage, even one with a time frame as short as theirs.

She slid her hands to the back of his neck, into his dark hair…softer than she'd imagined for such a hard man. Pulling him closer, she pressed her lips to his. He deepened the kiss, his tongue gliding over hers as she relished the invasion.

She wanted all of him. Because now she didn't have to think—she could *feel*. The rasp of his growing stubble. The prickle of her scalp as his fingers tightened in her hair. His lips teasing, testing, as he eased her backwards onto the bed. The heavy weight of him as he lay over her and pressed her down, down into the soft covers.

Her legs fell open, cradling his hips between hers. The ridge of hardness at his groin notched into her with a delicious burn. She writhed under him, shifting restlessly as she tried to alleviate the ache there, losing herself in the erotic grind of their bodies. Her skin overheated till she felt desperate to tear her clothes away.

This was a flame only Christo could quench.

He was rocking against her. The tightness low inside her twisting tighter and harder. He tore at her robe, his breath mingling with hers as they panted and moved against each other. His searching fingers drifted over her breast, teasing at her nipple till heat seared between her thighs. She moaned, but his kiss trapped the sound.

Thea tore her mouth from his and gasped for air. 'Please… Please…'

She toyed with the buttons of his shirt. No thought other than having him naked and inside her, quelling the ache now at a fever pitch.

'I have you,' he murmured. 'I'll look after you.'

It wasn't enough. Her whole body screamed to be filled by him. She didn't care. Nothing mattered any more but this. His hips worked against hers. The edge of oblivion was close. So close. She wrapped her legs tight round him. Gripped his back and arched into him as he rolled her nipple between his fingers and kissed and kissed, his tongue delving into her mouth.

Then nothing.

Everything stopped.

Why? Why was he so still?

She groaned, and didn't care how frustrated, how desperate she sounded.

'Oh, no!'

Anna's voice?

Christo turned his head towards it as his hands gently closed her robe, his body still covering her.

'What do you want?' he growled.

Christo was coiled tight, but there was the slightest tremble through his huge frame, and she wasn't sure whether it was unsatisfied desire, or anger at being disturbed. She buried her head in the side of his neck to hide her face, breathing in the clean scent of him mingled with something musky and erotic. Desire and arousal…

'The breakfast plates. I'll—'

'Please leave.' The words were a hiss through his clenched teeth.

'I'm sorry…'

The clink of cutlery, shoes scuffing on carpet and then the snick of the door signalled Anna's departure.

And a return of Thea's common sense.

What had she been doing? All of this was evidence of how easily she could be ensnared. Her heart raced. Not in a way that was pleasant or spoke of passion, but thready and panicked.

'Koukla mou,' Christo said, stroking his thumbs over her jaw.

No, she couldn't do this. He still wanted her. His interest hadn't diminished and he remained hard and ready. But for her it was like being plunged into a stream of meltwater. She shifted and pushed. Because she couldn't be under him anymore.

He rolled from her as she sat up and tied her robe tight—too tight. How needy she'd been. He must leave. She could never allow him to see her like this again.

'Don't you need to be back at work?' She reached trembling fingers to her lips, which were tender and bee-stung from his kisses.

Christo raked his hand through his hair, a crease forming between his brows. 'I could stay.'

His eyes were hot on hers. The invitation in them, clear and tempting. Too much more and she'd burst into flames. But she couldn't—not now. Even though the memory of his touch, his hardness between her thighs, burned relentlessly.

Thea chewed the inside of her mouth. Clenched her hands into fists and let her nails bite the soft flesh of her palms. She mustn't forget the only reason she was here was the deal, and what her father had done to force her compliance.

It was nothing more than business. Her body had never been part of the bargain, no matter the ache at her core and how much every cell protested Christo's absence.

She shook her head. 'No. Go. Take over the world or whatever you plan on doing today.'

He hesitated, then stood. Still hard. The zip of his trousers was straining; his shirt was crushed. He looked delicious and disarrayed, like she'd never seen him before. Warmth coursed through her—a heady rush of power. *She'd* done that to him. This implacable man was now softened and less than perfect. Looking…human. Devastatingly handsome. Her husband.

But in the end it was all meaningless.

Christo took a step back, smiled, but something about it appeared stiff and brittle, not reaching his eyes. 'World domination isn't as entertaining in your absence.'

He leaned over, touched his lips to her forehead. Then he brushed a gentle hand over her hair, straightened and left the room.

As she curled back into herself Thea hated it that his last moment of tenderness caused a tear to slip down her cheek.

CHAPTER SEVEN

CHRISTO SAW OFF his dinner party guests. Exchanged crushing handshakes. Suffered pats on the back and the words, 'Give my regards to Hector.'

His father had always been the centre of any party. Splashing millions around in a way Christo never would. Yet he needed to secure the loyalty of these people if his plan to save Atlas was to succeed. To cement ties which would stand when Hector was gone.

There was so much work to do, and tonight, he still had another part to play. He'd be accompanying the men to an exclusive club. Without their wives. That suggestion by one of his guests had been telling in itself.

Perhaps Thea would share a coffee with him before he left? She'd been wary of him since he'd arrived home, earlier than expected, after leaving her looking so tumbled and wanton on her bed. His day of meetings had been shot to pieces because fantasies of Thea naked and himself buried deep inside her had consumed his every thought. Especially now he knew how they ignited together.

The same thoughts obviously hadn't plagued her. He could tell by the way she avoided his gaze, flitted away from him when he tried to get close. He couldn't abide that reticence. He wanted the fire, the passion. Her pleas for him to satisfy her ringing loud in his ears.

His hunger for her was something he longed to explore. Like the hills and valleys of her glorious body which so far he'd barely touched. Still, the sensible part of him cautioned that he must keep the distance he'd deliberately maintained till now. A challenging task when his hunger for her remained undiminished, despite the lies.

Although his broker had called, advising him that the

solar company she'd recommended was on its way to making him millions. So what she'd told him about her money-making abilities appeared true.

This dissonance in his picture of her unsettled him. She remained an enigma, and in his ordered world he hated puzzles.

The apartment was hushed and in near darkness as he walked towards the dining room to find her. Only the glow from the myriad candles on the long table seating twenty flickered in the room.

Christo hesitated near the door. Thea gleamed in the low lights. She was elegant and understated in black, yet she'd shone more brightly than any of the other women, with their colourful clothes and sparkling jewels. She drifted around the table, blowing out candle after candle. Their waxy smell thick in the air.

She stopped in front of the table's centre, her face illuminated in the golden light of a squat candle in the middle of an arrangement, which held a well of melted wax around its flame. She dipped the tip of her finger into it, blowing till the thin coating of wax hardened. Then she picked up the candle and tipped a stream of molten liquid onto her open palm.

Christo started forward, gut clenching hard. He should stop her. It must burn. Yet all he could do was watch, transfixed, as she toyed with the fire. Replacing the candle, Thea licked her fingers and pinched out the flame, then another, and another. Each one was extinguished with a quiet hiss.

He couldn't take any more.

She jumped as he stepped into the honeyed light. 'I thought you'd already left.'

He didn't miss the curl of her hand, closing over her wax-covered palm, as he strolled round the table towards her.

'I'm going soon,' he said, keeping his voice calm.

She stood like a cornered animal. Eyes wide, body stiff. He didn't want that. He wanted her soft and pliant and pleading to be sated.

'What were you doing?'

'Putting out the candles.'

Thea was the expert at never really answering a question. Why had she mastered that skill? He could ask, but chose not to. He didn't think she'd tell him even if he did.

'You'll burn yourself.'

'I never have before.'

And there was the tiny truth he'd longed for—though he wasn't sure what it meant. He searched her face for any hint. Her expression gave him nothing, but she looked pale. Like a Technicolor picture fading to sepia, all the vibrancy leached from her. Unlike when they'd kissed this morning. Then, she'd glowed.

'I wanted to thank you for tonight,' he said.

She had an innate sense for the role of gracious hostess, charming men and women alike. For that he was indebted to her.

'There's no need. I had a job to do.'

How selfish he'd been. He should have rescheduled the party, as he'd offered. A splinter of concern pricked at him. She'd only toyed with her dinner tonight, and he noticed her dress hung loosely on her curves.

'You aren't well. Don't think I haven't appreciated your efforts.'

'I'm used to it. It's little different from my father's demands.'

He hated the comparison to her father. Just as he hated the dull, dead tone to her voice and the lack of light in her eyes. Where had all her flash and fire gone?

'I thought you might like to share a coffee with me before I leave.'

Perhaps he could forgo his obligations for one night. Instead coax Thea to indulge in the pleasure of burning together once more.

She cocked her head, narrowed her gaze. In that moment she made him feel like a schoolboy, asking out his first date.

He had an insane desire to peer down at his shoes and scuff them on the carpet.

'Where are you headed?' she asked, her face bland and unreadable.

Another request from him left unanswered.

'We're meeting at someone's club.'

Somewhere that was by invitation only. Discreet. Where morals could be compromised or forgotten. The sort of place he despised.

The prospect of spending time there exhausted him. At least being newly married he could reject the menu he'd be offered there without anyone questioning it. Tonight would cost him only money, not his soul. All he had to do was keep his father's associates happy and try to recover what Hector had wrecked—ensure the upcoming celebration of Atlas Shipping's seventy-fifth year didn't become a wake instead.

'Ah. More *business*.'

He didn't miss the raised eyebrow, her loaded tone. He could show her again how they combusted together. *Then* she'd ask him to stay.

Christo took a step forward. Thea stepped back, eyes wary. He hesitated. She didn't desire this like he did. So he couldn't ignore his gentlemen guests' request to take tonight's party elsewhere.

'Sadly,' he said, and meant it. But he knew too well when he wasn't wanted.

'I won't keep you from your fun.' She gave a wan smile. 'I'm tired. I want to go to bed.'

Thea blew out the last candle, plunging the room into darkness. He watched as she walked down the hall, slender fingers still clenched over her wax-encrusted palm.

Thea sat up with a jolt, heart pounding, a slick ache between her thighs. She pushed her palms into her eyes and rubbed till bright flashes burst behind her lids.

She was trying and failing, to scrub away a dream of she

and Christo entwined. Touching. Tasting. Indulging in her sleep, what she wouldn't take for herself when awake. The vestiges of desire clung, making her nipples hard knots, abrading even under the soft fabric of her top.

She could ease the ache herself. It wouldn't take much—not the way she felt…

No. Christo would remain off-limits in both fantasy and reality. It was safer that way.

She picked up her phone to check the time, noticed the message alert flashing bright. Two in the morning, meaning it was about eight in the morning at home in Athens. A message. *Alexis.* Could it be?

Thea grappled with the handset. Fumbled her password twice before succeeding.

Her heart leapt for a moment, then her shoulders dropped as she saw the name. Not Alexis. Demetri.

You're taking your time.

He was referring to the information her father had demanded about Christo's business. She wanted no part of this, or their shady schemes. Whatever information her father and Demetri requested, it wasn't for honest reasons.

Thea typed her reply. Damn her clumsy, trembling fingers.

Go to hell.

A response pinged back.

Will see Alexis there first if you don't get what we want.

She swallowed the tight ball closing her throat. There it was. The threat. The reason they'd reported him to the police. Her fault—again.

She tossed her phone onto the bed. Choked back a sob. She had no way of easing the emotional pain threatening to crack her. The crushing pressure that made her want to scratch at her skin, to flay it from her body till she bled.

Not even the bright burn of that candle wax had diminished the relentless ache. Thea rubbed at her palm, still tingling after all these hours. What a foolish move that had been—especially with Christo witnessing her weakness. She recognised that moment earlier for what it had evidenced. Desperation. Where was all her caution, her control?

She curled into a ball on the bed for a few moments and then rose, refusing to lie there and feel sorry for herself. She needed to do something—anything to keep moving, give herself time to think.

Her stomach griped with the twin agony of nerves and hunger pangs, punishing her for not having eaten enough. That was as good a motivation as any.

She traipsed down the unlit hall towards the kitchen. The astonishing New York skyline glittered through every window, lighting up the space in its silvery glow. She glanced over the view, unmoved.

Once at the refrigerator, she grabbed some bread, cheese and milk—ate in the comforting darkness because she didn't care what she put into her stomach so long as that crippling inertia didn't steal over her again.

The apartment lay silent. Sergei and Anna were sensibly asleep. Christo was still out. It was better that she didn't see him. Her emotions regarding the man were a tangle she couldn't sort through. Simpler to avoid it. Anyhow, they'd be returning to Greece soon. Back to the numbing routine of Christo working long hours and her futile efforts to find Alexis.

She needed someone with different skills. Perhaps Sergei would help? Anna had told her he'd been in the Special

Forces in his home country. But how to convince a man as immovable as a hunk of concrete to assist her?

Thea was contemplating any number of ways to approach Sergei on the way back to her room. No option stood out. But as she padded down the hallway noises stopped her. A rustle, a smothered giggle...

She moved towards the sound, beckoned by the soft, golden glow coming from the direction of Christo's study. The door was slightly ajar. She heard whispers. Male and female. The clatter of pens falling. She walked faster. Heart pounding. Drawn towards the light with a sense of dread.

She's heard enough to recognise that murmured intimacies were being exchanged. They didn't have a real marriage, but surely Christo wouldn't bring someone back here? After he'd touched her? So clearly displayed his desire? Though she knew men lied about fidelity all the time. Men like her father. And where else would Christo go if he didn't want to be caught and their marriage exposed as a fraud?

She didn't understand why the thought seized her with a sense of humiliation as she approached the door.

She heard a breathy sigh, a male groan—*'Agapi mou...'*—and her humiliation exploded in a screaming hot conflagration which roared through her. She couldn't see anything through the crack of the door, but to *hell* with Christo bringing someone to the apartment after demanding that theirs must appear like a real marriage in all respects. How *dared* he? After kissing her? Making her *feel*?

She flung the door back. Stormed in. Wild. Not caring what she'd find.

Wide eyes. Gasps of shock. The scramble of two people caught out. Anna was on Christo's desk, her hair a tumbled mess, her skirt hitched high on her thighs. And Sergei was standing there. Stripped to the waist.

'Mrs Callas—I can explain,' Sergei said as Anna clutched at her open blouse.

Thea held up her hand to stop him. What she'd interrupted had only just started. Relief washed over her like a warm shower—to be quickly replaced by a calculated resolve.

Sergei didn't attempt more excuses, only glanced down at Anna, cupped her jaw in what seemed like a moment of reassurance. But that look… Tight with concern and brimming with something else. Softness, intent… She recognised it instantly. *Love.*

In that moment Thea was assailed by two thoughts. The first was a terrifying craving for Christo to look at her with the same expression Sergei had given Anna. The second was the realisation that she now had the means to make her bodyguard do anything she desired.

'No need for explanations,' she said, her voice firm and hard. 'We won't mention this again. But I want you to find Alexis Anastos for me. And, Sergei…? You will *not* tell Mr Callas.'

CHAPTER EIGHT

'IF HE'S STILL in Greece he remains well hidden, even though his bank accounts are frozen.'

Thea stiffened at the sound of Sergei's voice as he approached her where she sat on the private terrace under an ancient olive tree. She put down her coffee. The dappled morning light shifted over an uneaten breakfast. Despite Sergei's efforts since they'd returned to Athens, Alexis hadn't been found. Reason told her to remain calm. But the clawing fear that he was out there alone, without money or help, tore in her abdomen.

'Thank you,' she said, as Sergei positioned himself at the end of the table. 'Do you think he might have left the country?'

'Anything's possible.'

She read between his words. Crossing borders illegally cost money. And right now Alexis had nothing. That meant he needed her help.

'Keep looking.'

Sergei cleared his throat. 'I'm not comfortable about this.'

She picked up her coffee and took a long sip, peering at him over the rim of the cup. They'd had this discussion many times before Sergei had finally agreed to help her.

'I wasn't comfortable about finding you half-naked in my husband's office. Let's both bear it as best we can—for Anna's sake.'

His expression didn't change. He stood inhumanly still, legs apart, hands behind his back, staring blankly over her head. 'Of course.'

'Remember—I'll keep your secrets if you keep mine.'

Thea loathed this. Loathed the things she'd said to garner his cooperation. It was clear he'd do anything to protect the woman he loved, so that was whose job she'd threatened. He didn't need to know she'd never tell Christo. In fact Anna was turning into more of a friend than an employee. But Thea was trying to protect someone *she* loved too. And she'd go to any lengths—just like Sergei would.

'Excellent.' She slid a piece of paper towards him. 'Now that's settled, today I want to go here.'

That simple act, making her request, led to the slow unknotting of the muscles in her neck. Sergei couldn't object, and here was a way to relieve some of the tension winding her so tight she felt her bones were bound to splinter.

Sergei picked up the note, looked at it, at her and then back at the note. A muscle ticked in his cheek. 'Mr Callas was specific in his instructions when he engaged me, and—'

'Again, there's no need for Christo to know.' Anger bubbled inside her, hot and thick. Sergei's job wasn't to keep her safe. Christo had merely subcontracted the role of her nanny and jailer because he couldn't be bothered doing it himself.

'I can keep the fact I'm looking for someone behind Mr Callas's back a secret. But...' He held up the scrap of paper with a name and address on it between his fingers, hissing his words through gritted teeth. 'A tattoo?'

'Your job is to keep to our agreement. Mine's to deal with Christo.' She narrowed her eyes. 'Every action has consequences. Take responsibility for yours and let me worry about my own.'

Sergei looked heavenward and muttered something. It might have been a curse, or even a prayer. She waited for him to finish.

'Do you know where this place is?' she asked.

'Yes.' He screwed up the piece of paper and stuffed it into his trouser pocket. 'It's where I get mine. Shall I call for the car now?'

She raised her cup to him in a toast. 'Perfect.'

They drove to the tattoo parlour without speaking. Sergei was taciturn at the best of times. Today his silence seemed ominous. As they parked, she tried not to think about how Christo would feel, or why his good opinion mattered.

Sergei scanned the narrow back street. After a short while he opened her door and ushered her out. 'Would you like me to come in and hold your hand?' His words were dry as alum.

She patted his rock-solid forearm. 'I bet I have more tattoos than you.'

He raised an eyebrow. 'I doubt it. Perhaps when you're done we could compare?'

Thea laughed. His sense of humour was unexpected. She saw why Anna liked him. 'Now, how would we explain *that* scene to Mr Callas?'

Sergei grunted in reply as they walked into the bright white waiting room. He took his place, standing to attention near the door.

Thea was invited through by a large man with more ink than bare skin. Not her usual artist, but it didn't matter. She riffled through a portfolio of his work. He appeared skilled. Anyway, she knew what she wanted. She couldn't turn back now. The need for it slid through her veins like a drug.

She took off her shirt, felt her heartbeat slowing to a sleepy rhythm.

The man moved behind her. '*Nice*. And you want another where?'

'At the end. Follow what I designed with Marco last time. Make sure it stays below the bra line.'

She lay forward, relaxing as the man prepared. Calm spread over her at the familiar routine, soft and cocooning as a goose down quilt. *This* was her reward. For the forced marriage. For every hurt. No matter how hard people tried to shape her into their own image, no one could steal the essence of her. Here was her proof—in the secrets scribed on her body.

'Ready?' the man asked.

'Yes.' It was almost a sigh of relief. She smiled and closed her eyes as the needle bit into her skin.

Something had changed. Thea seemed happier. There was a sense of peace about her now, as they sat down to breakfast. She glowed with a mysterious, ethereal kind of beauty that tugged at him.

Christo had seen that look in women who were pregnant, the secret joy. Strange imagining that with her when it was impossible. Yet still the thought trickled through him with a slide of warmth.

Rather than picking at the food, as she'd done since New York, today she ate a large meal. It pleased him in an inexplicable way to see her looking more settled. He wasn't sure why he cared. Yet he felt a deep satisfaction in her new-found happiness.

A partnership. That was how their relationship had begun to feel. Something he'd never expected when he'd checked off the list of things he must do to ensure Atlas's safety.

What would it be like to have a true partnership? A woman in his mind, his bed, his heart?

He looked over the table at his wife. Strange how he'd never thought he'd ever be married. Especially now there was an odd companionship in their forced togetherness. Some comfort in having another person in his home who might learn to care, as he was learning.

Thea. A luminous mystery…so much of her hidden. The desire to unlock her secrets, stuck under his skin. To inflame the passion which kindled between them. No games. No reining anything in. Both of them allowed free flight to every fantasy.

He'd felt in New York how it would be, with the force of a blow. All his desires exploding into life in the bright burst that was Thea.

She looked at him and smiled, a soft tilt to her lips. The

allure of her rushed through him, and a clutch of need gripped him in a way he'd never felt.

'There are some more people you'll meet at the party,' he said, trying to ignore the pull that drew him to her.

Thea sipped a coffee, her lipstick leaving a pale pink stain on the cup. 'Who are they and what should I know?'

'More business contacts.'

'What about friends?'

'No.'

A faint frown marred her brow. 'Do you have any?' she said, like it was a surprise to her that he could be close to anyone.

Christo hesitated. Thea was nearer to the truth than she realised. But why did he feel the need to explain? They had a business deal. He would simply dictate the terms and she'd do what he wanted, without the need to bare his soul. Yet that look of hers judged him, as lethal as a stab to the heart.

'Of course.'

Except he spent all his time bolstering Atlas. Nothing else had mattered for longer than he remembered. Including other people. He scrubbed his hands over his face, every part of him weary.

She shrugged. 'Tell me what I need to know and I'll be ready.'

Thea always assimilated the information he gave her and used it in the most gracious of ways. Making every person she met feel special, as if they were old friends. There was strength in her. She didn't want this, yet she carried on with persistence and dedication. And that part of her glowed more brightly than mere beauty ever could, lighting the darkest places of him.

'Tonight, perhaps we could have dinner on the terrace and discuss it.' There, under the olive trees, seemed to be her favourite place.

He smiled. Thea smiled back and the warmth of it filled him to overflowing.

'I'd love to.'

She sounded genuinely pleased. He contemplated staying home from work today. Taking time away from shoring up support for Atlas and spending it here. With her.

A low pulse picked up a throbbing tempo in his gut. He was sure they could find something pleasurable to do together...

'Mr Callas?'

His thoughts were interrupted by Anna.

'Your car's here.'

Christo's shoulders sagged. More work. Stitching together the gaping holes left by his father. But he'd win this battle and release Atlas from its debts. Release Thea in the process. Yet something about that prospect sat bitter in his mouth.

He stood. Anna was looking on, so he kissed Thea on the lips. Her rich scent curled into him and something deep inside clenched with need. Better he leave for work than risk exploring that hunger.

As he passed Thea, he noticed a vivid red mark on the back of her white blouse. 'You've blood on your shirt.'

Thea lifted her head, a look of concern flickering over her face before disappearing. Her features reverted to a blank calm. 'I had a bite. It must have been bigger than I realised.'

She smiled again, but this one was flat and lifeless.

'Perhaps someone should take a look?'

She rolled her eyes. 'It's nothing. A mosquito bite, and I scratched too hard.'

He accepted her explanation reluctantly. After all she was an adult, could look after herself.

'Now, go,' she said, with a flick of her hand, her engagement ring twinkling in the fresh morning light. 'Sergei can look after me. That's why you hired him, isn't it?'

She turned back to her breakfast and he felt strangely dismissed.

* * *

An amateur mistake, wearing white. Thea stormed into her room and tore off her shirt, throwing it on the dresser. She should have been more careful. Yet she wasn't thinking clearly, being ruled by emotion. It was causing her to make stupid mistakes.

She reached behind her, peeled off the dressing and turned to look in the mirror. Okay, more bleeding than she'd had before, but not infected—at least she didn't think so. This tattoo hurt more than usual too, but that was bound to be its position on her spine.

She peered over her shoulder at the flock of birds soaring across her back, showing that no matter how many people tried to cage her, in the end she'd be free.

Christo couldn't hold her. Nor could her father. They'd all try, but she'd slip through the bars one day and fly away for ever. Until then she'd add bird after bird. Marks to commemorate each insult as a reminder that her time would come.

Thea grappled with the dressing, twisting awkwardly as she tried to replace it. Only a few days and the tattoo would heal. She'd just be more careful. Perhaps she should wear a black shirt?

Then in the mirror she saw a movement. *Christo*. Watching with fury twisting ugly across his features.

'What the hell is this?'

She snatched up her shirt. Clutched it to her chest. And all the simmering feelings bubbled and boiled and spilled over in a scalding flood.

'Get out!' Her composure was gone in a torrent of white-hot anger. She trembled as it burned through her. 'You've no right to be in here.'

'I have every right. This is my house.' He towered in the doorway. Jaw hard. Mouth stretched in a thin, brutal line. 'You'll explain this.'

'It's my body. I can do what I like with it.'

Christo's lip curled into a sneer. 'What else have you been doing with it when my back's been turned?'

'I'm sure your imagination can conjure any number of horrors.'

The cool air of the room chilled her overheated skin. Or perhaps it was the cold rage in Christo's eyes. She felt too exposed, with the shirt held in front of her and his icy gaze flicking to her tattoos reflected in the mirror behind.

'And you will document each one for me,' he said. 'My study. One hour.'

Christo hadn't thought himself a fool for years—not since childhood. Not since he'd believed his parents' false promises time and again, till he'd stopped believing anything. Yet here Thea was, sitting in front of him, her whole presence mocking as if he was one.

He'd gone to check on her. Genuinely worried. And what had he found? Evidence of betrayal. Lies. People always told lies. Especially those you allowed close to you. Never again.

It was clear she didn't care. Leaning back in the chair opposite, arms crossed, a victorious gleam in her eye. That was why she'd looked so happy—because she'd thought she'd won.

It might not be a real marriage, but he'd made vows and he'd keep them till the end. He'd expected the same of her.

Where to begin when the rage scorched through him? He searched for the chill usually running in his veins. *She* did this to him—made him unreasonable. And he was usually a reasonable man.

'Sergei's employment has been terminated.'

'That's unfair. I want you to reinstate him. He's an excellent bodyguard.'

'He told me everything.'

Actually, Sergei had only admitted to an error of judgement—trying to protect Thea's shattered honour, no doubt. But Christo knew there was little that would make a consummate professional like Sergei forget where his allegiances lay. An illicit affair with his employer's beautiful young wife was the only explanation.

But Christo wanted the truth from Thea's lips, not Sergei's. The truth that she hadn't stuck to their bargain of fidelity, that she was like his parents. An opportunistic liar.

As he stared her down, myriad emotions flickered across her face. It was like watching a movie on fast forward. Surprise, disbelief, sorrow. Until she plastered on her usual smooth veneer of calm.

'Love can make a man do uncharacteristic things. Of course you don't believe in love, so you would never know.'

Christo gritted his teeth. His suspicions were right. A pain knifed him deep inside, causing an aching wound to his soul. He'd craved her. Kissed her. And for what? Merely to repeat Hector's mistakes?

'You're so like your father.'

Damn his mother's words—the last she'd spoken to him. They hadn't been meant as a compliment.

He cast them into the wasteland of his memory. They had no place here. He'd married Thea for convenience, not love. So why did evidence of her betrayal tear to the very heart of him?

He gripped the arms of his chair till his nails bit into the leather. 'I'm sure you're easy to love when you want to get your own way.'

The cool calm thawed and her eyes widened a fraction. Triumph leapt inside him, a bitter white-hot flame. He'd caught her out.

'You think...? Me?'

She sounded incredulous—another act.

'That I'd trade myself to Sergei to get what I want? I may be many things, but I'd never do that.'

'Don't lie to me.' Christo flew from his chair, hands trembling. Every part of him was too hot, too tight for his suit. He tore off his tie before it choked him. 'I won't be taken for a fool like my father!'

Turning a blind eye to his wife's outrageous behaviour. Ignoring it till she ran off with her latest lover. Christo thought he'd avoided his genetics, the weakness allowing him to be conned by women. He had believed Thea was more. But glorious curves and luscious kisses had caused him to look past the truth of another duplicitous female.

'I'm not lying. Even though you've done nothing to earn my trust.'

He placed his hands on the desktop and leaned forward. Thea didn't move, her expression placid, as if she'd done nothing wrong at all.

'Sergei was protective,' he hissed. 'There's only one reason a man behaves that way!'

She laughed at him—a cold jeer. It was the way his father had been laughed at for years by his mother in the charade of their marriage.

'As you know so well, being the great protector that you are.'

He refused to be mocked. 'How quickly you move on from one man to the next. I hope using Sergei was worth it to get back at me. What happened? Did you seduce him when you realised Alexis was unavailable?'

Thea leapt from her seat, chest heaving. 'Alexis is my *brother*!'

A dreadful quiet fell in the room, taking on a life of its own. Heavy, oppressive, punctuated by Thea's ragged breaths. A clock on the wall ticked seconds in an ominous rhythm.

'He was like the brother I should have had.'

She only had one brother. Didn't she?

More lies.

'You want to know why I did this?' she asked.

Thea grabbed the bottom of her shirt and tore, buttons scattering as she hurled the ruined fabric to the floor, then whipped round, displaying her back. Christo stared at the birds sweeping across her skin, at the spidery detail of the feathers in their vivid colours.

'The first, I was eighteen. For all the times my father prevented me from seeing my mother. For the way she begged the staff to allow her to visit her little girl. I learned then the value of secrets and lies. This is a reminder of the sacrifices she made. How she fought to be free.'

The birds looked joyous as they twisted their way from the slender curve of her waist across her lower back and up her spine. Christo counted. Nine. Nine bluebirds.

'The one in the middle—the largest—it hurt the most. But not as much as what I did to earn it. Demetri promised me to one of his business associates. To close a deal.'

Christo froze in horror. *No.*

'Luckily the man desired a "compliant" woman,' she spat, 'not one who'd fight. So I remained untouched. Demetri wasn't so forgiving. He always enjoyed hurting little girls.'

'But your father…' Surely he should have protected her?

She gave a mirthless laugh. She was still facing away from him, hands now defiantly planted on her hips, her nails digging into her flesh.

'My father didn't need his fists to make an impression. He'd take my phone—prevent my contact with the outside world to ensure compliance. I thought I'd go mad at times. In the end I behaved. Or he thought I did.'

He couldn't stand here and let her continue baring herself like this. 'Thea. Stop.' The words were rough as ground glass in his throat.

She shot a look behind her. 'Oh, please… You wanted to know and I'm keen to enlighten you. This bird, at my side…'

She catalogued a litany of deprivations. Too many for someone so young. He wanted to rage. To tear her family apart on her behalf. To *fix* this.

'But this last one. This one is all for *you*, Christo, my

beloved husband. When I told my father I wouldn't marry you Demetri stepped in to convince me. Alexis and Demetri fought. Then the police…'

She stopped. Slumped a little. Her shoulders rose and fell. Then she straightened.

'That's when my father discovered who Alexis was. He said he'd go to jail for assault unless I married you.' Her voice broke and trembled.

He wanted to reach for her. Hold her. Make it better, somehow. But the painful truth of their deal and what it had cost her was etched on her back, red and angry-looking. His fault and his shame.

The realisation sat leaden in his stomach.

'And you think I used my body, used Sergei, to get him to do what I wanted?'

She turned, bared to him apart from her bra. Christo couldn't keep his gaze from her devastated eyes.

'He doesn't deserve to be fired for doing what a good man should. Yes, Sergei's protecting the one he loves—but it's not me. I just blackmailed him into doing what I wanted.'

Defiant, she bent down for her shirt and shrugged it over her shoulders as she made for the door. When she reached it, she stopped.

'I've learned that blackmail is a blunt but effective instrument. As you know too well, being so good at it yourself.'

She left the room, clicking the door softly behind her.

The sound held more quiet horror than if she'd slammed it in his face.

Christo stood outside Thea's room, a bundle of papers in his hand. Even though he was the last person she'd want to see, he couldn't leave her alone. Not after what she'd disclosed. He wanted to prove to Thea that he wasn't like Tito or Demetri, that he could be trusted.

He took a steadying breath and tapped on the door, trying to ensure it sounded like a request to enter, not a demand. If she wanted her space he'd give it to her, but there were things that had to be said.

When there was no reply he turned the handle. Thea sat on her bed, leaning forward. She hadn't changed out of her ruined shirt, which still hung open. Her hands were clenched into rigid fists on her thighs.

He eased into the room.

She didn't look at him. Eyes fixed to the floor.

'I have the papers I promised,' he said, crouching down in front of her. 'Our settlement for when my father dies... the divorce. If you sign them, they'll be filed as soon as the will takes effect.'

'Do you have a pen?' Thea's voice was the barest whisper.

'You should read them first.'

'I don't care. I want nothing of yours.'

He handed her the sheaf of documents, which she glanced through. Then he drew a pen from his pocket. She took it and scrawled her name on the last page. His gut roiled as she signed, in a feeling of loss, a regret he had no right to have when for him, relationships had no permanence.

She thrust the documents at him, the papers quavering in her hand. 'Fill in what you need to when the time comes.'

Christo took them from her, dropped them on the floor beside him. 'No one should have gone through what you have.'

'And you care? I'm just a means to your end.'

Her fingers clenched tight again. He knew what she was doing now. Castigated himself for not realising before.

He took her hands in his. Stroked his thumbs over the blanched knuckles, absorbing the tremble running through her. She relaxed a fraction. He opened her fingers. Her nails had scored red crescents into her palms. He circled his thumbs over the livid marks, trying to smooth them away.

'You hurt yourself...'

Her eyes flicked to him. They were red-rimmed, her face flushed.

'This, the candles, the tattoos…'

He continued soothing her palms. Her hands burning hot under his thumbs.

'Not the tattoos. They're a reminder.'

'Of things you should never have experienced. If I'd known—'

'You wouldn't have done anything differently.'

Sunlight flooded in through the window behind her. It was such a glorious blue-sky day outside, and yet she spoke truths that broke a storm inside him.

Her accusation was right. He would have done anything to save Atlas Shipping. The knowledge sat heavy on his chest, making it tight and hard to breathe.

He couldn't change the past, but he could help with the present. 'Tell me about Alexis.'

The tremble in her body intensified, as if she was barely holding herself together. He steadied her hands between his.

'He's my half-brother,' she whispered, as if she were disclosing some terrible secret.

'And your father didn't know about him?'

Thea lifted her head, looked at him straight on. She chewed on her bottom lip, which quivered under her teeth.

'My parents were promised to each other from birth—an arrangement to merge two families' wealth. But my mother fell in love with someone else. At seventeen, she had Alexis. He was taken away. Adopted. My father still married her. He was only interested in the money he'd gain from it.'

Thea seemed so tired and worn down, with no fight left in her. As if it was an effort for her not to curl into herself and disappear.

'How did Alexis become your bodyguard?' asked Christo.

'My mother spent half her life trying to find him. When

she did, she told him he had a little sister. He said he'd find a way to look after me.'

She stopped. Took a shuddering breath. Christo squeezed her hands in reassurance.

'He worked in security. A position became vacant in my father's home. He applied. When he finally told me who he was it was like life began again.'

Thea sat up, pulling her hands from his. She wrapped her open shirt around her, hugging herself.

'The theft…it's a lie. When I agreed to marry you, I negotiated some money. Fifty thousand euros. Alexis was supposed to leave the country. Start again. But I couldn't save him.'

She dropped her head, toying with her engagement ring—another symbol of her failed efforts to protect her brother.

Christo's heart ached for her. She blamed herself, and yet Thea's only failure was in trusting that her father and Demetri would keep their side of the bargain.

'Do you know where he is?'

She shook her head. 'Sergei's been looking.'

He understood the blackmail now. The last resort for a desperate woman.

'He doesn't have my resources. I'll engage Raul's company. If anyone can find him, Raul can.'

Her eyelids fluttered shut. She clasped her hands as if giving a silent prayer. 'Thank you.'

He stood. Thea's trembling had turned into a shiver which racked her body. Her face and chest were flushed red. Christo reached out to cup her cheek. She burned.

'You're not well,' he said.

She tried to wave him away, but it seemed as if she was having trouble raising her arm. He pulled his phone from his pocket and called his doctor. Demanded he come to the house within the hour.

'I only need rest,' she said.

The slightest nudge and she'd collapse to the bed. He was sure of it. 'Then lie down...sleep a while,' he murmured.

Thea eased onto the pillows with no argument, curling on her side. Christo covered her with a blanket, tucking it tight around her as her teeth chattered.

His concern escalated. 'The doctor will be here soon.' Whilst he was no expert, her tattoo looked too pink. He only hoped she'd been looking after it as she should.

She stared at him, eyes glazed.

'I'm sorry,' he said. 'If there was any way this could have been different...'

He stroked her hair and Thea's fever-bright eyes drifted shut. Her breathing slowed in the rhythm of sleep. He pulled over a chair and sat next to the bed.

And as he watched her fitful rest he made a promise to do everything in his power to ensure Alexis's safety and to punish Tito and Demetri for what they'd done to her.

CHAPTER NINE

THEA WALKED INTO her bedroom and flopped into a chair, escaping the chaos downstairs. A flurry of party planners had transformed the huge lounge and entertainment area into a sumptuous ballroom for the evening. The home's modern lines had been draped and swathed until they mimicked the art deco opulence of the *Queen Mary*—the perfect setting for Atlas Shipping's anniversary celebrations.

She checked her watch. In a few short hours the party would begin—Christo's crowning achievement, where she'd be expected to glitter and shine. Even now a shaky kind of heat trembled through her. But this wasn't a hangover from the illness. It was something else altogether.

She'd taken a week to recover fully from what the doctor had assured Christo was a virus, and not an infected tattoo. After three days of being confined to her sickbed she'd risen to find that on the surface everything had returned to normal. Anna fussed about her assiduously. Sergei returned to work, taciturn as ever. The sun still rose, the night still fell, she ate, she slept…but *everything* was different.

It had changed as the fever racked her body. Christo's voice had grounded her, soothing as the cool run of a mountain stream. Each time she'd woken in those days, he'd been there, eyes stormy green and intent, dark stubble shading his jaw.

She suspected he hadn't left her bedside throughout her brief incapacitation. His gentle touches to check her temperature, to reassure, had melted her bones and left her wanting. Now all she craved was the soft lilt of his voice and his masculine touch. Because somehow what she'd shared with him had changed everything.

She walked into her dressing room, pulled out the gown

she planned to wear that night and laid it on the bed. The slither of fear snaked through her veins. Christo had warned her that Tito and Demetri were coming. Here, to this home, where she'd finally found some measure of comfort and safety.

This place…they'd taint it. She shivered. Why had Christo invited them when he knew what they'd done to her? He'd promised her there was good reason, just as he'd promised to protect her. If only she could find the means within herself to trust him…

'Mrs Callas?'

Thea looked up as Anna walked into the room, clutching an armful of boxes. 'I thought I told you to call me Thea.'

Anna smiled, bouncing on her toes. She seemed so happy—glowing. No more the shy woman Thea had first met. Obviously her relationship with Sergei was going well.

Was that what love could do to a person? Since it wasn't something she expected for herself, best not to muse on that.

'These are from Mr Callas,' Anna said in a breathless kind of way as she placed the packages on the bed.

Thea plucked a card from under the outrageous silver bow on the largest box, opened the envelope and read Christo's bold script.

Wear these tonight.

She glanced at her choice of dress for the evening, lying on the bed. A floor-length sheath. Black. Restrained and classical. Other women might compete to outdo each other. Not her.

Though curiosity made her fingers itch. What had Christo bought? It wouldn't hurt to look at what he'd chosen, would it?

She picked up the smallest box, stroking over the soft blue velvet. Jewellery? She eased the lid open and her hand flew to her mouth as the exposed contents glittered under the lights. Earrings. A twinkling confection of rubies and diamonds.

Thea lifted one and the chandelier fall of it trembled in her grasp. She couldn't help it. Slipped them into her ears and turned to the mirror. The flash of gems dangled low.

Anna gasped. 'They're beautiful. Like drops of blood and tears.'

'Tears?' Thea's voice cracked as she said it.

'Happy tears,' Anna said. 'Why wouldn't a woman be happy with a gift like that?'

Because it was too much.

And yet there was more.

Thea reached for the large box, tugging at the ends of the perfect bow holding it closed. Inside lay a garment of vivid red. She eased it from the folds of white tissue. Now it was her turn to gasp. A halter neck evening dress lined with satiny carmine silk lay inside. The whole of it was beaded, and it sparkled in a way that matched the earrings.

'I've never seen anything like it...' Anna whispered.

But Thea had observed what Anna hadn't. The back of the dress plunged. When it was on, it would leave her exposed.

Heart pounding, she flung it onto the bed as if the fabric had burned her. How could Christo demand she wear this? Even with her hair long and free, as she'd planned, her tattoos would be on view.

Heat flushed her cheeks. Did he intend to humiliate her?

Anna's voice intruded. 'The last box, Mrs... Thea?'

Strappy sandals to match the dress and earrings. Perfection in gold, adorned with red and clear jewels.

'Aren't you going to try them on?' Anna asked.

'I don't know if I should...'

'You must.' Anna planted her hands on her hips. 'What man doesn't want to show off his beautiful wife?'

Was that it? Surely not.

She glanced back at the dress, discarded on the bed.

Like nothing she'd ever owned. Brand-new. Couture. All hers. She fingered the exquisite fabric, soft, yet heavy in her hands.

Anna grabbed the black dress from the bed and went to the walk-in wardrobe.

Thea took a deep breath and began unbuttoning her blouse. She'd do this—then refuse the gift and return to her first choice.

She stepped into the gown. The silk lining slipped cool and seductive against her skin. She sat on the bed and toed into the shoes before rising. Beaded lace fell heavy against her.

Anna returned to the room, eyes wide. 'You're going to take everyone's breath away.'

Thea walked to the full-length mirror. Lace of blood-coloured perfection slid across her body. A dress meant to display a woman's shape. It flared at the bottom, so when she walked the lower half swished, beads glittering with every footstep. She turned and cast an eye over her shoulder. The back plunged tantalisingly low, but not indecently, framing the birds which soared over her spine.

Why had he chosen this? She couldn't wear it. Even though the fabric sang against her skin.

Thea walked back to her wardrobe with Anna trailing behind. She'd wear the dress she'd picked earlier. It wasn't showy, like this one, which allowed all her private wounds to be displayed.

'What beautiful tattoos,' Anna said quietly. 'So real... like they're ready to fly away.'

'Thank you.' Thea flicked through the hangers, looking for her black gown. Where had Anna hidden it? 'But I usually keep them covered. I can't wear this dress.'

'Why hide them?' Anna looked bemused. 'Mr Callas knows you have them, and he chose this dress for you—so he doesn't care.'

'No, he doesn't. It's perfect.'

Christo's voice behind them was as smooth and sleek against her skin as the silk lining of the dress.

Anna excused herself and slid from the room.

'You're lurking again.' Thea turned to face him. 'You know my thoughts on that.'

'That I'm untrustworthy?' His hands clenched and released, his fingers flexing restlessly.

Right now he most definitely did not look like a man who could be trusted. A shadow of stubble shaded his jaw. His hair looked as if he'd raked his hands through it one too many times. And all the while his hooded eyes devoured her in a dark, gleaming sweep from her neck to her feet and back again.

His charcoal three-piece suit was the only thing giving him any air of respectability. The rest of him looked irretrievably disreputable. A liquid heat bloomed deep and low inside.

'Yes. And I'm not wearing the dress.'

'Don't you like it?'

She ran her hands down the exquisite fabric. Too many emotions were coursing through her. 'No… Yes. It's beautiful.'

'Then why are you afraid?' The corners of his lips tipped in a knowing smile.

'I'm not afraid. I just want to wear the dress I picked for myself.'

He cocked his head to the side, looking at her as if she was some curious bejewelled butterfly. 'Let me guess. Plain? Black? One you can hide behind?'

'Stop saying those things!'

'Wear the gown I chose for you.'

He pointed to the mirror behind her. She turned.

'One that shows the magnificent woman you are.'

As she looked at her reflection Christo closed in behind her, his warmth solid at her back. The scent of him was intoxicating. Crisp. Wild. Pure male.

He reached out and placed his hands on the tops of her arms. She absorbed the quiet intimacy as his thumbs began to make slow circles. A shiver of pleasure at that beguiling touch began at the base of her neck and sparkled down her arms. There was a rightness in this picture. Something settling about them standing together like this.

'Your father and Demetri…'

He caught her reflected gaze, his hands continuing that gentle stroking. It was as if he was trying to delve into the soul of her.

'I'm sorry they have to be here. It can't be avoided.'

Thea looked to the floor. At the glittering perfection of her dress. Her twinkling shoes. He didn't need to see the vulnerability his decision had wrought in her.

'You won't tell me the reason?' she asked.

'I want more information before saying anything else.' Christo hesitated. 'You've been hurt enough by them. I won't add to your pain. If there was any other way…'

'You've said that before.' She shrugged. 'Yet here we are.'

He bent down, whispered in her ear. The breath caressing her throat.

'Courage, Thea.'

His voice rushed over her, hot and thick, with the same jolt as her morning coffee. Then he released her and stepped back. She mourned the loss of his hands on her skin.

'I'll see you downstairs in an hour.'

Thea's heart thundered as she walked down the curving staircase. She steadied herself on the balustrade. One moment she thought Christo understood her. The next…?

'Courage, Thea.'

What did he know of courage? Living his life of privilege. Not knowing fear. The dress didn't frighten her. Mere scraps of fabric couldn't hurt you. She knew where the real monsters hid—and tonight they'd be here, in this house.

She took a few breaths to calm herself and walked towards the ballroom. As she rounded a huge potted palm there Christo stood, towering in a perfectly tailored tuxedo, greeting his guests. The superfine wool moulded to the slim taper of his waist. His hands in the pockets of his trousers pulled them tight over his backside.

She stopped, hesitated, smoothed damp palms over the beaded fabric she wore. All the people terrified her. All this pretence. But she still had time; he hadn't seen her. She should change.

Instead she froze, her chest tightening. Where had all the air gone? Perspiration pricked the back of her neck as her hands curled into tight fists. She needed to walk backwards, walk *somewhere*, yet she couldn't take another step.

Thea knew the moment Christo realised she was there. His imposing shoulders straightened. His hands slid from his pockets and he turned.

'*Thea.*'

His low velvet voice penetrated the tension corseting her chest. He strode towards her, arm outstretched. She played the game. Placed her hand in his, felt it engulfed. He lifted it to his mouth, kissing the palm where seconds earlier her nails had bitten into her soft flesh. And in that act he stole her breath, caused a burn to heat her cheeks.

He looked down at her, his gaze all-seeing. And for a moment she lost herself in the calm ocean of his eyes. Her breathing eased. Her pounding heart steadied. Christo *did* understand. He understood too well.

'You look exquisite. I can see why red's your favourite colour.'

Her cheeks heated, no doubt flaming into the shade of her dress. 'Thank you. But it's too generous a gift.'

'It's nothing less than you deserve for all you've done. But sadly for now we must work. Perhaps later…?'

He raised an eyebrow and the corner of his mouth lifted in a lazy smile. A flush of warmth stole over her, Christo's invitation was clear. She could say yes and see what came of it.

Memories of that drizzly day in New York flooded into her consciousness. His hard, aroused body. Those deep, drugging kisses. A heavy pulse beat between her legs...

No, she had a part to play. That was all she could trust. Nothing more.

'You work too hard,' she said, focusing on what they had to do tonight.

Christo surveyed the crowd, as if he was making sure everyone appeared satisfied. But Thea could see what others didn't notice. The tightness around his eyes. The dull shadows underneath.

'My father would be proud.' He let out a slow breath, looked down at the floor. *'"Fun, fun, fun. That's all you want to have,"* he'd say to me. Other boys at school had holidays with their families. Hector sent me to work picking olives. I was nine.'

The thought of him being sent out to work so young was...shocking. She'd sometimes wondered about Christo as a small boy, what had made him the man he was. He always seemed so serious she wasn't sure he knew how to have fun. Perhaps with good reason.

She stared out at the throng of people. At least they seemed to be enjoying themselves as waiters threaded in and out with food and wine.

She said, 'That's—'

'Life. I learned long ago not to care.'

Thea wasn't so sure. His voice sounded flat and dead, as if he had to force himself not to dwell on it.

'Your father must be sorry he can't be here tonight,' she said.

Christo pinned her with his gaze, eyes hard and stormy. Time ticked for a few heartbeats, too much unsaid between them.

'I'm sure he is.'

'What about your mother?' Where had she been when her son was sent away to pick olives as a little boy? 'Surely she'll want to celebrate your success?'

'Ha! My mother?' He tensed, a muscle at the side of his jaw ticking. 'She's never cared. Always claimed I was an impossible child. Why would she feign interest now? The woman's as maternal as a cuckoo.'

How could his mother say such a thing? But his words explained too much. At least she'd had one parent love her unconditionally, and Alexis too. Didn't he have anyone?

'Christo…' Thea placed a hand on his arm, trying to offer some small comfort.

He shrugged her away. Snagged two glasses of champagne from a waiter and handed one chilled flute to her with a brittle smile.

'We should talk to some guests.'

His words spoke only of obligation. She didn't want to talk to the guests. She wanted to wrap her arms around the wounded boy she'd glimpsed in his tired eyes. The one driven by his father, abandoned by his mother. But he'd reject her sympathy, she was sure.

So instead she followed Christo into the crowd, the crush surrounding them. He patted people on the back, made small talk, smiled. But the smile didn't meet his eyes.

Thea smiled too, playing her part. No one commented on her tattoos, as she'd feared. A heady rush thrummed through her. She'd never hide them again. They weren't wounds. They spoke instead of her strength and survival.

As they turned to talk with yet another person who wanted a piece of her husband she saw them. In a corner. Talking to someone she didn't know. Her father and Demetri.

A tight knot of nausea gripped her belly. She stiffened.

Christo glanced in the direction she was looking. Then he frowned, turning to face her. She peered around him, unable to take her eyes from the two men.

Like a predator watching its prey, Demetri's cold stare met hers. Her heart raced, preparing for flight. She'd lived in a kind of peace without them in the same house. But even another continent was too close.

She wrapped her arms round her waist.

'I won't let them near you,' Christo said.

He slid his hand to the dip in her back and rested it there. The touch steadied her heart. His solid presence calmed the tightness in her stomach.

He looked over his shoulder, then back to her. 'Forget them. I have a small surprise for you.'

His voice was soft and low, as if soothing a terrified animal. He kept his body between her and the men of her family.

Thea realised he was shielding her from their gaze. She believed Christo now. As long as she was with him he'd protect her from Tito and Demetri. She shook off the sticky tendrils of fear. Those men would only win if she let them.

'My dress and jewels weren't enough of a surprise?'

His features darkened into that glorious brooding which made her heart skip a beat. With one hand he swept her hair back over her shoulder and toyed with an earring. When had his touching her become normal?

Thea allowed herself to melt into it, heat pooling in her belly. For a small while her world was reduced to Christo's gentle caress, encouraging the pretence that this could be something different. And for a brief, bright moment she wished it was real.

He shrugged. 'They're trinkets.'

She shook herself out of the dream, her stomach twisting, wondering how often he bestowed *'trinkets'* upon other women.

What on earth was happening to her? She'd no right to these thoughts. Theirs was a convenient arrangement, and most women in this situation would be overjoyed by expensive gifts. She should learn to become one of them.

Thea gave him what she hoped was a gracious smile. 'How long are you going to keep me wondering?'

'Not long. I've invited Elena tonight.'

Her heart leapt with real joy. She hadn't spoken to her friend since her marriage—apart from a brief text from Elena saying her father was angry. Thea had a terrible feeling it had something to do with Elena's efforts to help *her*.

'Is she here yet?'

'Soon. But first come and meet the American ambassador and his wife. I think you'll like them.'

He swept her through the room, introducing her to more guests, never leaving her side. His hand was always at her back, its gentle pressure reassuring. His fingers stroked her body with the sway of her hips.

She became hyper-aware of every subtle touch. The way the luscious fabric of her gown fell against her as she moved. The caress of the satiny silk lining over her skin. Christo's choice. Christo's dress.

It was almost like his hands all over her. How much better would they feel than the silk that clothed her…? She craved it—craved his fingers exploring every curve, every secret place. The dark mystery that was Christo lit a burn deep inside her, flushing across her skin. Her nipples pebbled against the bodice of her dress, making every movement exquisite agony. She leaned into Christo's hard body, *all* of her attuned to him.

He tightened his arm around her. 'Elena's arrived,' he said, waking her from heated fantasies.

'Where?' Did he notice the huskiness of her voice? Christo gave no hint of it.

'In the corner—near the statue of Poseidon.'

She glimpsed her friend in a yellow dress and waved, trying to get her attention through the crush of guests.

'I'll take you to her. You've done enough smiling at strangers for me.'

'No. I'll go myself. You've too many people who need to congratulate you.'

Thea moved to leave Christo, slipping from his hold. The cool air where his hand had been felt like a loss.

He raised his eyebrows, stroking his hand down her arm till his fingers entwined in hers. He squeezed. 'You're sure?'

Thea looked up at him, her gaze snagging on the soft warmth in his green eyes, on his full lips which quirked at the corners.

The breath jagged in her throat. She needed to leave before she embarrassed herself. 'I'll be back shortly.'

'Take your time. You need some fun.' He kissed her hand in a perfect display of chivalry and let her go.

She hurried towards where she'd last seen her friend, excited to talk to her about how her life felt as if it were achieving some form of happiness, even in this arranged marriage.

'Thea.'

She froze. That familiar voice. Like being tossed into an icy river.

'You've been ignoring your father since you married. Talk to me a while.'

The old man himself stood there, arms out wide as if wanting to give her a hug. Smiling, but not with his eyes. They were a cold, muddy brown, fixed on her like a shark seeing prey in the water. She looked around furtively, but Christo was nowhere to be seen. The blood seeped to her toes and her vision blurred.

No. She was stronger than this. Her father was the weak one, bullying women. 'I've nothing to say to you.'

'Young love! You've forgotten your family.' He laughed.

The mirthless sound ran like frigid water through her veins. 'Family? I've no family here.'

Tito's eyes narrowed. There was nothing but disdain on his face now. 'What would your husband have to say to that?'

Thea gritted her teeth. 'He's no part of this conversation.

You sold me off for your own interests and then broke your promise to me about Alexis!'

To anyone watching it would look as though father and daughter were having a close conversation. But a war was being waged here. One she wouldn't lose.

'Your bastard half-brother will be interested to know how you're playing with his future.' Her father continued to give her that dead smile. 'I gave you clear instructions. Where's the information I want?'

She'd never even considered giving her father any information about Christo's company, and yet here was more confirmation that Alexis had paid the price for her decisions. The ache of it cut deep inside.

'Get the information yourself! You don't own me now. You passed that privilege on to Christo and he won't help you.'

Her father moved in close, looming over her. She wavered, the sick feeling at his proximity clawing at her throat. But she wouldn't cower, and she wouldn't hide. Not anymore.

'I'm sure you could convince him to do anything you wanted.' Her father's hard mouth turned up in a sneer, as if he'd stepped in something bad. 'Using your charms, your lies. It's in your breeding, with that mother of yours.'

She took a step back, the roil of her anger burning fierce. How dared he mention Maria, when he'd tried to obliterate her memory for so many years?

'Demetri has the same mother. Or have your forgotten that convenient fact? Watch your back, Father.'

'I can ruin Christo and you with him. Don't think it's beneath me.'

She folded her arms and narrowed her eyes. 'I don't think anything's beneath you. You'd eat from the gutter if it advantaged you.'

'Careful, Thea. You want money and privilege? I'll take all of this away if you don't do what I ask.'

She laughed. The deluded man thought he had the power of God. 'How can you take it? You'd never have sold me off to anyone who wasn't richer than Croesus.'

'Christo hasn't told you anything?'

Tito's eyes widened, and his smile morphed into one of pure evil. What was he planning?

A terrible chill slid through her. 'I don't under—'

Her father looked over her shoulder. 'Here's your brother to talk some sense into you.'

A shadow loomed behind her. Her father's words could slice like a dagger, but Demetri inflicted real pain. From pulling her hair as a child, he had progressed, unchecked by a father who didn't care about the little girl who was a constant reminder of the wife who'd left him.

Demetri's hand clamped tight on her arm. 'Sense? She's a disgrace.'

'Don't touch me!'

But no one would notice. She was on her own. These men had perfected sleight of hand, could hurt in ways which would never be seen.

'Have you looked at her back, Father? She's displaying a monstrosity.' Demetri leaned down to hiss in her ear. 'I suspected you were cheap, but you've outdone yourself.'

He pulled her around slyly, so no one would notice. He was clever that way. Her arm burned in his tight grip. But she wouldn't let him see her fear. She never had.

'How could your husband allow you to deface yourself?' her father spat.

She wrenched her arm from Demetri's crushing fingers. He'd never touch her again—not if she could help it. Thea drew herself up to face them, proudly displaying her tattoos—the symbols of her ultimate freedom. Even Christo had recognised that.

Christo.

He was cutting through the crowd. Purpose etched on his face. Eyes hard. Mouth a thin, cruel line. Looking as if he was ready to draw blood as his gaze slid from her father to Demetri. Blind fury from this man who always seemed implacable.

Her heart beat a little faster as he shouldered through his guests.

'You can ask me yourself.'

Christo's eyes were focused on her. She forgot everything, lost in his hot green gaze. Forgot the hatred tightening in her belly, the burning of her arm where Demetri's fingers had been.

Her father watched him, took a step back and plastered on his usual fake smile. 'An excellent party, Christo. It does Atlas Shipping's history great justice.'

Tito Lambros played the charming man well. She knew better. He might sound warm and interested. She could feel the strike of cold steel underneath.

Christo pushed between her and Demetri, towering over the men in her family.

'Are you troubling Thea?'

No niceties from her husband. His voice was stark and brutal. He wrapped his arm around her waist, drawing her close.

'Someone needs to keep her under control,' said Demetri.

Christo turned to her brother and pinned him with a withering look. 'What are you afraid of, Demetri? That if you let Thea be herself she'll outwit you? I'm sorry to say she already has.'

'She's making a mockery of us—displaying herself in that dress,' her father drawled, looking her up and down as if she was tainted.

'The only thing I see is an exquisite woman wearing the gift I gave her.' Christo's hand squeezed her hip. 'If you and your son don't appreciate that, you can leave our home.'

Her father held up his hands as if in surrender. Thea knew too well it was only for show.

'A piece of advice, Christo, from an older man who's

been married to a younger woman. It's easy to be blinded by beauty. Let your wife rule your home at your peril. Take your father—'

'I'll only take advice on marriage from a person who's had a successful one.'

Thea had never really taken notice of how her father, brother and Christo were together. Now she saw. Their dislike was palpable, and the air vibrated with mutual loathing.

'Then we'll leave you both to your obvious happiness.' Her father turned to her and fixed her with his reptilian gaze. 'Remember what I said. We'll have lunch. It's been too long since we've seen you.'

She shivered. The thought of sitting down to a meal with her father was about as welcome as the thought of being thrown into a tank of piranha fish.

'Yes,' said Demetri, looking at them both with contempt. 'Tonight isn't the time. It's all about celebrating your husband's exploits.'

As Demetri moved to go Christo gripped his arm, his tanned knuckles blanching as he did so. The two men stood there, glaring at each other. Demetri's gaze was tinged with fear; Christo's brimmed with pure hatred.

His lips contorted in a false smile, vicious and predatory. 'Touch Thea again and I will make you bleed.'

She gasped. The threat so bold, the violence underlying it so blatant.

Demetri said nothing. He nodded his head and wrenched his arm away, scuttling into the crowd.

Thea wilted. The only thing holding her upright was Christo's strong arm around her waist.

Dipping his head, he murmured, 'We need some time. Come with me.'

He steered her through the crowd to a quiet corner behind some freshly installed midnight-blue velvet curtains. Her whole body shook. Christo wrapped his arms around her. Drew her close. He'd said he'd protect her, and he had. That meant more to her than she could ever have imagined.

She rested her head on his chest, relishing his warmth. He stroked her back as her shivering subsided, whispering gentle words.

'I should never have left you alone… I didn't believe they'd be brazen enough… Not in our home…'

Everyone would think they were having a touching moment. No one would realise he was stitching her back together. Soothing her with his quiet strength. The solid beat of his heart.

'I'm fine now,' she said, pulling away. 'I need to go and find Elena. You invited her here for me.'

Christo cupped her jaw, looked into her eyes. She hated that he could see everything—especially her weakness.

'Are you sure? You don't have to stay any longer. I can say you were tired.'

She shook her head. 'Now you've put my father and Demetri in their place it'll be okay.'

Or would it? Considering what her father had said, the threats he'd made? She needed to warn Christo.

'My father said he could ruin you. Take everything away. Is that true?'

A flash of red heightened his cheeks and Christo dropped his head, a frown marring his perfect features. He shoved his hands in the pockets of his trousers. 'I should have told you.'

'About what?'

His shoulders rose and fell with a slow breath. 'Atlas owes money to your father's bank. Hector let the payments fall behind. Our marriage prevented your father calling in the debt.'

A terrible chill ran through her. Her father's ruthlessness in business was renowned. He would have used the situation to his every advantage. Christo had said in the beginning that he needed her. She hadn't realised how badly.

'How did this happen?'

Christo's jaw clenched hard. The party carried on around them. Champagne flowed. Such a celebration. And yet there was nothing to celebrate at all.

'My father should have learned. But, no. On a quest for the love of a woman he looked in the wrong place. *Again*.'

'Where was your mother?'

'Long gone. With a flamenco dancer, I believe.' He gave a mirthless laugh. 'My birth was a cunningly laid trap to secure my father's fortune, since he wouldn't have any *bastardos* walking the streets. They married, I was born, it ended—although they never divorced. She came back occasionally, when his purse strings were pulled too tight. He adored her, despite everything. I suspect he still does. But love makes fools of men.'

Thea knew now why Christo didn't believe in love. What kind of example had either of them been set? Both had been trapped in broken, hateful families.

'I'm sorry.'

Christo shook his head, his mouth twisted in a sneer of disgust. 'Hector always sought replacements to fill the hole my mother left. It was as if his only son didn't matter. He became involved with an antiquities dealer. Beautiful, exotic. He threw away a fortune on priceless treasures for her. The business suffered as my father ignored it. That's why he had to go begging to your father—to hide his humiliation. I found out too late.'

He looked around the room, hard lines of rage bracketing his mouth. 'Then I discovered some of the objects he'd purchased had been illegally obtained. I suspect from shipments of looted items. That alone could have ruined us. I'd like to believe my father didn't know, but the fool would have done anything for the alluring Miss Carvallo.'

Thea's heart rate spiked. She knew that name. 'Ramona Carvallo?'

Christo's eyes narrowed. 'Yes.'

'I think I've met her—at my father's home.'

He reached up his hand, sliding it through her hair to cup the back of her neck. His thumb traced a gentle line along her jaw, forcing her to look at him. Deep into the green storm of his eyes. He moved his head towards her, leaned down, his lips to her ear. And Thea's eyes drifted shut at the light brush of his warm breath on her skin.

'Look over my shoulder at the woman in the corner of the room. Purple dress. Do you recognise her?'

Thea didn't want to wake from this dream where they meant something to each other. She relished the intimacy even if its purpose was serious. Still, she did as he asked.

When her eyes focused, she saw her. 'Ramona Carvallo,' she whispered.

Christo's lips began drifting a fiery path down her neck. She sighed and melted into the heat of him. What they were doing might be hiding the true purpose of this conversation, but she craved every inch of his body melded against hers.

'Why invite her here?' she asked. Having this woman in his home might only inflame the very scandal he was trying to avoid.

Christo pulled back, his pupils dark, his breathing heavy. Matching hers. She regretted the broken intimacy.

'Raul's organising security,' he said. 'His operatives are in the crowd...watching.'

'What for?'

'Your father used information about the smuggled objects as leverage against my father—the risk of disgrace, jail... I wondered how your father had found out about them. I suspect Tito and Ramona were working together. I want to see if your father reacts to her. People make mistakes. Especially arrogant, entitled people. I'm relying on it happening here.'

'And if it doesn't?'

'Then it won't change anything you and I have agreed.'

That was the least of her worries. She realised now the

reason why he'd been working those long hours. The parties, the meetings…what he'd required of her. He wasn't only inheriting the company. He was saving it.

'I also hope to find out whether your father purchased anything questionable.'

'So you can use it against him like he did to Hector?'

'To stop him stealing Atlas? Yes.'

Could her father have bought illegal objects to add to his collection? Whilst she wasn't aware he'd ever actually broken the law, she wouldn't put it past him. He believed himself to be above everyone else. And after all he'd done to her she'd give anything to stop her father taking what wasn't his.

'He owns a vast collection of old things,' she said.

Heat flared in Christo's eyes. She wished it was for her, but she knew it was for the hope he'd described. Still, there was more she needed to tell him. The information her father had requested took on more significance now.

'There's something else,' she said. 'He demanded I get him information about Atlas. Shipping details. Ports of docking and unloading. Names of the captains on each vessel's journey.'

'Interesting…' Christo said.

It was. Most of those details were publicly available. She'd only investigated out of curiosity. Her father didn't need her to find out anything. A shipping broker could have done the job as easily.

'And did you give your father the information?'

Christo's voice was cool, his face impassive. He didn't trust her, even after what she'd divulged. A pang of hurt scored her insides.

'Never! That's why they said Alexis stole money. To ensure my compliance.' Her voice cracked.

Christo wrapped his arms around her again, drawing her tight to him. 'Thea. I'm sorry. Raul will find him.'

Unless her father got to Alexis first.

She slumped into Christo, exhaustion washing over her.

The night was going to be long, and all she wanted was to stay like this for ever. In Christo's arms. Where, for once, everything felt natural and right. But there was no 'for ever' for them—only now. And if that was all she had she'd take it. Because this wasn't Christo's fault—or hers. They were both pawns in a rich man's game.

And as she nestled into Christo's chest, soaking up the heat into her frozen heart, she knew. The blackmail… This marriage… It wasn't about a debt. Her father wanted Christo's ships.

CHAPTER TEN

HE'D FAILED. NOT on all measures tonight. But on the most important his failure had been acute—because he'd failed Thea.

Christo dropped his head, stared at the floor. A piece of lint was attached to his shoe. He kicked off the polished black leather. Tore at his bow tie and tossed it on the couch. The taint of bile rose in his throat.

His presumptions tonight disgusted him. What had he been thinking? He'd dared Thea to wear that dress. To show everyone the woman he saw each day. Show her magnificence. Show she was a force of nature, alive and powerful in a flash of arterial red.

She'd cut every man off at the knees when she'd walked into the room. His baser parts had brimmed with pride at having her by his side as she'd threaded her arm through his. Yet he'd brought the enemy into his home. Drawn her father and brother to her and hadn't been there to stop them.

It haunted him. Her standing there, surrounded. Demetri clasping her arm in that brutal grip. Volcanic heat clawed his gut. He flexed his fingers. How dared *anyone* lay their hands on her? After all she'd confessed, the least she was due was his protection and he couldn't even give her that properly.

He unbuttoned his shirt. Shrugged it off. Poured a cognac. He'd let another burn, that of the amber liquid, scorch away the guilt.

The celebrations had been a success. He'd done his duty by Atlas. Raul could assess the rest. Demetri and Tito's arrogance had overcome their good sense. It showed they could be caught out if watched closely enough.

He gulped from the glass, downing the contents in one mouthful. He'd try to sleep—a futile activity since Thea had entered his house. He'd wake to visions of smooth skin and breathless sighs as he immersed himself in a soft, warm body. The dreams were fevered, formless things, but he knew who he was with. Who shared with him the pleasure they unleashed. Thea. Always Thea.

He had no right to her. But the feel of her supple body in his arms tonight, her head on his chest as she melted into him...

Even as he'd been soothing her he'd been craving her. The only one he desired. Of all the women who'd sought him out over the years, he coveted the one who didn't want him. The relentless hunger of it ached inside him.

You're married to her.

No! He had to shut out that voice, whispering the impossible. Her trust had been betrayed by too many. He still had some honour left. A thin shred, which frayed a little more every time she came near, but he'd protect it. Try to stitch it up with more resolve than he'd ever shown in the past when he'd seen something he wanted to reach out and take.

She'd leave this marriage untouched. This constant ache was his penance for every selfish deed of his past. He *would* be better. For her.

A tentative knock sounded at the door. It opened a crack and the soft music of her voice filled the space. 'I want to thank you.'

His heart plummeted as Thea drifted into the room, still dressed in the glittering gown he'd chosen. The soft lace accentuated her hypnotic curves. His goddess. A dream that couldn't be. Thea had loaned him her life just for a short while. She wasn't his to keep.

Yet seductive whispers of *Kiss her...* filled his head. He shut them down.

'You've nothing to thank me for.' The words were ground out like broken glass, cutting with each utterance. He did want her thanks. He wanted it all.

'You stood up for me.'

Her eyes gleamed bright in the soft lamplight. His desire to comfort her overwhelmed him. To wrap her up tight and stroke away her pain. All dangerous ideas designed to get her into his arms again.

'It was no more than anyone would have done,' he said.

She shook her head. 'You know that's not true.'

He noticed the marks on her skin from Demetri's rough fingers. She'd bruise. Cold, dark certainty chilled through his veins. He'd break the man who had done that to her.

He took a step forward. Stopped. 'Your arm—'

She shrugged it off. 'I've had worse.'

Her acceptance crushed him. The things she'd endured... 'You're safe now. Your father and brother will *never* hurt you again.'

She looked up at him with warm amber eyes. The fire from them beat any drink in a glass.

'I know.'

She'd invaded his senses. He wanted to immerse himself in her scent of sweet spice. *Touch her...* Touch those red marks on her arm.

He reached out and stroked them. Her skin was smooth silk under his fingertips. Her pupils dilated and she blinked, long and slow. Her lashes feathered her cheek. A lick of heat curled deep inside him and clenched tight.

'I trust you, Christo.'

Her voice brushed feather-soft against his skin. *Take her...* He'd sweep her into his arms. Ravish her plush scarlet lips. Replace pain with gasping pleasure.

Christo glimpsed her reflection in the mirror behind them. That sinuous flock of birds soared across her spine. He would never forget that one of those birds had been tattooed there for him. He was required to atone for it.

'You shouldn't,' he said, though still every part of him yearned to protect her. For ever.

He removed his hand from the warmth of her and

clenched his fists by his sides. Relegated himself to a life of cold. 'I do what advantages me and no one else.'

Was she cold too? Goose bumps bloomed on her arms. Her lips parted. Her eyes were alight, blazing and fierce. The silence stretched the space between them till every part of him screamed to fill it. Her thoughts were so loud he could almost hear them.

I see through you.

To the child he'd once been. Unloved. Unlovable.

She cocked her head. 'Who's the liar now?'

Aching hunger gripped his gut. He couldn't give her what she deserved. *Love.* It wasn't an emotion he felt and she needed someone to cherish her. She contained too much life and passion to be kept by a man like him.

Yet how he longed to release it all. To scorch himself clean. He abhorred any man who'd seen her before. He wanted to be her past, present and future. It was a cruel, impossible desire.

She had her past. He'd seen snatches of it from the file Raul had created. Grainy pictures and the hidden treasure she'd permitted him to glimpse. Though no matter how deeply he delved he'd never unwrap all of her, wound in mystery as she was.

'It's a warning. One you should heed.'

He should send her away, safe to her room. Drink some more and drown out the dreams which lured him to purgatory each night.

'Goodnight, Thea.'

He was close to her now. How they'd moved together he couldn't tell. Were they his steps or hers?

She reached up, hesitated. Her slender hand hovered in the space between them. Then her eyes dropped to his mouth and she touched him. A tentative brush on his jaw. The burn of anticipation for things he'd never take roared through him. If he stood there, unmoving, she'd stop. He'd allow her this faltering exploration. Succumb to weakness and accept her soft caresses. It was all he could ever allow himself.

She traced his bottom lip, and the sting of pleasure rippled through him as her searching fingers trapped his gusting breaths. Her gaze followed everywhere she touched. Like his throat, where she hesitated on the pulse of his heart slamming into his ribs. Her lips tilted. Then cool fingers on heated flesh traced the muscles of his chest, as if the wonders of the universe were written in Braille on his skin. The merest brush over his nipple made his breath hitch.

His eyes drifted shut, trying to lock her out. Still her hand explored every ridge of his abdomen, till he was on fire. An inferno threatened to devour him.

He snapped his hand over hers. 'Stop.'

Every part of him screamed for her to go on. He'd never craved anything more. Atlas Shipping? He'd sign it all away for her fingers to continue their cartography of his body. But she wasn't his. He wouldn't take her.

He opened his eyes. Hers were heavy-lidded, with a sultry golden glow. She stepped back, slid her hand from under his. Broke their touch. The loss of her was immediate and brutal. But a quiet, knowing smile tilted the corners of her mouth.

Thea reached around and drew down the tiny zipper at the back of her dress. Christo watched the mirror behind her, as if in slow motion. Each notch of the zip punched another hit of lust into his gut. She tugged at the bow holding the halter neck and shrugged the dress free. Red lace slithered over her body, caressing each curve as it fell. She stood there. Bare except for the glittering heels and the tiny scrap of a G-string covering the apex of her thighs. The dress swirled at her feet, the colour of blood.

That should be his blood on the floor. His sacrifice to this goddess, all honeyed skin and slender waist and perfect breasts, her nipples taut and ripe. Ready for him.

'Thea…' His voice rasped, unrecognisable. A plea? A

prayer of thanks? He couldn't tell. He wanted all she was offering. Wanted to consume her. But he'd leave nothing behind if he had his way.

'Please, Christo…'

He shook his head, trembling with the effort of ignoring the desire raging through him. 'Not for me.'

'You're worth it.'

He wasn't. But those words… They broke him.

He strode forward. Wrapped his arms around her and grasped the smooth, warm flesh under his hands. Her skin was warm satin against his palms. She melted into him. Sighed as he took her lips with his. His tongue plundered her luscious mouth. She was tentative at first, before softening into the rhythm, willing and hungry.

She lifted her hands to his hair and he shivered at the scrape of her fingernails against his scalp. He slipped his hands to her buttocks, round and bare, holding her against his hard, aching body.

She ground against him, mewling and desperate. If he didn't get her to the bed soon they'd both finish here. He hooked his fingers into her flimsy underwear, slid it past her hips and let it fall to the floor. He battled with the fly of his trousers and cast them aside with his briefs. Thank God he was only half dressed, so he wouldn't have to waste more time. He was a wreck of desire.

He swept Thea into his arms and lowered her onto the bed. She scrambled back against the pillows, her body splayed out like an offering. Waiting. He slid a hand along the smooth swell of her calf. She dropped her head back and moaned. He eased off one stiletto, and then the other, all the while indulging in a visual feast of her golden skin and luxurious curves. Glowing, wanton and perfect.

'I'm coming for you, Thea.'

She shivered as he crawled over the top of her, his vision fogged by the red roar of arousal. Her dusky pink nipples peaked in hard points. He bent down and lavished one with the attention of his tongue. Her low cries of pleasure pierced the room. She smelled of spices and musk. Exotic. Delectable. Driving him on. Driving him to madness.

He was so hard he'd shatter before long. And Thea's body trembled at each touch. He needed her warm softness to envelop him. His mouth watered at the thought of the night ahead. Devouring her body. Pleasuring her till dawn. Taking the pleasure he'd denied himself. Now she was *his*.

He lay next to her, sliding his hand down her stomach, easing his fingers into the dark triangle of hair at the apex of her thighs, exploring the hot, plush folds of her. She arched into him as he stroked her there. He wanted to watch her fall apart, but that would be the end of him. She was everything. Too much. Like a dream he'd awoken into.

He rolled away. Grappled with protection. If he let her touch him he'd explode. He moved over her again. Settled between trembling thighs which had fallen open for him. He was beyond sanity, almost beyond all control. And then that thinnest of threads snapped. She was here. She was ready. *Thea*.

In one fluid movement he thrust hard and took what was his. And as he buried himself in the heart of her body he realised he'd made a terrible mistake.

Too fast. Too much. Too *everything*. The fire consumed her, deep inside. And Christo above her. Still, silent apart from his ragged breaths. She was trying not to breathe. Not to move. If she didn't, it might not hurt.

Was it meant to be like this? She'd had orgasms before, on her own. They were fun, and she'd assumed with someone else it would be even better.

But tonight? All the pleasure, and then…

She stiffened.

Christo dropped his forehead to hers. His strong, muscular arms bracketed the sides of her head, his heavy weight pressing her down.

'You should have told me.'

His voice was gentle. Kind. Her humiliation, complete.

'It didn't seem important.'

Virginity wasn't, was it? An outdated notion, she'd always thought. Till now.

His muscles quivered. Was it hard for him to hold himself like that? She wasn't sure. He'd been so hungry. Passionate. *Aroused.* Though she hadn't really anything to go by, when he'd said he was coming for her she'd almost burst into flames. And then as he'd crawled towards her, wild and wanting...

The size of him. For a moment passion had fled and fear had invaded, leaching in like poison. Then he'd plunged into her, and now they were here.

'It's everything, Thea.'

His breath brushed her cheek. He tried to move—a slight shift as if to gently withdraw. Her hands that had been bunching the sheets in tight fingers now grabbed his hips to still him.

'No. It's done.'

She wanted him, craved to give him all of herself. How could this have gone so wrong?

'That doesn't give me much comfort.'

His laugh was mirthless. Pained. Though her own pain seemed to be dulling. Maybe she was getting used to him. The burn felt different now—less fire more insistence. A sensation she couldn't place.

She moved her hands to his arms and stroked his taut biceps. Her each inhalation was a mere sip of air. What had started out as a grand seduction, had turned into a disaster.

Christo leaned down and brushed his lips over hers. 'You said you trusted me. Do you still trust me, Thea?'

She nodded. Because she did. Implicitly. She knew he'd never intended what had happened tonight.

'You need to breathe,' he said. 'Slowly.'

She looked into his eyes, green pools of swirling emotion.

'Relax. I know what I'm doing.'

She breathed and he withdrew. The relief was exquisite, but a terrible feeling of loss remained. She didn't understand it at all.

He cradled her in his arms. 'I've disappointed you,' she said, her voice cracking.

'No.' He held her close against his chest. All the while running his hand over her quaking body. 'You've honoured me.'

He kissed the side of her neck, feather-light. Goose bumps flowered from every touch of his lips, shivering over her. He continued to stroke her everywhere his gentle fingers could reach. Smoothing out the tense muscles till she relaxed.

He whispered into her ear. 'In this bed there's only pleasure. I promise.' Heat flashed over her, a new burn replacing the old. That confusing ache between her legs remained. Grew. She wanted him again—but how could that be?

He kissed her. His lips soft and gentle. Exploring slowly, waiting for her. She kissed him back. Every sweep of his tongue encouraged her to drown in the pleasure of his mouth. His hands drifted over her skin, stroking her nipples with the pad of his thumb till they were tight and all too sensitive. She wanted his tongue on them again. That sharp spike of pleasure spearing straight to her core.

As if reading her mind, he took her left nipple into his mouth, lavishing it with attention as his hand slipped between her legs.

Her stomach clenched with fear, but he soothed it away with his gentle insistent touch, coaxing her. The fire took hold, deep and low. He stroked, finding the perfect spot. There. *There.* The spark arced between her nipple and the juncture of her thighs. Pleasure. Pain. Beyond comprehension.

He slid one finger deep inside. Withdrew it. Then two. She gasped. The air was thick and hard to breathe. He kept moving, in a slow, hypnotic rhythm. Oh, this… *This* was how it was meant to be. All-consuming.

The rhythm inside her was mirrored by his tongue at her nipple. He moved his thumb to the sensitive nerves between her legs. A light circling and the heat bloomed in a rush from her centre, roaring outwards. There was nothing but the feel of him. Lips, tongue, fingers. The wet slickness of her.

She needed him inside her again. Was desperate for him to fill her. He didn't, just continued the relentless rhythm.

'Christo…'

His name undid her. She screamed it to the room, and then she flew. Gripped him hard as wave after wave of perfection flooded over her. Her mind soared and her body followed. Convulsing. Gasping. Out of control. True freedom.

The spasms subsided. He withdrew his hand. Every part of her was shimmering with pleasure as he lay over her again and eased into her body. Gently. With reverence. She sighed. There was no pain. Only relief.

She placed her hands on his buttocks. Gripped him as the muscles tensed with each thrust. She understood desire now. Understood why it could drive a person mad.

Christo. Inside her. Close. Perfect. Elemental.

The pressure built again as she rode with him, two bodies in unison. Each thrust plunged him deeper and deeper into the soul of her. Into the sticky, sweet mess of it. And this time it was less sharp, but no less devastating. A long, blissful ache that built and built till her control shattered right along with his.

He moaned her name. Pained? Pleasured? She wasn't sure. And then she let herself be swept away on the tide of it again.

CHAPTER ELEVEN

CHRISTO SLID INTO consciousness as the hazy veil of slumber lifted, to find his body curled around a luscious female form. The sun had barely begun to rise. Faint birdsong twittered in the garden. The room lay dusky and still, apart from her steady breaths.

Thea...

He buried his face in the warm silk of her hair. The honey-eyed smell of her wrapped seductively around him. Every part of him ached to ease into her warm, soft body again.

He wouldn't wake her. But the need clutched at his throat and threatened to cut off his breath. He had no rights here. He shouldn't have touched her. Even worse, he'd taken her virginity. The guilt of it scraped inside him.

He'd been fooled by those photographs in Raul's dossier. She'd been right from the beginning. He was no better than the rest of them. He'd seen only what he'd wanted to and taken selfishly. No matter how much she claimed to desire him, he'd used her in the crudest fashion.

It made him sick to his gut. Even though his body screamed for her, rigid with desire.

They were married. He could take her and what would it matter?

But it did. He'd said he'd protect her. From her father and brother, sure. But from himself too. He was just another man wanting to use her for his own aims. No matter how he tried to dress it up in some cloak of honour.

He dragged his reluctant body away from hers, putting some space between them. She stirred, sighed and sank back into the pillows. He watched her sleep. Stared at the dip and curve of her waist. The flare of her hip. Her hair like spilled coffee on the pillow.

Then there were the tattoos. When he'd first seen them, in his arrogance he'd thought they marred her. Not now. He reached out, his hand tracing the serpentine flock that swooped across her spine, each one a tribute to her strength in the face of deprivation.

He stroked his finger across the last bird. *His*. Acid burned his throat. His mark on her. He could never forget.

Thea stretched, lean limbs tightening. Then she turned, her eyes heavy with sleep. A soft smile played on her plush, plum-coloured mouth. She looked wanton. Well kissed.

He bunched his hands by his sides, but there was no hiding the arousal which had plagued him since he'd woken. Her eyes flicked to it, and back to him. She licked her lips. He had to do something—because he wasn't going to take any more from her. Even if she thought she wanted to give it freely.

'When are you going to add another bird?' His voice was rough with lust. He cleared his throat.

Her brows knitted. Confusion flitted over her face. 'Why would I do that?'

'I hurt you.'

The simple truth. One she couldn't deny.

Thea put her hand to his cheek. It rested there. Soft and cool against his burning skin.

'You gave me wings.'

She'd misunderstood him. He'd taken from her. Taken something he'd had no right to.

'You were in pain.'

Her thumb stroked gently back and forth across his cheek. Her eyes locked onto his, dark and serious.

'A few nerves. It was nothing.'

He took her hand in his and squeezed. 'I've marked you. Worse than your brother. Worse than your father.'

She sat up, filling his vision with her unique glow. Her hair tumbled over her shoulders to skim her rosy pink nipples. He wanted to drag her down, let her light spill into him. Flood the dark corners of his soul.

'No, Christo.' Her eyes were wide with horror. 'Never compare yourself to them. It was perfect.'

He should turn away, but the view of her luscious body filled him. His gaze raked over her. She looked down at him, grasped the sheet in front of her and dragged it to her chest. Her cheeks flushed. That picture of innocence made her look even more beautiful, and it was a reminder.

'Your virginity isn't something you should have given me. Anyone else—'

'I've never met anyone I thought worthy.'

Her words sliced through him. Her eyes were wide and soulful. They tore at his heart.

'You're worthy of me,' she whispered.

How could he tell her he was not that person?

He wasn't good enough. Not even his parents wanted him. But he craved to be a better man—one who'd never hurt her.

That bereft, lost look in her eyes haunted him. Christo hauled her close and she fell into his arms. He threaded his hands through her hair, dropping his lips to hers. He lost himself in her sweet intoxication. He couldn't give her much, but he could give her this.

He rolled away from her and she whimpered in protest, smiling as he returned, sheathed, protected and ready. He eased her leg over his hip, bringing her close. She arched towards him. He was hard. Desperate to be inside her. Each breathy sigh pleaded with him to thrust into her body. But he held back. There'd be no clumsy attempt this morning. He wanted it slow and aching. So he could watch her tremble and fall apart as he filled her with consuming pleasure.

He reached his hands around to her perfect buttocks, drawing her close. She sighed as her eyes drifted shut. He slid his hands between her legs, teasing between her thighs till she begged—'Please...'—and he slid one finger inside. Another circled her clitoris till she trembled in his arms.

She lifted her head and looked at him. Eyes glassy,

breaths short and panting. He angled his hips towards her and entered her with a slow slide that almost undid him. She moaned—a deep, satisfying thing that punched low and hard. He kept his hand between them, teasing as he pulled her leg higher over his hip and maintained the aching rhythm between her thighs.

He looked into her glazed, desire-drugged face. He wanted her. More than life. The curl of need at his every move into her body twisted tight and threatened to snap him. He was close. So close. But he'd ensure her pleasure first. Her nipples had tightened and her breathing had become ragged. Every part of her was taut, as if she were hanging by a gossamer thread. Like she needed permission to let go.

'Come for me, Thea.'

A final thrust and she gasped, as if starved for air. He lost all restraint as Thea threw her head back and sobbed out his name like some prayer to the heavens. Then the brittle seam holding him together ripped wide and he tore apart with her.

They lay for a while, his forehead against hers. Their panting breaths filled the room. Then he scooped her into his arms, showering her with soft kisses. He made a silent promise. He'd keep Thea safe for as long as he had her.

She raised her head. Her eyes were unfocused, her mouth red and soft.

'Christo…?'

She wanted answers he couldn't give.

He stroked a tendril of damp hair from her cheek. The birds outside sang louder now, but the dawn hadn't broken fully. They had a few more hours to rest. A few more hours and then she'd leave his bed and he must never do this again. How could he, when he had nothing to offer her? Until then he had time to revel in her touch.

The grief of how little was left stabbed at the heart of him. He cradled her to his chest. 'Sleep, *koukla mou*.' He closed his eyes as she softened in his arms.

CHAPTER TWELVE

'I'LL BE GONE a week—perhaps more.'

And so he'd left her. Alone.

Thea had offered to travel with him, but Christo had refused. For the few days before he'd left there'd been no breakfasts together. Even at night he'd turned her away. Said there was no longer any need for the charade, that everyone accepted their marriage as a proper one.

The rejection twisted her inside, but it didn't quell her desire. Nothing doused the fever he'd awakened. She dreamed of hard, entwined bodies, only to wake exhausted. Filled her days with thoughts only of him.

What had he done to her? This was like some illness. She couldn't escape the memory of pleasure, of the fire he'd lit. It consumed her.

Thea wanted more. Much more. She understood their arrangement, but surely both of them could be adults and enjoy the time they had together?

It will burn you to ashes.

She didn't care. The only thing that would soothe her was Christo. His body was like cool water on the flames.

'When are you going to add another bird?'

Such a strange thing to say. Surely he couldn't believe he'd hurt her after she'd cried out his name and lain sated in his arms? But he did—she was convinced of it. The way he'd avoided her before he left... Treated her with such care and reverence... Arranged full use of his yacht, warning the staff on his island that she may come...

But all she wanted to do was follow him around the world. Surprise him with some of the more exotic lingerie she still hadn't worn.

He wouldn't be able to resist. Because she had seen the

fire in him too. The hazel eyes which darkened to jade whenever she was near. The kiss goodbye that had pretended to be a chaste brush on the cheek but had ended in his low groan. Still he had denied himself.

And yet she recognised that Christo was gripped by some strange sense of honour. She had to prove to him that she understood.

Sure, Christo had promised he would soon have enough information about her father's illegal activities. Inviting him and her brother to the party had been a success. But she needed to repay Christo for the care he'd shown her, no matter what he said.

Which was why she was taking a risk.

She'd come up with a plan to go to her former home and look for more proof of her father's link with Ramona Carvallo. The problem was, she didn't know what to look for. All she could be certain of was that the house held answers, somewhere.

A dark shiver ran through her at the thought of crossing that threshold again, but she ignored it. She had to be strong for Christo. It was the only way.

Thea walked to the front of the house, where Sergei waited with the car. She slid into the back seat, her heart pounding in a sickening rhythm.

There was no need for fear. Her father wouldn't be there—she'd checked. And the staff still had some loyalty to her. She'd been the one to buy them Christmas gifts and to care when their children were ill. In turn they'd cared for her as her father never had. Tito Lambros might pay them, but they didn't like him.

Still, she needed a ruse in case he returned unexpectedly. It was a slim prospect, but she wanted to protect the people who'd been her only real family in that house as much as she protected herself. Everyone would believe her if she said she was looking for the necklace her mother had given her. She unclasped it from around her neck and dropped it into the pocket of her handbag.

The drive wasn't a long one, but as Sergei pulled up at the golden gates and high white walls she was reminded how much she loathed the crass opulence of the place.

'I'll get out here. Wait for me around the corner in the side street. You'll see a small wooden door.'

Sergei narrowed his eyes. 'Are you sure, Mrs Callas?'

No, she wasn't sure about this. The old, dark fears had begun to cloud her vision, chatter in her head. But she looked Sergei straight in the eye.

'Yes. I won't be long.'

She got out of the car. The heat of the day assaulted her, threatening to choke the air from her lungs. Thea pressed the buzzer and the gate opened. She stopped, took a deep breath and walked through, up the long, sloping drive. Each footfall took her closer to the house which held all her grief and tears.

When her mother had left, her world ended. Her father knew judges, lawyers. He'd fought to keep Thea not because he loved her, but because he'd wanted revenge. And still Maria had made her way back. Through the side door where Sergei now waited. Secreted in the servants' quarters so they could snatch a few minutes of happiness before she had to leave again.

Demetri had been lost even then. And one day her mother had become lost to her as well.

She forced away the memories as she made her way to the massive doors of the house. They cracked open as she arrived, and she was welcomed like a lost child. A few of the older staff remembered her mother's death. She'd never forgotten their kindness that had made the harsh, cruel days a little softer.

They ushered her inside. No, she wouldn't take coffee today, she said. She was only looking for her mother's necklace, which she thought she'd tucked away safely in her room. Yes, it was a shame her father wasn't here to see her. They all nodded, as if they understood. Though none of them could know the true extent of her suffering here.

Thea hurried up the stairs, her stomach cramping as she moved deeper into the house. Her nerves eased a little as she went into her room to fulfil the story she'd concocted. This space had been her one place of respite in the whole home, but still it oppressed her.

She fingered the necklace in her bag for reassurance. There was no time to dwell on the past. She had to move quickly to get out of this place.

Thea opened a few drawers and cupboards, to ensure the room looked searched, then set off down the hall for her father's study. On the way she passed Demetri's suite. The door was closed, but still a wave of nausea crippled her.

She stopped and leaned on the wall for a moment, regaining her composure. She was safe. He didn't live here anymore. But the memories had never left. The hair-pulling and tripping as a child, which had escalated to far worse. Her father never caring.

She swallowed and kept walking. She reached her father's study and slipped into the room. During those times he'd cut her off from the world she'd managed to sneak in and access the computer here. A poorly guarded thing, because her father thought himself impenetrable. She'd never looked for anything incriminating, only interested in getting messages to Elena and having some meagre contact with the outside world, but she felt sure there was something here that would help Christo.

Thea wiped clammy palms on her dress. She sat in the hard leather chair and fished a USB from her handbag. Switching on the computer, she waited until the lock screen appeared, asking for the password. Her father rarely changed it. When he did, in all his arrogance, he made it the name of his latest acquisition.

Her fingers trembled on the keyboard as she tried the last password—the name of his yacht, *Siren*. It failed. What

could it be now? She took a few breaths to steady herself.
There was time. His new mistress Athena? That might be
it. Nothing. The date of her wedding? No. Her heartbeat
spiked in panic. Atlas Shipping? Because she was sure her
father coveted that too.

Nothing worked.

She pressed her palms to her eyes. She'd failed. Failed
Christo. The realisation sat like a leaden weight in her stomach. What to do now?

She looked up, feeling small and ill. Like the little girl her
father and Demetri had tried to defeat. Well, they wouldn't
beat her. She cast her eyes around the room. Looked at all
the treasures—those old, mouldering things Tito loved more
than his living, breathing daughter. A new statue stood in
the corner. Some bronzed sculpture of a Hindu god. She'd
never seen it before. What if it hadn't been honestly purchased?

Thea shut down the computer, grabbed her phone from
her bag and took a picture. *Artefacts.* She left the study and
ran from room to room, snapping photographs of antiquities.
It was a long shot, but the house was huge and there were
rooms she hadn't explored since she was a child, many of
them closed off. Now she opened every door, taking pho-
tos of what she could.

Finally she entered a small room she'd never seen before.
It contained a desk and a bank of monitors, showing views
from all areas of the house. A security room. She stared at
the screens as if they might disclose some secrets. Show
her a place she hadn't searched. They all flicked scratchily
between different views except for one. It was fixed on the
front door and drive.

And then she saw it. The sleek black car. A man getting
out. Stopping briefly at the entrance. Looking up at the security camera for a second.

Demetri.

Thea froze. Then she ran.

* * *

Christo bounded up the stairs two at a time. Even in his jet it had been a gruelling flight after his tour of South East Asia's ports. Still, entering through the door of his home he felt seized with a burst of energy. He had news about Alexis.

Christo walked past his suite towards Thea's room, tearing at his tie and jacket on the way. He knocked on the door and opened it before there was any answer. Her scent permeated the air. Spice and honey. His heartbeat accelerated a notch. She hadn't made the space her own. It still looked like the guest suite she'd taken over. Clearly to her it was a temporary residence, one she'd leave soon enough.

He rubbed at the strange burning in his chest. He shouldn't be here. Not after giving the silent promise that he'd never touch her again. Though, to his shame, the horror of hurting her had subsided and his dreams were now plagued with visions of her golden skin and liquid amber eyes.

The memory of her perfume had sustained him through every smog-soaked city he'd visited. And on those lonely nights when he'd lain naked between expensive hotel sheets he'd burned to have her with him, head thrown back, gasping for breath as pleasure overwhelmed her.

He wouldn't act on any of it. But seeing her again—seeing her smile when he gave her the news about her brother— that was all the reward he needed.

Christo stalked downstairs, searching. Thea wasn't by the pool, lazing in the sunshine, showing off the slick honey-bronze skin he'd fantasised about too many times to count. Nor was she in her favourite place, at the table under a gnarled olive tree overhanging one of the more secluded terrace areas.

He'd joked that she hid from him there, and yet more often than not they'd both migrate to the dappled shade and drink coffee, whilst Thea tried to embarrass him in front of the staff with increasingly fanciful untruths.

He laughed—then stopped. Lies. Their whole liaison was built on them.

He looked up at the hazy sky peeking through green-grey leaves. Nothing here was based on truth but her naked body. Their soft, luscious kisses. They spoke of a truth all their own. And the way she'd screamed his name… There had been no lies there.

Something about her absence chastened him. She obviously didn't care when or if he returned. Nothing he wasn't used to. His parents had taught him well to have no expectations of being remembered. And, of course, it wasn't as if he'd left Thea a detailed itinerary. Part of his attempt to remind her that their relationship was a business arrangement.

Although his body didn't feel as if it was all business. He ached for her with a bone-deep hunger. Still, she could have found out about his return if she'd asked the right people. No, he'd clearly been harbouring vain hopes that she might have missed him. A ridiculous notion, and one he needed to overcome immediately.

He walked inside and checked the time. After a quick shower he could be back in his office, since there was nothing to keep him here.

As he walked towards the central stairs and his suite, he saw Anna.

She smiled. 'Mr Callas. Welcome home.'

He nodded as he passed her. 'Thank you.'

She'd probably know where Thea had gone, but it was none of his business. Still, he stopped and turned.

'Do you know where my wife is?'

A casual request. It would have been unusual if he *hadn't* asked. That was all.

'She's gone to her father's.'

Christo stilled. That wasn't a place she'd have travelled to willingly. His gut tightened.

'When?' The word came out sharper than he would have liked.

Anna frowned. 'An hour ago…maybe more?'

Hours? There was no prospect that she'd spend more

than minutes there. Had she been called over? She could be alone with that pig Demetri. Without anyone to protect her.

'Why did she go?'

'She said she had to find—'

'Has anyone heard from her? Or from Sergei?'

Christo tore the phone from his pocket and dialled the bodyguard's number. The phone rang. Nothing. He tried Thea. The same.

He looked back towards Anna. She blushed.

'Have I heard from Sergei? No…'

'From Thea? Please, it's important.'

'No. Nothing…'

Christo raked his hands through his hair, sucked in a steadying breath. He'd go to the Lambros home. Confront them. Get Thea back. If they'd touched her…

He swore.

'I'm leaving.'

Anna nodded. 'I'll call your driver.'

'No.'

He needed speed. As fast as his driver was, he'd take too much interest in Christo's safety. Christo didn't care about himself. All he wanted was to find Thea and bring her home. Protect her, as he'd promised.

'My keys. For the fastest car.'

'I don't know which—'

'Sports car. Black.'

'But all your cars are bl—'

There was no time for this. *'I'll find them.'*

If they'd hurt Thea he'd tear them apart, no matter the consequences. Christo clenched his fists. And if Sergei had allowed it to happen the man would never work again.

He calculated the time. It would take him twenty minutes to reach the house. And ten minutes to raze their world to the ground if they didn't tell him where she was.

His footsteps echoed against the walls. The door to the garage lay ahead.

Voices. He stopped. The door opened. *Thea.*

She walked through, sheathed in an inky black dress with her hair slicked back. Sergei followed her into the hall. His usually impassive face was cracked and worried.

Christo rushed forward, anger breaking like a wave on a reef. 'Did they hurt you?'

She looked up, her face pale and grey as moonlight. He caught her as she slumped into him.

'I need to go upstairs. Shower.'

Her voice was soft and fragile as a moth's wing. Christo swung her into his arms, where she clung. So light...so brittle. Like if he squeezed too hard she'd shatter.

He stalked past the staff, all their faces tinged with concern. The realisation hit him. They cared for her. Deeply. In the time she'd been with him she'd made her mark.

His jaw clenched as a strange thought came over him. This was how it should have been on their wedding night. Sweeping her into his arms. Carrying her upstairs to their room. Making love to her. *Loving* her. It should have been the happiest day of her life rather than what she'd actually had.

The guilt flooded over him, tainting him like a slick of oil. He needed to wash them both clean of it.

Christo carried her into his suite, set her down in the bathroom. A thready pulse flickered at the base of her throat. She stepped out of her shoes as he turned on the shower, scalding hot. Steam fogged the room.

'Why, Thea?'

She looked down at her feet and shook her head. He moved behind her and undid her zip, let the dress fall from her body. He unhooked her bra, slid her underwear down her legs till she stood there naked. He removed the pins from her tight bun and ran his fingers through her hair as it tumbled around her shoulders. He took off his watch, kicked off his shoes. Not caring that he was clothed, Christo walked her under the coursing water and held her close.

She trembled in his arms. Her skin was still cold even with the heat pounding it.

Christo took some soap, slicking it over her back and down her arms. He turned her around, checking for any sign she'd been hurt. She leaned forward, splaying her hands on the wall for support as he kept up his slow exploration.

It could almost have been worship as he knelt at her feet, looking up as the water sluiced down her spine through ribbons of dark hair. The light above shone like a halo over her head. He worked slowly. Massaged the taut, bunched muscles of her calves till they relaxed. Stroked the smooth skin of her thighs until she moaned, soft and long.

The sound punched his gut. Whatever haunted her, he'd wash her clean of it. Then he stood. His trousers were tight, the fine wool shrunken. Moving to her hair, he washed it, his nails scraping her scalp. Her head tipped back, her eyes closed, and mascara running down her cheeks in black streaks. He wiped away the last traces with a flannel.

When he was sure he'd washed off as much of the taint of the day as he could, he cast his ruined clothes aside. Turned off the scalding water and lashed a thick towel around his waist.

Then he grabbed a bathrobe from the back of the door and dressed her in it with care. In the oversized garment she looked tiny, vulnerable. He towelled her hair, swept her into his arms and carried her to the bed. The bed he'd sworn never to take her to again. But she needed him now.

He settled with her on the covers, cradling her as she nestled into him, female perfection in his arms. Her damp hair lay cool against his chest. He held her tight. She had to know she was safe. Here, with him.

And he asked the question again. 'Why did you go to your father's?'

There was nothing for a heartbeat, and then her slender shoulders rose and fell in a heavy sigh.

'I went there for you.'

CHAPTER THIRTEEN

No. *No.* SHE shouldn't have placed herself at risk. Not for him. He'd never have asked, knowing what he did now about her father and brother. To think she'd thrust herself in harm's way—and for what? There was nothing worth the price she might have paid.

'Thea. I'd *never* have asked you.'

'I know. But my father... Demetri. They won't let you go. They said they'd destroy you. I had to do something.'

He tightened his arms around her. In that moment he would have given her anything. Anything she wanted. 'I told you—Raul and I have enough.'

'I knew I could access the house. I thought maybe on the computers... I wanted to give you more.'

Christo tensed. He had strong circumstantial evidence. Enough for the authorities. But irrefutable proof... Surely it wasn't that easy?

'I tried, but couldn't figure out the password. He'd changed it.'

Christo relaxed. Of course. Nothing was ever easy for him. It didn't matter anyway—all he cared about was what had caused the fear he'd had to cleanse from her skin. Because if anyone had hurt her he'd chase them to the gates of Hades and cast them into its pits for eternity.

'What happened?'

'No one was supposed to be there. Then Demetri arrived. I couldn't avoid him.' Her voice cracked. 'I pretended I was looking for my mother's necklace. I'd taken it there. It was in my handbag. I showed it to him.'

He cradled her close. 'Did he believe you?'

'He said that my mother never changed her will. That my

father inherited everything so the necklace was his. Demetri snatched it away and kept it.' She shuddered.

That she'd risked herself for him, tore Christo's heart in two.

'I'll get it back. I promise you.'

She didn't seem to hear him, her voice broken and strained. 'It was worth nothing. A St Christopher medal. My mother gave it to me…said we would be travelling…it would keep us safe. She arranged to take me away one day. I waited in the kitchens by the door. Waited and waited and she didn't come. She was run down by a car in the street near the house. She was coming for me and she died.'

A tight curl of rage twisted in his chest. Demetri would not keep that heirloom from Thea. He had no right to it other than out of a belief driven by his own bitterness and hatred.

Christo began to move, but she held him tight.

'Don't leave me.'

He settled back into the covers. 'I won't.'

Right now, he'd give her whatever she asked. He kissed the top of her head. Her hair was now drying in a tangled mass. He ran his fingers through it to straighten it, easing out the knots. He still had information for her—some measure of happiness he could offer as part of his penance. The news from Raul.

'We've found Alexis.'

Thea stiffened in his arms. Then the sobbing began— heaving gulps with no control. Crying till his chest was soaked with her tears.

'He's been living rough, but Raul has him safe. It's better that you don't know where he is for now.'

'Thank you.'

The sobs subsided to a quiet weeping. He continued combing his fingers through the silken strands of her hair, smoothing them into a coffee-coloured river on his chest.

Trying to soothe the pain their marriage had caused her yet again.

'Raul can take a message to him. No other communication's wise until we deal with these false charges.'

Thea nodded, then spoke, her breath warm against his chest. 'I took pictures.' Her words scraped out, barely a whisper.

'Of what?'

Thea grew heavy against him, her limbs soft and supple. He ached to ease her onto her back. To caress her body till she wept from pleasure, not heartache. But he wouldn't take any more from her. He'd taken enough.

'The old things he loves better than me. The antiquities...'

And as Christo wrapped his arms around her he realised that she might have saved him after all.

A dull ache throbbed at Thea's temples. She'd handed her phone to Christo and told him to go. To download the photographs and send them to Raul. Not that she'd wanted him to leave. What she wanted was to kiss him until his lips and tongue erased the day from her body and soul. But all he'd do was hold her.

She must have slept. The shadows were now long. A golden glow filled the room. She rolled over in bed and saw him. A tall, dark shape in the doorway. She held out her hand. He walked in and took it, kissing her fingertips, the bed dipping as he sat on its edge.

'Did Raul find anything?'

'He'll search the lost antiquities registers. It'll take time.'

Christo brushed a stray lock of hair from her face. She closed her eyes and relished the stroke of his fingertips, her body liquefying at his touch. He was so solid. She felt no fear when he was close. Only a calm, dreamlike stillness. Like a drug to balm her anxious soul.

His finger ran along the edge of the collar of her robe,

following it to where it plunged between her breasts. 'Promise me something, Thea.'

His face was dark and serious. So beautiful. As she'd always imagined the embodiment of a god. Tall. Pure. Perfectly etched lines.

Her breath hitched as the gentle stroke of his fingers started through her hair. 'What?'

'Never take a risk for me again. It's not worth it.'

She touched her hand to the side of his face. It was what he hadn't said that spoke volumes. Christo had never been shown love as a child. He couldn't understand. *He* was worth it.

'Then don't leave me again,' she said.

He smiled, but only with his mouth. His eyes looked soft and sad. Her heart cracked. He continued stroking her. Gentle caresses that drove her to the edge of insanity. Her skin heated and prickled under the robe. An ache throbbed between her thighs. If only his hand would drift lower...trail burning fingertips down her abdomen to stoke the heat between her legs till they both caught fire and burned.

'I've taken enough. I won't have you trading your safety as well.'

She had a kernel of a thought—bright and bold. 'Are you saying you're indebted to me?'

'Yes.'

'Then I want—'

'Anything.'

'Make love to me.'

He stopped, and that was the cruellest torture of all. She'd combust right here if he didn't keep touching her. How could he have such control? Every nerve sang for him. Tight, shimmering and alive with his closeness.

'You said *anything*, Christo.'

The ghost of a smile played on his lips. 'I did.'

He leaned forward, placing his forearms on either side of her head. His nose touched hers, his breath caressing her cheek. He brushed his lips along the shell of her ear. Trailed kisses down her neck. She arched her back, a shiver of anticipation running through her. Her breath was coming in soft pants. Her hands worked at the tie of her robe.

'Patience,' he whispered. 'Lie still.'

She did as he asked. Waited.

The slow slide of his lips on her skin traced her jaw in languid kisses till he reached her mouth. His lips hovered above hers. She moaned. His mouth captured the sound, his tongue plundering as it joined hers in an erotic dance.

She wrapped her arms around his muscular torso, his back flexing and tense. His left hand moved to the tie of her robe and undid the knot in one swift pull, easing the fabric open so cool air washed over her. He cupped the underside of her left breast. Traced his fingers to the nipple which he rolled with exquisite care between his fingers.

An arrow of heat tore through her body, shocking between her legs. He skimmed a hand down her side and her thighs relaxed, moved apart. Inviting him.

'My beautiful wife…' he murmured.

She lay almost naked. He was fully clothed. The brush of his cotton shirt against her sensitive skin. The crisp smell of starch, the soft, smooth wool of his trousers. Her every nerve stood on end in anticipation. She squirmed and gasped and moaned at the suck and swipe of his tongue as he teased each nipple in turn.

'You want something? Hmm?'

The only sound she could utter was one of frustration. It had been over a week since his hands had been on her body. She was plump, ripe, desperate to be devoured.

Christo's tongue traced down her abdomen. He blew on the moist trail. Goose bumps bloomed on her overheated skin. He circled her navel and moved lower, then lower.

Thea held her breath. Waiting. He dipped between her legs, teasing softly. She gasped, almost leaping from the bed. He held her hips still.

'It's all for you.'

He slid his hands under her backside, cupping it, bringing her body to his mouth. His tongue explored with maddening precision. She raked her hands through his hair before gripping tight. Tried to hold him in place whilst the rest of her fought to escape the blinding sensation hitting her like lightning.

It was too much. The insistent stroke of his tongue. The crisp cotton where her legs touched his shirt. The stubble of his chin scratching the soft skin of her inner thigh as he feasted. Her world became the swirl of his tongue. The sparks of bright light flickering and shimmering behind her closed eyes. The noises she made. Breathy sounds, pleading for release as he taunted her with pleasure, taking her higher and higher till she was ready to soar, afraid to leap because it would ruin her.

He stopped for a second. She groaned in protest as a wicked smile played on his decadent lips.

'If I have to spend all night…' his breath toyed between her legs '…you'll come for me.'

She whimpered as a sheen of perspiration misted her skin. Her body trembled in fever and need till he dropped his head.

With one sharp, hard flick of his tongue she flew, screaming his name to the heavens.

'Christo!'

Only Christo.

CHAPTER FOURTEEN

THEA WASN'T SURE how to seduce a man. Particularly when said man was her husband. But if her own orgasms were any measure she was doing spectacularly well. Christo had denied her nothing. Using his body to pleasure her till she trembled and broke again and again, before falling into an exhausted sleep in his arms.

Sure, he'd had orgasms too. But he held something back, focused on her pleasure. She wanted to drive him as mindless as he did her. Crack the control he always seemed to hold on to like a shield.

Oh, he wanted her. Whenever she was near him his eyes coloured to the dark green of a hailstorm. His nostrils flared as she came close, right before he swept her into his arms and took her on another journey to ecstasy. And she could always feel him through his clothes. So hard and ready. But when she tried to take over and give him something with no thought for herself he didn't relent. Only whispering the words, *'It's all for you.'*

Well, tonight it was all for him. She knew a thing or two about control, and this was a battle she'd win.

She looked in the mirror and fluffed her hair till it hung messy and wanton. He liked it long and loose, so he could bury his hands in it as he held her tight for a searing kiss. She shivered. *No.* This was about Christo. His pleasure, not hers.

She smoothed her dress. Black. Fitted. The fabric soft and silky against her curves. She'd decided against a bra. A teardrop gold pendant hung low in her cleavage. She turned to look at the back. Saw the way it hugged her rounded backside. It was her least favourite feature. Though Christo seemed to love it, from the way he'd grab her and draw her close as they kissed.

Thea smiled over her shoulder. She had an idea… She bunched up her dress and shimmied out of her underwear. Nerves fluttered in her belly. *There.* He'd know the minute he touched her. She'd soon see if he could stop himself tonight. He'd lose himself in her. She'd ensure it.

She'd organised a candlelit meal on her favourite terrace. Secluded, peaceful. She reached the beautifully appointed table and took a glass of champagne to quell her nerves. She had no doubt Christo would make her mindless with pleasure, but could she do the same for him?

Best not to think too hard… Simply act. Touch, tease, tempt…

'Thea.'

She whipped around as the sound of his voice caressed down her spine. He tugged his tie through the collar of his shirt, winding it around his hand before tucking it in a pocket. Then he undid the two top buttons. She swallowed, her mouth dry.

'Have some champagne.'

She poured for him. As usual, he feasted on her with his gaze. Scorched her with a head-to-toe appraisal that had her wanting to shed her clothes and bare herself to him.

How could he do this to her? Needing this man had never been part of their arrangement. Yet the ferocity of her desire seemed as natural as breathing.

He took the glass she handed to him and placed it on the tabletop, drew her close. His lips were upon hers before she could think. His tongue explored her mouth greedily as his hands slid over her body. She turned liquid, her core aching.

He pulled back, an eyebrow quirked. 'Nothing under the dress?' He chuckled, a low and throaty sound that wound through her on a fiery journey. *'Koukla mou…'*

She'd taunted him in the past to say those words with feeling. Tonight they were rough and coated with desire. The way she'd dreamed of them being said. And the need in his voice punctuated every syllable.

She slid her arms around his neck and looked into his face. The hunger smouldering there almost cut her off at the knees.

'Have dinner with me,' she said. 'Let me take you to bed. Make love to you.'

'I thought that was what we'd been doing.'

'You know what I mean, Christo. You said you'd give me anything. Now I want to give you something in return.'

He brushed a lock of hair behind her ear and smiled. 'Ah, the demon that's been unleashed. My beautiful temptress. You should've been called Eve.'

'I want you.'

She dropped her hand between them and brushed it across the hard bulge in his groin. His breath hitched.

'I want *this*. One word and you'll have me on my knees, showing you how much.'

'Never kneel for me, Thea.'

Kneel for him? She'd worship him.

'You're worth more than you know.'

He hesitated, a look of something like uncertainty on his face. It was striking in a man she'd once thought was certain of everything.

'I'm not—'

'Shh…'

Thea placed a finger on his lips and stopped him. She wrapped her arms around his neck. He dragged her close and plundered her mouth. Drove her back till she hit the balustrade. His hand went to her left breast, teasing the nipple until it pinched and hardened through the soft fabric of her clothes.

She'd have him here. Now. Out under the stars. She didn't care who could see. She'd never get enough of this man.

He groaned her name. Hitched up the back of her dress and smoothed his large, warm palms over her bare buttocks. Slid a hand between her legs and stroked her.

'Wet. Perfect. Ready for me.'

'Always. *Please.*'

Thea gripped the front of his shirt, crushing the smooth white fabric. If he didn't do something soon she'd combust.

She fumbled with the front of his belt, trying to undo it.

'Protection…' he said.

'No time. Don't care.'

He took a step back and stilled her hands. 'We do have time. You should care.'

He couldn't do this to her again. She wanted to feel him naked against her. Hear him groan and shout her name as he found release, lost control, all because of her.

She stifled a sob. 'I need to be yours.'

Christo bundled her into his arms and whispered fiercely in her ear. 'We'll go to my suite, and I *will* use protection.' His thumbs grazed her nipples and she shivered. 'Then I am going to bend you over and take you so deeply you won't remember where you end and I begin. And you will *never* doubt that tonight you're mine.'

This wasn't going to plan, but she didn't care. Christo didn't believe her words, so she'd show it with her body. In bed, she'd prove how worthy he was.

He took her hand. They began walking towards the house. At the French doors leading inside he looked down at her tenderly. 'Should I carry you?'

Carry her over the threshold? The meaning loomed large. *Yes.*

But before she could answer Sergei rounded the corner with Anna. They stopped.

Christo glared at the interruption. 'What?'

Anna looked at her toes. Sergei merely stared straight ahead. When he spoke, his voice was impassive.

'Mr Callas. It's your father.'

If time could stand still, he'd have chosen hours ago. Out on the terrace with Thea's arms around his neck, her eyes burning into him. The words *'You're worth more than you know...'* on her lips.

But time had stopped here. In a darkened room, with an old man.

Christo sat in a chair by the bed. Wherever he'd gone now, at least his father looked peaceful. That was what the nurse had said. It had been a good death, whatever the hell that meant.

He'd sped here and he'd been too late. A private nurse had sat with him in his final moments. Laid him out. Christo didn't know how he felt about that. It was as if his insides were hollowed out. His skin and bones a mere shell around nothingness.

He stood and walked to the door. The nurse hovered outside. 'Once again, Mr Callas, I'm sorry.'

Christo nodded. 'My father did things in his own way and in his own time.'

'He left me a note to give you. For this moment.' She handed over a white envelope and placed a hand on his arm. 'It was my pleasure to look after him for you.'

She smiled. Patted him and walked away. Leaving Christo alone in the long hallway.

He strode out of the house as if death itself was chasing him. His chest heaved with the need for air. He burst out through the front door and bent at the waist, gasping for breath.

It was over. Time to go and start making arrangements. Try to maintain the lie of his father's legacy.

Christo slid into the car he'd parked at the front of his father's house and drove through the darkened streets. The whole world lay asleep, which was what he wanted to be too. Insensible to everything.

He drove through the gates of his home into the garage, where he sat for a moment. The white envelope taunted him from the passenger seat. He tore it open and read.

Dear Christo,
Now is a time to dwell on the living, not the dead...

There were instructions for the funeral. Who to invite, who to forbid. Advice on the allowance made for his mother, which would keep her in some style, but would not be enough to make either her or her lover happy. There was some talk about his joy at his son's marriage and his hope for grandchildren.

Hope. For a future which wasn't Christo's to have, not knowing how to love. Selfishness was the only lesson taught to him.

He crushed the empty envelope in his hand. Turning over the letter, he read the final page.

I know you won't grieve for me. That I was not much of a father.
I can't change how harshly I treated you, though the past is what made you the man you are now. But of all the hopes and regrets a foolish man has at the end, the one message that stays with me is this:
Never believe you weren't wanted.

What did that mean? He hadn't been wanted by his mother. She'd barely even acknowledged his existence once her future was secure. And as for his father—unloved by the wife who'd craved the money and not the man, searching for love again and again and in the process almost destroying Atlas.

The capacity to love didn't run in his parents' veins. Their blood had been passed to him.

And now he'd tried weaving Thea into his poisoned web of selfishness and subterfuge. He'd effectively held her captive. Then she'd offered to make love to him without protection. She had to know that meant the risk of pregnancy. That if she conceived their child there was no letting her go.

But now the reason to keep her had gone.

He dropped his head to the steering wheel. The gnawing ache of realisation filled him with endless torment.

He didn't know how long he sat there. Only that his muscles were stiff and the world was cold.

A shadow crossed the driver's window and the door cracked open.

'You can't stay here all night.'

Thea's voice was a soft caress on his wounded soul. She took his hand and led him through the darkened house to his room, where she peeled off his clothes, stripping him layer by layer. Then she lay down on his bed. Inviting him to her. Inviting him home.

He fell into her. This woman who gave and gave. But if she stayed too long he would take everything, leaving her a husk.

The leaden weight of the evening crushed him. He couldn't move. Wrapped in comforting arms which smoothed over his body, curling around him as if she was bandaging all the pain, he'd rest a while. Let the beautiful light of her soul illuminate all his dark places.

He still had time. Because just before his darkness extinguished her flame he would let her go.

CHAPTER FIFTEEN

A WEDDING. A FUNERAL. Christo knew what came next but had been putting off the inevitable. The will had been read, his mother's hysterics managed and the estate divided. There was no reason to cling to what couldn't be.

Coward.

He knotted his tie, tightening it like a noose around his neck. As he did so Thea rose from the bed naked and wrapped her body around his, wishing him a good day at work in the best possible way.

He slid his hand into her soft, warm hair. The silken strands held the exotic scent that was all her. He breathed her in. Each morning their ritual was the same. He'd get ready early, in the hope of leaving without seeing her, but something would always draw him back to the bedroom where they now spent every night. She'd ignited a hunger in him that wouldn't be sated.

Thea tipped her head back and smiled. 'Will you be home early tonight?' Her voice was husky, holding the promise of another indulgent evening.

How could he be in the presence of such a woman? This goddess like Aphrodite risen from the ocean? Someone who gave and gave, when all he wanted to do was take?

But he'd made her a promise. One he'd keep.

He had no knowledge of how to love. His parents had seen to that. Obsession? Yes. Sex? For sure. But Thea deserved more. Her youth and her life had been stolen from her by her father, her brother and now him. She deserved to *choose* a man to love—not be sold to the highest bidder for another's benefit. To be free from her cage. To have fun and go out, with her own money and resources.

That was what she'd planned and that was what he'd give

her. No matter how much the thought squeezed his heart till it almost stopped beating.

He dropped his mouth to hers and claimed it. Her lips were soft and drugging and she sighed, opening to him. His tongue slid in to taste her. Pure nectar. As sweet as honey. Her breathy sigh chased away all common sense as her body taunted and tempted him. He returned the kiss as if it was his last day on earth.

She moaned. 'Do you have to go to work at all?'

Yes. Today was his most important day. The day when he'd try to be the man Thea deserved.

She'd thank him. Maybe not now, but in the end.

'I have meetings. Don't wait up for me tonight.'

One more night with her and he might not do what needed to be done.

He pulled Thea in for a last, lingering kiss. The bright glow of her beauty warmed him. When he let her go that light would be gone. Darkness would take over again. It was what he knew, so he'd welcome it like an old friend. They could reacquaint themselves over a bottle of cognac in a lengthy future of lonely nights together.

He called his driver and left for his first and most important destination of the day.

The ostentation of the Lambros Bank's headquarters disgusted him. But it was where the story of Christo and Thea would end. When he'd called for a meeting Tito and Demetri had asked him to come here. No doubt they wanted to impress, to instil fear. It wouldn't work. He feared no one. Especially not these craven men. His only aim was to ensure that by the end of today Thea had everything she deserved.

He strode into the building and punched the lift button for the top floor. Their arrogance was laid out in front of him as the lift doors slid open on the pompous gilt and antiquities adorning the executive suite's foyer. There he sat in a cold leather chair. Waiting as he knew they'd make him.

He didn't care. It gave him a few more moments to cherish the gift of Thea. He twisted the wedding ring on his finger, felt the smooth gold warm under his touch. Still shiny and new. Witness to the privilege of being her husband. Of doing this for her.

'Mr Callas?' An immaculate blonde woman greeted him with a smiling mouth and unsmiling eyes. 'They'll see you now. Sincere apologies for the delay.'

There was nothing sincere about the look on her face. He followed her dismissive gesture through a wooden door into an office of cream marble and garish gold. Tito Lambros sat at a massive desk which looked as if it had been hewn from a solid piece of stone. As cold and hard as the man behind it. Demetri was perched on its front corner like a bird of prey waiting to strike. A large painting hung behind Tito, full of darkness and violence.

Christo raised an eyebrow. 'Jesus casting out the moneylenders. By El Greco, I believe?'

'I didn't know you had an interest in art,' Tito drawled.

Christo cocked his head, his voice full of menace. 'I've acquired an eye for hidden treasures.'

'As indeed this was. Locked away for centuries. A private collector found himself in some difficulty, so I helped. Or rather his sale of the painting to me did.'

'A strange picture for a banker to own...'

'You think? It's an attempt to get rid of us, and yet we're still here. It shows that in the end we always win.' Tito gave a slow and evil smile. 'I see it as a telling reminder to those who want to believe otherwise.'

Christo smiled back. Ah, the fall would be so sweet when it came...

He took a seat, without being invited.

'Once again, I'm sorry about your father,' Tito went on. 'Of course it means Atlas Shipping is now yours. To succeed with or fail. It would be a shame for my daughter if it were the latter.'

His daughter. Even now Tito hadn't relinquished her. That would change soon.

'Thea hasn't anything to fear from me.'

He'd failed her once. He would never fail her again.

He turned to Demetri. 'You took something of hers. A necklace her mother gave her. I want it back.'

'That cheap trinket?' His lips curled into a sneer. 'I misplaced it.'

'Then that carelessness will cost you,' Christo said, his voice sharp and cold as a steel blade.

'My son's only careless with meaningless things,' Tito said. 'Luckily I have it.'

He opened the drawer next to him, pulled out a slim gold chain with a pendant and tossed it across the desk. Christo caught it in one hand.

'But you didn't come for a necklace. Why are you here?'

Now the game would be played—a game he planned to win.

Christo slipped the pendant into his suit pocket and lounged back in his chair. 'You lied. Thea wasn't a willing partner in this marriage. I'm granting her a divorce.'

Demetri pushed himself up from the corner of his father's desk. 'That's not what was agreed. You owe my father.'

'Atlas Shipping owes your father's bank. Personally, I owe him nothing. Except contempt.'

'How dared you? That loan—'

Thea's father lifted two fingers and Demetri was silenced.

'That loan was a noose, designed to throttle me at the appropriate moment,' Christo said. 'But now Atlas's loan repayments are up to date. I rectified that oversight of my father's. And by the end of the week the loan will be repaid in full.'

Tito regarded Christo over steepled fingers. 'Paying back early means penalty interest—which you can't afford. It'll ruin you or take you close.'

Christo smiled blandly. 'You underestimate my abilities.'

'Perhaps… But you can't rectify all your father's mistakes. The antiquity smuggling, for one. If that's disclosed your ruination will be complete.'

Christo grinned. Tito Lambros had no idea how deep a mire he was wading into.

'I was hoping you'd come to that. My father left several letters before he died. One was to his solicitor, documenting what he knew about the stolen treasures he had unwittingly allowed Atlas to transport. Most interesting were his comments about *your* suspected involvement. And then there's your link to a particular ship's captain…'

A man who'd become suspiciously lax about documentation and the cargo that went onto each vessel. That was the information they'd sought from Thea, trying to weave her into their web of deceit. Getting more to blackmail her with when the need arose.

'I've terminated his services, if you're curious. Interpol want to talk to him.'

Tito sat back in his chair, his eyes darting to Demetri. 'Your father's letters won't be believed. They're the words of a dying man, bitterly regretting the errors he made, and trying to blame someone else for his folly.'

And this was where Thea's help had saved him—yet even now she didn't realise how much she'd done.

Christo took a long, slow breath, savouring the moment. 'Perhaps. But the authorities will be interested to see the security footage from that secret room you have in your house. If I sent it to the lost antiquities register what would they find?'

Demetri stared at his father, wide-eyed.

Tito paled.

Christo had them—and he wouldn't rest till they were finished. He stood, leaning forward and splaying his hands on the frigid marble of Tito's desk.

'All those times you locked Thea away, her only contact came from breaking into the computer in your office to speak to her friends. You may have changed your passwords there, but you forgot the passwords on your security system. It was only a matter of my consultants working through the list Thea gave me to find the right one. Apparently the hack isn't complicated if you know how.'

'You're lying.' Tito's voice came out hoarse and raw.

'You want to test that theory?'

The two men said nothing.

Christo smiled. 'Now, let's talk about the penalty interest…'

Two hours later Christo sauntered to his car. He slid into the back seat, took a folder from his briefcase and pulled out a sheaf of documents. Flicking through them, he came to Thea's signature on the back page. He traced a finger over the feminine writing, sitting there with pain embedded in him like a knife as he stared at the blank space where his own signature would go.

'Where to next, Mr Callas?' his driver asked.

He swallowed the agony down. Later he'd dwell. For now, he could never forget that everything he did was for her. All for her.

'To my lawyer's,' he said.

Christo slipped a pen out of the top pocket of his suit jacket. Scrawling his name on the line below Thea's, he did what he had promised all those months ago. He set her free.

CHAPTER SIXTEEN

THEA FINISHED HER morning coffee. Christo hadn't come for breakfast, and last night he hadn't graced their bed. She'd woken that morning to cold sheets where his warm body normally lay and she'd been struck by the realisation that even after one night apart she missed him. Missed his touch, the way it filled her with liquid heat, with something aching, trembling. Out of control.

She didn't know how she'd lived without it. In such a short time he'd become her every waking thought. Her night-time passion. Her secret addiction.

Should she look for him?

Thea knew he and Raul had been working long hours on the meagre information she'd given them. Trying to connect her father to something illegal and free Christo from Tito's clutches. Perhaps that was what he'd been doing last night.

Anyway, this morning there was no time to find him. She and Elena were going out together. Maybe to do some shopping now she could spend something of her own money rather than save for a grand escape. It would be fun for a change, and it was her time for a bit of fun. She hadn't thought about escaping for a long while.

She'd missed Elena desperately, thinking she and her friend would be separated permanently. Now the freedom to do normal things other women of her age did filled Thea with an almost girlish glee. For the first time in her life she felt valued. Cared for as an individual, not as a possession to be traded. Another thing to thank Christo for.

That list was ever increasing.

Thea smiled as she stretched in the morning sun, contemplating the number of ways she would thank her husband. A seductive pulse beat low in her belly...

As pleasant as it was, luxuriating in those thoughts, none of them would get her to Elena any faster. She sighed. Christo would have to wait.

Checking her watch, she made her way through the house, running into Anna.

'Thea—Mr Callas wants to see you. He's in his study.'

Thea grinned and her heart missed a few beats. She almost skipped to his office, not waiting to knock before she pushed the door open and walked in, snicking it shut behind her.

Christo sat at his massive oak desk. He clearly hadn't been home last night. The clothes he wore were the same as yesterday. His usually pristine shirt was crushed and his hair messed, as if he'd run his hand through it too many times. In most men it would look unkempt. In Christo it made him ruggedly handsome.

Thea's breath caught. The man could ignite her with a glance and she didn't care. The walls no longer closed in on her in quiet moments. She wasn't afraid of being trapped. Not anymore.

Christo raised tired eyes to hers. And there was something else she noticed. The lack of heat in them.

Every look he'd cast her way in the past weeks had threatened to singe her to ashes. Today there was nothing but... *devastation.*

Thea's heart pounded. Not even after his father had died had she seen him like this. Something terrible had happened.

'Christo, what's wrong?'

He motioned with his hand. 'Take a seat.'

So cool. Businesslike. It made her nervous.

She dropped into a solid leather chair opposite him. Leaned back. Crossed her legs. Tried to look casual and relaxed when inside she was bound in knots.

'I have to meet Elena soon.'

'This won't take long.'

His Adam's apple rose and fell as he swallowed. Her hands clenched reflexively into tight fists. The cut of her nails into her palms settled her racing heart a fraction.

'Is it about my father? Has Raul found anything?'

Christo shook his head. 'That wasn't a condition of granting what you wanted.'

His voice was so cold it chilled her bones.

He picked up a pen, tapped it on the leather desktop. 'You've fulfilled your obligations. That's all I ever required.'

She didn't understand. None of this made sense. 'What are you talking about?'

It was as if he wasn't looking at her, but at a point over her shoulder. She turned, the leather of her seat creaking under her, but there was no one there.

'Since Hector's gone and the estate's been settled, it's time to talk about bringing our arrangement to an end.'

She jerked back as if he'd slapped her. After what they'd shared... All their nights together... How could he do this now? Surely things had changed. How dared he do this without talking to her first about the future?

'You don't get to say that without looking me in the eyes.' She gritted her teeth. '*Look* at me, Christo.'

He didn't, instead leafing through some papers on his desk.

'How did you think it was going to end, Thea?'

She hadn't thought about an ending in such a long time. Now she understood the truth in her throbbing heart. She didn't know how she wanted it to end, only that she didn't want it to end immediately.

'As for your settlement,' he said, as if he was running through some awful shopping list, 'your investment's grown. That solar start-up in the States paid off. I've added half a million euros to the amount you had in the bank.'

Obviously Christo didn't feel the same way as her. Nothing had changed for him. She couldn't breathe. A tight band had wrapped around her chest.

'Christo. Please.' He was handing her everything she'd ever dreamed of and yet she wanted none of it.

'Ours was only ever a short-term arrangement. You wanted a life. I'm granting it to you. Along with a fully furnished house in Glyfada.'

At the beach? She loved the beach. But it was just another possession. Another *thing*. She wanted to hurl it right back at him.

'Is this what you want?' she asked.

He looked at her now, and all she saw was blankness. Nothing but the cold, dark heart of him. The man from the night of her marriage, from the negotiations with her father. Where was the gentle, passionate person she thought she'd discovered? It was as if he'd never existed.

Christo gave a curt nod. 'I signed the divorce papers yesterday and delivered them to my lawyer. It's done.'

'No!'

'There are no happily-ever-afters here,' he said, lifting the papers he'd been looking through and tapping them on the desktop till they were straight.

He put them in a folder and slid it across to her.

'In addition to those settlements I've negotiated a ten-million-euro payment from your father. You'll be a wealthy woman. Free to do whatever you want. The removal company will come tomorrow to pack your things. I've taken the liberty of delivering your motorcycle to your new home. I'll leave all the necessary keys with Anna. The estate agent will show you around.'

She didn't know this man. The man who stuck a knife in her heart with no remorse. There was nothing left of the husband who'd made love to her till she'd wept from pleasure. This man only caused pain.

'You've been busy.'

He was casting her out. Moving on. Had these past months meant nothing to him?

'You've kept me from the business I have to attend to. You wanted a life. I want my life back.'

The thought of him taking back his life made her ill. Living without her, seeing other women... She swallowed down the saliva flooding her mouth. Swallowed past the tight, choking feeling that crept into her throat, as if the world was trying to throttle her. He'd planned this all along, using her in the process. Well, she wouldn't let him see her humiliation.

'The wedding and engagement rings are yours to keep,' he said.

She looked at the still twinkling gems on her finger. Funny how she'd forgotten they were even there, and yet they were mocking her now. She wrenched them from her hand and tossed them on the leather desktop. Christo watched their trajectory as they bounced and fell in front of him.

'Since I'm not married any more I don't want them,' she hissed. 'Give them to your next bride of convenience.'

He shrugged, then stood and walked out from behind the desk. 'Your father has retracted his complaint against Alexis. He says it was an accounting error. The charges are in the process of being dropped. When that's happened, Raul will give you Alexis's new number.'

She slumped in the chair. At least some good had come from this disaster.

Christo stopped as he reached her. Sliding his hand into his pocket, he placed something carefully on the desktop. Thea saw the gleaming gold of her mother's necklace. She picked it up. The metal was warm from his hand. Tears pricked her eyes, burned her nose as she blinked hard.

She didn't look back as Christo walked away from her, as the door of his office clicked open. She felt his hesitation, heard the scuff of leather soles on carpet.

'Goodbye, Thea.'

The door closed behind him and he was gone from her life for ever.

CHAPTER SEVENTEEN

THEA TOYED WITH her lunch, chasing a rogue olive around the plate. Another meal. Another hour passing in this, the eighty-seventh day since she'd walked from Christo's home with everything and nothing.

Not that she'd been counting since that moment. Not at all. Not since those awful minutes when she'd left his office and a distraught Anna had handed her a bunch of keys and an envelope. No, it was done now.

She sipped at a glass of wine, which could have been vinegar for all she cared. Today her mission was to choose a gown for a function at the American Embassy in a few days' time. She was having fun. It was what she'd always wanted. It should have been perfect. No, it *was* perfect. It was…

'Are you missing Alexis?' Elena sat opposite, her lunch long devoured. She peered at Thea over a pair of oversized sunglasses.

A week earlier Alexis had left for Australia to visit his father. And, yes, she missed him. Their reunion had been full of joy and hugs and tears, and it hadn't been long enough after everything that had happened. Now he was spending six months travelling the world, and when he returned to Greece he was taking up a role in Raul's security company. She suspected that was Christo's doing too…

'*Paidi mou.* You're not happy.'

Wasn't she happy? She had everything she'd ever desired. A house. Wealth. Freedom. And what she *didn't* want—her father's money—she'd put to good use in funding a refuge for women who were escaping family violence. Achieving something worthwhile.

She had a wide circle of acquaintances. Her life was hers to control. All the freedom she'd ever wanted and yet those old fears returned late at night. Of being trapped in a cage. Rattling the bars till cold sweat prickled down her neck. The same fear which once had her clenching her fists till her nails bit into her palms.

Now those fears took her out early, riding her motorcycle in the predawn air. Riding till the sun rose. Pretending she could fly. Always pretending...

Elena reached out and squeezed her hand. 'What happened, Thea?'

Why did she feel so rooted to the ground when she could do anything she wanted?

Thea stared into her empty glass.

Christo.

She'd hated him in those days after she'd left his home. In those lonely days when she'd forgotten the words he'd repeated so often. *'It's all for you.'* Now, everywhere she turned, that was all she heard. His voice, whispering that truth in her ear.

When she'd walked into the exquisite house he'd chosen for her...when she'd waved Alexis away at the airport... when she'd heard the rumour that Demetri had betrayed her father to the authorities to save himself.

Christo had given it all to her. Everything she craved. Almost. But the most important part was missing. Leaving an ache which hadn't eased.

Thea looked up at her friend.

'I fell in love.'

Those simple words freed her. She smiled at the power of her admission. Felt a spark telling her that if she acknowledged that truth, anything was possible.

'I love Christo.'

Elena slapped her thigh. 'I knew it! So what are you going to do about it?'

Thea flopped in her seat. She had no answers. Did Christo love her in return? He'd loved her body—there she had no doubts. As for the rest...she didn't know. Their last conversation had left her questioning everything, hearing the chill in his voice as he froze her out of his life. But his actions… His desolation when he'd let her go…

Because in the end everything he'd done had all been for her. She couldn't sit back ignoring the truth any longer. She loved him. She wanted him. And moping about it was not an acceptable option.

'I've got to go.'

She stood, bumping the table as she rose. Her wine glass teetered. She steadied it.

Elena raised her eyebrows. 'Where?'

There was only one thing to do. Her first real choice. No more pretending.

'To tell Christo I love him.'

Thea rode her motorcycle through the open gates of Christo's mansion, pulling to a stop near the immense pots overflowing with the magenta riot of bougainvillea. As she removed her helmet the cast-iron gates behind her slid to a close. She tried to ignore the ominous clang as they locked.

Swinging from her seat, she stuffed her gloves into the helmet and hung it from the handlebars. Everything would be fine.

Tell that to her terrified heart.

She stopped and took a few deep breaths, catching the scent of citrus blossom drifting on the warm air, reminding her of a day when all she'd wanted to do was run. Well, she wasn't running away now. Instead, she strode to the front door, which opened as she reached it.

Anna.

Thea pulled her into a tight hug. 'I hope I haven't made things difficult for you by coming?'

'As I said when you called, you're worth the trouble. Anyway, nothing could make things more difficult than they are now.'

Anna led her into the bright foyer and closed the door behind them.

Thea unzipped her jacket, the cool air of the house washing over her. 'If anything happens today, you'll always have a job with me.'

Anna waved her hand, a tightness pinching her eyes. 'I'm not worried about my job… I'm hoping you can help Mr Callas.'

At his name, Thea felt a shock of adrenalin spike through her.

'How is he?'

'Unforgiving. Of himself, mostly. But there's more. Your room…he got rid of all the furniture. Curtains. Tore up the carpet. It's all bare. He refuses to allow us to speak of you. It's like you were never here.'

Thea's stomach heaved, pain knifing her deep inside. Did he really want her out of his life so badly? Maybe it had been a mistake coming here. Her hands curled into fists, the nails cutting into her palms. *No.* Fear wasn't going to win. She wouldn't run from this.

Thea flexed her fingers. 'Take me to him.'

Anna gave a tight smile. 'He's shut in his office—as usual.'

They walked in silence up the stairs. Past the magnificent paintings she'd first seen all those months ago. Then, this place had pressed in on her like a prison. Now, a feeling of calm washed over her. She'd come home—if only Christo would see that too.

Anna glanced back at Thea as they stood outside his closed door. She mouthed *Good luck*, then turned back and knocked.

'Come.'

That voice. Stern and uncompromising, it slid through her like fire in her blood. Her body trembled—but not from fear. From the agony of being away from this man for so long.

Anna opened the door and Thea slid past her, not giving Christo any time. He looked up at her, his eyes blank. Then confused. Then—

'What the hell are you doing here? Anna!'

The door had already snicked shut. Anna had sensibly gone.

'Don't blame her. I can be very persuasive when I want.'

He unfurled from his chair. All muscle and towering height. Funny, she'd never been intimidated by that. She noticed his clothes hung slightly looser. His trousers a touch lower on his hips. He wore a business shirt, top buttons open. Lean. Hungry. Predatory.

He canted forward, palms on the desktop. 'Answer my question.'

Oh, he'd give her nothing. She'd have to work hard for everything today.

She loosened the tie in her hair. Ruffled her hands through its long waves, flattened by her helmet. He watched, those green eyes tracing its fall over her shoulders, moving down to the split of her unzipped jacket, her heavy studded belt, to her boots and back.

When his eyes met hers again they were wild and dark. She smiled. 'You offered me my rings. I didn't want them then, but I do now.'

He stood back and his shoulders dropped. What was that look on his face now? Like a cloud passing over the sun? It could have been relief or disappointment. He turned towards the safe hidden in a cupboard behind his desk. She saw nothing but the broad expanse of his shoulders, narrow hips, standing stiff and severe.

'You should have called…' Christo's voice scored down her spine, rough as fingernails.

'I was told you were unlikely to speak to me.'

'You could have left a message.'

'It was the right time to visit.'

The safe cracked open. He withdrew a box, turned and placed it on the desk in front of him.

'I shouldn't be surprised. You said you liked shiny things.'

She shrugged. 'Being a young, single millionairess, it's all about the sparkle.'

'You don't need those to do that.' He nodded to the box. 'You're the belle of every ball.'

A glimmer of hope lit deep inside. She raised her eyebrows. 'Keeping an eye on me?'

'People say things…' Christo's throat worked as he swallowed. He shook his head. 'You have what you came for.'

No, she hadn't. Not yet.

She wiggled her fingers. 'I should put them on. Would you do the honours?'

He stared at her outstretched hand. The white line her rings had left was only recently faded.

His lips narrowed. 'What's this game?'

'No game. Not afraid of a few diamonds, are you?'

Christo grabbed the box, wrenched it open and snatched out the rings. He stalked round to her. 'They mean nothing,' he said as he reached for her hand. 'Not now.'

His fingers shook as he slid the rings onto hers. Once they were in place he snapped back as if he'd been burned. Oh, Christo. So strong. So hard. Denying himself what he truly wanted.

Thea held up her hand and looked at the glistening gems. They appeared to be newly cleaned.

'That feels better. You didn't do that before. Put the engagement ring on my finger.'

They were close now. She could see the rapid rise and fall of his chest as he breathed hard, the throbbing pulse at his throat.

'There was nothing romantic about our arrangement.'

She smiled and his eyes dropped to her mouth. His lips parted, then closed. He still desired her, but out of some misplaced nobility he believed that what he'd done was right. It was time to prove how wrong he was.

'I know your secret. You're a romantic man at heart. You crave it, if only you'd admit that to yourself.'

'You misunderstand me. I gave you everything you wanted. Go.'

His words were a plea, wounded and raw. And at his pain her bright, blinding love for him burst inside.

'You gave me money. I want something more.'

'There's nothing for you here.'

'Everything's here. I've come for your heart.'

Thea dropped to her knees in front of him. Looking up, she took his hands in hers.

'Because I love you with all of mine.'

Christo watched her kneel before him. All sorts of visions flickered through his head. Of dark nights, a warm bed and Thea. Always Thea. He'd attempted to exorcise the house of her short existence there, but even after removing everything from her room the ghost of her still haunted it. Her smell, her shadow was everywhere. Turning every day into a prison, a purgatory from which there was no escape.

'What madness is this?'

His voiced grated out, raw and ragged. He tried to pull his hands away but she held firm, gazing up at him with her cognac eyes. That look slid inside his veins. His one true addiction was setting him alight.

'Courage, Christo.'

He stilled. Courage? He was looking at the bravest person he knew. Him…? He was the coward who'd driven her to this. On her knees, begging him. The guilt of it clawed in his chest.

'You wanted your freedom,' he said.

Still she held tight. The heat of her infernal fingers scorched him. The light in her eyes reached into his dark places. Damn her. It would take him an age to recover from this.

'You touched me and I discovered what freedom was. It's inside myself, not outside the walls which surrounded me. It's loving with all that I am and all that I have. I'm free with *you*.'

When he looked at her face he saw it shining from within. Love. It poured from her and into him. How could she feel this way when he had nothing to give? And yet the pain of her absence cut through him.

He fell to his knees in front of her. 'I told you never to kneel. You should kneel to no man.'

'I'm not kneeling to *any* man. I'm kneeling to the man I love. The man with whom I want to spend the rest of my life. For better. For worse. Though I can't imagine anything worse than the pain of this time without you.'

'What are you asking?'

'Marry me.'

Time stopped. In this room, on his knees, looking into the soul of the woman he now knew he'd loved for months. She was handing him her heart. Did he have the courage to accept it and honour her the way he should?

'I don't know that I'm worthy.'

'You prove yourself worthy every day. I see it. Your staff see it. The only person who doesn't believe is you. So answer my question.'

He cupped her face in his hands. This incredible woman. He'd give her anything to ensure her happiness. Even his cracked and broken self. Because she wanted him. Believed in him.

He'd punished himself enough over the years, absorbing his parents' disapprobation. But why accept their opinions about him when he rejected their judgement on everything else? Perhaps he did deserve the love Thea showed him now.

There was only one way to find out.

'*I zoí mou, s'agapó.* My life, I love you.'

He'd fight every day to keep that smile on her face. He stood, pulling her with him. Holding her tight. Accepting all she offered.

'Yes. Was there any doubt of my answer?'

She nuzzled into his chest. 'Life's full of doubt. But I see you like you saw me. Only a man who truly loved me would have let me go.'

And only a woman who truly loved him would have asked for him back.

'My brave, beautiful Thea.'

'I must be brave. It seems I have a wedding to plan.'

She ran her hands through his hair and all he could think about was the bedroom down the hall and staying there for days.

No, she deserved more.

He grabbed his phone and called the harbour master. 'Yanis—ready the yacht. I'm travelling tomorrow. First light. With my fiancée.'

Thea raised her eyebrows.

'You can plan the wedding,' he said, 'but I intend to start the honeymoon early.'

He swung her into his arms and she squealed with laughter. 'I was right when I said you were a romantic.'

'It's all for you, Thea,' he murmured, brushing his lips across hers.

She cupped his face in her hands. 'No, not for me. From now on it's for *us*.'

He smiled at this woman who would hold his heart for ever.

'Always.'

EPILOGUE

WHITE MUSLIN CURTAINS billowed in the warm breeze from the Aegean. Each time they parted Christo caught a glimpse of the azure blue sea surrounding their island. Exquisite, but nothing matched the woman sprawled with him, replete on the rumpled sheets. Her bare skin like honey against the crisp white cotton.

Their trip here had been an escape after visiting Maria's grave on Karpathos. Tidying the space, leaving flowers. For him, comforting his wife. Such a strong woman Maria had borne in Thea, it left him in awe. That day at the cemetery Christo gave a silent word of thanks to the mother-in-law he'd never known, for giving him such an incredible young woman to cherish.

Six months on from their honeymoon on this island, and he was still immersed in the fulfilment of every day. The magnificent whitewashed mansion had become their haven and escape where they relived their renewed vows and commitment to one another. With Raul and Elena as witnesses, it was all they'd needed, standing barefoot on the golden sand here and declaring their love. Nothing more, nothing less.

There was a rustle beside him. He remained still, lying on his stomach as Thea sat up. She leaned across his body, her long hair trailing over his back sending goose bumps of pleasure shivering across his skin. Her warm breath ghosted over his right shoulder blade, before she dropped her mouth in a gentle kiss. Right over where he now had his own tattoo, of a bluebird like hers.

'Did it hurt?'

'You've asked me this before.' He felt her smile against his skin. 'Many times.' And each time he answered with the truth, she'd kiss *all* of him better. Inflicting her own kind of agony with her lips and hands. Now, it was his turn to smile. She bent down and kissed the upturned corner of his mouth.

'Tell me again,' she murmured, tracing the tattoo's outline with her clever fingers. He closed his eyes, allowing her to explore for a while, even though his body had other ideas which involved him being far more assertive, and preferably inside of her.

'Excessively.' He'd wanted to experience a little of what she'd gone through. Anyhow, the pain had been worth it to honour Thea, and nothing compared to her past hardships. It was also a reminder of what bound them together. The bluebird a symbol of joy, not suffering.

There'd be no more suffering, not if he could help it.

'My darling, brave husband.'

'I'm hardly brave.' He shrugged. 'My wife leaves me in her shadow.'

'You have your own fine attributes.'

Christo looked over his shoulder and raised an eyebrow. 'Well endowed?'

Thea tossed back her head, hair tumbling in unruly waves over her glorious, naked torso. Her throaty laugh sending a lick of pleasure right through him. It was his mission to hear it every day, because of him. He made sure she laughed loud and often. How he loved the sound.

'Now you're digging for compliments,' she said, the laughter warming her voice. 'When you know the answer to that question.'

Her skin flushed a beautiful pink. She'd perfected the art of looking seductive and coy all at once, and it never failed to intoxicate him. Their lovemaking left Christo in a constant state of deep, bone-numbing satisfaction. But it wasn't only in bed that his life had reached the status of perfection. It was in the day-to-day. A true partnership of hearts and minds. The simple things like cooking a meal together. Helping raise money for her women's refuge. Choosing colours for a nursery which wasn't needed yet, although they'd talked of children. Thea assured him it was good to be prepared and he relished her joy in the task. Who knew there were so many different shades of yellow? He'd come to learn them all.

Having her in his life and in his arms completed him in ways he'd never thought possible. The ultimate privilege. Anything seemed achievable, because of her. 'Now you're being elusive about my attributes.'

'Well,' she said, looking up at the ceiling as if thinking hard. Nibbling on her plump lower lip in a way which heated his blood. He shifted on the mattress, rolling onto his back. 'My husband's protective.'

'About you, of course.'

'And dogged.'

'Mmm…' His pursuit of her father and brother had been relentless and deserved. He wouldn't lower himself to even mentioning them in Thea's presence any more. The legal tangle they were mired in over stolen antiquities filled enough newspapers. The scandal complete. If Thea chose to read about what befell them, that was up to her. He hoped she forgot they'd ever existed.

'You're modest too,' she said. A smile of amusement hinted on her lips. He'd kiss that smile away soon enough. Christo stroked his fingers lazily over the skin of her thigh, her own responding goose bumps teasing his fingertips.

'Now my wife exaggerates.'

He sat up and wrestled a giggling Thea underneath him, before her body melted soft and pliant on the cool sheets. She wrapped her arms round his neck, threading her fingers into his hair. 'You're loving.' Her eyes gleamed the rich fire of cognac in candlelight. 'And lovable. Never forget that.'

How could he, when they told each other each day? When they showed it with their bodies and hearts and souls. He believed it now, the ghosts of his childhood well and truly exorcised.

'I'm loved.' He brushed his lips across hers as she drew him into a kiss. 'I love you.'

And Christo relished the lifetime of days ahead, to show Thea exactly how much.

* * * * *

MILLS & BOON

Coming next month

ITALY'S MOST SCANDALOUS VIRGIN
Carol Marinelli

Dante's want for her was perpetual, a lit fuse he was constantly stamping out, but it was getting harder and harder to keep it up. His breathing was ragged; there was a shift in the air and he desperately fought to throw petrol on the row, for his resistance was fast fading. 'What did you think, Mia, that we were going to walk into the church together? A family united? Don't make me laugh...'

No one was laughing.

'Take your tea and go to bed.' Dante dismissed her with an angry wave of his hand, but even as he did so he halted, for it was not his place to send her to bed. 'I didn't mean that. Do what you will. I will leave.'

'It's fine. I'm going up.' She retrieved the tray.

'We leave tomorrow at eleven,' he said again as they headed through to the entrance.

'Yes.'

She turned then and gave him a tight smile, and saw his black eyes meet hers, and there was that look again between them, the one they had shared at the dining table. It was a look that she dared not decipher.

His lips, which were usually plump and red, the only splash of colour in his black and white features, were for once pale. There was a muscle leaping in his cheek, and she was almost sure it was pure contempt, except her body was misreading it as something else.

She had always been aware of his potent sexuality, but now Mia was suddenly aware of her own.

Conscious that she was naked beneath the gown, her breasts felt full and heavy, aware of the lust that danced inappropriately in the air between them. The prison gates were parting further and she was terrified to step out. 'Goodnight,' she croaked, and climbed the stairs, almost tipping the tray and only able to breathe when she heard the door slam.

Tea forgotten, she lay on the bed, frantic and unsettled. So much for the Ice Queen! She was burning for him in a way she had never known until she'd met Dante.

Mia had thought for a long time that there was something wrong with her, something missing in her make-up, for she'd had little to no interest in sex. Even back at school she would listen in on her peers, quietly bemused by their obsessive talking about boys and the things they did that to Mia sounded filthy. Her mother's awkward talk about the facts of life had left Mia revolted. The *fact of Mia's life*: it was something she didn't want! There was no reason she could find. There had been no trauma, nothing she could pin it to. Just for her, those feelings simply did not exist. Mia had tried to ignite the absent fire and had been on a couple of dates, but had found she couldn't even tolerate kisses, and tongues positively revolted her. She couldn't bear to consider anything else.

And while this marriage had given her a unique chance to heal from the appalling disaster that had befallen her family, the deeper truth was that it had given her a chance to hide from something she perhaps ought to address.

A no-sex marriage had felt like a blessing when she and Rafael had agreed to it.

Yet the ink had barely dried on the contract when she had found out that though those feelings might be buried deep, they were there after all.

Mia had been just a few days into the pretend position of Rafael's PA, and the carefully engineered rumours had just started to fly, when Dante Romano had walked in. A mere moment with him had helped her understand all she had been missing, for with just a look she found herself reacting in a way she never had before.

His dark eyes had transfixed her, the deep growl of his voice had elicited a shiver low in her stomach, and even his scent, as it reached her, went straight to form a perfect memory. When Dante had asked who she was, his voice and his presence had alerted, startled and awoken her. So much so that she had half expected him to snap his fingers like a genie right before her scalding face.

Three wishes?
You.
You.
You.

Continue reading
ITALY'S MOST SCANDALOUS VIRGIN
Carol Marinelli

Available next month
www.millsandboon.co.uk

COMING SOON!

We really hope you enjoyed reading this book.
If you're looking for more romance, be sure to
head to the shops when new books are
available on

Thursday 23rd July

MILLS & BOON

THE HEART OF ROMANCE

A ROMANCE FOR EVERY KIND OF READER

MODERN

Prepare to be swept off your feet by sophisticated, sexy and seductive heroes, in some of the world's most glamourous and romantic locations, where power and passion collide.
8 stories per month.

HISTORICAL

Escape with historical heroes from time gone by. Whether you passion is for wicked Regency Rakes, muscled Vikings or rugg Highlanders, awaken the romance of the past.
6 stories per month.

MEDICAL

Set your pulse racing with dedicated, delectable doctors in the high-pressure world of medicine, where emotions run high ar passion, comfort and love are the best medicine.
6 stories per month.

True Love

Celebrate true love with tender stories of heartfelt romance, f the rush of falling in love to the joy a new baby can bring, and focus on the emotional heart of a relationship.
8 stories per month.

Desire

Indulge in secrets and scandal, intense drama and plenty of si hot action with powerful and passionate heroes who have it all wealth, status, good looks…everything but the right woman.
6 stories per month.

HEROES

Experience all the excitement of a gripping thriller, with an in romance at its heart. Resourceful, true-to-life women and stro fearless men face danger and desire - a killer combination!
8 stories per month.

DARE

Sensual love stories featuring smart, sassy heroines you'd want best friend, and compelling intense heroes who are worthy of
4 stories per month.

To see which titles are coming soon, please visit

millsandboon.co.uk/nextmonth